THE CASTLE OF OTRANTO

THE MYSTERIES OF UDOLPHO *(Abridged)*

NORTHANGER ABBEY

THE CASTLE OF OTRANTO
BY HORACE WALPOLE

THE MYSTERIES OF UDOLPHO
BY ANN RADCLIFFE
(Abridged)

NORTHANGER ABBEY
BY JANE AUSTEN

Edited with an Introduction by
ANDREW WRIGHT

Holt, Rinehart and Winston, Inc.
NEW YORK · CHICAGO · SAN FRANCISCO
TORONTO · LONDON

CONTENTS

INTRODUCTION

"May there not be something," asked Bishop Richard Hurd in his anonymously issued *Letters on Chivalry and Romance* (1762), "in the Gothic Romance peculiarly suited to the views of a genius, and to the ends of poetry? And may not the philosophic moderns have gone too far in their perpetual ridicule and contempt of it?" Indeed the very word "Gothic" had been a term of reproach during the first half of the eighteenth century, and Bishop Hurd was by way of being a pioneer in his effort to make the Gothic acceptable. For it is true that the very spirit of Gothic was antithetical to that of the earlier eighteenth century. Yet, and in reaction to the radiance of the Augustans, it was during the latter part of the century that the Gothic tale had its greatest vogue. *The Castle of Otranto* (dated 1765 though actually issued in 1764) is the principal forerunner; *The Mysteries of Udolpho* (1794), together with M. G. Lewis's *The Monk* (1796), set off the evidently insatiable fever; and *Northanger Abbey* (1818), though begun before the turn of the century and actually published many years after it was first offered for sale, takes the genre to the playful realm, that of parody and burlesque; and it is no accident—it is an explicable historical development—that Thomas Love Peacock's exquisite spoof *Nightmare Abbey* was published in the same year as Jane Austen's.

Nor has the Gothic gone altogether out of fashion, though not since the first or second decade of the nineteenth century has the genre commanded so much frightened attention—except, perhaps, in modern films. Yet that the Gothic is more than an apparatus, that its impulse lies deep in the human psyche, is evident not in the excesses to which the Gothic lent itself in its various literary and subliterary manifestations (Mary Shelley's justly maligned *Frankenstein* also appeared in 1818) but in the superbly realized work of such various writers as Byron, Scott, and Shelley, the Brontes, Hawthorne and Poe, Hardy and Henry James, Faulkner and Graham Greene. It is not too much to say that an understanding of the literature of the last two hundred years requires a knowledge of the nature of Gothic. The works represented in the following pages afford an opportunity to examine the genre at the time of its greatest efflorescence, in the works of three writers of profoundly different tempers, writing from avowedly different motives, and addressing quite different audiences.

Michael Sadleir dates what he calls "the Gothic romantic epoch" from about 1775 to 1815. And yet the period, including its main prefiguration in *The Castle of Otranto,* has many roots in the Augustan age. Quite apart from the human fact that reasonableness, however sweet, is a diet insufficient for human needs, and was felt to be so by even the most ardent champions of luminosity in the earlier eighteenth century, there were at that time interests as well as needs from which the Gothic flame was to be kindled.

The *Arabian Nights* were translated into French early in the eighteenth century, and subsequently into English; they were popular as offering views of the distant—the distant in time, geography, belief, and character. To the most diverse writers these tales had a decided appeal; the effects can be observed in a wide variety of English oriental tales that both precede and parallel the Gothic movement itself; the range is from the dejected reasonableness of Samuel Johnson's *Rasselas* (1759) to the sadistic (or masochistic) orgy of unreason that is William Beckford's *Vathek: An Arabian Tale* (1786). The earlier eighteenth century was also an era of voyages, real and imaginary. Rich young men—Horace Walpole was one of them—took the Grand Tour; the less well endowed confined themselves to imaginary journeys, of which *Robinson Crusoe* (1719) and *Gulliver's Travels* (1726) are now the best remembered of very many such productions. Even Henry Fielding wrote in this genre, a series of essays in *The Champion* which he called "The Voyages of Mr. Job Vinegar" (1740). But the popularity of the oriental tale and of the imaginary voyage (which were sometimes, as in *Vathek,* combined) is itself but a pair among many facts that can be brought forward to demonstrate that the origins of the Gothic are deep in the so-called classical period of English literature.

Of these roots—including a cult of medievalism and influences from both France and Germany—the strongest is that of sentiment, the groundwork of the Earl of Shaftesbury's enormously influential *Characteristicks of Men, Manners, Opinions, Times* (1711): "moral sentiment," he averred, is what enables man to distinguish right from wrong, and "moral sentiment" is what propels men toward a realization of the good, the beautiful, and the true. Shaftesbury is simply representative of a large number of Englishmen in the era before the one in which the Gothic novel emerged. From the belief in sentiment—whether it leads to the inward musings of a *Clarissa Harlowe* (1747–1748), the rural regret of a *Vicar of Wakefield* (1761–1762), the restless self-pity of a *Humphry Clinker* (1771), or the blatant celebration of emotional response in *A Sentimental Journey* (1768) and Henry Mackenzie's *The Man of Feeling* (1771)— can flow the dark rivers of the Gothic tale. Entirely apposite was the English taste for melancholy, manifest well before the appearance of a study of the subject, Dr. George Cheyne's *The English Malady* (1733), and borne out in the work of Robert Blair and Edward Young, whose poems "The Grave" (1743) and "Night Thoughts" (1742–1745) had many imitators. There was even philosophical treatment of the subject, very notably by Edmund Burke, who argued in his *Philosophical Enquiry into the Origin of Our Ideas of the Sublime and the Beautiful* (1756) that the sublime is based on terror.

But the Gothic was not merely the sum of its precedents; it became a new amalgam. The difference in degree became a difference in kind. Indeed the elements making up the Gothic are all separately identifiable as representing tendencies that may lead in other directions, but the Gothic as a literary genre has a distinct and solid central feature, because it could contain or suggest all these elements, together with the human characteristics that these elements make possible: the central Gothic feature is the castle. Montague Summers, an enthusiast for the Gothic tale, puts it vigorously; he speaks of

the remote and ruined castle with its antique courts, deserted chambers, pictured windows that exclude the light, haunted galleries amid whose mouldering gloom is heard the rustle of an unseen robe, a sigh, a hurried footfall where no mortal step should tread; the ancient manor, hidden away in the heart of a pathless forest, a home of memories of days gone before when bright eyes glanced from casement and balcony over the rich domain, the huge-girthed oaks, the avenues and far-stretching vistas, the cool stream winding past the grassy lawns, but now tenanted only by a silver-headed retainer and his palsied dame; the huge fortress set high upon some spar of the Apennines, dark machicolated battlements and sullen towers which frown o'er the valleys below, a lair of masterless men, through whose dim corridors prowl armed bandits, whose halls ring with hideous revelry or anon are silent as the grave; the lone and secret convent amid the hills, ruled by some proud abbess whose nod is law, a cloister of which the terraces overlook vast precipices shagged with larch and darkened by the gigantic pine, whose silences are only disturbed by the deep bell that knolls to midnight office and prayer.

Appropriately enough, Horace Walpole's most ardent devotion was lavished on and reserved for his miniature Gothic castle at Strawberry Hill, an English confection of fanciful irregularity, turreted and battlemented, lovingly furbished, refurbished, and furbished again, over a period of four decades. Walpole was born in 1717; his father, Sir Robert Walpole, was the Whig First Minister from 1721–1742, immensely wealthy and the most powerful man in England for many years. Horace Walpole's education was aristocratic—Eton; King's College, Cambridge; and inevitably the Grand Tour, with his schoolfellow, Thomas Gray. Collector, traveler, antiquarian, Member of Parliament, gardener, writer of superbly elegant and witty letters, Walpole is often regarded as the acme of the eighteenth-century English gentleman. Throughout his long life (he was nearly eighty when he died), he was at all events the amateur and the dilettante; his manner, however, made him seem more disengaged than he actually was; his *Catalogue of Royal and Noble Authors* (1758), for instance, is a work of devoted if not always perfectly accurate scholarship; and the list of his publications provides ample evidence that Walpole's whim was in any event iron. Above all, the letters, so numerous and circumstantial, so replete with insight, with wit, with—indeed—high art: these are monuments of both assiduity and determination.

But *The Castle of Otranto* is playfully calculated, though the impulse to write it was compelling. In one of his most famous letters, to the Reverend William Cole (March 9, 1765), Walpole tells of the dream which caused him to begin writing his tale:

Shall I even confess to you what was the origin of this romance? I waked one morning in the beginning of last June from a dream, of which all I could recover was, that I had thought myself in an ancient castle (a very natural dream for a head like mine filled with Gothic story) and that on the uppermost bannister of a great staircase I saw a gigantic hand in armour. In the evening I sat down, and began to write, without knowing in the least what I intended to say or relate. The work grew on my hands and I grew so fond of it. . . . In short I was so engrossed with my tale, which I completed in less than two months, that one evening, I wrote from the time I had drunk my tea, about six o'clock, till half an hour after one in the morning, when my hand and fingers were so weary, that I could not hold the pen to finish the sentence, but left Matilda and Isabella talking, in the middle of a paragraph.

Furthermore, though he did not come to realize the fact until five years later, he was unconsciously thinking of Trinity College, Cambridge, which he had visited in the previous year; Otranto is a conflation of Strawberry and Trinity.

Published pseudonymously as "translated by William Marshall, Gent. from the original Italian of Onuphrio Muralto," the first edition of *The Castle of Otranto* was issued on Christmas eve of 1764. The second edition, published in the following April, jettisoned the pretense as to authorship. Walpole was by then glad to admit that he had written the book, for it had been extremely well received.

"The Translator's Preface" is agreeably flippant. The pretended translator of a pretended author pretends to speculate on the motive behind the writing of the book:

It is not unlikely, that an artful priest . . . might avail himself of his abilities as an author to confirm the populace in their ancient errors and superstitions. If this was his view, he has certainly acted with signal address. Such a work as the following would enslave a hundred vulgar minds, beyond half the books of controversy that have been written from the days of Luther to the present hour.

He even pretends to find a moral in the story, but his mask is very lightly worn indeed. This preface was, however, omitted in the second edition, and a new, longer, and more solemn preface takes its place. Both prefaces are reprinted in the following pages, and the reader is encouraged to take his cue to the spirit of the second, from the spirit of the first.

Some readers have taken with excessive solemnity Walpole's pronouncement that *The Castle of Otranto* represents "an attempt to blend the two kinds of Romance, the ancient and the modern"; his defense of the way he characterizes the domestics ("My rule was Nature"); his elaborate comparison of himself to Shakespeare. But the key to his attitude to the book is doubtless contained in a letter to Hannah More two decades later: *The Castle of Otranto,* he wrote, "was fit for nothing but the age in which it was written, an age in which much was known; that required only to be amused, nor cared whether its amusements were conformable to truth and the models of good sense."

Nonetheless, Walpole's novel contains all the Gothic ingredients: the castle in the Kingdom of Naples, the medieval setting, the dark prophecy, the usurped heir, the mysterious lineage, not to mention the sighing portrait, the plumed helmet, the subterraneous passage, the "vault totally dark," the giant, the suicide, the hermit, the drops of blood, the deathbed scene complete with thunder and lightning, and poison. But Walpole, as he does not intend his story seriously, takes little trouble to make his characters come to life, even when they are intended to be alive, and he cheerfully alters personality to suit the requirements of the story. As Hugh Honour says in his excellent British Council pamphlet on Walpole: "Dark and Gothic as their surroundings are, the inhabitants of Otranto think and talk very much like the people of Walpole's London, though they occasionally spice their conversation with a little tushery to give period flavour." But *The Castle of Otranto* must be taken very seriously indeed as the main precursor of a long line of Gothic tales, some of them far more earnest in purpose, and many of them more ample in scope. *The Castle of Otranto* has, among Gothic tales, the rare merit of brevity.

Ann Radcliffe (1764–1823), though a less interesting person than Horace Walpole, is the more considerable novelist. Born Ann Ward in the year *The Castle of Otranto* was issued, she was nearly half a century younger than Walpole. Married at twenty-three to William Radcliffe, a law student who became a newspaper editor, she was the author of some half-dozen prose romances, of which *The Mysteries of Udolpho* (1794) and *The Italian* (1797) stand out. For the last twenty-five years of her life she published nothing, but *Gaston de Blondville* and a long metrical romance were both published posthumously in 1826.

In the 1790s her work was the talk of London, and she was greatly praised: "the Shakespeare," one admirer went so far as to say, "of Romance Writers." In fact, her romances, for all their crudity of construction, tapped a source that tells the story of the popularity of the Gothic tale altogether. Lionel Stevenson puts the matter succinctly in his *English Novel: A Panorama:*

In departing from realism Mrs. Radcliffe stumbled upon the whole realm of the unconscious. The standard situations in her stories are those which recur in everyone's nightmares—wandering alone in an unrecognizable, eerie place, or trying to flee from unidentified but frightful pursuers in an endless tunnel or staircase, or being imprisoned in a tiny cell that seems to be closing in. No matter how crudely Mrs. Radcliffe described these things, she had the knack of stimulating the reader's own dream-making function, which then took over and supplied the private horrors of each individual imagination. Probably, too, her central theme—a pure, pale maiden persecuted by a vicious but dominating sadist—became a powerful sex symbol for both male and female readers. Unuttered risks of incest sometimes hover around the heroine through the uncertainty of her parentage. Even the heroine's excessive refinement, preventing the slightest mention of crime or of any strong emotion, helps to strengthen the morbid suggestiveness.

The action of *The Mysteries of Udolpho* takes place, sup-

posedly, in 1584, a time sufficiently distant from Ann Radcliffe's to invoke the spell cast by remoteness. But the
disguise is thin, and the characters are pure English, pure
eighteenth century. Equally blatant is the geographical
pretense. Again remoteness rather than verisimilitude is the
aim. The principal geography is the south of France—
Gascony, Provence, Languedoc, with many glances at and
thoughts about the Pyrenees; and Italy, from the brilliance
of Venice to the dark Apennine enclave, Udolpho itself.
Ann Radcliffe lavishes words on the geography of her novel,
but her descriptions are intended to elicit an emotional
response rather than the shock of recognition. At least, the
novel abounds in anachronisms and in geographical blun-
ders; Mrs. Radcliffe once traveled to Holland and Germany,
but (so far as is known) she never saw France or Italy.

For *The Mysteries of Udolpho* is a novel of sensibility,
and Emily St. Aubert is right out of the sentimental tales
with which Ann Radcliffe obviously occupied herself. As is
customary, the heroine has an extraordinarily well-furnished
mind and a generous measure of accomplishments: "a general view of the sciences, and an exact acquaintance with
every part of elegant literature." Furthermore, she plays the
lute, "with such sweet pathos," and she is a poet whose muse
inspires her more often, perhaps, than the reader of her
book finds agreeable. Besides, she is an only child, and she
tells an unsuccessful suitor, " 'My heart can never know a
second affection.' " It is easy to laugh at her, and Jane Austen
does so with fine mockery; but Emily emerges as a credible
heroine of sensibility, with a coherence that compels both
attention and respect.

Not all the other characters are equally successful. But
Emily's father is a figure whose retreat from the great world
to the country pleasures of La Vallée is adequately exem-
plary of sensibility. Montoni is a well-drawn villain, especially as his villainy becomes the blacker in the atmosphere

of Udolpho. Valancourt, the ultimately successful suitor, is appealing from the beginning, because his awakening love for Emily causes him to pursue her and her father on the journey undertaken to improve the old man's health, and because he succumbs to the lures of Paris; from these he must recover and repent before he can be united to Emily.

Ann Radcliffe is so much a woman of the eighteenth century that—even notoriously—the mysteries of Udolpho are every single one of them ultimately explicable as natural rather than supernatural phenomena. To Ann Radcliffe there were no ghosts, and the skeptical turn of her mind would seem to be a peculiar qualification to bring to the writing of novels of mystery. But the reasonableness of Ann Radcliffe is very probably a reason for her success. In *The Monk* (1796), M. G. Lewis tapped another vein, but Ann Radcliffe's readers could enjoy the exhilaration of terror without surrendering themselves to irrationality. Or, for that matter, without abandoning propriety.

The Mysteries of Udolpho is about 300,000 words long; it was originally published in four volumes—and it should be read entire, because like other long novels its total effect depends in part upon the pace and the cumulative impact of leisurely and ample tale telling. In making selections from the novel, the editor intends to provide no more than a sample. But in order that the reader may come to understand something of the very pace of the novel, the first four chapters of Volume I are included, uncut. Subsequent selections are intended to give the high points of the Udolpho experience, and at the same time to present the portions of the novel to which Jane Austen applied the knives of parody and burlesque. But Jane Austen mocked a genre rather than any particular work, and it would be a mistake to search in *Northanger Abbey* for parallels to be found uniquely in *The Mysteries of Udolpho*. In fact, as R. W. Chapman points out in his scholarly edition of *Northanger Abbey*, there is in Chapter Eight of Ann Radcliffe's *The Romance of the Forest* (1791) a closer parallel to Catherine Morland's adventures than anything to be found in *The Mysteries of Udolpho*.

Jane Austen, to be sure, was intimately acquainted with the works of Ann Radcliffe, and an ardent reader of Gothic novels. *Northanger Abbey* is entirely explicit on this point. But to Jane Austen, whose temperament preferred fresh air and sunshine, the darkly Gothic mysteries elicited not terror but delight at the absurdity of horrid fiction. Her experience of life was distinctly different. The spinster daughter of a country parson in a numerous family, Jane Austen was born in Hampshire in 1775 and lived quietly away from the mainstream of contemporary society. Her education was sketchy, but her reading was fairly wide—and she was incontestably a genius.

Among the manifestations of her superb self-knowledge is her recognition of her own limits: "3 or 4 Families in a Country Village is the very thing to work on," she once wrote to her niece; and she resisted the blandishments offered by James Stainer Clarke, the pompous and self-consequential librarian to the Prince Regent. Himself a clergyman, he suggested that Jane Austen "delineate in some future Work the Habits of Life and Character and enthusiasm of a Clergyman—who should pass his time between the metropolis & the Country"—who should, in fact, be an idealized portrait of himself. Jane Austen's reply is wholly characteristic. "I am quite honoured by your thinking me capable of drawing such a clergyman as you gave the sketch of in your note of November 16th. But I assure you I am *not*. The comic part of the character I might be equal to, but not the good, the enthusiastic, the literary." This correspondence took place in 1815, two years before Jane

Austen's death, but from girlhood she had known all about how to have such fun.

Of all her novels *Northanger Abbey* is probably the simplest, and though it was not published until 1818, it was written in 1797 and 1798, sold in 1803 to the publisher Crosby who advertised the book but for reasons unknown did not in fact publish it then. Even though after 1803 it is probable, as R. W. Chapman says in *Jane Austen Facts and Problems,* "that revision and experiment went on," *Northanger Abbey* is unquestionably much of it early work.

As a burlesque of the Gothic novel *Northanger Abbey* would seem to contain all the ingredients of this genre, except the hero and heroine, who are emphatically normalized, partly no doubt for the purpose of heightening the ridicule. Like all burlesques the book exhibits two sets of values: one is guyed, the other is shown to be "truer." Here the illusions of Gothic—and indeed all other—sentimentality are contrasted to the more durable values of good sense; the Gothic world is one of fancy, the world as apprehended by good sense is "real." But *Northanger Abbey* goes beyond these boundaries: Jane Austen here explores the limitations of good sense itself. And she shows us that though the Gothic world must be rejected as inadequate and false, the real world cannot be apprehended by good sense alone.

In sketching Catherine Morland's background, appearance, and disposition, her author manages to suggest the most striking contrast to Emily St. Aubert (miscalled by Jane Austen "St. Aubin"). Catherine "never could learn or understand any thing before she was taught; and sometimes not even then, for she was often inattentive, and occasionally stupid. . . . What a strange, unaccountable character!" So she was at the age of ten, but, on the brink of a six weeks' visit to Bath, she has grown: "her heart was affectionate, her disposition cheerful and open, without conceit or affectation of any kind—her manners just removed from the awkwardness and shyness of a girl; her person pleasing, and, when in good looks, pretty—and her mind about as ignorant and uninformed as the female mind at seventeen usually is."

Her experiences on first arriving at Bath (rather than Venice) are a combination of what might be expected from the Gothic heroine, and the very reverse. The Allens, whose guest she is, are an untroubled Wiltshire couple; her first experience of the Upper Rooms produces ennui rather than rapture; the young man she meets is no vehement seducer from southern Europe, but a talkative, sardonic clergyman from Gloucestershire named Henry Tilney, whose father is a general, and who lectures Catherine on the inadequacies of young ladies as letter writers. On the other hand, she meets Isabella Thorpe, a sentimental confidante out of a novel, who induces her to read *The Mysteries of Udolpho;* she encounters the flashy, cruel, and dishonest John Thorpe, who endeavors to take her, against her will, to Blaize Castle.

But far more than her Gothic indoctrination at Bath is her own emergence as a human being—though she is not to be cured of the Gothic infection until her experience at Northanger Abbey itself. At once she is drawn to Isabella Thorpe, led by youth and a natural credulousness; but John Thorpe affects her differently even at the beginning of their acquaintance. He is stout, loud, impudent, boastful, insensitive, and dishonest—and Catherine "could not entirely repress a doubt, while she bore with the effusions of his endless conceit, of his being altogether agreeable." Indeed she is soon forced to make a conscious and quite firm judgment against him when he lies to her in order to persuade her to accompany him to Blaize Castle. Made to think for herself on this occasion, and increasingly allied with the Tilneys, she is gradually able to see even Isabella with greater objectivity. Meanwhile, Catherine's greater intimacy with the Tilneys and a mistaken impression on the general's part as to her wealth leads to an invitation to Northanger Abbey—

the Udolpho, as Catherine imagines in advance, of her life.

With beautifully comic anticlimax, Jane Austen traces Catherine's Gothic adventures. Having expected "long damp passages . . . narrow cells and [a] ruined chapel . . . some awful memorials of an injured and ill-fated nun," she finds "lodges of a modern appearance . . . a smooth, level road of fine gravel, without obstacle, alarm or solemnity of any kind." In her bedroom, which is far from horrifying in most respects, she finds a mysterious chest—which contains nothing out of Ann Radcliffe; she later spies another chest which frightens her out of a full night's sleep—this contains a document probably never to be seen, and certainly never told of, at Udolpho. She steals to the room where Mrs. Tilney died, expecting to see such evidence as frightened and exhilarated Emily St. Aubert, but finds something quite else. And at last Catherine is purged of her Gothic illusions.

At all events, these illusions had never transformed, they had only intoxicated her; her emergence as a human being of good sense is far more important. And if the relationship to the Thorpes shows Catherine the value of common sense in evaluating life's difficulties, the relationship to the Tilneys —except the Gothic trimmings—discloses the limits of this virtue. She meets, and is attracted to, though she is rather baffled by, Henry Tilney; she becomes the friend of Eleanor; she is treated with affectionate kindness by the rather terrifying General Tilney—and then suddenly she is dismissed without explanation. She is stunned, almost overcome with grief, and returns home to Wiltshire in deep humiliation; there she meets with the unfailing kindness and sympathy of her family and the Allens, whose calm good sense she is at last able to value highly. But almost before she has been able to absorb the lesson, she learns that good sense cannot deal with the crisis that has forced her sudden expulsion: "Her anxiety," she realizes, "had foundation in fact," and the happy ending is a triumph of character, rather than of good sense, of manageable circumstance. The final sentence of *Northanger Abbey* burlesques the didacticism of the genre which Jane Austen has been treating. Equally, this sentence suggests that mere simplicity in the approach to human behavior may be less than enough: "I leave it to be settled," Jane Austen writes, "by whomsoever it may concern, whether the tendency of this work be altogether to recommend parental tyranny, or reward filial disobedience."

A.W.

Columbus, Ohio
May 1963

A NOTE ON THE TEXTS

The text of *The Castle of Otranto* is that of the second edition of 1765 (I have, however, used the so-called Translator's Preface from the first edition; the second edition does not reproduce it). Other than correcting obvious misprints, I have refrained from modernizing, except to set the proper names in roman type rather than in italics. In order to prevent confusion, I have also supplied quotation marks throughout. The selections from *The Mysteries of Udolpho* have been made by the present editor, and the text as printed is that of the first edition of 1794. The text of *Northanger Abbey* is that of R. W. Chapman for the authoritative Oxford edition of the novels (3d edition, Oxford, 1933), and is reproduced with the kind permission of the Oxford University Press.

SELECT BIBLIOGRAPHY

The Gothic Tale

Baker, Ernest A. *The History of the English Novel,* Vols. V and VI. London, 1934–1935.

Foster, James R. *History of the Pre-Romantic Novel in England.* New York, 1949.

Penzoldt, Peter. *The Supernatural in Fiction.* London, 1952.

Summers, Montague. *A Gothic Bibliography.* London, 1941.

———. *The Gothic Quest: A History of the Gothic Novel.* London, 1938.

Tompkins, J. M. S. *The Popular Novel in England, 1770–1800.* London, 1932 (reprinted, Lincoln, Nebraska, 1961).

Varma, Devendra P. *The Gothic Flame: Being a History of the Gothic Novel in England.* London, 1957.

Horace Walpole

Doughty, Oswald. *Introduction* to The Castle of Otranto. London, 1929.

Honour, Hugh. *Horace Walpole.* (British Council pamphlet). London, 1957.

Ker, W. P. "Horace Walpole," in his *Collected Essays.* London, 1925, I, 109–127.

Ketton-Cremer, R. W. *Horace Walpole: A Biography,* rev. ed. London, 1946.

Ann Radcliffe

Each of the authors listed under "The Gothic Tale" devotes considerable attention to Ann Radcliffe in the works cited. In addition, the following may be consulted:

Grant, Aline. *Ann Radcliffe*. Denver, 1951.

Summers, Montague. "A Great Mistress of Romance: Ann Radcliffe, 1764–1823." *Transactions of the Royal Society of Literature*, 2d ser., XXXV (1917), 39–78.

Jane Austen

Chapman, R. W. *Jane Austen: A Critical Bibliography*, 2d ed. Oxford, 1955.

McKillop, A. D. "Critical Realism in Northanger Abbey," in Robert C. Rathburn and Martin Steinmann, Jr., eds. *From Jane Austen to Joseph Conrad*, Minneapolis, 1958, pp. 35–45.

Sadleir, Michael. *The Northanger Novels: A Footnote to Jane Austen*. (English Association Pamphlet No. 68). Oxford, 1927.

Wright, Andrew. *Jane Austen's Novels: A Study in Structure*, rev. ed. London, 1961.

THE CASTLE OF OTRANTO
THE MYSTERIES OF UDOLPHO *(Abridged)*
NORTHANGER ABBEY

The Castle of Otranto

BY

HORACE WALPOLE

THE

CASTLE of OTRANTO,

A

GOTHIC STORY.

—— *Vanæ*
Fingentur species, tamen ut Pes, & Caput uni
Reddantur formæ. ——

HOR.

THE SECOND EDITION.

L O N D O N:

Printed for WILLIAM BATHOE in the *Strand,*
and THOMAS LOWNDS in *Fleet-Street.*

M. DCC. LXV.

THE TRANSLATOR'S PREFACE

[NOTE: *This preface was omitted from the second edition.*]

The following work was found in the library of an ancient Catholic family in the north of England. It was printed at Naples, in the black letter, in the year 1529. How much sooner it was written does not appear. The principal incidents are such as were believed in the darkest ages of christianity; but the language and conduct have nothing that savours of barbarism. The style is the purest Italian. If the story was written near the time when it is supposed to have happened, it must have been between 1095, the æra of the first crusade, and 1243, the date of the last, or not long afterwards. There is no other circumstance in the work, that can lead us to guess at the period in which the scene is laid. The names of the actors are evidently fictitious, and probably disguised on purpose; yet the Spanish names of the domestics seem to indicate that this work was not composed until the establishment of the Arragonian kings in Naples had made Spanish appellations familiar in that country. The beauty of the diction, and the zeal of the author (moderated, however, by singular judgment) concur to make me think, that the date of the composition was little antecedent to that of the impression. Letters were then in their most flourishing state in Italy, and contributed to dispel the empire of superstition, at that time so forcibly attacked by the reformers. It is not unlikely, that an artful priest might endeavour to turn their own arms on the innovators; and might avail himself of his abilities as an author to confirm the populace in their ancient errors and superstitions. If this was his view,

3

he has certainly acted with signal address. Such a work as the following would enslave a hundred vulgar minds, beyond half the books of controversy that have been written from the days of Luther to the present hour.

This solution of the author's motives is, however, offered as a mere conjecture. Whatever his views were, or whatever effects the execution of them might have, his work can only be laid before the public at present as a matter of entertainment. Even as such, some apology for it is necessary. Miracles, visions, necromancy, dreams, and other preternatural events, are exploded now even from romances. That was not the case when our author wrote; much less when the story itself is supposed to have happened. Belief in every kind of prodigy was so established in those dark ages, that an author would not be faithful to the *manners* of the times, who should omit all mention of them. He is not bound to believe them himself, but he must represent his actors as believing them.

If this *air* of the *miraculous* is excused, the reader will find nothing else unworthy of his perusal. Allow the possibility of the facts, and all the actors comport themselves as persons would do in their situation. There is no bombast, no similes, flowers, digressions, or unnecessary descriptions. Every thing tends directly to the catastrophe. Never is the reader's attention relaxed. The rules of the drama are almost observed throughout the conduct of the piece. The characters are well drawn, and still better maintained. Terror, the author's principal engine, prevents the story from ever languishing; and it is so often contrasted by pity, that the mind is kept up in a constant vicissitude of interesting passions.

Some persons may, perhaps, think the characters of the domestics too little serious for the general cast of the story; but, besides their opposition to the principal personages, the art of the author is very observable in his conduct of the subalterns. They discover many passages essential to the story, which could not be well brought to light but by their naiveté and simplicity: in particular, the womanish terror and foibles of Bianca, in the last chapter, conduce essentially towards advancing the catastrophe.

It is natural for a translator to be prejudiced in favour of his adopted work. More impartial readers may not be so much struck with the beauties of this piece as I was. Yet I am not blind to my author's defects. I could wish he had grounded his plan on a more useful moral than this: that *the sins of fathers are visited on their children to the third and forth generation*. I doubt whether, in his time, any more than at present, ambition curbed its appetite of dominion from the dread of so remote a punishment. And yet this moral is weakened by that less direct insinuation, that even such anathema may be diverted, by devotion to St. Nicholas. Here, the interest of the Monk plainly gets the better of the judgment of the Author. However, with all its faults, I have no doubt but the English reader will be pleased with a sight of this performance. The piety that reigns through-out, the lessons of virtue that are inculcated, and the rigid purity of the sentiments, exempt this work from the censure to which romances are but too liable. Should it meet with the success I hope for, I may be encouraged to re-print the original Italian, both for variety and harmony. The latter is peculiarly excellent for simple narrative. It is difficult, in English, to relate without falling too low, or rising too high; a fault obviously occasioned by the little care taken to speak pure language in common conversation. Every Italian or Frenchman of any rank piques himself on speaking his own tongue correctly and with choice. I cannot flatter myself with having done justice to my author in this respect: His stile is as elegant, as his conduct of the passions is masterly. It is a pity that he did not apply his talents to what they were evidently proper for, the theatre.

I will detain the reader no longer, but to make one short remark. Though the machinery is invention, and the names of the actors imaginary, I cannot but believe, that the ground-work of the story is founded on truth. The scene is undoubtedly laid in some real castle. The author seems frequently, without design, to describe particular parts. *The chamber,* says he, *on the right-hand; the door on the left-hand; the distance from the chapel to Conrad's apartment.* These, and other passages, are strong presumptions that the author had some certain building in his eye. Curious persons, who have leisure to employ in such researches, may possibly discover in the Italian writers the foundation on which our author has built. If a catastrophe, at all resembling that which he describes, is believed to have given rise to this work, it will contribute to interest the reader, and will make the Castle of Otranto a still more moving story.

SONNET ✓

To the Right Honorable Lady Mary Coke

The gentle Maid,whose hapless tale
These melancholy pages speak;
Say, gracious Lady, shall she fail
To draw the tear adown thy cheek?

No; never was thy pitying breast
Insensible to human woes:
Tender, tho' firm, it melts distress
For weaknesses it never knows.

Oh! guard the marvels I relate
Of fell ambition scourg'd by fate,
  From reason's peevish blame.

Blest with thy smile, my dauntless sail
I dare expand to Fancy's gale,
  For sure thy smiles are Fame.

H. W.

PREFACE

To this second Edition

The favourable manner in which this little piece has been received by the public, calls upon the author to explain the grounds on which he composed it. But before he opens those motives, it is fit that he should ask pardon of his readers for having offered his work to them under the borrowed personage of a translator. As diffidence of his own abilities, and the novelty of the attempt, were his sole inducements to assume that disguise, he flatters himself he shall appear excuseable. He resigned his performance to the impartial judgment of the public; determined to let it perish in obscurity, if disapproved; nor meaning to avow such a trifle, unless better judges should pronounce that he might own it without a blush.

It was an attempt to blend the two kinds of Romance, the ancient and the modern. In the former, all was imagination and improbability: in the latter, nature is always intended to be, and sometimes has been, copied with success. Invention has not been wanting; but the great resources of fancy have been dammed up, by a strict adherence to common life. But if in the latter species Nature has cramped imagination, she did but take her revenge, having been totally excluded from old Romances. The actions, sentiments, conversations, of the heroes and heroines of ancient days were as unnatural as the machines employed to put them in motion.

The author of the following pages thought it possible to reconcile the two kinds. Desirous of leaving the powers of fancy at liberty to expatiate through the boundless realms of invention, and thence of creating more interesting situations, he wished to conduct the mortal agents in his drama according to the rules of probability; in short, to make them think, speak and act, as it might be supposed mere men and women would do in extraordinary positions. He had observed, that in all inspired writings, the personages under the dispensation of miracles and witnesses to the most stupendous phenomena, never lose sight of their human character: whereas in the productions of romantic story, an improbable event never fails to be attended by an absurd dialogue. The actors seem to lose their senses, the moment the laws of Nature have lost their tone. As the public have applauded the attempt, the author must not say he was entirely unequal to the task he had undertaken: yet if the new route he has struck out shall have paved a road for men of brighter talents, he shall own with pleasure and modesty, that he was sensible the plan was capable of receiving greater embellishments than his imagination or conduct of the passions could bestow on it.

With regard to the deportment of the domestics, on which I have touched in the former preface, I will beg leave to add a few words. The simplicity of their behaviour, almost tending to excite smiles, which at first seem not consonant to the serious cast of the work, appeared to me not only not improper, but was marked designedly in that manner. My rule was Nature. However grave, important, or even melancholy, the sensations of Princes and heroes may be, they do not stamp the same affections on their domestics: at least the latter do not, or should not be made to express their passions in the same dignified tone. In my humble opinion, the contrast between the sublime of the one and the *naivetè* of the others, sets the pathetic of the former in a stronger light. The very impatience which a reader feels, while delayed by the coarse pleasantries of vulgar actors from arriving at the knowledge of the important catastrophe he expects, perhaps heightens, certainly proves, that he has been artfully interested in the depending event. But I had higher authority than my own opinion for this conduct. The great master of nature, Shakespeare, was the model I copied. Let me ask if his tragedies of *Hamlet* and *Julius Cæsar* would not lose a considerable share of their spirit and wonderful beauties, if the humour of the grave-diggers, the fooleries of Polonius, and the clumsy jests of the Roman citizens were omitted, or vested in heroics? Is not the eloquence of Antony, the nobler and affectedly-unaffected oration of Brutus, artificially exalted by the rude bursts of nature from the mouths of their auditors? These touches remind one of the Grecian sculptor, who to convey the idea of a Colossus within the dimensions of a seal, inserted a little boy measuring his thumb.

No, says Voltaire in his edition of Corneille, this mixture of buffoonery and solemnity is intolerable—Voltaire is a genius*—but not of Shakespeare's magnitude. Without re-

---

* The following remark is foreign to the present question, yet excusable in an Englishman, who is willing to think that the severe criticisms of so masterly a writer as Voltaire on our immortal countryman, may have been the effusions of wit and precipitation, rather than the result of judgment and attention. May not the Critic's skill in the force and powers of our language have been as incorrect and incompetent as his knowledge of our history? of the latter his own pen has dropped glaring evidence. In his Preface to Thomas Corneille's Earl of *Essex*, Monsieur de Voltaire allows that the truth of history has been grossly perverted in that piece. In excuse he pleads, that when Corneille wrote, the *Noblesse* of *France* were much unread in English story; but now, says the commenator, that they study it, such misinterpretation would not be suffered—yet forgetting that the period of ignorance is lapsed, and that it is not very necessary to instruct the knowing, he undertakes from the overflowing of his own reading to give the Nobility of his own country a detail of Queen Elizabeth's favourites—of whom, says he, Robert Dudley was the first, and the Earl of Leicester the second.— Could one have believed that it could be necessary to inform Monsieur de Voltaire himself, that Robert Dudley and the Earl of Leicester were the same person?

curring to disputable authority, I appeal from Voltaire to himself. I shall not avail myself of his former encomiums on our mighty poet; though the French critic has twice translated the same speech in *Hamlet,* some years ago in admiration, latterly in derision; and I am sorry to find that his judgment grows weaker, when it ought to be farther matured. But I shall make use of his own words, delivered on the general topic of the theatre, when he was neither thinking to recommend or decry Shakespeare's practice; consequently at a moment when Voltaire was impartial. In the preface to his *Enfant Prodigue,* that exquisite piece of which I declare my admiration, and which, should I live twenty years longer, I trust I shall never attempt to ridicule, he has these words, speaking of Comedy [but equally applicable to Tragedy, if Tragedy is, as surely it ought to be, a picture of human life; nor can I conceive why occasional pleasantry ought more to be banished from the tragic scene, than pathetic seriousness from the comic] *On y voit un melange de serieux et de plaisanterie, de comique et de touchant;* souvent meme une seule avanture *produit tous ces contrastes. Rien n'est si commun, qu'une maison dans laquelle* un pere gronde, une fille occupèe de sa passion pleure; *le fils se moque des deux, et quelques parens prennent part differemment à la scene,* &c. *Nous n'inferons pas de là que toute Comedie doive avoir des scenes de bouffonerie et des scenes attendrissantes: il y a beaucoup de tres bonnes pieces ou il ne regne que de la gayetè; d'autres toutes serieuses; d'autres melangèes: d'autres ou l'attendrissement va jusques aux larmes:* il ne faut donner l'exclusion à aucun genre: *et si l'on me demandoit, quel genre est le meilleur, je repondrois, celui qui est le mieux traitè.* Surely if a Comedy may be *toute serieuse,* Tragedy may now and then, soberly, be indulged in a smile. Who shall prescribe it? shall the critic, who in self-defence declares that *no kind* ought to be excluded from Comedy, give laws to Shakespeare?

I am aware that the preface from whence I have quoted

these passages, does not stand in Monsieur de Voltaire's name, but in that of his editor; yet who doubts that the editor and author were the same person? or where is the editor, who has so happily possessed himself of his author's stile and brilliant ease of argument? These passages were indubitably the genuine sentiments of that great writer. In his epistle to Maffei, prefixed to his *Merope,* he delivers almost the same opinion, though I doubt with a little irony. I will repeat his words, and then give my reason for quoting them. After translating a passage in Maffei's *Merope,* Monsieur de Voltaire adds, *Tous ces traits sont naifs: tout y est convenable à ceux que vous introduisez sur la scene, et aux mœurs que vous leur donnez. Ces familiaritès naturelles eussent etè, à ce que je crois, bien recuès dans Athenes; mais Paris et notre parterre veulent une autre espece de simplicitè.* I doubt, I say, whether there is not a grain of sneer in this and other passages of that epistle; yet the force of truth is not damaged by being tinged with ridicule. Maffei was to represent a Grecian story: Surely the Athenians were as competent judges of Grecian manners and of the propriety of introducing them, as the *Parterre* of Paris. On the contrary, says Voltaire [and I cannot but admire his reasoning] there were but ten thousand citizens at Athens, and Paris has near eight hundred thousand inhabitants, among whom one may reckon thirty thousand judges of dramatic works.—Indeed!—but allowing so numerous a tribunal, I believe this is the only instance in which it was ever pretended that thirty thousands persons, living near two thousand years after the æra in question, were, upon the mere face of the poll, declared better judges than the Grecians themselves of what ought to be the manners of a Tragedy written on a Grecian story.

I will not enter into a discussion of the *espece de simplicitè,* which the *Parterre* of Paris demands, nor of the shackles with which *the thirty thousand judges* have cramped their poetry, the chief merit of which, as I gather from repeated passages in *The New Commentary on Corneille,* consists in vaulting in spite of those fetters; a merit which, if true, would reduce poetry from the lofty effort of imagination, to a puerile and most contemptible labour—*difficiles nugæ* with a witness! I cannot however help mentioning a couplet, which, to my *English* ears, always sounded as the flattest and most trifling instance of circumstantial propriety; but which Voltaire, who has dealt so severely with nine parts in ten of Corneille's works, has singled out to defend in Racine;

> *De son appartement cette porte est prochaine,*
> *Et cette autre conduit dans celui de la* Reine.

IN ENGLISH,

> *To Cæsar's closet through this door you come,*
> *And t'other leads to the Queen's drawing-room.*

Unhappy Shakespeare! hadst thou made Rosencrans inform his compeer, Guildenstern, of the ichnography of the palace of Copenhagen, instead of presenting us with a moral dialogue between the Prince of Denmark and the gravedigger, the illuminated pit of Paris would have been instructed *a second time* to adore thy talents.

The result of all I have said, is, to shelter my own daring under the canon of the brightest genius this country, at least, has produced. I might have pleaded, that having created a new species of romance, I was at liberty to lay down what rules I thought fit for the conduct of it: But I should be more proud of having imitated, however faintly, weakly, and at a distance, so masterly a pattern, than to enjoy the entire merit of invention, unless I could have marked my work with genius as well as with originality. Such as it is, the Public have honoured it sufficiently, whatever rank their suffrages allot to it.

CHAPTER I

Manfred, Prince of Otranto, had one son and one daughter: The latter a most beautiful virgin, aged eighteen, was called Matilda. Conrad, the son, was three years younger, a homely youth, sickly, and of no promising disposition; yet he was the darling of his father, who never showed any symptoms of affection to Matilda. Manfred had contracted a marriage for his son with the Marquis of Vicenza's daughter, Isabella; and she had already been delivered by her guardians into the hands of Manfred, that he might celebrate the wedding as soon as Conrad's infirm state of health would permit. Manfred's impatience for this ceremonial was remarked by his family and neighbours. The former indeed, apprehending the severity of their Prince's disposition, did not dare to utter their surmises on this precipitation. Hippolita, his wife, an amiable lady, did sometimes venture to represent the danger of marrying their only son so early, considering his great youth, and greater infirmities; but she never received any other answer than reflections on her own sterility, who had given him but one heir. His tenants and subjects were less cautious in their discourses: They attributed this hasty wedding to the Prince's dread of seeing accomplished an ancient prophecy, which was said to have pronounced, that *the Castle and Lordship of Otranto should pass from the present family, whenever the real owner should be grown too large to inhabit it.* It was difficult to make any sense of this prophecy; and still less easy to conceive what it had to do with the marriage in question. Yet these mysteries, or contradictions, did not make the populace adhere the less to their opinion.

15

Young Conrad's birth-day was fixed for his espousals. The company was assembled in the chapel of the Castle, and every thing ready for beginning the divine office, when Conrad himself was missing. Manfred impatient of the least delay, and who had not observed his son retire, dispatched one of his attendants to summon the young Prince. The servant, who had not staid long enough to have crossed the court to Conrad's apartment, came running back breathless, in a frantic manner, his eyes staring, and foaming at the mouth. He said nothing, but pointed to the court. The company were struck with terror and amazement. The Princess Hippolita, without knowing what was the matter, but anxious for her son, swooned away. Manfred, less apprehensive than enraged at the procrastination of the nuptials, and at the folly of his domestic, asked imperiously, what was the matter? The fellow made no answer, but continued pointing towards the court-yard; and at last, after repeated questions put to him, cried out, "Oh! the helmet! the helmet!" In the mean time, some of the company had run into the court, from whence was heard a confused noise of shrieks, horror, and surprise. Manfred, who began to be alarmed at not seeing his son, went himself to get information of what occasioned this strange confusion. Matilda remained endeavouring to assist her mother, and Isabella staid for the same purpose, and to avoid showing any impatience for the bridegroom, for whom, in truth, she had conceived little affection.

The first thing that struck Manfred's eyes was a groupe of his servants endeavouring to raise something that appeared to him a mountain of sable plumes. He gazed without believing his sight. "What are ye doing?" cried Manfred wrathfully; "where is my son?" A volley of voices replied, "Oh! My Lord! The Prince! The Prince, the helmet! the helmet!" Shocked with these lamentable sounds, and dreading he knew not what, he advanced hastily,—but what a sight for a father's eyes!—he beheld his child dashed to pieces, and almost buried under an enormous helmet, an hundred times more large than any casque ever made for human being, and shaded with a proportionable quantity of black feathers.

The horror of the spectacle, the ignorance of all around how this misfortune had happened, and above all, the tremendous phænomenon before him, took away the Prince's speech. Yet his silence lasted longer than even grief could occasion. He fixed his eyes on what he wished in vain to believe a vision; and seemed less attentive to his loss, than buried in meditation on the stupendous object that had occasioned it. He touched, he examined the fatal casque; nor could even the bleeding mangled remains of the young Prince, divert the eyes of Manfred from the portent before him. All who had known his partial fondness for young Conrad, were as much surprised at their Prince's insensibility, as thunder-struck themselves at the miracle of the helmet. They conveyed the disfigured corpse into the hall, without receiving the least direction from Manfred. As little was he attentive to the Ladies who remained in the chapel: On the contrary, without mentioning the unhappy Princesses, his wife and daughter, the first sounds that dropped from Manfred's lips were, "Take care of the lady Isabella."

The domestics, without observing the singularity of this direction, were guided by their affection to their mistress, to consider it as peculiarly addressed to her situation, and flew to her assistance. They conveyed her to her chamber more dead than alive, and indifferent to all the strange circumstances she heard, except the death of her son. Matilda, who doated on her mother, smothered her own grief and amazement, and thought of nothing but assisting and comforting her afflicted parent. Isabella, who had been treated by Hippolita like a daughter, and who returned that tenderness with equal duty and affection, was scarce less assiduous about the Princess; at the same time endeavouring to partake and lessen the weight of sorrow which she saw Matilda strove to suppress, for whom she had conceived the warmest sympathy of friendship. Yet her own situation could not help finding its place in her thoughts. She felt no concern for the death of young Conrad, except commiseration; and she was not sorry to be delivered from a marriage which had promised her little felicity, either from her destined bridegroom, or from the severe temper of Manfred, who, though he had distinguished her by great indulgence, had imprinted her mind with terror, from his causeless rigour to such amiable Princesses as Hippolita and Matilda.

While the Ladies were conveying the wretched mother to her bed, Manfred remained in the court, gazing on the ominous casque, and regardless of the crowd which the strangeness of the event had now assembled around him. The few words he articulated, tended solely to inquiries, whether any man knew from whence it could have come? Nobody could give him the least information. However, as it seemed to be the sole object of his curiosity, it soon became so to the rest of the spectators, whose conjectures were as absurd and improbable, as the catastrophe itself was unprecedented. In the midst of their senseless guesses, a young peasant, whom rumour had drawn thither from a neighbouring village, observed that the miraculous helmet was exactly like that on the figure in black marble of Alfonso the Good, one of their former Princes, in the church of St. Nicholas. "Villain! What sayest thou!" cried Manfred, starting from his trance in a tempest of rage, and seizing the young man by the collar; "how darest thou utter such treason? thy life shall pay for it." The spectators, who as little comprehended the cause of the Prince's fury as all the rest they had seen, were at a loss to unravel this new circumstance. The young peasant himself was still more astonished, not conceiving how he had offended the Prince: Yet recollecting himself, with a mixture of grace and humility, he disengaged himself from Manfred's gripe, and then with an obeisance, which discovered more jealousy of innocence, than dismay; he asked, with respect, of what he was guilty! Manfred, more enraged at the vigour, however decently exerted, with which the young man had shaken off his hold, than appeased by his submission, ordered his attendants to seize him, and, if he had not been withheld by his friends, whom he had invited to the nuptials, would have poignarded the peasant in their arms.

During this altercation, some of the vulgar spectators had run to the great church, which stood near the castle, and came back open-mouth'd, declaring, that the helmet was missing from Alfonso's statue. Manfred, at this news, grew perfectly frantic; and, as if he sought a subject on which to vent the tempest within him, he rushed again on the young peasant, crying, "Villain! Monster! Sorcerer! 'tis thou hast done this! 'tis thou hast slain my son!" The mob, who wanted some object within the scope of their capacities, on whom they might discharge their bewildered reasonings, caught the words from the mouth of their Lord, and re-ecchoed, "Ay, ay; 'tis he, 'tis he: He has stolen the helmet from good Alfonso's tomb, and dashed out the brains of our young Prince with it,"—never reflecting how enormous the disproportion was between the marble helmet that had been in the church, and that of steel before their eyes; nor how impossible it was for a youth, seemingly not twenty, to wield a piece of armour of so prodigious a weight.

The folly of these ejaculations brought Manfred to himself: Yet whether provoked at the peasant having observed the resemblance between the two helmets, and thereby led to the farther discovery of the absence of that in the church; or wishing to bury any fresh rumours under so impertinent a supposition; he gravely pronounced that the young man was certainly a necromancer, and that till the church could take cognizance of the affair, he would have the Magician, whom they had thus detected, kept prisoner under the helmet itself, which he ordered his attendants to raise, and place the young man under it; declaring he should be kept there without food, with which his own infernal art might furnish him.

It was in vain for the youth to represent against this preposterous sentence: In vain did Manfred's friends endeavour to divert him from this savage and ill-grounded resolution. The generality were charmed with their Lord's decision, which, to their apprehensions, carried great appearance of justice, as the Magician was to be punished by the very instrument with which he had offended: Nor were they struck with the least compunction at the probability of the youth being starved, for they firmly believed, that, by his diabolic skill, he could easily supply himself with nutriment.

Manfred thus saw his commands even chearfully obeyed, and appointing a guard with strict orders to prevent any food being conveyed to the prisoner, he dismissed his friends and attendants, and retired to his own chamber, after locking the gates of the castle, in which he suffered none but his domestics to remain.

In the mean time, the care and zeal of the young Ladies had brought the Princess Hippolita to herself, who amidst the transports of her own sorrow, frequently demanded news of her Lord, would have dismissed her attendants to watch over him, and at last enjoined Matilda to leave her, and visit and comfort her father. Matilda, who wanted no affectionate duty to Manfred, though she trembled at his austerity, obeyed the orders of Hippolita, whom she tenderly recommended to Isabella; and enquiring of the domestics for her father, was informed that he was retired to his chamber, and had commanded that nobody should have admittance to him. Concluding that he was immersed in sorrow for the death of her brother, and fearing to renew his tears by the sight of his sole remaining child, she hesitated whether she should break in upon his affliction; yet solicitude for him, backed by the commands of her mother, encouraged her to venture disobeying the orders he had given, a fault she had never been guilty of before. The gentle timidity of her nature made her pause for some minutes at his door. She heard him traverse his chamber backwards and forwards with disordered steps; a mood which increased her apprehensions. She was however just going to beg admittance, when Manfred suddenly opened his door; and as it was now twilight, concurring with the disorder of his mind, he did not distinguish the person, but asked angrily, who it was? Matilda replied trembling, "My dearest father, it is I, your daughter." Manfred stepping back hastily, cried, "Begone, I do not want a daughter;" and flinging back abruptly, clapped the door against the terrified Matilda.

She was too well acquainted with her father's impetuosity to venture a second intrusion. When she had a little recovered the shock of so bitter a reception, she wiped away her tears to prevent the additional stab that the knowledge of it would give to Hippolita, who questioned her in the most anxious terms on the health of Manfred, and how he bore his loss. Matilda assured her he was well, and supported his misfortune with manly fortitude. "But will he not let me see him?" said Hippolita mournfully; "will he not permit me to blend my tears with his, and shed a mother's sorrows in the bosom of her Lord? Or do you deceive me, Matilda? I know how Manfred doated on his son: Is not the stroke too heavy for him? has he not sunk under it?—You do not answer me—alas! I dread the worst!—raise me, my maidens; I will, I will see my Lord. Bear me to him instantly: He is dearer to me even than my children." Matilda made signs to Isabella to prevent Hippolita's rising; and both those lovely young women were using their gentle violence to stop and calm the Princess, when a servant, on the part of Manfred, arrived and told Isabella that his Lord demanded to speak with her.

"With me?" cried Isabella. "Go," said Hippolita, relieved by a message from her Lord: "Manfred cannot support the sight of his own family. He thinks you less disordered than we are, and dreads the shock of my grief. Console him, dear Isabella, and tell him I will smother my own anguish rather than add to his."

As it was now evening, the servant, who conducted Isabella, bore a torch before her. When they came to Manfred, who was walking impatiently about the gallery, he started and said hastily, "Take away that light, and begone." Then shutting the door impetuously, he flung himself upon a bench against the wall, and bad Isabella sit by him. She obeyed trembling. "I sent for you, Lady," said he,—and then stopped under great appearance of confusion. "My Lord!"— "Yes, I sent for you on a matter of great moment," resumed he,—"dry your tears, young Lady—you have lost your bridegroom."—"Yes, cruel fate!" "And I have lost the hopes of my race!—but Conrad was not worthy of your beauty"— "How! my Lord," said Isabella; "sure you do not suspect me of not feeling the concern I ought. My duty and affection would have always"—"Think no more of him," interrupted Manfred; "he was a sickly puny child, and heaven has perhaps taken him away, that I might not trust the honours of my house on so frail a foundation. The line of Manfred calls for numerous supports. My foolish fondness for that boy blinded the eyes of my prudence—but it is better as it is. I hope in a few years, to have reason to rejoice at the death of Conrad."

Words cannot paint the astonishment of Isabella. At first she apprehended that grief had disordered Manfred's understanding. Her next thought suggested that this strange discourse was designed to ensnare her: She feared that Manfred had perceived her indifference for his son: And in consequence of that idea she replied, "Good my Lord, do not doubt my tenderness: my heart would have accompanied my hand. Conrad would have engrossed all my care; and wherever fate shall dispose of me, I shall always cherish his memory, and regard your Highness and the virtuous Hippolita as my parents." "Curse on Hippolita!" cried Manfred: "Forget her from this moment as I do. In short, Lady, you have missed a husband undeserving of your charms: They shall now be better disposed of. Instead of a sickly boy, you shall have a husband in the prime of his age, who will know how to value your beauties, and who may expect a numerous offspring." "Alas! My Lord," said Isabella, "my mind is too sadly engrossed by the recent catastrophe in your family to think of another marriage. If ever my father returns, and it shall be his pleasure, I shall obey, as I did when I consented to give my hand to your son: But until his return, permit me to remain under your hospitable roof, and employ the melancholy hours in asswaging yours, Hippolita's, and the fair Matilda's affliction."

"I desired you once before," said Manfred angrily, "not to name that woman: from this hour she must be a stranger to you, as she must be to me;—in short, Isabella, since I cannot give you my son, I offer you myself."—"Heavens!" cried Isabella, waking from her delusion, "what do I hear! You! My Lord! You! My father-in-law! the father of Conrad! the husband of the virtuous and tender Hippolita!"—"I tell you," said Manfred imperiously, "Hippolita is no longer my wife, I divorce her from this hour. Too long has she cursed me by her unfruitfulness: my fate depends on having sons,—and this night I trust will give a new date to my hopes." At those words he seized the cold hand of Isabella, who was half dead with fright and horror. She shrieked and started from him. Manfred rose to pursue her, when the moon, which was now up and gleamed in at the opposite casement, presented to his sight the plumes of the fatal helmet, which rose to the height of the windows, waving backwards and forwards in a tempestuous manner, and accompanied with a hollow and rustling sound. Isabella, who gathered courage from her situation, and who dreaded nothing so much as Manfred's pursuit of his declaration, cried, "Look! My Lord; see, heaven itself declares against your impious intentions!"—"Heaven nor hell shall impede my designs," said Manfred, advancing again to seize the Princess. At that instant the portrait of his grandfather, which hung over the bench where they had been sitting, uttered a deep sigh, and heaved its breast. Isabella, whose back was turned to the picture, saw not the motion, nor knew whence the sound came, but started, and said, "Hark, my Lord! What sound was that?" and at the same time made towards the door. Manfred, distracted between the flight of Isabella, who had now reached the stairs, and yet unable to keep his eyes from the picture which began to move, had however advanced some steps after her, still looking backwards on the portrait, when he saw it quit its pannel, and descend on the floor with a grave and melancholy air. "Do I dream?" cried Manfred returning, "or are the devils themselves in league against me? speak, infernal spectre! or, if thou art my grandsire, why dost thou too conspire against thy wretched descendant, who too dearly pays for—" E'er he could finish the sentence, the vision sighed again, and made a sign to Manfred to follow him. "Lead on!" cried Manfred; "I will follow thee to the gulph of perdition." The spectre marched sedately, but dejected, to the end of the gallery, and turned into a chamber on the right-hand. Manfred accompanied him at a little distance, full of anxiety and horror, but resolved. As he would have entered the chamber, the door was clapped to with violence by an invisible hand. The Prince, collecting courage from this delay, would have forcibly burst open the door with his foot, but found that it resisted his utmost efforts. "Since hell will not satisfy my curiosity," said Manfred, "I will use the human means in my power for preserving my race; Isabella shall not escape me."

That Lady, whose resolution had given way to terror the moment she had quitted Manfred, continued her flight to the bottom of the principal staircase. There she stopped, not knowing whether to direct her steps, nor how to escape from the impetuosity of the Prince. The gates of the castle she knew were locked, and guards placed in the court. Should she, as her heart prompted her, go and prepare Hippolita for the cruel destiny that awaited her; she did not doubt but Manfred would seek her there, and that his violence would incite him to double the injury he meditated, without leaving room for them to avoid the impetuosity of his passions. Delay might give him time to reflect on the horrid measures he had conceived, or produce some circumstance in her favour, if she could for that night at least avoid his odious purpose.—Yet where conceal herself! how avoid the pursuit he would infallibly make throughout the castle! As these thoughts passed rapidly through her mind, she recollected a subterraneous passage which led from the vaults of the castle to the church of St. Nicholas. Could she reach the altar before she was overtaken, she knew even Manfred's violence would not dare to prophane the sacredness of the place; and she determined, if no other means of deliverance offered, to shut herself up for ever among the holy virgins, whose convent was contiguous to the cathedral. In this resolution, she seized a lamp that burned at the foot of the staircase, and hurried towards the secret passage.

The lower part of the castle was hollowed into several intricate cloysters; and it was not easy for one under so much anxiety to find the door that opened into the cavern. An awful silence reigned throughout those subterraneous regions, except now and then some blasts of wind that shook the doors she had passed, and which grating on the rusty hinges, were reecchoed through that long labyrinth of darkness. Every murmur struck her with new terror;—yet more she dreaded to hear the wrathful voice of Manfred urging his domestics to pursue her. She trod as softly as impatience would give her leave,—yet frequently stopped and listened to hear if she was followed. In one of those moments she thought she heard a sigh. She shuddered, and recoiled a few paces. In a moment she thought she heard the step of some person. Her blood curdled; she concluded it was Manfred. Every suggestion that horror could inspire rushed into her mind. She condemned her rash flight, which had thus exposed her to his rage in a place where her cries were not likely to draw any body to her assistance.—Yet the sound seemed not to come from behind,—if Manfred knew where she was, he must have followed her: She was still in one of the cloysters, and the steps she had heard were too distinct to proceed from the way she had come. Cheared with this reflection, and hoping to find a friend in whoever was not the Prince; she was going to advance, when a door that stood a jar, at some distance to the left, was opened gently: But e'er her lamp, which she held up, could discover who opened it, the person retreated precipitately on seeing the light.

Isabella, whom every incident was sufficient to dismay, hesitated whether she should proceed. Her dread of Manfred soon outweighed every other terror. The very circumstance of the person avoiding her, gave her a sort of courage. It could only be, she thought, some domestic belonging to the castle. Her gentleness had never raised her an enemy, and conscious innocence bade her hope that, unless sent by the Prince's order to seek her, his servants would rather assist than prevent her flight. Fortifying herself with these reflections, and believing by what she could observe, that she was near the mouth of the subterraneous cavern, she approached the door that had been opened; but a sudden gust of wind that met her at the door, extinguished her lamp, and left her in total darkness.

Words cannot paint the horror of the Princess's situation. Alone in so dismal a place, her mind imprinted with all the terrible events of the day, hopeless of escaping, expecting every moment the arrival of Manfred, and far from tranquil on knowing she was within reach of somebody, she knew not whom, who for some cause seemed concealed thereabouts, all these thoughts crouded on her distracted mind, and she was ready to sink under her apprehensions. She addressed herself to every Saint in heaven, and inwardly implored their assistance. For a considerable time she remained in an agony of despair. At last, as softly as was possible, she felt for the door, and having found it, entered trembling into the vault from whence she had heard the sigh and steps. It gave her a kind of momentary joy to perceive an imperfect ray of clouded moonshine gleam from the roof of the vault, which seemed to be fallen in, and from whence hung a fragment of earth or building, she could not distinguish which, that appeared to have been crushed inwards. She advanced eagerly towards this chasm, when she discerned a human form standing close against the wall.

She shrieked, believing it the ghost of her betrothed Conrad. The figure advancing, said in a submissive voice, "Be not alarmed, Lady; I will not injure you." Isabella a little encouraged by the words and tone of voice of the stranger, and recollecting that this must be the person who had opened the door, recovered her spirits enough to reply, "Sir, whoever you are, take pity on a writched Princess, standing on the brink of destruction: Assist me to escape from this fatal castle, or in few moments I may be made miserable for ever." "Alas!" said the stranger, "what can I do to assist you? I will die in your defence; but I am unacquainted with

the castle, and want—" "Oh;" said Isabella, hastily interrupting him, "help me but to find a trap-door that must be
hereabout, and it is the greatest service you can do me, for
I have not a minute to lose." Saying these words, she felt
about on the pavement, and directed the stranger to search
likewise for a smooth piece of brass inclosed in one of the
stones. "That," said she, "is the lock, which opens with a
spring, of which I know the secret. If we can find that, I
may escape—if not, alas! courteous stranger, I fear, I shall
have involved you in my misfortunes: Manfred will suspect
you for the accomplice of my flight, and you will fall a
victim to his resentment." "I value not my life," said the
stranger, "and it will be some comfort to lose it, in trying to
deliver you from his tyranny." "Generous youth," said Isabella, "how shall I ever requite—" As she uttered those
words, a ray of moonshine streaming through a cranny of
the ruin above shone directly on the lock they sought—"Oh!
transport!" said Isabella, "here is the trap-door!" and taking
out a key, she touched the spring, which starting aside, discovered an iron ring. "Lift up the door," said the Princess.
The stranger obeyed; and beneath appeared some stone
steps descending into a vault totally dark. "We must go
down here," said Isabella: "Follow me; dark and dismal as
it is, we cannot miss our way; it leads directly to the church
of St. Nicholas—but perhaps," added the Princess modestly,
"you have no reason to leave the castle, nor have I farther
occasion for your service: in few minutes I shall be safe
from Manfred's rage—only let me know to whom I am so
much obliged." "I will never quit you," said the stranger
eagerly, "until I have placed you in safety—nor think me,
Princess, more generous than I am; though you are my
principal care—" The stranger was interrupted by a sudden
noise of voices that seemed approaching, and they soon
distinguished these words: "Talk not to me of necromancers;
I tell you she must be in the castle: I will find her in spite

of enchantment—" "Oh! heavens," cried Isabella, "it is the voice of Manfred! make haste or we are ruined! and shut the trap-door after you." Saying this, she descended the steps precipitately, and as the stranger hastened to follow her, he let the door slip out of his hands: it fell, and the spring closed over it. He tried in vain to open it, not having observed Isabella's method of touching the spring: nor had he many moments to make an essay. The noise of the falling door had been heard by Manfred, who directed by the sound, hastened thither, attended by his servants with torches. "It must be Isabella;" cried Manfred before he entered the vault; "she is escaping by the subterraneous passage, but she cannot have got far."— What was the astonishment of the Prince, when, instead of Isabella, the light of the torches discovered to him the young peasant, whom he thought confined under the fatal helmet: "Traitor!" said Manfred, "how camest thou here? I thought thee in durance above in the court." "I am no traitor," replied the young man boldly, "nor am I answerable for your thoughts." "Presumptuous villain!" cried Manfred, "dost thou provoke my wrath? tell me; how hast thou escaped from above? thou hast corrupted thy guards, and their lives shall answer it." "My poverty," said the peasant calmly, "will disculpate them: Though the ministers of a tyrant's wrath, to thee they are faithful, and but too willing to execute the orders which you unjustly imposed upon them." "Art thou so hardy as to dare my vengeance?" said the Prince—"but tortures shall force the truth from thee. Tell me, I will know thy accomplices." "There was my accomplice!" said the youth smiling, and pointing to the roof. Manfred ordered the torches to be held up, and perceived that one of the cheeks of the enchanted casque had forced its way through the pavement of the court, as his servants had let it fall over the peasant, and had broken through into the vault, leaving a gap through which the peasant had pressed himself some minutes before he was found by Isabella. "Was that the way by which thou didst descend?" said Manfred. "It was;" said the youth. "But what noise was that," said Manfred, "which I heard as I entered the cloyster?" "A door clapped:" said the peasant; "I heard it as well as you." "What door?" said Manfred hastily. "I am not acquainted with your castle;" said the peasant; "this is the first time I ever entered it; and this vault the only part of it within which I ever was." "But I tell thee," said Manfred (wishing to find out if the youth had discovered the trap-door) "it was this way I heard the noise: My servants heard it too"—"My Lord," interrupted one of them officiously, "to be sure it was the trap-door, and he was going to make his escape." "Peace! blockhead," said the Prince angrily; "if he was going to escape, how should he come on this side? I will know from his own mouth what noise it was I heard. Tell me truly; thy life depends on thy veracity." "My veracity is dearer to me than my life;" said the peasant: "nor would I purchase the one by forfeiting the other." "Indeed! young philosopher!" said Manfred contemptuously; "tell me then, what was the noise I heard?" "Ask me what I can answer," said he, "and put me to death instantly if I tell you a lie." Manfred growing impatient at the steady valour and indifference of the youth, cried, "Well then thou man of truth! answer; was it the fall of the trap-door that I heard?" "It was;" said the youth. "It was!" said the Prince; "and how didst thou come to know there was a trap-door here?" "I saw the plate of brass by a gleam of moonshine;" replied he. "But what told thee it was a lock?" said Manfred; "How didst thou discover the secret of opening it?" "Providence, that delivered me from the helmet, was able to direct me to the spring of a lock;" said he. "Providence should have gone a little farther, and have placed thee out of the reach of my resentment," said Manfred: "When Providence had taught thee to open the lock, it abandoned thee for a fool, who did not know how to make use of its favours. Why didst thou not pursue the path pointed out for thy escape? Why didst thou shut the trap-door before you hadst descended the steps?" "I might ask you, my Lord," said the peasant, "how I, totally unacquainted with your castle, was to know that those steps led to any outlet? but I scorn to evade your questions. Wherever those steps lead to, perhaps I should have explored the way—I could not be in a worse situation than I was. But the truth is, I let the trap-door fall: Your immediate arrival followed. I had given the alarm—what imported it to me whether I was seized a minute sooner or a minute late?" "Thou art a resolute villain for thy years;" said Manfred—"yet on reflection I suspect thou dost but trifle with me: Thou hast not yet told me how thou didst open the lock." "That I will show you, my Lord;" said the peasant, and taking up a fragment of stone that had fallen from above, he laid himself on the trap-door, and began to beat on the piece of brass that covered it; meaning to gain time for the escape of the Princess. This presence of mind, joined to the frankness of the youth, staggered Manfred. He even felt a disposition towards pardoning one who had been guilty of no crime. Manfred was not one of those savage tyrants who wanton in cruelty unprovoked. The circumstances of his fortune had given an asperity to his temper, which was naturally humane; and his virtues were always ready to operate, when his passions did not obscure his reason.

While the Prince was in this suspense, a confused noise of voices ecchoed through the distant vaults. As the sound approached, he distinguished the clamours of some of his domestics, whom he had dispersed through the castle in search of Isabella, calling out, "Where is my Lord? where is the Prince?" "Here I am;" said Manfred, as they came nearer; "have you found the Princess?" The first that arrived, replied, "Oh! my Lord! I am glad we have found you"— "Found me!" said Manfred; "have you found the Princess!"

"We thought we had, my Lord," said the fellow, looking terrified—"but"—"But what?" cried the Prince; "has she escaped?"—"Jaquez and I, my Lord"—"Yes, I and Diego," interrupted the second, who came up in still greater consternation—"Speak one of you at a time," said Manfred; "I ask you where is the Princess?" "We do not know;" said they both together; "but we are frightened out of our wits"—"So I think, blockheads," said Manfred; "what is it has scared you thus?"—"Oh! my Lord," said Jaquez, "Diego has seen such a fight! your Highness would not believe your eyes"—"what new absurdity is this!" cried Manfred—"give me a direct answer, or by heaven"—"Why, my Lord, if it please your Highness to hear me," said the poor fellow; "Diego and I"—"Yes I and Jaquez," cried his comrade—"Did not I forbid you to speak both at a time?" said the Prince: "You, Jaquez, answer; for the other fool seems more distracted than thou art:" "What is the matter? my gracious Lord," said Jaquez, "if it please your Highness to hear me: Diego and I according to your Highness' orders went to search for the young Lady; but being comprehensive that we might meet the ghost of my young Lord, your Highness's son, God rest his soul, as he has not received christian burial"—"Sot!" cried Manfred in a rage, "it is only a ghost then that thou hast seen?" "Oh! worse! worse! my Lord," cried Diego: "I had rather have seen ten whole ghosts"—"Grant me patience!" said Manfred; "these blockheads distract me—out of my sight, Diego! and thou, Jaquez, tell me in one word, art thou sober? art thou raving? thou wast wont to have some sense: has the other sot frightened himself and thee too? speak! what is it he fancies he has seen?" "Why, my Lord," replied Jaquez trembling, "I was going to tell your Highness, that since the calamitous misfortune of my young Lord, God rest his precious soul! not one of us your Highness' faithful servants, indeed we are, my Lord, though poor men; I say, not one of us has dared to set a foot about the castle, but two together: So Diego and I, thinking that my young Lady might be in the great gallery; went up there to look for her, and tell her your Highness wanted something to impart to her—" "O blundering fools!" cried Manfred: "And in the mean time she has made her escape, because you were afraid of goblins!—Why, thou knave! she left me in the gallery; I came from thence myself." "For all that, she may be there still for ought I know;" said Jaquez; "but the devil shall have me before I seek her there again!—poor Diego! I do not believe he will ever recover it!" "Recover what?" said Manfred; "am I never to learn what it is has terrified these rascals?—but I lose my time; follow me slave; I will see if she is in the gallery"—"For heaven's sake, my dear good Lord," cried Jaquez, "do not go to the gallery! Satan himself I believe is in the great chamber next to the gallery——" Manfred, who hitherto had treated the terror of his servants as an idle panic, was struck at this new circumstance. He recollected the apparition of the portrait, and the sudden closing of the door at the end of the gallery—his voice faltered, and he asked with disorder, "What is in the great chamber?" "My Lord," said Jaquez, "When Diego and I came into the gallery, he went first, for he said he had more courage than I. So when we came into the gallery, we found nobody. We looked under every bench and stool; and still we found nobody"—"Were all the pictures in their places?" said Manfred. "Yes, my Lord," answered Jaquez; "but we did not think of looking behind them"—"Well, well!" said Manfred, "proceed." "When we came to the door of the great chamber," continued Jaquez, "we found it shut"—"and could you not open it?" said Manfred. "Oh! yes, my Lord, would to heaven we had not!" replied he—"Nay, it was not I neither, it was Diego: he was grown fool-hardy, and would go on, though I advised him not"—"If ever I open a door that is shut again"—"Trifle not," said Manfred shuddering, "but tell me what you saw in the great chamber on opening the door"—"I! my Lord!" said Jaquez, "I saw nothing; I was behind Diego;—but I heard the noise"—"Jaquez," said Manfred in a solemn tone of voice; "tell me I adjure thee by the souls of my ancestors, what was it thou sawest? what was it thou heardst?" "It was Diego saw it, my Lord, it was not I;" replied Jaquez; "I only heard the noise. Diego had no sooner opened the door, then he cried out, and ran back—. I ran back too, and said, 'Is it the ghost?' 'The ghost? No, no,' said Diego, and his hair stood on end—'it is a giant I believe; he is all clad in armour, for I saw his foot and part of his leg, and they are as large as the helmet below in the court.' As he said these words, my Lord, we heard a violent motion and the ratling of armour, as if the giant was rising, for Diego has told me since, that he believes the giant was lying down, for the foot and leg were stretched at length on the floor. Before we could get to the end of the gallery, we heard the door of the great chamber clap behind us, but we did not dare turn back to see if the giant was following us—yet now I think on it, we must have heard him if he had pursued us—but for heaven's sake, good my Lord, send for the chaplain and have the castle exorcised, for, for certain, it is enchanted." "Ay, pray do, my Lord," cried all the servants at once, "or we must leave your Highness's service"—"Peace! dotards;" said Manfred, and follow me; I will know what all this means." "We! my Lord!" cried they with one voice, "we would not go up to the gallery for your Highness' revenue." The young peasant, who had stood silent, now spoke. "Will your Highness," said he, "permit me to try this adventure? my life is of consequence to nobody: I fear no bad angel, and have offended no good one." "Your behaviour is above your seeming;" said Manfred, viewing him with surprise and admiration—"hereafter I will reward your bravery—but now," continued he with a sigh, "I am so circumstanced, that I dare trust no eyes but my own—however, I give you leave to accompany me."

Manfred, when he first followed Isabella from the gallery, had gone directly to the apartment of his wife, concluding the Princess had retired thither. Hippolita, who knew his step, rose with anxious fondness to meet her Lord, whom she had not seen since the death of their son. She would have flown a transport mixed of joy and grief to his bosom, but he pushed her rudely off, and said, "Where is Isabella?" "Isabella, my Lord!" said the astonished Hippolita. "Yes; Isabella;" cried Manfred imperiously; "I want Isabella." "My Lord," replied Matilda, who perceived how much his behaviour had shocked her mother, "She has not been with us since your Highness summoned her to your apartment." "Tell me where she is;" said the Prince; "I do not want to know where she has been." "My good Lord," said Hippolita, "your daughter tells you the truth: Isabella left us by your command, and has not returned since;—but, my good Lord, compose yourself: retire to your rest: This dismal day has disordered you, Isabella shall wait your orders in the morning." "What then, you know where she is!" cried Manfred: "Tell me directly, for I will not lose an instant—and you, woman," speaking to his wife, "order your chaplain to attend me forthwith." "Isabella," said Hippolita calmly, "is retired, I suppose to her chamber: She is not accustomed to watch at this late hour. Gracious my Lord," continued she, "let me know what has disturbed you: has Isabella offended you?" "Trouble me not with questions," said Manfred, "but tell me where she is." "Matilda shall call her," said the Princess—"Sit down, my Lord, and resume your wonted fortitude."—"What, art thou jealous of Isabella," replied he, "that you wish to be present at our interview?" "Good heavens! my Lord," said Hippolita, "what is it your Highness means?" "Thou wilt know ere many minutes are passed;" said the cruel Prince. "Send your chaplain to me, and wait my pleasure here." At these words he flung out of the room in search of Isabella; leaving the amazed

Ladies thunder-struck with his words and frantic deportment, and lost in vain conjectures on what he was meditating.

Manfred was now returning from the vault, attended by
the peasant and a few of his servants whom he had obliged
to accompany him. He ascended the stair-case without
stopping till he arrived at the gallery, at the door of which
he met Hippolita and her chaplain. When Diego had been
dismissed by Manfred, he had gone directly to the Princess'
apartment with the alarm of what he had seen. That excellent Lady, who no more than Manfred, doubted of the reality of the vision, yet affected to treat it as a delirium of the
servant. Willing, however, to save her Lord from any additional shock, and prepared by a series of grief not to tremble
at any accession to it; she determined to make herself the
first sacrifice, if fate had marked the present hour for their
destruction. Dismissing the reluctant Matilda to her rest,
who in vain sued for leave to accompany her mother, and
attended only by her chaplain, Hippolita had visited the
gallery and great chamber; and now with more serenity of
soul than she had felt for many hours, she met her Lord,
and assured him that the vision of the gigantic leg and foot
was all a fable; and no doubt an impression made by fear,
and the dark and dismal hour of the night on the minds of
his servants. She and the chaplain had examined the chamber, and found every thing in the usual order.

Manfred, though persuaded, like his wife, that the vision
had been no work of fancy, recovered a little from the tempest of mind into which so many strange events had thrown
him. Ashamed too of his inhuman treatment of a Princess,
who returned every injury with new marks of tenderness
and duty; he felt returning love forcing itself into his eyes—
but not less ashamed of feeling remorse towards one, against
whom he was inwardly meditating a yet more bitter out-
rage; he curbed the yearnings of his heart, and did not dare

to lean even towards pity. The next transition of his soul was to exquisite villainy. Presuming on the unshaken submission of Hippolita, he flattered himself that she would not only acquiesce with patience to a divorce, but would obey if it was his pleasure, in endeavouring to persuade Isabella to give him her hand—but e'er he could indulge this horrid hope, he reflected that Isabella was not to be found. Coming to himself, he gave orders that every avenue to the castle should be strictly guarded, and charged his domestics on pain of their lives to suffer no body to pass out. The young peasant, to whom he spoke favourably, he ordered to remain in a small chamber on the stairs, in which there was a pallat-bed, and the key of which he took away himself, telling the youth he would talk with him in the morning. Then dismissing his attendants, and bestowing a sullen kind of half-nod on Hippolita, he retired to his own chamber.

CHAPTER II

Matilda, who by Hippolita's order, had retired to her apartment, was ill-disposed to take any rest. The shocking fate of her brother had deeply affected her. She was surprised at not seeing Isabella: But the strange words which had fallen from her father, and his obscure menace to the Princess his wife, accompanied by the most furious behaviour, had filled her gentle mind with terror and alarm. She waited anxiously for the return of Bianca, a young damsel that attended her, whom she had sent to learn what was become of Isabella. Bianca soon appeared and informed her mistress of what she had gathered from the servants, that Isabella was no where to be found. She related the adventure of the young peasant, who had been discovered in the vault, tho' with many simple additions from the incoherent accounts of the domestics; and she dwelled principally on the gigantic leg and foot which had been seen in the gallery-chamber. This last circumstance had terrified Bianca so much, that she was rejoiced when Matilda told her that she would not go to rest, but would watch till the Princess should rise.

The young Princess wearied herself in conjectures on the flight of Isabella, and on the threats of Manfred to her mother. "But what business could he have so urgent with the chaplain?" said Matilda. "Does he intend to have my brother's body interred privately in the chapel?" "Oh! Madam," said Bianca, "now I guess. As you are become his heiress, he is impatient to have you married: He has always been raving for more sons; I warrant he is now impatient for grandsons. As sure as I live, Madam, I shall see you a bride at last—Good Madam, you won't cast off your faithful Bianca: you won't put Donna Rosara over me, now you are a great Princess." "My poor Bianca," said Matilda, "how fast your thoughts amble! I a great Princess! What hast thou seen in Manfred's behaviour since my brother's death that bespeaks any increase of tenderness to me? No, Bianca; his heart was ever a stranger to me—but he is my father, and I must not complain. Nay, if heaven shuts my father's heart against me, it overpays my little merit in the tenderness of my mother—O that dear mother! yes, Bianca, 'tis there I feel the rugged temper of Manfred. I can support his harshness to me with patience; but it wounds my soul when I am witness to his causeless severity towards her." "Oh! Madam," said Bianca, "all men use their wives so, when they are weary of them"—"And yet you congratulated me but now," said Matilda, "when you fancied my father intended to dispose of me." "I would have you a great lady," replied Bianca, "come what will. I do not wish to see you moped in a convent, as you would be if you had your will, and if my Lady, your mother, who knows that a bad husband is better than no husband at all, did not hinder you—bless me! what noise is that! St. Nicholas forgive me! I was but in jest." "It is the wind," said Matilda, "whistling through the battlements in the tower above: You have heard it a thousand times." "Nay," said Bianca, "there was no harm neither in what I said: It is no sin to talk of matrimony— and so, Madam, as I was saying; if my Lord Manfred should offer you a handsome young Prince for a bridegroom, you would drop him a curtsy, and tell him you had rather take the veil." "Thank heaven! I am in no such danger," said Matilda: "You know how many proposals for me he has rejected"—"And you thank him, like a dutiful daughter, do you, Madam?—but come, Madam; suppose, to-morrow morning he was to send for you to the great council chamber, and there you should find at his elbow a lovely young

Prince, with large black eyes, a smooth white forehead, and manly curling locks like jet; in short, Madam, a young Hero resembling the picture of the good Alfonso in the gallery, which you sit and gaze at for hours together"—"Do not speak lightly of that picture," interrupted Matilda sighing: "I know the adoration with which I look at that picture is uncommon—but I am not in love with a coloured pannel. The character of that virtuous Prince, the veneration with which my mother has inspired me for his memory, the orisons which I know not why she has enjoined me to pour forth at his tomb, all have concurred to persuade me that some how or other my destiny is linked with something relating to him"—"Lord! Madam, how should that be?" said Bianca: "I have always heard that your family was no way related to his: And I am sure I cannot conceive why my Lady, the Princess, sends you in a cold morning or a damp evening to pray at his tomb: He is no Saint by the Almanack. If you must pray, why does not she bid you address yourself to our great St. Nicholas? I am sure he is the Saint I pray to for a husband." "Perhaps my mind would be less affected," said Matilda, "if my mother would explain her reasons to me: But it is the mystery she observes, that inspires me with this—I know not what to call it. As she never acts from caprice, I am sure there is some fatal secret at bottom—nay, I know there is: In her agony of grief for my brother's death she dropped some words that intimated as much"—"Oh! dear Madam," cried Bianca, "What were they?" "No;" said Matilda, "if a parent lets fall a word, and wishes it recalled, it is not for a child to utter it." "What! was she sorry for what she had said!" asked Bianca.—"I am sure, Madam, you may trust me"—"With my own little secrets, when I have any, I may;" said Matilda; "but never with my mother's: A child ought to have no ears or eyes, but as a parent directs." "Well! to be sure, Madam, you was born to be a saint," said Bianca, "and there is no resisting one's vocation:

You will end in a convent at last. But there is my Lady Isabella would not be so reserved to me: She will let me talk to her of young men; and when a handsome cavalier has come to the castle, she has owned to me that she wished your brother Conrad resembled him." "Bianca," said the Princess, "I do not allow you to mention my friend disrespectfully. Isabella is of a chearful disposition, but her soul is pure as virtue itself. She knows your idle babling humour, and perhaps has now and then encouraged it, to divert melancholy, and enliven the solitude in which my father keeps us"—"Blessed Mary!" said Bianca starting, "there it is again!—dear Madam, Do you hear nothing?—this castle is certainly haunted!"—"Peace!" said Matilda, "and listen! I did think I heard a voice—but it must be fancy; your terrors, I suppose, have infected me." "Indeed! indeed! Madam," said Bianca, half-weeping with agony, "I am sure I heard a voice." "Does any body lie in the chamber beneath?" said the Princess. "Nobody has dared to lie there," answered Bianca, "since the great astrologer that was your brother's tutor, drowned himself. For certain, Madam, his ghost and the young Prince's are now met in the chamber below—for heaven's sake let us fly to your mother's apartment!" "I charge you not to stir;" said Matilda. "If they are spirits in pain, we may ease their sufferings by questioning them. They can mean no hurt to us, for we have not injured them—and if they should, shall we be more safe in one chamber than in another! Reach me my beads; we will say a prayer, and then speak to them." "Oh! dear Lady, I would not speak to a ghost for the world;" cried Bianca—as she said those words, they heard the casement of the little chamber below Matilda's open. They listened attentively, and in few minutes thought they heard a person sing, but could not distinguish the words. "This can be no evil spirit;" said the Princess in a low voice: "It is undoubtedly one of the family—open the window, and we shall know the voice." "I dare not indeed, Madam;" said Bianca. "Thou art a very fool;" said Matilda, opening the window gently herself. The noise the Princess made was however heard by the person beneath, who stopped; and they concluded had heard the casement open. "Is any body below?" said the Princess: "If there is, speak." "Yes;" said an unknown voice. "Who is it?" said Matilda. "A stranger;" replied the voice. "What stranger?" said she; "and how didst thou come there at this unusual hour, when all the gates of the castle are locked?" "I am not here willingly:" answered the voice—"but pardon me, Lady, if I have disturbed your rest: I knew not that I was overheard. Sleep had forsaken me: I left a restless couch, and came to waste the irksome hours with gazing on the fair approach of morning, impatient to be dismissed from this castle." "Thy words and accents," said Matilda, are of a melancholy cast: If thou art unhappy, I pity thee. If poverty afflicts thee, let me know it: I will mention thee to the Princess, whose beneficent soul ever melts for the distressed; and she will relieve thee." "I am indeed unhappy," said the stranger; "and I know not what wealth is: But I do not complain of the lot which heaven has cast for me: I am young and healthy, and am not ashamed of owing my support to myself—yet think me not proud, or that I disdain your generous offers. I will remember you in my orisons, and will pray for blessings on your gracious self and your noble mistress—if I sigh, Lady, it is for others, not for myself." "Now I have it, Madam;" said Bianca, whispering the Princess. "This is certainly the young peasant; and by my conscience he is in love—Well! this is a charming adventure!—do, Madam, let us sist him. He does not know you, but takes you for one of my Lady Hippolita's women." "Art thou not ashamed, Bianca!" said the Princess: "What right have we to pry into the secrets of this young man's heart? he seems virtuous and frank, and tells us he is unhappy: Are those circumstances that authorize us to make a property of him? how are we intitled to his confidence?" "Lord! Madam, how little you know of love!" replied Bianca: "Why lovers have no pleasure equal to talking of their mistress." "And would you have *me* become a peasant's confident?" said the Princess. "Well then, let me talk to him," said Bianca: "Though I have the honour of being your Highness' maid of honour, I was not always so great: Besides, if love levels ranks, it raises them too: I have a respect for any young man in love"—"Peace! simpleton;" said the Princess. "Though he said he was unhappy, it does not follow that he must be in love. Think of all that has happened to-day, and tell me if there are no misfortunes but what love causes. Stranger," resumed the Princess, "if thy misfortunes have not been occasioned by thy own fault, and are within the compass of the Princess Hippolita's power to redress, I will take upon me to answer that she will be thy protectress. When thou art dismissed from this castle, repair to holy father Jerome at the convent adjoining to the church of St. Nicholas, and make thy story known to him, as far as thou thinkest meet: He will not fail to inform the Princess, who is the mother of all that want her assistance. Farewell: It is not seemly for me to hold farther converse with a man at this unwonted hour." "May the Saints guard thee, gracious Lady!" replied the peasant—"but oh! if a poor and worthless stranger might presume to beg a minute's audience farther—am I so happy?—the casement is not shut—might I venture to ask"—"Speak quickly;" said Matilda; "the morning dawns a pace: Should the labourers come into the fields and perceive us—What wouldst thou ask?"—"I know not how—I know not if I dare—" said the young stranger faltering—"yet the humanity with which you have spoken to me emboldens—Lady! dare I trust you?"—"Heavens!" said Matilda, "What dost thou mean? with what wouldst thou trust me?—speak boldly, if thy secret is fit to be entrusted to a virtuous breast"—"I would ask," said the Peasant, recollecting himself, "whether what I have heard from the domestics is true, that the Princess is missing from the castle?" "What imports it to thee to know?" replied Matilda. "Thy first words bespoke a prudent and becoming gravity. Dost thou come hither to pry into the secrets of Manfred?—Adieu. I have been mistaken in thee." Saying these words, she shut the casement hastily, without giving the young man time to reply. "I had acted more wisely," said the Princess to Bianca with some sharpness, "if I had let thee converse with this peasant: His inquisitiveness seems of a piece with thy own." "It is not fit for me to argue with your Highness," replied Bianca; "but perhaps the questions I should have put to him, would have been more to the purpose, than those you have been pleased to ask him." "Oh! no doubt;" said Matilda; "you are a very discreet personage! may I know what *you* would have asked him?" "A by-stander often sees more of the game than those that play:" answered Bianca. "Does your Highness think, Madam, that his question about my Lady Isabella was the result of mere curiosity? No, no, Madam; there is more in it than you great folks are aware of. Lopez told me that all the servants believe this young fellow contrived my Lady Isabella's escape—now, pray, Madam, observe—you and I both know that my Lady Isabella never much fancied the Prince your brother—Well! he is killed just in the critical minute—I accuse nobody. A helmet falls from the moon—so, my Lord, your father says; but Lopez and all the servants say that this young spark is a magician, and stole it from Alfonso's tomb"—"Have done with this rhapsody of impertinence," said Matilda. "Nay, Madam, as you please;" cried Bianca—"yet it is very particular though, that my Lady Isabella should be missing the very same day, and that this young sorcerer should be found at the mouth of the trapdoor—I accuse nobody—but if my young Lord came honestly by his death"—"Dare not on thy duty," said Matilda, "to breathe a suspicion on the purity of my dear Isabella's fame"—"Purity, or not purity," said Bianca, "gone she is—a stranger is found that nobody knows: You question him yourself: He tells you he is love, or unhappy, it is the same thing—nay; he owned he was unhappy about others! and is any body unhappy about another, unless they are in love with them? and at the very next word, he asks innocently, poor soul! if my Lady Isabella is missing"—"To be sure," said Matilda, "thy observations are not totally without foundation—Isabella's flight amazes me: The curiosity of this stranger is very particular—yet Isabella never concealed a thought from me"—"So she told you," said Bianca, "to fish out your secrets—but who knows, Madam, but this stranger may be some Prince in disguise?—do, Madam, let me open the window, and ask him a few questions." "No," replied Matilda, "I will ask him myself, if he knows aught of Isabella: He is not worthy that I should converse farther with him." She was going to open the casement, when they heard the bell ring at the postern gate of the castle, which is on the right-hand of the tower, where Matilda lay. This prevented the Princess from renewing the conversation with the stranger.

After continuing silent for some time: "I am persuaded," said she to Bianca, "that whatever be the cause of Isabella's flight, it had no unworthy motive. If this stranger was accessary to it, she must be satisfied of his fidelity and worth. I observed, did not you, Bianca? that his words were tinctured with an uncommon effusion of piety. It was no ruffian's speech: His phrases were becoming a man of gentle birth." "I told you, Madam," said Bianca, "that I was sure he was some Prince in disguise"—"Yet," said Matilda, if he was privy to her escape, how will you account for his not accompanying her in her flight? why expose himself unnecessarily and rashly to my father's resentment?" "As for that, Madam," replied she, "if he could get from under the helmet, he will find ways of eluding your Father's anger. I do not doubt but he has some talisman or other about him" —"You resolve everything into magic;" said Matilda—"but a man, who has any intercourse with infernal spirits, does not dare to make use of those tremendous and holy words, which he uttered. Didst thou not observe with what fervour he vowed to remember *me* to heaven in his prayers?—yes; Isabella was undoubtedly convinced of his piety." "Commend me to the piety of a young fellow and a damsel that consult to elope!" said Bianca. "No, no, Madam; my Lady Isabella is of another guess mould than you take her for. She used indeed to sigh and lift up her eyes in your company, because she knows you are a Saint—but when your back was turned"—"You wrong her!" said Matilda: "Isabella is no hypocrite: She has a due sense of devotion, but never affected a call she has not. On the contrary, she always combated my inclination for the cloyster: And though I own the mystery she has made to me of her flight, confounds me; though it seems inconsistent with the friendship between us; I cannot forget the disinterested warmth with which she always opposed my taking the veil: she wished to see me married, though my dower would have been a loss to her and my brother's children. For her sake I will believe well of this young peasant." "Then you do think there is some liking between them;" said Bianca—While she was speaking, a servant came hastily into the chamber and told the Princess, that the Lady Isabella was found. "Where?" said Matilda. "She has taken sanctuary in St. Nicholas's church;" replied the servant: "Father Jerome has brought the news himself: he is below with his Highness." "Where is my Mother!" said Matilda. "She is in her own chamber, Madam, and has asked for you."

Manfred had risen at the first dawn of light, and gone to Hippolita's apartment, to inquire if she knew aught of

Isabella. While he was questioning her, word was brought that Jerome demanded to speak with him. Manfred, little suspecting the cause of the Friar's arrival, and knowing he was employed by Hippolita in her charities, ordered him to be admitted, intending to leave them together, while he pursued his search after Isabella. "Is your business with me or the Princess?" said Manfred. "With both," replied the holy man. "The Lady Isabella"—"What of her!" interrupted Manfred eagerly—"is at St. Nicholas's altar," replied Jerome. "That is no business of Hippolita;" said Manfred with confusion: "let us retire to my chamber, Father; and inform me how she came thither." "No; my Lord;" replied the good man with an air of firmness and authority, that daunted even the resolute Manfred, who could not help revering the saint-like virtues of Jerome: "My commission is to both; and with your Highness' good-liking, in the presence of both I shall deliver it—but first, my Lord, I must interrogate the Princess, whether she is acquainted with the cause of the Lady Isabella's retirement from your castle"—"No, on my soul;" said Hippolita: "does Isabella charge me with being privy to it?"—"Father," interrupted Manfred, "I pay due reverence to your holy profession; but I am sovereign here, and will allow no meddling priest to interfere in the affairs of my domestic. If you have ought to say, attend me to my chamber—I do not use to let my Wife be acquainted with the secret affairs of my State; they are not within a woman's province." "My Lord," said the holy man, "I am no intruder into the secrets of families. My office is to promote peace, to heal divisions, to preach repentance, and teach mankind to curb their headstrong passions. I forgive your Highness' uncharitable apostrophe: I know my duty, and am the minister of a mightier prince than Manfred. Hearken to him who speaks through my organs." Manfred trembled with rage and shame. Hippolita's countenance declared her astonishment and impatience to know where this would end: her silence more strongly spoke her observance of Manfred.

"The Lady Isabella," resumed Jerome, "commends herself to both your Highnesses; she thanks both for the kindness with which she has been treated in your castle: She deplores the loss of your son, and her own misfortune in not becoming the daughter of such wife and noble Princess, whom she shall always respect as *Parents;* she prays for uninterrupted union and felicity between you: [Manfred's colour changed] but as it is no longer possible for her to be allied to you, she intreats your consent to remain in sanctuary, till she can learn news of her father, or, by the certainty of his death, be at liberty, with the approbation of her guardians, to dispose of herself in suitable marriage." "I shall give no such consent;" said the Prince, "but insist on her return to the castle without delay: I am answerable for her person to her guardians and will not brook her being in any hands but my own." "Your Highness will recollect whether that can any longer be proper:" replied the Friar. "I want no monitor," said Manfred colouring, "Isabella's conduct leaves room for strange suspicions—and that young villain, who was at least the accomplice of her flight, if not the cause of it"—"The cause!" interrupted Jerome; "was a young man the cause!" "This is not to be borne!" cried Manfred. "Am I to be bearded in my own palace by an insolent Monk! thou art privy I guess, to their amours." "I would pray to heaven to clear up your uncharitable surmizes," said Jerome, "if your Highness were not satisfied in your conscience how unjustly you accuse me. I do pray to heaven to pardon that uncharitableness: And I implore your Highness to leave the Princess at peace in that holy place, where she is not liable to be disturbed by such vain and worldly fantasies as discourses of love from any man." "Cant not to me," said Manfred, "but return and bring the Princess to her duty." "It is my duty to prevent her return hither;" said Jerome. "She is where orphans and virgins are safest from the snares and wiles of this world; and nothing but a parent's authority shall take her thence." "I am her parent," cried Manfred, "and demand her." "She wished to have you for her parent;" said the Friar: "But heaven that forbad that connection, has for ever dissolved all ties betwixt you: And I announce to your Highness"—"Stop! audacious man," said Manfred, "and dread my displeasure." "Holy father," said Hippolita, "it is your office to be no respecter of persons: you must speak as your duty prescribes: But it is my duty to hear nothing that it pleases not my Lord I should hear. Attend the Prince to his chamber. I will retire to my oratory, and pray to the blessed virgin to inspire you with her holy councils, and to restore the heart of my gracious Lord to its wonted peace and gentleness." "Excellent woman!" said the Friar—"my Lord, I attend your pleasure."

Manfred, accompanied by the Friar, passed to his own apartment, where shutting the door, "I perceive, father," said he, "that Isabella has acquainted you with my purpose. Now hear my resolve, and obey. Reasons of state, most urgent reasons, my own and the safety of my people, demand that I should have a son. It is in vain to expect an heir from Hippolita. I have made choice of Isabella. You must bring her back; and you must do more. I know the influence you have with Hippolita: her conscience is in your hands. She is, I allow, a faultless woman: Her soul is set on heaven, and scorns the little grandeur of this world: you can withdraw her from it intirely. Persuade her to consent to the dissolution of our marriage, and to retire into a monastery—she shall endow one if she will; and she shall have the means of being as liberal to your order as she or you can wish. Thus you will divert the calamities that are hanging over our heads, and have the merit of saving the principality of Otranto from destruction. You are a prudent man, and though the warmth of my temper betrayed me into some unbecoming expressions, I honour your virtue, and wish to be indebted to you for the repose of my life and the preservation of my family."

"The will of heaven be done!" said the Friar. "I am but its worthless instrument. It makes use of my tongue, to tell thee, Prince, of thy unwarrantable designs. The injuries of the virtuous Hippolita have mounted to the throne of pity. By me thou art reprimanded for thy adulterous intention of repudiating her: By me thou art warned not to pursue the incestuous design on thy contracted daughter. Heaven that delivered her from thy fury, when the judgments so recently fallen on thy house ought to have inspired thee with other thoughts, will continue to watch over her. Even I, a poor despised Friar, am able to protect her from thy violence—I, sinner as I am, and uncharitably reviled by your Highness, as an accomplice of I know not what amours, scorn the allurements with which it has pleased thee to tempt mine honesty. I love my order; I honour devout souls; I respect the piety of thy Princess—but I will not betray the confidence she reposes in me, nor serve even the cause of religion by foul and sinful compliances—but for sooth! the welfare of the state depends on your Highness having a son. Heaven mocks the short-sighted views of man. But yester-morn, whose house was so great, so flourishing as Manfred's?—where is young Conrad now!—my Lord, I respect your fears—but I mean not to check them—let them flow, Prince! they will weigh more than heaven towards the welfare of thy subjects, than a marriage, which, founded on lust or policy, could never prosper. The scepter, which passed from the race of Alfonso to thine, cannot be preserved by a match which the church will never allow. If it is the will of the most High that Manfred's name must perish; resign yourself, my Lord, to its decrees; and thus deserve a crown that can never pass away—come, my Lord; I like this sorrow—let us return to the Princess: she is not apprised of your cruel intentions; nor did I mean more than to alarm you. You saw with what gentle patience, with what efforts of love, she heard, she rejected hearing the extent of your guilt. I know she longs to fold you in her arms, and assure you of her unalterable affection." "Father," said the Prince, "you mistake my compunction: true; I honour Hippolita's virtues; I think her a Saint; and wish it were for my soul's health to tie faster the knot that has united us—but alas! Father, you know not the bitterest of my pangs! it is some time that I have had scruples on the legality of our union: Hippolita is related to me in the fourth degree—it is true, we had a dispensation: but I have been informed that she had also been contracted to another. This it is that sits heavy at my heart: To this state of unlawful wedlock I impute the visitation that has fallen on me in the death of Conrad!—ease my conscience of this burden: dissolve our marriage, and accomplish the work of godliness which your divine exhortations have commenced in my soul."

How cutting was the anguish which the good man felt, when he perceived this turn in the wily Prince! He trembled for Hippolita, whose ruin he saw was determined; and he feared if Manfred had no hope of recovering Isabella, that his impatience for a son would direct him to some other object, who might not be equally proof against the temptation of Manfred's rank. For some time the holy man remained absorbed in thought. At length, conceiving some hope from delay, he thought the wisest conduct would be to prevent the Prince from despairing of recovering Isabella. Her the Friar knew he could dispose, from her affection to Hippolita, and from the aversion she had expressed to him for Manfred's addresses, to second his views, till the censures of the church could be fulminated against a divorce. With this intention, as if struck with the Prince's scruples, he at length said; "My Lord, I have been pondering on what your Highness has said; and if in truth it is delicacy of conscience that is the real motive of your repugnance to your virtuous Lady, far be it from me to endeavour to harden your heart. The church is an indulgent mother: unfold your griefs to her: she alone can administer comfort to your soul, either by satisfying your conscience, or upon examination of your scruples, by setting you at liberty, and indulging you in the lawful means of continuing your lineage. In the latter case, if the Lady Isabella can be brought to consent"—Manfred, who concluded that he had either over-reached the good man, or that his first warmth had been but a tribute paid to appearance, was overjoyed at this sudden turn, and repeated the most magnificent promises, if he should succeed by the Friar's mediation. The well-meaning Priest suffered him to deceive himself, fully determined to traverse his views, instead of seconding them.

"Since we now understand one another," resumed the Prince, "I expect father, that you satisfy me in one point. Who is the youth that I found in the vault? He must have been privy to Isabella's flight: Tell me truly; is he her lover? or is he an agent for another's passion? I have often suspected Isabella's indifference to my son: a thousand circumstances croud on my mind that confirm that suspicion. She herself was so conscious of it, that while I discoursed her in the gallery, she outran my suspicions, and endeavoured to justify herself from coolness to Conrad." The Friar, who knew nothing of the youth, but what he had learnt occasionally from the Princess, ignorant what was become of him, and not sufficiently reflecting on the impetuosity of Manfred's temper, conceived that it might not be amiss to sow the seeds of jealousy in his mind: They might be turned to some use hereafter, either by prejudicing the Prince against Isabella, if he persisted in that union; or by diverting his attention to a wrong scent, and employing his thoughts on a visionary intrigue, prevent his engaging in any new pursuit. With this unhappy policy, he answered in a manner to confirm Manfred in the belief of some connection between Isabella and the youth. The Prince, whose passions wanted little fuel to throw them into a blaze, fell into a rage at the idea of what the Friar suggested. "I will fathom to the bottom of this intrigue;" cried he; and quitting Jerome abruptly, with a command to remain there till his return, he hastened to the great hall of the castle, and ordered the peasant to be brought before him.

"Thou hardened young impostor!" said the Prince, as soon as he saw the youth; "what becomes of thy boasted veracity now? it was Providence, was it, and the light of the moon, that discovered the lock of the trap-door to thee? Tell me, audacious boy, who thou art, and how long thou hast been acquainted with the Princess—and take care to answer with less equivocation than thou didst last night, or tortures shall wring the truth from thee." The young man, perceiving that his share in the flight of the Princess was discovered, and concluding that any thing he should say could no longer be of service or detriment to her, replied, "I am no impostor, my Lord, nor have I deserved opprobrious language. I answered to every question your Highness put to me last night with the same veracity that I shall speak now: And that will not be from fear of your tortures, but because my soul abhors a falshood. Please to repeat your questions, my Lord; I am ready to give you all the satisfaction in my power." "You know my questions," replied the Prince, "and only want time to prepare an evasion. Speak directly; who art thou? and how long hast thou been known to the Princess?" "I am a labourer at the next village;" said the peasant; "my name is Theodore. The Princess found me in the vault last night: Before that hour I never was in her presence." "I may believe as much or as little as I please of this;" said Manfred; "but I will hear thy own story, before I examine into the truth of it. Tell me, what reason did the Princess give thee for making her escape? thy life depends on thy answer." "She told me," replied Theodore, "that she was on the brink of destruction, and that if she could not escape from the castle, she was in danger in a few moments of being made miserable for ever." "And on this slight foundation, on a silly girl's report," said Manfred, "thou didst hazard my displeasure!" "I fear no man's displeasure," said Theodore, "when a woman in distress puts herself under my protection—" During this examination, Matilda was going to the apartment of Hippolita. At the upper end of the hall, where Manfred sat, was a boarded gallery with latticed windows, through which Matilda and Bianca were to pass. Hearing her father's voice, and seeing the servants assembled round him, she stopped to learn the occasion. The prisoner soon drew her attention: The steady and composed manner in which he answered, and the galantry of his last reply, which were the first words she heard distinctly interested her in his favour. His person was noble, handsome, and commanding, even in that situation: But his countenance soon engrossed her whole care. "Heavens! Bianca," said the Princess softly, "do I dream? or is not that youth the exact resemblance of Alfonso's picture in the gallery?" She could say no more, for her father's voice grew louder at every word. "This bravado," said he, "surpasses all thy former insolence. Thou shalt experience the wrath with which thou darest to trifle. Seize him," continued Manfred, "and bind him—the first news the Princess hears of her champion shall be, that he has lost his head for her sake." "The injustice of which thou art guilty towards me," said Theodore, "convinces me that I have done a good deed in delivering the Princess from thy tyranny. May she be happy, whatever becomes of me!" "This is a lover!" cried Manfred in a rage: "A peasant within sight of death is not animated by such sentiments. Tell me, tell me, rash boy, who thou art, or the rack shall force thy secret from thee." "Thou hast threatened me with death already," said the youth, "for the truth I have told thee: If that is all the encouragement I am to expect for sincerity, I am not tempted to indulge thy vain curiosity farther." "Then thou wilt not speak!" said Manfred; "I will not," replied he. "Bear him away into the court-yard;" said Manfred; "I will see his head this instant severed from his body—" Matilda fainted at hearing those words. Bianca shrieked, and cried "Help! help! the Princess is dead!" Manfred started at this ejaculation, and demanded what was the matter! The young peasant, who heard it too, was struck with horror, and asked eagerly the same question; but Manfred ordered him to be hurried into the court, and kept there for execution, until he had informed himself of the cause of Bianca's shrieks. When he learned the meaning, he treated it as a womanish panic, and ordering Matilda to be carried to her apartment, he rushed into the court, and calling for one of his guards, bad Theodore kneel down, and prepare to receive the fatal blow.

The undaunted youth received the bitter sentence with a resignation that touched every heart, but Manfred's. He wished earnestly to know the meaning of the words he had heard relating to the Princess; but fearing to exasperate the tyrant more against her, he desisted. The only boon he deigned to ask, was, that he might be permitted to have a confessor, and make his peace with heaven. Manfred, who hoped by the confessor's means to come at the youth's history, readily granted his request: and being convinced that Father Jerome was now in his interest, he ordered him to be called and shrieve the prisoner. The holy man, who had little foreseen the catastrophe that his imprudence occasioned, fell on his knees to the Prince, and adjured him in the most solemn manner not to shed innocent blood. He accused himself in the bitterest terms for his indiscretion, endeavoured to disculpate the youth, and left no method untried to soften the tyrant's rage. Manfred, more incensed than appeased by Jerome's intercession, whose retractation now made him suspect he had been imposed upon by both, commanded the Friar to do his duty, telling him he would not allow the prisoner many minutes for confession. "Nor do I ask many, my Lord," said the unhappy young man. "My sins, thank heaven! have not been numerous; nor exceed what might be expected at my years. Dry your tears, good father, and let us dispatch: This is a bad world; nor have I had cause to leave it with regret." "Oh! wretched youth!" said Jerome; "how canst thou bear the sight of me with patience? I am thy murderer! it is I have brought this dismal hour upon thee!" "I forgive thee from my soul," said the youth, "as I hope heaven will pardon me. Hear my confession, father; and give me thy blessing." "How can I prepare thee for thy passage, as I ought?" said Jerome. "Thou canst not be saved without pardoning thy foes—and canst thou forgive that impious man there!" "I can;" said Theodore; "I do"—"And does this not touch thee! cruel Prince!" said the Friar. "I sent for thee to confess him," said Manfred sternly; "not to plead for him. Thou didst first incense me against him—his blood be on thy head!" "It will! it will!" said the good man, in an agony of sorrow. "Thou and I must never hope to go, where this blessed youth is going! "Dispatch!" said Manfred: "I am no more to be moved by the whining of priests, than by the shrieks of women." "What!" said the youth; "is it possible that my fate could have occasioned what I heard! is the Princess then again in thy power?" "Thou dost but remember me of my wrath;" said Manfred: "prepare thee, for this moment is thy last." The youth, who felt his indignation rise, and who was touched with the sorrow which he saw he had infused into all the spectators, as well as into the Friar, suppressed his emotions, and putting off his doublet, and unbuttoning his collar, knelt down to his prayers. As he stooped, his shirt slipped down below his shoulder, and discovered the mark of a bloody arrow. "Gracious heaven!" cried the holy man starting, "what do I see! it is my child! my Theodore!"

The passions that ensued, must be conceived; they cannot be painted. The tears of the assistants were suspended by wonder, rather than stopped by joy. They seemed to enquire in the eyes of their Lord what they ought to feel. Surprise, doubt, tenderness, respect, succeeded each other in the countenance of the youth. He received with modest submission the effusion of the old man's tears and embraces: Yet afraid of giving a loose to hope, and suspecting from what had passed the inflexibility of Manfred's temper, he cast a glance towards the Prince, as if to say, canst thou be unmoved at such a scene as this?

Manfred's heart was capable of being touched. He forgot his anger in his astonishment: Yet his pride forbad his owning himself affected. He even doubted whether this discovery was not a contrivance of the friar to save the youth. "What may this mean?" said he: "How can he be thy son? is it consistent with thy profession or reputed sanctity to avow a peasant's offspring for the fruit of thy irregular amours!" "Oh! God," said the holy man, "dost thou question his being mine? could I feel the anguish I do, if I were not his father? Spare him! good Prince, spare him! and revile me as thou pleasest." "Spare him! spare him," cried the attendants, "for this good man's sake!" "Peace!" said Manfred sternly: "I must know more, ere I am disposed to pardon. A Saint's bastard may be no saint himself." "Injurious Lord!" said Theodore; "add not insult to cruelty. If I am this venerable man's son, though no Prince, as thou art, know, the blood that flows in my veins"—"Yes," said the Friar, interrupting him, "his blood is noble; nor is he that abject thing, my Lord, you speak him. He is my lawful son; and Sicily can boast of few houses more ancient than that of Falconara—but alas! my Lord, what is blood! what is nobility! We are all reptiles, miserable, sinful creatures. It is piety alone that can distinguish us from the dust whence we sprung, and whither we must return"—"Truce to your ser-

mon!" said Manfred: "You forget, you are no longer Friar
Jerome, but the Count of Falconara. Let me know your history: You will have time to moralize hereafter, if you should
not happen to obtain the grace of that sturdy criminal
there." "Mother of God!" said the Friar, "is it possible my
Lord can refuse a father the life of his only, his long-lost
child! Trample me, my Lord, scorn, afflict me, accept my
life for his, but spare my son!" "Thou canst feel then," said
Manfred, "what it is to lose an only son!—a little hour ago
thou didst preach up resignation to me: *My* House, if fate so
pleased, must perish—but the Counts of Falconara"—"Alas!
my Lord!" said Jerome, "I confess I have offended! but aggravate not an old man's sufferings! I boast not of my family, nor think of such vanities—it is nature that pleads for
this boy; it is the memory of the dear woman that bore him
—is she Theodore, is she dead?"—"Her soul has long been
with the blessed," said Theodore. "Oh! how?" cried Jerome,
"tell me—No—she is happy! Thou art all my care now!—
most dread Lord! will you—will you grant me my poor boy's
life?" "Return to thy convent;" answered Manfred; "conduct the Princess hither; obey me in what else thou knowest;
and I promise thee the life of thy son"—"Oh! my Lord,"
said Jerome, "is my honesty the price I must pay for this
dear youth's safety"—"For me!" cried Theodore: "Let me
die a thousand deaths, rather than stain thy conscience.
What is it the tyrant would exact of thee? is the Princess still
safe from his power? protect her, thou venerable old man;
and let all the weight of his wrath fall on me." Jerome endeavoured to check the impetuosity of the youth; and ere
Manfred could reply, the trampling of horses was heard,
and a brazen trumpet, which hung without the gate of the
castle, was suddenly sounded. At the same instant the sable
plumes on the enchanted helmet, which still remained at
the other end of the court, were tempestuously agitated, and
nodded thrice, as if bowed by some invisible wearer.

CHAPTER III

Manfred's heart mis-gave him when he beheld the plumage on the miraculous casque shaken in concert with the sounding of the brazen trumpet. "Father!" said he to Jerome, whom he now ceased to treat as Count of Falconara, "what mean these portents? If I have offended—" The plumes were shaken with greater violence than before. "Unhappy Prince that I am!" cried Manfred—"Holy Father! will you not assist me with your prayers?" "My Lord," replied Jerome, "heaven is no doubt displeased with your mockery of its servants. Submit yourself to the church; and cease to persecute her ministers. Dismiss this innocent youth; and learn to respect the holy character I wear: Heaven will not be trifled with: you see—" The trumpet sounded again. "I acknowledge I have been too hasty:" said Manfred. "Father, do you go to the wicket, and demand who is at the gate." "Do you grant me the life of Theodore?" replied the Friar. "I do;" said Manfred; "but inquire who is without!"

Jerome falling on the neck of his son, discharged a flood of tears, that spoke the fullness of his soul. "You promised to go to the gate;" said Manfred. "I thought," replied the Friar, "your Highness would excuse my thanking you first in this tribute of my heart." "Go, dearest Sir," said Theodore; "obey the Prince: I do not deserve that you should delay his satisfaction for me."

Jerome, inquiring who was without, was answered, "A Herald." "From whom?" said he. "From the Knight of the gigantic sabre;" said the Herald; "and I must speak with the usurper of Otranto." Jerome returned to the Prince, and did not fail to repeat the message in the very words it had been uttered. The first sounds struck Manfred with terror; but when he heard himself styled usurper, his rage rekindled, and all his courage revived. "Usurper!—insolent villain!" cried he, "who dares to question my title? retire, Father! this is no business for Monks: I will meet this presumptuous man myself. Go to your convent, and prepare the Princess's return: Your son shall be a hostage for your fidelity: His life depends on your obedience." "Good heaven! my Lord," cried Jerome, "your Highness did but this instant freely pardon my child—have you so soon forgot the interposition of heaven?" "Heaven," replied Manfred, "does not send Heralds to question the title of a lawful Prince—I doubt whether it even notifies its will through Friars—but that is your affair, not mine. At present you know my pleasure; and it is not a saucy Herald, that shall have your son, if you do not return with the Princess."

It was in vain for the holy man to reply. Manfred commanded him to be conducted to the postern-gate, and shut out from the castle; And he ordered some of his attendants to carry Theodore to the top of the black tower, and guard him strictly; scarce permitting the Father and son to exchange a hasty embrace at parting. He then withdrew to the hall, and seating himself in princely state, ordered the Herald to be admitted to his presence.

"Well! thou insolent!" said the Prince, "what wouldst thou with me!" "I come," replied he, "to thee Manfred, usurper of the principality of Otranto, from the renowned and invincible Knight; the Knight of the gigantic sabre: in the name of his Lord, Frederic Marquis of Vicenza, he demands the Lady Isabella, daughter of that Prince, whom thou hast basely and traiterously got into thy power, by bribing her false guardians during his absence: and he requires thee to resign the principality of Otranto, which thou hast usurped from the said Lord Frederic, the nearest of blood to the last rightful Lord Alfonso the good. If thou dost not instantly comply with these just demands, he defies thee to single combat to the last extremity." And so saying, the Herald cast down his warder.

"And where is this braggart, who sends thee?" said Manfred. "At the distance of a league," said the Herald: "he comes to make good his Lord's claim against thee, as he is a true Knight and thou an usurper and ravisher."

Injurious as this challenge was, Manfred reflected that it was not his interest to provoke the Marquis. He knew how well-founded the claim of Frederic was; nor was this the first time he had heard of it. Frederic's ancestor's had assumed the style of Princes of Otranto, from the death of Alfonso the good without issue; but Manfred, his Father, and grandfather, had been too powerful for the house of Vicenza to dispossess them. Frederic, a martial and amorous young Prince, had married a beautiful young Lady, of whom he was enamoured, and who had died in childbed of Isabella. Her death affected him so much, that he had taken the cross and gone to the holy land, where he was wounded in an engagement against the infidels, made prisoner, and reported to be dead. When the news reached Manfred's ears, he bribed the guardians of the Lady Isabella to deliver her up to him as a bride for his son Conrad, by which alliance he had proposed to unite the claims of the two houses. This motive, on Conrad's death, had cooperated to make him so suddenly resolve on espousing her himself; and the same reflection determined him now to endeavour at obtaining the consent of Frederic to this marriage. A like policy inspired him with the thought of inviting Frederic's champion into his castle, lest he should be informed of Isabella's flight, which he strictly enjoined his domestics not to disclose to any of the Knight's retinue.

"Herald," said Manfred as soon as he had digested these reflections, "return to thy master, and tell him, ere we liquidate our differences by the sword, Manfred would hold some converse with him. Bid him welcome to my castle, where by my faith, as I am a true Knight, he shall have courteous reception, and full security for himself and followers. If we cannot adjust our quarrel by amicable means, I swear he shall depart in safety, and shall have full satisfaction according to the laws of arms: So help me God and his holy Trinity!" The Herald made three obeisances and retired.

During this interview Jerome's mind was agitated by a thousand contrary passions. He trembled for the life of his son, and his first thought was to persuade Isabella to return to the castle. Yet he was scarce less alarmed at the thought of her union with Manfred. He dreaded Hippolita's unbounded submission to the will of her Lord; and though he did not doubt but he could alarm her piety not to consent to a divorce, if he could get access to her; yet should Manfred discover that the obstruction came from him, it might be equally fatal to Theodore. He was impatient to know whence came the Herald, who with so little management had questioned the title of Manfred: yet he did not dare absent himself from the convent, lest Isabella should leave it, and her flight be imputed to him. He returned disconsolately to the monastery, uncertain on what conduct to resolve. A Monk, who met him in the porch and observed his melancholy air, said, "Alas! brother, is it then true that we have lost our excellent Princess Hippolita?" The holy man started, and cried, "What means thou, brother! I come this instant from the castle, and left her in perfect health." "Martelli," replied the other Friar, "passed by the convent but a quarter of an Hour ago on his way from the castle, and reported that her Highness was dead. All our brethren are gone to the chapel to pray for her happy transit to a better life, and willed me to wait thy arrival. They know thy holy attachment to that good Lady, and are anxious for the affliction it will cause in thee—indeed we have all reason to weep; she was a mother to our House—but this life is but a pilgrimage; we must not murmur—we shall all follow her! may our end be like hers!" "Good brother, thou dreamest," said Jerome: "I tell thee I come from the castle, and left the Princess well—where is the Lady Isabella?"—"Poor Gentlewoman!" replied the Friar; "I told her the sad news, and offered her spiritual comfort; I reminded her of the transitory condition of mortality, and advised her to take the veil: I quoted the example of the holy Princess Sanchia of Arragon"—"Thy zeal was laudable," said Jerome impatiently; "but at present it was unnecessary: Hippolita is well—at least I trust in the Lord she is; I heard nothing to the contrary—yet methinks, the Prince's earnestness—well, brother, but where is the Lady Isabella?" "I know not;" said the Friar: "She wept much, and said she would retire to her chamber." Jerome left his comrade abruptly, and hasted to the Princess, but she was not in her chamber. He inquired of the domestics of the convent, but could learn no news of her. He searched in vain throughout the monastery and the church, and dispatched messengers round the neighbourhood, to get intelligence if she had been seen; but to no purpose. Nothing could equal the good man's perplexity. He judged that Isabella, suspecting Manfred of having precipitated his wife's death, had taken the alarm, and withdrawn herself to some more secret place of concealment. This new flight would probably carry the Prince's fury to the height. The report of Hippolita's death, though it seemed almost incredible, increased his consternation; and though Isabella's escape bespoke her aversion of Manfred for a husband, Jerome could feel no comfort from it, while it endangered the life of his son. He determined to return to the castle, and made several of his brethren accompany him to attest his innocence to Manfred, and, if necessary, join their intercession with his for Theodore.

The Prince, in the mean time, had passed into the court,

and ordered the gates of the castle to be flung open for the reception of the stranger Knight and his train. In a few minutes the cavalcade arrived. First came two harbingers with wands. Next a herald, followed by two pages and two trumpets. Then an hundred foot-guards. These were attended by as many horses. After them fifty footmen, cloathed in scarlet and black, the colours of the Knight. Then a led horse. Two heralds on each side of a gentleman on horse-back bearing a banner with the arms of Vicenza and Otranto quarterly—a circumstance that much offended Manfred—but he stifled his resentment. Two more pages. The Knight's confessor telling his beads. Fifty more foot-men, clad as before. Two Knights habited in complete armour, their beavers down, comrades to the principal Knight. The squires of the two Knights, carrying their shields and devices. The Knight's own squire. An hundred gentlemen bearing an enormous sword, and seeming to faint under the weight of it. The Knight himself on a chestnut steed, in complete armour, his lance in the rest, his face entirely concealed by his vizor, which was surmounted by a large plume of scarlet and black feathers. Fifty foot-guards with drums and trumpets closed the procession, which wheeled off to the right and left to make room for the principal Knight.

As soon as he approached the gate, he stopped; and the herald advancing, read again the words of the challenge. Manfred's eyes were fixed on the gigantic sword, and he scarce seemed to attend to the cartel: But his attention was soon diverted by a tempest of wind that rose behind him. He turned and beheld the plumes of the enchanted helmet agitated in the same extraordinary manner as before. It required intrepidity like Manfred's not to sink under a concurrence of circumstances that seemed to announce his fate. Yet scorning in the presence of strangers to betray the courage he had always manifested, he said boldly, "Sir Knight, whoever thou art, I bid thee welcome. If thou art of mortal mould, thy valour shall meet its equal: And, if thou art a true Knight, thou wilt scorn to employ sorcery to carry thy point. Be these omens from heaven or hell, Manfred trusts to the righteousness of his cause and to the aid of St. Nicholas, who has ever protected his house. Alight, Sir Knight, and repose thyself. To-morrow thou shalt have a fair field; and heaven befriend the juster side!"

The Knight made no reply, but dismounting, was conducted by Manfred to the great hall of the castle. As they traversed the court, the Knight stopped to gaze at the miraculous casque; and kneeling down, seemed to pray inwardly for some minutes. Rising, he made a sign to the Prince to lead on. As soon as they entered the hall, Manfred proposed to the stranger to disarm, but the Knight shook his head in token of refusal. "Sir Knight," said Manfred, "this is not courteous; but by my good faith I will not cross thee; nor shalt thou have cause to complain of the Prince of Otranto. No treachery is designed on my part; I hope none is intended on thine: Here take my gage: [giving him his ring] your friends and you shall enjoy the laws of hospitality. Rest here, until refreshments are brought: I will but give orders for the accommodation of your train, and return to you." The three Knights bowed as accepting his courtesy. Manfred directed the stranger's retinue to be conducted to an adjacent hospital, founded by the Princess Hippolita for the reception of pilgrims. As they made the circuit of the court to return towards the gate, the gigantic sword burst from the supporters, and falling to the ground opposite to the helmet, remained immoveable. Manfred almost hardened to preternatural appearances, surmounted the shock of this new prodigy; and returning to the hall, where by this time the feast was ready, he invited his silent guests to take their places. Manfred, however ill his heart was at ease, endeavoured to inspire the company with mirth. He put several questions to them, but was answered only by signs. They raised their vizors but sufficiently to feed themselves, and that sparingly. "Sirs," said the Prince, "ye are the first guests I ever treated within these walls, who scorned to hold any intercourse with me: Nor has it oft been customary, I ween, for Princes to hazard their state and dignity against strangers and mutes. You say you come in the name of Frederic of Vicenza: I have ever heard that he was a gallant and courteous Knight; nor would he, I am bold to say, think it beneath him to mix in social converse with a Prince that is his equal, and not unknown by deeds in arms. —Still ye are silent—well! be it as it may—by the laws of hospitality and chivalry ye are masters under this roof: Ye shall do your pleasures—but come, give me a goblet of wine; ye will not refuse to pledge me to the healths of your fair mistresses." The principal Knight sighed and crossed himself, and was rising from the board—"Sir Knight," said Manfred, "what I said was but in sport: I shall constrain you in nothing: use your good liking. Since mirth is not your mood, let us be sad. Business may hit your fancies better: Let us withdraw; and hear if what I have to unfold, may be better relished than the vain efforts I have made for your pastime."

Manfred then conducting the three Knights into an inner chamber, shut the door, and inviting them to be seated, began thus, addressing himself to the chief personage.

"You come, Sir Knight, as I understand, in the name of the Marquis of Vicenza, to re-demand the Lady Isabella his daughter, who has been contracted in the face of holy church to my son, by the consent of her legal guardians; and to require me to resign my dominions to your Lord, who gives himself for the nearest of blood to Prince Alfonso, whose soul God rest! I shall speak to the latter article of your demands first. You must know, your Lord knows, that I enjoy the principality of Otranto from my father Don Manuel, as he received it from his father Don Ricardo.

Alfonso, their predecessor, dying childless in the Holy Land, bequeathed his estates to my grandfather Don Ricardo, in consideration of his faithful services"—the stranger shook his head—"Sir Knight," said Manfred warmly, "Ricardo was a valiant and upright man; he was a pious man, witness his munificent foundation of the adjoining church and two convents. He was peculiarly patronized by St. Nicholas—my grandfather was incapable—I say, Sir, Don Ricardo was incapable—excuse me, your interruption has disordered me. —I venerate the memory of my grandfather—well! Sirs, he held this estate; he held it by his good sword and by the favour of St. Nicholas—so did my father; and so, Sirs, will I, come what come will—but Frederic, your Lord, is nearest in blood—I have consented to put my title to the issue of the sword—does that imply a vitious title?—I might have asked, where is Frederic your Lord? Report speaks him dead in captivity. You say, your actions say, he lives—I question it not—I might, Sirs, I might—but I do not. Other Princes would bid Frederic take his inheritance by force, if he can: They would not stake their dignity on a single combat. They would not submit it to the decision of unknown mutes!—pardon me, Gentlemen, I am too warm: But suppose yourselves in my situation: As ye are stout Knights, would it not move your choler to have your own and the honour of your ancestors called in question?—but to the point. Ye require me to deliver up the Lady Isabella—Sirs, I must ask if ye are authorized to receive her?" The Knight nodded. "Receive her"—continued Manfred; "well! you are authorized to receive her—but, gentle Knight, may I ask if you have full powers?" The Knight nodded. "It is well," said Manfred: "Then hear what I have to offer—ye see, Gentlemen, before you the most unhappy of men! [he began to weep] afford me your compassion; I am intitled to it: Indeed I am. Know, I have lost my only hope, my joy, the support of my house—Conrad died yester morning." The

Knights discovered signs of surprise. "Yes, Sirs, fate has disposed of my son. Isabella is at liberty"—"Do you then restore her?" cried the chief Knight, breaking silence. "Afford me your patience," said Manfred. "I rejoice to find, by this testimony of your good-will, that this matter may be adjusted without blood. It is no interest of mind dictates what little I have farther to say. Ye behold in me a man disgusted with the world: The loss of my son has weaned me from earthly cares. Power and greatness have no longer any charms in my eyes. I wished to transmit the scepter I had received from my ancestors with honour to my son—but that is over! Life itself is so indifferent to me, that I accepted your defiance with joy: A good Knight cannot go to the grave with more satisfaction than when falling in his vocation. Whatever is the will of heaven, I submit; for alas! Sirs, I am a man of many sorrows. Manfred is no object of envy—but no doubt you are acquainted with my story." The Knight made signs of ignorance, and seemed curious to have Manfred proceed. "Is it possible, Sirs," continued the Prince, "that my story should be a secret to you? have you heard nothing relating to me and the Princess Hippolita?" They shook theirs heads—"No! thus then, Sirs, it is. You think me ambitious: Ambition alas! is composed of more rugged materials. If I were ambitious, I should not for so many years have been a prey to all the hell of conscientious scruples—but I weary your patience: I will be brief. Know then, that I have long been troubled in mind on my union with the Princess Hippolita.—Oh! Sirs, if ye were acquainted with that excellent woman! if ye knew that I adore her like a mistress, and cherish her as a friend—but man was not born for perfect happiness! she shares my scruples, and with her consent I have brought this matter before the church, for we are related within the forbidden degrees. I expect every hour the definitive sentence that must separate us for ever—I am sure you feel for me—I see you do—pardon these tears! The Knights gazed on each other, wondering where this would end. Manfred continued. The death of my son betiding while my soul was under this anxiety, I thought of nothing but resigning my dominions, and retiring for ever from the sight of mankind. My only difficulty was to fix on a successor, who would be tender of my people, and to dispose of the Lady Isabella, who is dear to me as my own blood. I was willing to restore the line of Alfonso, even in his most distant kindred: And though, pardon me, I am satisfied it was his will that Ricardo's lineage should take place of his own relations; yet where was I to search for those relations? I knew of none but Frederic your Lord; he was a captive to the infidels, or dead; and were he living, and at home, would he quit the flourishing state of Vicenza for the inconsiderable principality of Otranto? If he would not, could I bear the thought of seeing a hard unfeeling Viceroy set over my poor faithful people?—for, Sirs, I love my people, and thank heaven am beloved by them—but ye will ask, whither tends this long discourse? briefly then, thus, Sirs. Heaven in your arrival seems to point out a remedy for these difficulties and my misfortunes. The Lady Isabella is at liberty; I shall soon be so—I would submit to any thing for the good of my people—were it not the best, the only way to extinguish the feuds between our families, if I was to take the Lady Isabella to wife—you start—but though Hippolita's virtues will ever be dear to me, a Prince must not consider himself; he is born for his people—" A servant at that instant entering the chamber apprized Manfred that Jerome and several of his brethren demanded immediate access to him.

The Prince, provoked at this interruption, and fearing that the Friar would discover to the strangers that Isabella had taken sanctuary, was going to forbid Jerome's entrance. But recollecting that he was certainly arrived to notify the Princess's return, Manfred began to excuse himself to the

Knights for leaving them for a few moments, but was prevented by the arrival of the Friars. Manfred angrily reprimanded them for their intrusion, and would have forced them back from the chamber; but Jerome was too much agitated to be repulsed. He declared aloud the flight of Isabella, with protestations of his own innocence. Manfred distracted at the news, and not less at its coming to the knowledge of the strangers, uttered nothing but incoherent sentences, now upbraiding the Friar, now apologizing to the Knights, earnest to know what was become of Isabella, yet equally afraid of their knowing, impatient to pursue her, yet dreading to have them join in the pursuit. He offered to dispatch messengers in quest of her,—but the chief Knight no longer keeping silence, reproached Manfred in bitter terms for his dark and ambiguous dealing, and demanded the cause of Isabella's first absence from the castle. Manfred, casting a stern look at Jerome, implying a command of silence, pretended that on Conrad's death he had placed her in sanctuary until he could determine how to dispose of her. Jerome who trembled for his son's life, did not dare contradict this falshood, but one of his brethren, not under the same anxiety, declared frankly that she had fled to their church in the preceding night. The Prince in vain endeavoured to stop this discovery, which overwhelmed him with shame and confusion. The principal stranger, amazed at the contradictions he heard, and more than half persuaded that Manfred had secreted the Princess, notwithstanding the concern he expressed at her flight, rushing to the door, said, "Thou traitor-Prince! Isabella shall be found." Manfred endeavoured to hold him, but the other Knights assisting their comrade, he broke from the Prince, and hastened into the court, demanding his attendants. Manfred finding it vain to divert him from the pursuit, offered to accompany him; and summoning his attendants, and taking Jerome and some of the Friars to guide them, they issued from the castle; Manfred privately giving orders, to have the Knight's company secured, while to the Knight he affected to dispatch a messenger to require their assistance.

The company had no sooner quitted the castle, than Matilda, who felt herself deeply interested for the young peasant, since she had seen him condemned to death in the hall, and whose thoughts had been taken up with concerting measures to save him, was informed by some of the female attendants that Manfred had dispatched all his men various ways in pursuit of Isabella. He had in his hurry given this order in general terms, not meaning to extend it to the guard he had set upon Theodore, but forgetting it. The domestics, officious to obey so peremptory a Prince, and urged by their own curiosity and love of novelty to join in any precipitate chace, had to a man left the castle. Matilda disengaging herself from her women, stole up to the black tower, and unbolting the door, presented herself to the astonished Theodore. "Young man," she said, "though filial duty, and womanly modesty condemn the step I am taking, yet holy charity, surmounting all other ties, justifies this act. Fly; the doors of thy prison are open: My father and his domestics are absent; but they may soon return: Be gone in safety; and may the angels of heaven direct thy course!" "Thou art surely one of those angels!" said the enraptured Theodore: "None but a blessed saint could speak, could act —could look like thee!—may I not know the name of my divine protectress! methought thou namedst thy father: Is it possible! can Manfred's blood feel holy pity?—lovely Lady, thou answerest not—but how art thou here thyself? why dost thou neglect thy own safety, and waste a thought on a wretch like Theodore? let us fly together: The life thou bestowest shall be dedicated to thy defence." "Alas! thou mistakest;" said Matilda sighing: "I am Manfred's daughter, but no dangers await me." "Amazement!" said Theodore: "But last night I blessed myself for yielding thee the service thy gracious compassion so charitably returns me now." "Still thou art in an error!" said the Princess; "but this is no time for explanation. Fly, virtuous youth, while it is in my power to save thee; Should my father return, thou and I both should indeed have cause to tremble." "How!" said Theodore; "thinkest thou, charming maid, that I will accept of life at the hazard of aught calamitous to thee? better I endured a thousand deaths."—"I run no risk," said Matilda, "but by thy delay. Depart; it cannot be known that I assisted thy flight." "Swear by the saints above," said Theodore, "that thou canst not be suspected; else here I vow to await whatever can befal me." "Oh! thou art too generous;" said Matilda; "but rest assured that no suspicion can alight on me." "Give me thy beauteous hand in token that thou dost not deceive me," said Theodore; "and let me bathe it with the warm tears of gratitude."—"Forbear;" said the Princess; "this must not be." "Alas!" said Theodore, "I have never known but calamity until this hour—perhaps shall never know other fortune again: Suffer the chaste raptures of holy gratitude; 'Tis my soul would print its effusions on thy hand." "Forbear, and be gone," said Matilda:— "How would Isabella approve of seeing thee at my feet?" "Who is Isabella?" said the young man with surprize. "Ah me! I fear," said the Princess, "I am serving a deceitful one! —hast thou forgot thy curiosity this morning?" "Thy looks, thy actions, all thy beauteous self seems an emanation of divinity," said Theodore, "but thy words are dark and mysterious,—speak, Lady; speak to thy servant's comprehension."—"Thou understandest but too well!" said Matilda: "But once more I command thee to be gone: Thy blood, which, I may preserve, will be on my head, if I waste the time in vain discourse." "I go, Lady," said Theodore, "because it is thy will, and because I would not bring the grey hairs of my father with sorrow to the grave. Say but, adored

Lady, that I have thy gentle pity."—"Stay;" said Matilda; "I will conduct thee to the subterraneous vault by which Isabella escaped; it will lead thee to the church of St. Nicholas, where thou mayst take sanctuary."—"What!" said Theodore, "was it another, and not thy lovely self that I assisted to find the subterraneous passage?" "It was;" said Matilda; "but ask no more: I tremble to see thee still abide here: Fly to the sanctuary."—"To sanctuary!" said Theodore: "No, Princess; sanctuaries are for helpless damsels, or for criminals. Theodore's soul is free from guilt, nor will wear the appearance of it. Give me a sword, Lady, and thy father shall learn that Theodore scorns an ignominious flight." "Rash youth!" said Matilda, "thou wouldst not dare to lift thy presumptuous arm against the Prince of Otranto?" "Not against thy father; indeed I dare not:" said Theodore: "Excuse me, Lady; I had forgotten,—but could I gaze on thee, and remember thou art sprung from the tyrant Manfred?—but he is thy father, and from this moment my injuries are buried in oblivion." A deep and hollow groan, which seemed to come from above, startled the Princess and Theodore. "Good heaven! we are overheard!" said the Princess. They listened; but perceiving no farther noise, they both concluded it the effect of pent-up vapours: And the Princess preceding Theodore softly, carried him to her father's armory, where equipping him with a complete suit, he was conducted by Matilda to the postern-gate. "Avoid the town," said the Princess, "and all the western side of the castle: 'Tis there the search must be making by Manfred and the strangers: But hie thee to the opposite quarter. Yonder behind that forest to the east is a chain of rocks, hollowed into a labyrinth of caverns that reach to the seacoast. There thou mayst lie concealed, till thou canst make signs to some vessel to put on shore and take thee off. Go! heaven be thy guide!—and sometimes in thy prayers remember—Matilda!" Theodore flung himself at her feet, and seizing her lilly hand, which with struggles she suffered him to kiss, he vowed on the earliest opportunity to get himself knighted, and fervently intreated her permission to swear himself eternally her knight—E'er the Princess could reply, a clap of thunder was suddenly heard, that shook the battlements. Theodore, regardless of the tempest, would have urged his suit; but the Princess, dismayed, retreated hastily into the castle, and commanded the youth to be gone with an air that would not be disobeyed. He sighed, and retired, but with eyes fixed on the gate, until Matilda closing it, put an end to an interview, in which the hearts of both had drunk so deeply of a passion, which both now tasted for the first time.

Theodore went pensively to the convent, to acquaint his father with his deliverance. There he learned the absence of Jerome, and the pursuit that was making after the Lady Isabella, with some particulars of whose story he now first became acquainted. The generous galantry of his nature prompted him to wish to assist her; but the Monks could lend him no lights to guess at the route she had taken. He was not tempted to wander far in search of her, for the idea of Matilda had imprinted itself so strongly on his heart, that he could not bear to absent himself at much distance from her abode. The tenderness Jerome had expressed for him concurred to confirm this reluctance; and he even persuaded himself that filial affection was the chief cause of his hovering between the castle and monastery, until Jerome should return at night; Theodore at length determined to repair to the forest that Matilda had pointed out to him. Arriving there, he sought the gloomiest shades, as best suited to the pleasing melancholy that reigned in his mind. In this mood he roved insensibly to the caves which had formerly served as a retreat to hermits, and were now reported round the country to be haunted by evil spirits. He recollected to have heard this tradition; and being of a brave and adventurous disposition, he willingly indulged his curiosity in exploring the secret recesses of this labyrinth. He had not penetrated far before he thought he heard the steps of some person who seemed to retreat before him. Theodore, though firmly grounded in all our holy faith enjoins to be believed, had no apprehension that good men were abandoned without cause to the malice of the powers of darkness. He thought the place more likely to be infested by robbers than by those infernal agents who are reported to molest and bewilder travellers. He had long burned with impatience to approve his valour—drawing his sabre, he marched sedately onwards, still directing his steps, as the imperfect rustling sound before him led the way. The armour he wore was a like indication to the person who avoided him. Theodore now convinced that he was not mistaken, redoubled his pace, and evidently gained on the person that fled, whose haste increasing, Theodore came up just as a woman fell breathless before him. He hasted to raise her, but her terror was so great, that he apprehended she would faint in his arms. He used every gentle word to dispel her alarms, and assured her that far from injuring, he would defend her at the peril of his life. The Lady recovering her spirits from his courteous demeanour, and gazing on her protector, said, "Sure I have heard that voice before!" "Not to my knowledge," replied Theodore, "unless as I conjecture thou art the Lady Isabella."—"Merciful heaven!" cried she, "thou art not sent in quest of me, art thou?" and saying those words, she threw herself at his feet, and besought him not to deliver her up to Manfred. "To Manfred!" cried Theodore—"no, Lady, I have once already delivered thee from his tyranny, and it shall fare hard with me now, but I will place thee out of the reach of his daring." "Is it possible," said she, "that thou shouldst be the generous unknown whom I met last night in the vault of the castle? sure thou art not a mortal, but my guardian angel: On my knees let me thank"—"Hold, gentle Princess," said Theodore, "nor demean thyself before a poor and friendless young man. If heaven has selected me for thy deliverer, it will accomplish its work, and strengthen my arm in thy cause—but come, Lady, we are too near the mouth of the cavern; let us seek its inmost recesses: I can have no tranquillity until I have placed thee beyond the reach of danger." "Alas! what mean you, Sir?" said she. "Though all our actions are noble, though your sentiments speak the purity of your soul, is it fitting that I should accompany you alone into these perplexed retreats? should we be found together, what would a censorious world think of my conduct?" "I respect your virtuous delicacy," said Theodore; "nor do you harbour a suspicion that wounds my honour. I meant to conduct you into the most private cavity of these rocks, and then at the hazard of my life to guard their entrance against every living thing. Besides, Lady," continued he drawing a deep sigh, "beauteous and all perfect as your form is, and though my wishes are not guiltless of aspiring, know, my soul is dedicated to another; and although"—a sudden noise prevented Theodore from proceeding. They soon distinguished these sounds, "Isabella! What ho! Isabella!"—the trembling Princess relapsed into her former agony of fear. Theodore endeavoured to encourage her, but in vain. He assured her he would die rather than suffer her to return under Manfred's power; and begging her to remain concealed, he went forth to prevent the person in search of her from approaching.

At the mouth of the cavern he found an armed Knight, discoursing with a peasant, who assured him he had seen a Lady enter the passes of the rock. The Knight was preparing to seek her, when Theodore, placing himself in his way, with his sword drawn, sternly forbad him at his peril to advance. "And who art thou who darest to cross my way?" said the Knight haughtily. "One who does not dare more than he will perform," said Theodore. "I seek the Lady

Isabella;" said the Knight, "and understand she has taken refuge among these rocks. Impede me not, or thou wilt repent having provoked my resentment." "Thy purpose is as odious, as thy resentment is contemptible," said Theodore. "Return whence thou camest, or we shall soon know whose resentment is most terrible." The stranger, who was the principal Knight that had arrived from the marquis of Vicenza, had galloped from Manfred as he was busied in getting information of the Princess, and giving various orders to prevent her falling into the power of the three Knights. Their chief had suspected Manfred of being privy to the Princess's absconding; and this insult from a man, who he concluded was stationed by that Prince to secrete her, confirming his suspicions, he made no reply, but discharging a blow with his sabre at Theodore, would soon have removed all obstruction, if Theodore, who took him for one of Manfred's captains, and who had no sooner given the provocation than prepared to support it, had not received the stroke on his shield. The valour that had so long been smothered in his breast, broke forth at once; he rushed impetuously on the Knight, whose pride and wrath were not less powerful incentives to hardy deeds. The combat was furious, but not long: Theodore wounded the Knight in three several places, and at last disarmed him as he fainted with the loss of blood. The peasant, who had fled at the first onset, had given the alarm to some of Manfred's domestics, who by his orders were dispersed through the forest in pursuit of Isabella. They came up as the Knight fell, whom they soon discovered to be the noble stranger. Theodore, notwithstanding his hatred to Manfred, could not behold the victory he had gained without emotions of pity and generosity: But he was more touched, when he learned the quality of his adversary, and was informed that he was no retainer, but an enemy of Manfred. He assisted the servants of the latter in disarming the Knight, and in endeavouring to staunch the blood that flowed from his wounds. The Knight recovering his speech, said in a faint and faltering voice, "Generous foe, we have both been in an error: I took thee for an instrument of the tyrant; I perceive thou hast made the like mistake—it is too late for excuses—I faint—if Isabella is at hand—call her—I have important secrets to—" "He is dying!" said one of the attendants; "has nobody a crucifix about them? Andrea, do thou pray over him"—"Fetch some water," said Theodore, "and pour it down his throat, while I hasten to the Princess"—Saying this, he flew to Isabella, and in a few words told her modestly, that he had been so unfortunate by mistake as to wound a Gentleman from her father's court, who wished e'er he died to impart something of consequence to her. The Princess, who had been transported at hearing the voice of Theodore as he called to her to come forth, was astonished at what she heard. Suffering herself to be conducted by Theodore, the new proof of whose valour recalled her dispersed spirits, she came where the bleeding Knight lay speechless on the ground—but her fears returned, when she beheld the domestics of Manfred. She would again have fled, if Theodore had not made her observe that they were unarmed, and had not threatened them with instant death, if they should dare to seize the Princess. The stranger, opening his eyes, and beholding a woman, said—"Art thou, pray tell me truly—art thou Isabella of Vicenza?" "I am;" said she: "good heaven restore thee!"—"Then thou—then thou—" said the Knight, struggling for utterance—"seest—thy father—give me one"—"Oh! amazement! horror! what do I hear! what do I see!" cried Isabella. "My father! you my father! how came you here, Sir? for heaven's sake speak!—oh! run for help, or he will expire!"—" 'Tis most true," said the wounded Knight, exerting all his force; "I am Frederic thy father—yes, I came to deliver thee—It will not be—give me a parting kiss, and take—" "Sir," said Theodore, "do not exhaust yourself: suffer us to convey you to the castle"—"To the castle!" said Isabella; "is there no help nearer than the castle? would you expose my father to the tyrant? if he goes thither, I dare not accompany him—and yet, can I leave him!" "My child," said Frederic, "it matters not for me whither I am carried: A few minutes will place me beyond danger—but while I have eyes to doat on thee, forsake me not, dear Isabella! This brave Knight—I know not who he is, will protect thy innocence—Sir, you will not abandon my child, will you!" Theodore shedding tears over his victim, and vowing to guard the Princess at the expence of his life, persuaded Frederic to suffer himself to be conducted to the castle. They placed him on a horse belonging to one of the domestics, after binding up his wounds as well as they were able. Theodore marched by his side; and the afflicted Isabella, who could not bear to quit him, followed mournfully behind.

CHAPTER IV

The sorrowful troop no sooner arrived at the castle, than
they were met by Hippolita and Matilda, whom Isabella
had sent one of the domestics before to advertise of their
approach. The Ladies causing Frederic to be conveyed into
the nearest chamber, retired, while the surgeons examined
his wounds. Matilda blushed at seeing Theodore and Isabella together; but endeavoured to conceal it by embracing
the latter, and condoling with her on her father's mischance.
The surgeons soon came to acquaint Hippolita that none
of the Marquis's wounds were dangerous; and that he was
desirous of seeing his daughter and the Princess. Theodore,
under pretence of expressing his joy at being freed from his
apprehensions of the combat being fatal to Frederic, could
not resist the impulse of following Matilda. Her eyes were
so often cast down on meeting his, that Isabella, who regarded Theodore as attentively as he gazed on Matilda,
soon divined who the object was that he had told her in
the cave engaged his affections. While this mute scene
passed, Hippolita demanded of Frederic the cause of his
having taken that mysterious course for reclaiming his
daughter; and threw in various apologies to excuse her Lord
for the match contracted between their children. Frederic,
however incensed against Manfred, was not insensible to
the courtesy and benevolence of Hippolita: But he was still
more struck with the lovely form of Matilda. Wishing to
detain them by his bedside, he informed Hippolita of his
story. He told her, that, while prisoner to the infidels, he
had dreamed that his daughter, of whom he had learned no
news since his captivity, was detained in a castle, where she

was in danger of the most dreadful misfortunes: And that if he obtained his liberty, and repaired to a wood near Joppa, he would learn more. Alarmed at this dream, and incapable of obeying the direction given by it, his chains became more grievous than ever. But while his thoughts were occupied on the means of obtaining his liberty, he received the agreeable news that the confederate Princes, who were warring in Palestine, had paid his ransom. He instantly set out for the wood that had been marked in his dream. For three days he and his attendants had wandered in the forest without seeing a human form: But on the evening of the third they came to a cell, in which they found a venerable hermit in the agonies of death. Applying rich cordials, they brought the saint-like man to his speech. "My sons," said he, "I am bounden to your charity—but it is in vain—I am going to my eternal rest—yet I die with the satisfaction of performing the will of heaven. When first I repaired to this solitude, after seeing my country become a prey to unbelievers—it is alas! above fifty years since I was witness to that dreadful scene! St. Nicholas appeared to me, and revealed a secret, which he bade me never disclose to mortal man, but on my deathbed. This is that tremendous hour, and ye are no doubt the chosen warriors to whom I was ordered to reveal my trust. As soon as ye have done the last offices to this wretched corse, dig under the seventh tree on the left-hand of this poor cave, and your pains will—Oh! good heaven receive my soul!" With those words the devout man breathed his last. "By break of day," continued Frederic, "when we had committed the holy relicks to earth, we dug according to direction—but what was our astonishment, when about the depth of six feet we discovered an enormous sabre—the very weapon yonder in the court. On the blade, which was then partly out of the scabbard, though since closed by our efforts in removing it, were written the following lines—no; excuse me, Madam," added the Marquis, turning to Hippolita, "if I forbear to repeat them: I respect your sex and rank, and would not be guilty of offending your ear with sounds injurious to ought that is dear to you—" He paused. Hippolita trembled. She did not doubt but Frederic was destined by heaven to accomplish the fate that seemed to threaten her house. Looking with anxious fondness at Matilda, a silent tear stole down her cheek: But recollecting herself, she said; "Proceed, my Lord: Heaven does nothing in vain: Mortals must receive its divine behests with lowliness and submission. It is our part to deprecate its wrath, or bow to its decrees. Repeat the sentence, my Lord; we listen resigned." Frederic was grieved that he had proceeded so far. The dignity and patient firmness of Hippolita penetrated him with respect, and the tender silent affection with which the Princess and her daughter regarded each other, melted him almost to tears. Yet apprehensive that his forbearance to obey, would be more alarming, he repeated in a faltering and low voice the following lines:

> *Where e'er a casque that suits this sword is found,*
> *With perils is thy daughter compass'd round.*
> Alfonso's *blood alone can save the maid,*
> *And quiet a long restless Prince's shade.*

"What is there in these lines," said Theodore impatiently, "that affects these Princesses? why were they to be shocked by a mysterious delicacy, that has so little foundation?" "Your words are rude, young man," said the Marquis; "and tho' fortune has favoured you once"—"My honoured Lord," said Isabella, who resented Theodore's warmth, which she perceived was dictated by his sentiments for Matilda, "discompose not yourself for the glosing of a peasant's son: He forgets the reverence he owes you; but he is not accustomed—" Hippolita, concerned at the heat that had arisen, checked Theodore for his boldness, but with an air acknowledging his zeal; and changing the conversation, demanded of Frederic where he had left her Lord? As the Marquis was going to reply, they heard a noise without, and rising to inquire the cause, Manfred, Jerome, and part of the troop, who had met an imperfect rumour of what had happened, entered the chamber. Manfred advanced hastily towards Frederic's bed to condole with him on his misfortune, and to learn the circumstances of the combat, when starting in an agony of terror and amazement, he cried, "Ha! what art thou? thou dreadful spectre! is my hour come?"—"My dearest, gracious Lord," cried Hippolita, clasping him in her arms, "what is it you see? why do you fix your eye-balls thus!"—"What!" cried Manfred breathless —"dost thou see nothing, Hippolita? is this ghastly phantom sent to me alone—to me, who did not"—"For mercy's sweetest self, my Lord," said Hippolita, "resume your soul, command your reason. There is none here, but us, your friends" —"what, is not that Alfonso?" cried Manfred: "Dost thou not see him? can it be my brain's delirium?"—"This! my Lord," said Hippolita; "this is Theodore, the youth who has been so unfortunate—"Theodore!" said Manfred mournfully, and striking his forehead—"Theodore, or a phantom, he has unhinged the soul of Manfred—but how comes he here? and how comes he in armour?" "I believe he went in search of Isabella," said Hippolita. "Of Isabella!" said Manfred, relapsing into rage—"yes, yes, that is not doubtful —but how did he escape from durance in which I left him? was it Isabella, or this hypocritical old Friar, that procured his enlargement?"—"And would a parent be criminal, my Lord," said Theodore, "if he meditated the deliverance of his child?" Jerome amazed to hear himself in a manner accused by his son, and without foundation, knew not what to think. He could not comprehend, how Theodore had escaped, how he came to be armed, and to encounter Frederic. Still he would not venture to ask any questions that might tend to inflame Manfred's wrath against his son. Jerome's silence convinced Manfred that he had contrived Theodore's release—"And is it thus, thou ungrateful old man," said the Prince addressing himself to the Friar, that thou repayest mine and Hippolita's bounties? And not content was traversing my heart's nearest wishes, thou armest thy bastard, and bringest him into my own castle to insult me!" "My Lord," said Theodore, "you wrong my father: Nor he nor I are capable of harbouring a thought against your peace. Is it insolence thus to surrender myself to your Highness' pleasure?" added he, laying his sword respectfully at Manfred's feet. "Behold my bosom; strike, my Lord, if you suspect that a disloyal thought is lodged there. There is not a sentiment engraven on my heart, that does not venerate you and yours." The grace and fervour with which Theodore uttered these words, interested every person present in his favour. Even Manfred was touched—yet still possessed with his resemblance to Alfonso, his admiration was dashed with secret horror. "Rise;" said he; "thy life is not my present purpose.—But tell me thy history, and how thou camest connected with this old traitor here." "My Lord," said Jerome eagerly—"Peace! impostor!" said Manfred; "I will not have him prompted." "My Lord," said Theodore, "I want no assistance: My story is very brief. I was carried at five years of age to Algiers with my mother, who had been taken by corsairs from the coast of Sicily. She died of grief in less than a twelvemonth—" The tears gushed from Jerome's eyes, on whose countenance a thousand anxious passions stood expressed. "Before she died," continued Theodore, "she bound a writing about my arm under my garments, which told me I was the son of the Count Falconara"—"It is most true," said Jerome; "I am that wretched father"—"Again I enjoin thee silence," said Manfred: "Proceed." "I remained in slavery," said Theodore, "until within these two years, when attending on my master in his cruizes, I was delivered by a Christian vessel, which

over-powered the pirate; and discovering myself to the captain, he generously put me on shore in Sicily—but alas! instead of finding a father, I learned that his estate, which was
situated on the coast, had, during his absence, been laid
waste by the Rover, who had carried my mother and me
into captivity: That his castle had been burnt to the ground,
and that my father on his return had sold what remained,
and was retired into religion in the kingdom of Naples, but
where, no man could inform me. Destitute and friendless,
hopeless almost of attaining the transport of a parent's embrace, I took the first opportunity of setting sail for Naples,
from whence, within these six days, I wandered into this
province, still supporting myself by the labour of my hands;
nor until yester-morn did I believe that heaven had reserved
any lot for me but peace of mind and contented poverty.
This, my Lord, is Theodore's story. I am blessed beyond my
hope in finding a father; I am unfortunate beyond my
desert in having incurred your Highness' displeasure." He
ceased. A murmur of approbation gently arose from the
audience. "This is not all;" said Frederic: "I am bound in
honour to add what he suppresses. Though he is modest, I
must be generous—he is one of the bravest youths on Christian ground. He is warm too; and from the short knowledge
I have of him, I will pledge myself for his veracity: If what
he reports of himself were not true, he would not utter it—
and for me, youth, I honour a frankness which becomes thy
birth. But now, and thou didst offend me: Yet the noble
blood which flows in thy veins, may well be allowed to boil
out, when it has so recently traced itself to its source. Come,
my Lord [turning to Manfred] if I can pardon him, surely
you may: It is not the youth's fault, if you took him for a
spectre." This bitter taunt galled the soul of Manfred. "If
beings from another world," replied he haughtily, "have
power to impress my mind with awe, it is more than living
man can do; nor could a stripling's arm—" "My Lord," in-

terrupted Hippolita, "your guest has occasion for repose: Shall we not leave him to his rest?" Saying this, and taking Manfred by the hand, she took leave of Frederic, and led the company forth. The Prince, not sorry to quit a conversation, which recalled to mind the discovery he had made of his most secret sensations, suffered himself to be conducted to his own apartment, after permitting Theodore, tho' under engagement to return to the castle on the morrow [a condition the young man gladly accepted] to retire with his father to the convent. Matilda and Isabella were too much occupied with their own reflections, and too little content with each other, to wish for farther converse that night. They separated each to her chamber, with more expressions of ceremony and fewer of affection, than had passed between them since their childhood.

If they parted with small cordiality, they did but meet with greater impatience, as soon as the sun was risen. Their minds were in a situation that excluded sleep, and each recollected a thousand questions which she wished she had put to the other overnight. Matilda reflected that Isabella had been twice delivered by Theodore in very critical situations, which she could not believe accidental. His eyes, it was true, had been fixed on her in Frederic's chamber; but that might have been to disguise his passion for Isabella from the fathers of both. It were better to clear this up—She wished to know the truth, lest she should wrong her friend by entertaining a passion for Isabella's lover. Thus jealousy prompted, and at the same time borrowed an excuse from friendship to justify its curiosity.

Isabella, not less restless, had better foundation for her suspicions. Both Theodore's tongue and eyes had told her his heart was engaged—it was true—yet perhaps Matilda might not correspond to his passion—she had ever appeared insensible to love: "All her thoughts were set on heaven— why did I dissuade her?" said Isabella to herself: "I am pun-

ished for my generosity—but when did they meet? where?—
it cannot be: I have deceived myself—perhaps last night was
the first time they ever beheld each other—it must be some
other object that has prepossessed his affections—if it is, I
am not so unhappy, as I thought; if it is not my friend
Matilda—how! can I stoop to wish for the affection of a
man, who rudely and unnecessarily acquainted me with his
indifference? and that at the very moment in which common courtesy demanded at least expressions of civility. I
will go to my dear Matilda, who will confirm me in this
becoming pride—man is false—I will advise with her on
taking the veil: She will rejoice to find me in this disposition; and I will acquaint her that I no longer oppose her
inclination for the cloyster." In this frame of mind, and
determined to open her heart entirely to Matilda, she went
to that Princess' chamber, whom she found already dressed,
and leaning pensively on her arm. This attitude, so corre-
spondent to what she felt herself, revived Isabella's suspicions, and destroyed the confidence she had purposed to
place in her friend. They blushed at meeting, and were too
much novices to disguise their sensations with address.
After some unmeaning questions and replies, Matilda demanded of Isabella the cause of her flight? The latter, who
had almost forgotten Manfred's passion, so entirely was she
occupied by her own, concluding that Matilda referred to
her last escape from the convent, which had occasioned the
events of the preceding evening, replied, "Martelli brought
word to the convent that your mother was dead"—"Oh!"
said Matilda interrupting her, "Bianca has explained that
mistake to me: on seeing me faint, she cried out, the Princess is dead! and Martelli who had come for the usual dole
to the castle"—"And what made you faint?" said Isabella,
indifferent to the rest. Matilda blushed, and stammered—
"My father—he was sitting in judgment on a criminal—"
"What criminal?" said Isabella eagerly—"A young man;"

said Matilda—"I believe—I think it was that young man that"—"What, Theodore?" said Isabella. "Yes;" answered she; "I never saw him before; I do not know how he had offended my father—but as he has been of service to you, I am glad my Lord has pardoned him"—"Served me?" replied Isabella; "do you term it serving me, to wound my father, and almost occasion his death! Though it is but since yesterday that I am blessed with knowing a parent, I hope Matilda does not think I am such a stranger to filial tenderness as not to resent the boldness of that audacious youth, and that it is impossible for me ever to feel any affection for one who dared to lift his arm against the author of my being. No, Matilda, my heart abhors him; and if you still retain the friendship for me that you have vowed from your infancy, you will detest a man who has been on the point of making me miserable for ever." Matilda held down her head, and replied; "I hope my dearest Isabella does not doubt her Matilda's friendship: I never beheld that youth until yesterday; he is almost a stranger to me: But as the surgeons have pronounced your father out of danger, you ought not to harbour uncharitable resentment against one, who I am persuaded did not know the Marquis was related to you." "You plead his cause very pathetically," said Isabella, "considering he is so much a stranger to you! I am mistaken, or he returns your charity." "What mean you?" said Matilda. "Nothing," said Isabella, repenting that she had given Matilda a hint of Theodore's inclination for her. Then changing the discourse, she asked Matilda what occasioned Manfred to take Theodore for a spectre? "Bless me," said Matilda, "did you not observe his extreme resemblance to the portrait of Alfonso in the gallery? I took notice of it to Bianca even before I saw him in armour; but with the helmet on, he is the very image of that picture." "I do not much observe pictures," said Isabella: "Much less have I examined this young man so attentively as you seem to have done—ah! Matilda, your heart is in danger—but let me warn you as a friend—he has owned to me that he is in love; it cannot be with you, for yesterday was the first time you ever met—was it not?" "Certainly:" replied Matilda; "but why does my dearest Isabella conclude from any thing I have said, that—" she paused—then continuing; "he saw you first, and I am far from having the vanity to think that my little portion of charms could engage a heart devoted to you—may you be happy, Isabella, whatever is the fate of Matilda!" "My lovely friend," said Isabella, whose heart was too honest to resist a kind expression, "it is you that Theodore admires; I saw it; I am persuaded of it; nor shall a thought of my own happiness suffer me to interfere with yours." This frankness drew tears from the gentle Matilda; and jealousy that for a moment had raised a coolness between these amiable maidens, soon gave way to the natural sincerity and candour of their souls. Each confessed to the other the impression that Theodore had made on her; and this confidence was followed by a struggle of generosity, each insisting on yielding her claim to her friend. At length, the dignity of Isabella's virtue reminding her of the preference which Theodore had almost declared for her rival, made her determine to conquer her passion, and cede the beloved object to her friend.

During this contest of amity, Hippolita entered her daughter's chamber. "Madam," said she to Isabella, "you have so much tenderness for Matilda, and interest yourself so kindly in whatever affects our wretched house, that I can have no secrets with my child, which are not proper for you to hear." The Princesses were all attention and anxiety. "Know then, Madam," continued Hippolita, "and you, my dearest Matilda, that being convinced by all the events of these two last ominous days, that heaven purposes the sceptre of Otranto should pass from Manfred's hands into those of the Marquis Frederic, I have been perhaps inspired with the thought of averting our total destruction by the union of our rival houses. With this view I have been proposing to Manfred my Lord to tender this dear, dear child to Frederic your father"—"Me to Lord Frederic!" cried Matilda—"Good heavens! my gracious mother—and have you named it to my father?" "I have," said Hippolita: "He listened benignly to my proposal, and is gone to break it to the Marquis." "Ah! wretched Princess!" cried Isabella; "what hast thou done! what ruin hast thy inadvertent goodness been preparing for thyself, for me, and for Matilda!" "Ruin from me to you and to my child!" said Hippolita; "what can this mean?" "Alas!" said Isabella, "the purity of your own heart prevents your seeing the depravity of others. Manfred, your Lord, that impious man"—"Hold;" said Hippolita, "you must not in my presence, young lady, mention Manfred with disrespect: He is my lord and husband, and" —"will not long be so," said Isabella, "if his wicked purposes can be carried into execution." "This language amazes me;" said Hippolita. "Your feeling, Isabella, is warm; but until this hour I never knew it betray you into intemperance. What deed of Manfred authorizes you to treat him as a murderer, an assassin?" "Thou virtuous, and too credulous Princess!" replied Isabella; "it is not thy life he aims at—it is to separate himself from thee! to divorce thee!" "To—to divorce me!" "To divorce my mother!" cried Hippolita and Matilda at once—"Yes;" said Isabella; "and to compleat his crime, he meditates—I cannot speak it!" "What can surpass what thou hast already uttered?" said Matilda. Hippolita was silent. Grief choked her speech; and the recollection of Manfred's late ambiguous discourses confirmed what she heard. "Excellent, dear Lady! Madam! Mother!" cried Isabella, flinging herself at Hippolita's feet in a transport of passion; "trust me, believe me, I will die a thousand deaths sooner than consent to injure you, than yield to so odious— oh!"—"This is too much!" cried Hippolita: "What crimes does one crime suggest! rise, dear Isabella; I do not doubt your virtue. Oh! Matilda, this stroke is too heavy for thee! weep not, my child; and not a murmur, I charge thee. Remember, he is *thy* father still!"—"But you are my mother too;" said Matilda fervently; "and *you* are virtuous, *you* are guiltless!—Oh! must not I, must not I complain!" "You must not," said Hippolita—"come, all will yet be well. Manfred, in the agony for the loss of thy brother, knew not what he said: perhaps Isabella misunderstood him: His heart is good—and, my child, thou knowest not all! There is a destiny hangs over us; the hand of Providence is stretched out—Oh! could I but save thee from the wreck!—yes," continued she in a firmer tone; "perhaps the sacrifice of myself may atone for all—I will go and offer myself to this divorce —it boots not what becomes of me. I will withdraw into the neighbouring monastery, and waste the remainder of life in prayers and tears for my child and—the Prince!" "Thou art as much too good for this world," said Isabella, "as Manfred is execrable—but think not, Lady, that thy weakness shall determine for me. I swear, hear me all ye angels"—"Stop, I adjure thee;" cried Hippolita: "Remember thou dost not depend on thyself; thou hast a father"— "My father is too pious, too noble," interrupted Isabella, "to command an impious deed. But should he command it; can a father enjoin a cursed act? I was contracted to the son? can I wed the father?—no, Madam, no; force should not drag me to Manfred's hated bed. I loath him, I abhor him: Divine and human laws forbid—and my friend, my dearest Matilda! would I wound her tender soul by injuring her adored mother? my own mother—I never have known another"—"Oh! she is the mother of both!" cried Matilda: "Can we, can we, Isabella, adore her too much?" "My lovely children," said the touched Hippolita, "your tenderness overpowers me—but I must not give way to it. It is not ours to make election for ourselves: Heaven, our fathers, and our husbands must decide for us. Have patience until you hear what Manfred and Frederic have determined. If the Marquis accepts Matilda's hand, I know she will readily obey. Heaven may interpose and prevent the rest. What means my child?" continued she, seeing Matilda fall at her feet with a flood of speechless tears—"but no; answer me not, my daughter: I must not hear a word against the pleasure of thy father." "Oh! doubt not my obedience, my dreadful obedience to him and to you!" said Matilda. "But can I, most respected of women, can I experience all this tenderness, this world of goodness, and conceal a thought from the best of mothers?" "What art thou going to utter?" said Isabella trembling. "Recollect thyself, Matilda." "No, Isabella," said the Princess, "I should not deserve this incomparable parent, if the inmost recesses of my soul harboured a thought without her permission—nay, I have offended her; I have suffered a passion to enter my heart without her avowal!—but here I disclaim it; here I vow to heaven and her"—"My child! my child!" said Hippolita, "what words are these! what new calamities has fate in store for us! Thou, a passion! Thou, in this hour of destruction"—"Oh! I see all my guilt!" said Matilda. "I abhor myself, if I cost my mother a pang. She is the dearest thing I have on earth—oh! I will never, never behold him more!" "Isabella," said Hippolita, "thou art conscious to this unhappy secret, whatever it is. Speak"—"What!" cried Matilda, "have I so forfeited my mother's love, that she will not permit me even to speak my own guilt? oh! wretched, wretched Matilda!" "Thou art too cruel;" said Isabella to Hippolita: "Canst thou behold this anguish of a virtuous mind, and not commiserate it?" "Not pity my child!" said Hippolita, catching Matilda in her arms—"Oh! I know she is good, she is all virtue, all tenderness, and duty. I do forgive thee, my excellent, my only hope!" The Princesses then revealed to Hippolita their mutual inclination for Theodore, and the purpose of Isabella to resign him to Matilda. Hippolita blamed their imprudence, and shewed them the improbability that either father would consent to bestow his heiress on so poor a man, though nobly born. Some comfort it gave her to find their passion of so recent a date, and that Theodore had had but little cause to suspect it in either. She strictly enjoined them to avoid all correspondence with him. This Matilda fervently promised: But Isabella, who flattered herself that she meant no more than to promote his union with her friend, could not determine to avoid him; and made no reply. "I will go to the convent," said Hippolita, "and order new masses to be said for a deliverance from these calamities."—"Oh! my mother," said Matilda, "you mean to quit us: You mean to take sanctuary, and to give my father an opportunity of pursuing his fatal intention. Alas! on my knees I supplicate you to forbear—will you leave me a prey to Frederic? I will follow you to the convent"—"Be at peace, my child:" said Hippolita: "I will return instantly. I will never abandon thee, until I know it is the will of heaven, and for thy benefit. "Do not deceive me," said Matilda. "I will not marry Frederic until thou commandest it.—Alas! What will become of me?" "Why that exclamation?" said Hippolita. "I have promised thee to return"—"Ah! my mother," replied Matilda, "stay and save me from myself. A frown from thee can do more than all my father's severity. I have given away my heart, and you alone can make me recall it." "No more," said Hippolita: "thou must not relapse, Matilda." "I can quit Theodore," said she, "but must I wed another? let me attend thee to the altar, and shut myself from the world for ever." "Thy fate depends on thy father;" said Hippolita: "I have ill bestowed my tenderness, if it has taught thee to revere aught beyond him. Adieu! my child: I go to pray for thee."

Hippolita's real purpose was to demand of Jerome, whether in conscience she might not consent to the divorce.

She had oft urged Manfred to resign the principality, which the delicacy of her conscience rendered an hourly burthen to her. These scruples concurred to make the separation from her husband appear less dreadful to her, than it would have seemed in any other situation.

Jerome, at quitting the castle overnight, had questioned Theodore severely why he had accused him to Manfred of being privy to his escape. Theodore owned it had been with design to prevent Manfred's suspicion from alighting on Matilda; and added, the holiness of Jerome's life and character secured him from the tyrant's wrath. Jerome was heartily grieved to discover his son's inclination for that Princess; and leaving him to his rest; promised in the morning to acquaint him with important reasons for conquering his passion. Theodore, like Isabella, was too recently acquainted with parental authority to submit to its decisions against the impulse of his heart. He had little curiosity to learn the Friar's reasons, and less disposition to obey them. The lovely Matilda had made stronger impressions on him than filial affection. All night he pleased himself with visions of love; and it was not till late after the morning-office, that he recollected the Friar's commands to attend him at Alfonso's tomb.

"Young man," said Jerome, when he saw him, "this tardiness does not please me. Have a father's commands already so little weight?" Theodore made awkward excuses, and attributed his delay to having overslept himself. "And on whom were thy dreams employed?" said the Friar sternly. His son blushed. "Come, come," resumed the Friar, "inconsiderate youth, this must not be: Eradicate this guilty passion from thy breast"—"Guilty passion!" cried Theodore: "Can guilt dwell with innocent beauty and virtuous modesty?" "It is sinful," replied the Friar, "to cherish those whom heaven has doomed to destruction. A tyrant's race must be swept from the earth to the third and fourth gen-

eration." "Will heaven visit the innocent for the crimes of
the guilty?" said Theodore. "The fair Matilda has virtues
enough"—"To undo thee:" interrupted Jerome. "Hast thou
so soon forgotten that twice the savage Manfred has pronounced thy sentence?" "Nor have I forgotten, Sir," said
Theodore, "that the charity of his daughter delivered me
from his power. I can forget injuries, but never benefits."
"The injuries thou hast received from Manfred's race," said
the Friar, "are beyond what thou canst conceive.—Reply
not, but view this holy image! Beneath this marble monument rest the ashes of the good Alfonso; a Prince adorned
with every virtue: The father of his people! the delight of
mankind! Kneel, head strong boy, and list, while a father
unfolds a tale of horror, that will expel every sentiment
from thy soul, but sensations of sacred vengeance—Alfonso!
much injured Prince! let thy unsatisfied shade sit awful on
the troubled air, while these trembling lips—ha! who comes
there?"—"The most wretched of women!" said Hippolita,
entering the choir. "Good Father, art thou at leisure?—but
why this kneeling youth? what means the horror imprinted
on each countenance? why at this venerable tomb—alas! hast
thou seen aught?" "We were pouring forth our orisons to
heaven," replied the Friar with some confusion, "to put an
end to the woes of this deplorable province. Join with us,
Lady! thy spotless soul may obtain an exemption from the
judgments which the portents of these days but too speak-
ingly denounce against thy house." "I pray fervently to
heaven to divert them:" said the pious Princess. "Thou knowest it has been the occupation of my life to wrest a blessing
for my Lord and my harmless children—One alas! is taken
from me! would heaven but hear me for my poor Matilda!
Father! intercede for her!"—"Every heart will bless her," cried
Theodore with rapture—"Be dumb, rash youth!" said Jerome. "And thou fond Princess contend not with the Powers
above! The Lord giveth, and the Lord taketh away: Bless

his holy name, and submit to his decrees." "I do most devoutly," said Hippolita: "But will he not spare my only comfort? must Matilda perish too?—ah! Father, I came—but dismiss thy son. No ear but thine must hear what I have to utter." "May heaven grant thy every wish, most excellent Princess!" said Theodore retiring. Jerome frowned.

Hippolita then acquainted the Friar with the proposal she had suggested to Manfred, his approbation of it, and the tender of Matilda that he was gone to make to Frederic. Jerome could not conceal his dislike of the motion, which he covered under pretence of the improbability that Frederic, the nearest of blood to Alfonso, and who was come to claim his succession, would yield to an alliance with the usurper of his right. But nothing could equal the perplexity of the Friar, when Hippolita confessed her readiness not to oppose the separation, and demanded his opinion on the legality of her acquiescence. The Friar catched eagerly at her request of his advice, and without explaining his aversion to the proposed marriage of Manfred and Isabella, he painted to Hippolita in the most alarming colours the sinfulness of her consent, denounced judgments against her if she complied, and enjoined her in the severest terms to treat any such proposition with every mark of indignation and refusal.

Manfred, in the mean time, had broken his purpose to Frederic, and proposed the double marriage. That weak Prince, who had been struck with the charms of Matilda, listened but too eagerly to the offer. He forgot his enmity to Manfred, whom he saw but little hope of dispossessing by force; and flattering himself that no issue might succeed from the union of his daughter with the Tyrant, he looked upon his own succession to the principality as facilitated by wedding Matilda. He made faint opposition to the proposal; affecting, for form only, not to acquiesce unless Hippolita should consent to the divorce. Manfred took that upon himself. Transported with his success, and impatient to see himself in a situation to expect sons, he hastened to his wife's apartment, determined to extort her compliance. He learned with indignation that she was absent at the convent. His guilt suggested to him that she had probably been informed by Isabella of his purpose. He doubted whether her retirement to the convent did not import an intention of remaining there, until she could raise obstacles to their divorce; and the suspicions he had already entertained of Jerome, made him apprehend that the Friar would not only traverse his views, but might have inspired Hippolita with the resolution of taking sanctuary. Impatient to unravel this clue, and to defeat its success, Manfred hastened to the convent, and arrived there, as the Friar was earnestly exhorting the Princess never to yield to the divorce.

"Madam," said Manfred, "what business drew you hither? why did you not await my return from the Marquis?" "I came to implore a blessing on your councils," replied Hippolita. "My councils do not need a Friar's intervention," said Manfred—"and of all men living is that hoary traitor the only one whom you delight to confer with?" "Profane Prince!" said Jerome; "is it at the altar that thou chusest to insult the servants of the altar?—but, Manfred, thy impious schemes are known. Heaven and this virtuous Lady know them—nay, frown not, Prince. The church despises thy menaces. Her thunders will be heard above thy wrath. Dare to proceed in thy curst purpose of a divorce, until her sentence be known, and here I lance her Anathema at thy head." "Audacious rebel!" said Manfred, endeavouring to conceal the awe with which the Friar's words inspired him; "Dost thou presume to threaten thy lawful Prince?" "Thou art no lawful Prince;" said Jerome; "thou art no Prince—go, discuss thy claim with Frederic; and when that is done" —"It is done," replied Manfred: "Frederic accepts Matilda's hand, and is content to wave his claim, unless I have no male issue"—as he spoke those words, three drops of blood fell from the nose of Alfonso's statue. Manfred turned pale, and the Princess sunk on her knees. "Behold!" said the Friar; "mark this miraculous indication that the blood of Alfonso will never mix with that of Manfred!" "My gracious Lord," said Hippolita, "let us submit ourselves to heaven. Think not thy ever obedient wife rebels against thy authority. I have no will but that of my Lord and the church. To that revered tribunal let us appeal. It does not depend on us to burst the bonds that unite us. If the church shall approve the dissolution of our marriage, be it so—I have but few years, and those of sorrow to pass. Where can they be worn away so well as at the foot of this altar, in prayers for thine and Matilda's safety?"—"But thou shalt not remain here until then," said Manfred. "Repair with me to the castle, and there I will advise on the proper measures for a divorce; but this meddling Friar comes not thither: My hospitable roof shall never more harbour a traitor—and for thy Reverence's offspring," continued he, "I banish him from my dominions. He, I ween, is no sacred personage, nor under the protection of the church. Whoever weds Isabella, it shall not be Father Falconara's started up son." "They start up," said the Friar, "who are suddenly beheld in the seat of lawful Princes; but they wither away like the grass, and their place knows them no more." Manfred casting a look of scorn at the Friar, led Hippolita forth; but at the door of the church, whispered one of his attendants to remain concealed about the convent, and bring him instant notice, if any one from the castle should repair thither.

CHAPTER V

Every reflection which Manfred made on the Friar's behaviour, conspired to persuade him that Jerome was privy
to an amour between Isabella and Theodore. But Jerome's
new presumption, so dissonant from his former meekness,
suggested still deeper apprehensions. The Prince even suspected that the Friar depended on some secret support
from Frederic, whose arrival coinciding with the novel
appearance of Theodore seemed to bespeak a correspondence. Still more was he troubled with the resemblance of
Theodore to Alfonso's portrait. The latter he knew had
unquestionably died without issue. Frederic had consented
to bestow Isabella on him. These contradictions agitated his
mind with numberless pangs. He saw but two methods of
extricating himself from his difficulties. The one was to resign his dominions to the Marquis—Pride, ambition, and
his reliance on ancient prophecies, which had pointed out
a possibility of his preserving them to his posterity, combated that thought. The other was to press his marriage
with Isabella. After long ruminating on these anxious
thoughts, as he marched silently with Hippolita to the
castle, he at last discoursed with that Princess on the subject of his disquiet, and used every insinuating and plausi-
ble argument to extract her consent to, even her promise of
promoting the divorce. Hippolita needed little persuasion
to bend her to his pleasure. She endeavoured to win him
over to the measure of resigning his dominions; but finding
her exhortations fruitless, she assured him, that as far as her
conscience would allow, she would raise no opposition to
a separation, though without better founded scruples than

what he yet alleged, she would not engage to be active in demanding it.

This compliance, though inadequate, was sufficient to raise Manfred's hopes. He trusted that his power and wealth would easily advance his suit at the court of Rome, whither he resolved to engage Frederic to take a journey on purpose. That Prince had discovered so much passion for Matilda, that Manfred hoped to obtain all he wished by holding out or withdrawing his daughter's charms, according as the Marquis should appear more or less disposed to co-operate in his views. Even the absence of Frederic would be a material point gained, until he could take farther measures for his security.

Dismissing Hippolita to her apartment, he repaired to that of the Marquis; but crossing the great hall through which he was to pass, he met Bianca. That damsel he knew was in the confidence of both the young ladies. It immediately occurred to him to sift her on the subject of Isabella and Theodore. Calling her aside into the recess of the oriel window of the hall, and soothing her with many fair words and promises, he demanded of her whether she knew ought of the state of Isabella's affections. "I! my Lord! no, my Lord—yes, my Lord—poor Lady! she is wonderfully alarmed about her father's wounds; but I tell her he will do well, don't your Highness think so?" "I do not ask you," replied Manfred, "what she thinks about her father: But you are in her secrets: Come, be a good girl and tell me; is there any young man—ha!—you understand me"—"Lord bless me! understand your Highness, no, not I: I told her a few vulnerary herbs and repose"—"I am not talking," replied the Prince impatiently, "about her father: I know he will do well"—"Bless me, I rejoice to hear your Highness say so; for though I thought it not right to let my young Lady despond, methought his Greatness had a wan look, and a something—I remember when young Ferdinand was wounded by the Venetian"—"Thou answerest from the point," interrupted Manfred; "but here, take this jewel, perhaps that may fix thy attention—nay, no reverences; my favour shall not stop here—come, tell me truly; how stands Isabella's heart." "Well! your Highness has such a way!" said Bianca—"to be sure—but can your Highness keep a secret? if it should ever come out of your lips"—"It shall not, it shall not," cried Manfred.—"Nay, but swear, your Highness" —"By my halidame, if it should ever be known that I said it"—"Why, truth is truth, I do not think my Lady Isabella ever much affectioned my young Lord your Son—yet he was a sweet youth as one should see—I am sure, if I had been a Princess—but bless me! I must attend my Lady Matilda; she will marvel what is become of me"—"Stay;" cried Manfred, "thou hast not satisfied my question. Hast thou ever carried any message, any letter"—"I! good gracious!" cried Bianca; "I carry a letter? I would not to be a Queen. I hope your Highness thinks, though I am poor, I am honest—did your Highness never hear what Count Marsigli offered me, when he came a wooing to my Lady Matilda?" "I have not leisure," said Manfred, to listen to thy tales. I do not question thy honesty: But it is thy duty to conceal nothing from me. How long has Isabella been acquainted with Theodore?" "Nay, there is nothing can escape your Highness!" said Bianca—"not that I know any thing of the matter—Theodore, to be sure, is a proper young man, and, as my Lady Matilda says, the very image of good Alfonso: Has not your Highness remarked it?" "yes, yes,—no—thou torturest me," said Manfred: "Where did they meet? when?"—"Who! My Lady Matilda?" said Bianca. "No, no, not Matilda: Isabella; when did Isabella, first become acquainted with this Theodore?" "Virgin Mary!" said Bianca, "how should I know?" "Thou dost know;" said Manfred; "and I must know; I will"—"Lord! your Highness is not jealous of young Theodore!" said Bianca—"Jealous! no, no: Why should I be jealous?—perhaps I mean to unite them—if I were sure Isabella would have no repugnance"—"Repugnance! no, I'll warrant her;" said Bianca; "he is as comely a youth as ever trod on Christian ground: We are all in love with him, there is not a soul in the castle, but would be rejoiced to have him for our Prince—I mean, when it shall please heaven to call your Highness to itself"—"Indeed!" said Manfred; "has it gone so far! oh! this cursed Friar!—but I must not lose time—go, Bianca, attend Isabella; but I charge thee, not a word of what has passed. Find out how she is affected towards Theodore: bring me good news, and that ring has a companion. Wait at the foot of the winding staircase: I am going to visit the Marquis, and will talk farther with thee at my return."

Manfred, after some general conversation, desired Frederic to dismiss the two Knights his companions, having to talk with him on urgent affairs. As soon as they were alone, he began in artful guise to sound the Marquis on the subject of Matilda; and finding him disposed to his wish, he let drop hints on the difficulties that would attend the celebration of their marriage, unless—at that instant Bianca burst into the room with a wildness in her look and gestures that spoke the utmost terror. "Oh! my Lord, my Lord!" cried she; "we are all undone! it is come again! it is come again!" "What is come again?" cried Manfred amazed—"Oh! the hand! the Giant! the hand!—support me! I am terrified out of my senses," cried Bianca, "I will not sleep in the castle to-night; where shall I go? my things may come after me to-morrow—would I had been content to wed Francesco! this comes of ambition!" "What has terrified thee thus, young woman?" said the Marquis: "Thou art safe here; be not alarmed." "Oh! your Greatness is wonderful good," said Bianca, "but I dare not—no, pray let me go—I had rather leave every thing behind me, than stay another hour under this roof." "Go to, thou hast lost thy senses," said

Manfred. "Interrupt us not; we were communing on important matters—my Lord, this wench is subject to fits—come with me, Bianca"—"Oh! the Saints! no," said Bianca—"for certain it comes to warn your Highness; why should it appear to me else? I say my hours morning and evening—oh! if your Highness had believed Diego! 'Tis the same hand that he saw the foot to in the gallery-chamber—Father Jerome has often told us the prophecy would be out one of these days"—"Bianca," said he, "mark my words—thou ravest;" said Manfred in a rage; "be gone, and keep these fooleries to frighten thy companions"—"What! my Lord," cried Bianca, "do you think I have seen nothing? go to the foot of the great stairs yourself—as I live I saw it." "Saw what? tell us, fair maid, what thou hast seen," said Frederic. "Can your Highness listen," said Manfred, "to the delirium of a silly wench, who has heard stories of apparitions until she believes them?" "This is more than fancy," said the Marquis; "her terror is too natural and too strongly impressed to be the work of imagination. Tell us, fair maiden, what it is has moved thee thus." "Yes, my Lord, thank your Greatness;" said Bianca—"I believe I look very pale; I shall be better when I have recovered myself—I was going to my Lady Isabella's chamber by his Highness' order"—"We do not want the circumstances," interrupted Manfred: "Since his Highness will have it so, proceed; but be brief." "Lord! your Highness thwarts one so!" replied Bianca—"I fear my hair—I am sure I never in my life—well! as I was telling your Greatness, I was going by his Highness' order to my Lady Isabella's chamber: She lies in the watchet-coloured chamber, on the right-hand, one pair of stairs. So when I came to the great stairs—I was looking on his Highness's present here"—"Grant me patience!" said Manfred, "will this wench never come to the point? what imports it to the Marquis, that I gave thee a bawble for thy faithful attendance on my daughter? we want to know what thou sawest."

"I was going to tell your Highness," said Bianca, "if you would permit me.—So as I was rubbing the ring—I am sure I had not gone up three steps, but I heard the rattling of armour; for all the world such a clatter, as Diego says he heard when the Giant turned him about in the gallery-chamber"—"What does she mean, my Lord!" said the Marquis; "is your castle haunted by giants and goblins?" "Lord! what, has not your Greatness heard the story of the Giant in the gallery-chamber?" cried Bianca. "I marvel his Highness has not told you—may hap you do not know there is a prophecy"—"This trifling is intolerable;" interrupted Manfred. "Let us dismiss this silly wench, my Lord, we have more important affairs to discuss." "By your favour," said Frederic, "these are no trifles: The enormous sabre I was directed to in the wood, yon casque, its fellow—are these visions of this poor maiden's brain?"—"so Jaquez thinks, may it please your Greatness," said Bianca. "He says this moon will not be out without our seeing some strange revolution. For my part I should not be surprized if it was to happen to-morrow; for, as I was saying, when I heard the clattering of armour, I was all in a cold sweat.—I looked up, and, if your Greatness will believe me, I saw upon the uppermost banister of the great stairs a hand in armour as big, as big—I thought I should have swooned—I never stopped until I came hither—would I were well out of this castle! My Lady Matilda told me but yester-morning that her Highness Hippolita knows something"—"Thou art an insolent!" cried Manfred—"Lord Marquis, it much misgives me that this scene is concerted to affront me. Are my own domestics suborned to spread tales injurious to my honour? Pursue your claim by manly daring; or let us bury our feuds, as was proposed, by the intermarriage of our children: But, trust me, it ill becomes a Prince of your bearing to practice on mercenary wenches"—"I scorn your imputation;" said Frederic: "until this hour I never set eyes on this damsel: I have given her no jewel!—my Lord, my Lord, your conscience, your guilt accuses you, and would throw the suspicion on me—but keep your daughter, and think no more of Isabella: The judgments already fallen on your house forbid my matching into it."

Manfred alarmed at the resolute tone in which Frederic delivered these words, endeavoured to pacify him. Dismissing Bianca, he made such submissions to the Marquis, and threw in such artful encomiums on Matilda, that Frederic was once more staggered. However, as his passion was of so recent a date, it could not at once surmount the scruples he had conceived. He had gathered enough from Bianca's discourse to persuade him that heaven declared itself against Manfred. The proposed marriages too removed his claim to a distance; and the principality of Otranto was a stronger temptation, than the contingent reversion of it with Matilda. Still he would not absolutely recede from his engagements; but purposing to gain time, he demanded of Manfred if it was true in fact that Hippolita consented to the divorce. The Prince, transported to find no other obstacle, and depending on his influence over his wife, assured the Marquis it was so, and that he might satisfy himself of the truth from her own mouth.

As they were thus discoursing, word was brought that the banquet was prepared. Manfred conducted Frederic to the great hall, where they were received by Hippolita and the young Princesses. Manfred placed the Marquis next to Matilda, and seated himself between his wife and Isabella. Hippolita comported herself with an easy gravity; but the young Ladies were silent and melancholy. Manfred, who was determined to pursue his point with the Marquis in the remainder of the evening, pushed on the feast until it waxed late; affecting unrestrained gaiety, and plying Frederic with repeated goblets of wine. The latter, more upon his guard than Manfred wished, declined his frequent challenges, on pretence of his late loss of blood; while the Prince, to raise his own disordered spirits, and to counterfeit unconcern, indulged himself in plentiful draughts, though not to the intoxication of his senses.

The evening being far advanced, the banquet concluded. Manfred would have withdrawn with Frederic; but the latter pleading weakness and want of repose, retired to his chamber, galantly telling the Prince, that his daughter should amuse his Highness until himself could attend him. Manfred accepted the party, and to the no small grief of Isabella accompanied her to her apartment. Matilda waited on her mother to enjoy the freshness of the evening on the ramparts of the castle.

Soon as the company were dispersed their several ways, Frederic, quitting his chamber, enquired if Hippolita was alone, and was told by one of her attendants, who had not noticed her going forth, that at that hour she generally withdrew to her oratory, where he probably would find her. The Marquis during the repast had beheld Matilda with increase of passion. He now wished to find Hippolita in the disposition her Lord had promised. The portents that had alarmed him, were forgotten in his desires. Stealing softly and unobserved to the apartment of Hippolita, he entered it with a resolution to encourage her acquiescence to the divorce, having perceived that Manfred was resolved to make the possession of Isabella an unalterable condition, before he would grant Matilda to his wishes.

The Marquis was not surprized at the silence that reigned in the Princess's apartment. Concluding her, as he had been advertised, in her oratory, he passed on. The door was ajar; the evening gloomy and overcast. Pushing open the door gently, he saw a person kneeling before the altar. As he approached nearer, it seemed not a woman, but one in a long woollen weed, whose back was towards him. The person seemed absorbed in prayer. The Marquis was about to return, when the figure rising, stood some moments fixed in meditation, without regarding him. The Marquis, expecting the holy person to come forth, and meaning to excuse his uncivil interruption, said, "Reverend Father, I sought the Lady Hippolita"—"Hippolita!" replied a hollow voice. "Camest thou to this castle to seek Hippolita?"—and then the figure, turning slowly round, discovered to Frederic the fleshless jaws and empty sockets of a skeleton, wrapt in a hermit's cowl. "Angels of grace protect me!" cried Frederic recoiling. "Deserve their protection!" said the Spectre. Frederic falling on his knees, adjured the Phantom to take pity on him. "Dost thou not remember me?" said the apparition. "Remember the wood of Joppa!" "Art thou that holy Hermit?" cried Frederic trembling—"can I do ought for thy eternal peace?"—"Wast thou delivered from bondage," said the spectre, "to pursue carnal delights? Hast thou forgotten the buried sabre, and the behest of Heaven engraven on it?"—"I have not, I have not;" said Frederic—"but say, blest spirit, what is thy errand to me? what remains to be done?" "To forget Matilda!" said the apparition—and vanished.

Frederic's blood froze in his veins. For some minutes he remained motionless. Then falling prostrate on his face before the altar, he besought the intercession of every saint for pardon. A flood of tears succeeded to this transport; and the image of the beauteous Matilda rushing in spite of him on his thoughts, he lay on the ground in a conflict of penitence and passion. E'er he could recover from this agony of his spirits, the Princess Hippolita with a taper in her hand entered the oratory alone. Seeing a man without motion on the floor, she gave a shriek, concluding him dead. Her fright brought Frederic to himself. Rising suddenly, his face bedewed with tears, he would have rushed from her presence; but Hippolita stopping him, conjured him in the most plaintive accents to explain the cause of his disorder, and by what strange chance she had found him there in that posture. "Ah! virtuous Princess!" said the Marquis, penetrated with grief—and stopped. "For the love of Heaven, my Lord," said Hippolita, "disclose the cause of this transport! what mean these doleful sounds, this alarming exclamation on my name? What woes has heaven still in store for the wretched Hippolita?—yet silent!—by every pitying angel, I adjure thee, noble Prince," continued she falling at his feet, "to disclose the purport of what lies at thy heart—I see thou feelest for me; thou feelest the sharp pangs that thou inflictest—speak for pity!—does ought thou knowest concern my child?"—"I cannot speak;" cried Frederic, bursting from her—"Oh! Matilda!"

Quitting the Princess thus abruptly, he hastened to his own apartment. At the door of it he was accosted by Manfred, who flushed by wine and love had come to seek him, and to propose to waste some hours of the night in music and revelling. Frederic, offended at an invitation so dissonant from the mood of his soul, pushed him rudely aside, and entering his chamber, flung the door intemperately against Manfred, and bolted it inwards. The haughty Prince, enraged at this unaccountable behaviour, withdrew in a frame of mind capable of the most fatal excesses. As he crossed the court, he was met by the domestic whom he had planted at the convent as a spy on Jerome, and Theodore. This man, almost breathless with the haste he had made, informed his Lord, that Theodore and some Lady from the castle were at that instant in private conference at the tomb of Alfonso in St. Nicholas's church. He had dogged Theodore thither, but the gloominess of the night had prevented his discovering who the woman was.

Manfred, whose spirits were inflamed, and whom Isabella had driven from her on his urging his passion with too little reserve, did not doubt but the inquietude she had expressed, had been occasioned by her impatience to meet

Theodore. Provoked by this conjecture, and enraged at her father, he hastened secretly to the great church. Gliding softly between the isles, and guided by an imperfect gleam of moonshine that shone faintly through the illuminated windows, he stole towards the tomb of Alfonso, to which he was directed by indistinct whispers of the persons he sought. The first sounds he could distinguish were—"Does it alas! depend on me? Manfred will never permit our union"— "No, this shall prevent it!" cried the tyrant, drawing his dagger, and plunging it over her shoulder into the bosom of the person that spoke"—"Ah! me, I am slain!" cried Matilda sinking; "good heaven, receive my soul!" "Savage inhuman monster! what hast thou done!" cried Theodore, rushing on him, and wrenching his dagger from him—"Stop, stop thy impious hand!" cried Matilda; "it is my father!" Manfred waking as from a trance, beat his breast, twisted his hands in his locks, and endeavoured to recover his dagger from Theodore to dispatch himself. Theodore scarce less distracted, and only mastering the transports of his grief to assist Matilda, had now by his cries drawn some of the monks to his aid. While part of them endeavoured in concert with the afflicted Theodore to stop the blood of the dying Princess, the rest prevented Manfred from laying violent hands on himself.

Matilda resigning herself patiently to her fate, acknowledged with looks of grateful love the zeal of Theodore. Yet oft as her faintness would permit her speech its way, she begged the assistants to comfort her father. Jerome by this time had learn'd the fatal news, and reached the church. His looks seemed to reproach Theodore: but turning to Manfred, he said, "Now, tyrant! behold the completion of woe, fulfilled on thy impious and devoted head! The blood of Alfonso cried to heaven for vengeance; and heaven has permitted its altar to be polluted by assassination, that thou mightest shed thy own blood at the foot of that

Prince's sepulchre!"—"Cruel man!" cried Matilda, "to aggravate the woes of a parent! may heaven bless my father, and forgive him as I do! My Lord, my gracious Sire, dost thou forgive thy child? indeed I came not hither to meet Theodore: I found him praying at this tomb, whither my mother sent me to intercede for thee, for her,—dearest father, bless your child, and say you forgive her"—"Forgive thee! murderous monster!" cried Manfred—"can assassins forgive? I took thee for Isabella; but heaven directed my bloody hand to the heart of my child!—oh! Matilda—I cannot utter it—canst thou forgive the blindness of my rage!" "I can, I do! and may heaven confirm it!" said Matilda— "but while I have life to ask it—Oh! my mother! what will she feel!—will you comfort her, my Lord? will you not put her away? indeed she loves you—oh! I am faint! bear me to the castle—can I live to have her close my eyes?"

Theodore and the monks besought her earnestly to suffer herself to be borne into the convent; but her instances were so pressing to be carried to the castle, that placing her on a litter, they conveyed her thither as she requested. Theodore supporting her head with his arm, and hanging over her in an agony of despairing love, still endeavoured to inspire her with hopes of life. Jerome on the other side comforted her with discourses of heaven, and holding a crucifix before her, which she bathed with innocent tears, prepared her for her passage to immortality. Manfred plunged in the deepest affliction, followed the litter in despair.

E'er they reached the castle, Hippolita, informed of the dreadful catastrophe, had flown to meet her murdered child: but when she saw the afflicted procession, the mightiness of her grief deprived her of her senses, and she fell lifeless to the earth in a swoon. Isabella and Frederic, who attended her, were overwhelmed in almost equal sorrow. Matilda alone seemed insensible to her own situation: every thought was lost in tenderness for her mother. Ordering the litter to stop, as soon as Hippolita was brought to herself, she asked for her father. He approached, unable to speak. Matilda seizing his hand and her mother's, locked them in her own, and then clasped them to her heart. Manfred could not support this act of pathetic piety. He dashed himself on the ground, and cursed the day he was born. Isabella, apprehensive that these struggles of passion were more than Matilda could support, took upon herself to order Manfred to be borne to his apartment, while she caused Matilda to be conveyed to the nearest chamber. Hippolita, scarce more alive than her daughter, was regardless of every thing but her: but when the tender Isabella's care would have likewise removed her, while the surgeons examined Matilda's wound, she cried, "Remove me! never! never! I lived but in her, and will expire with her." Matilda raised her eyes at her mother's voice, but closed them again without speaking. Her sinking pulse and the damp coldness of her hand soon dispelled all hopes of recovery. Theodore followed the surgeons into the outer chamber, and heard them pronounce the fatal sentence with a transport equal to frenzy—"Since she cannot live mine," cried he, "at least she shall be mine in death!—Father! Jerome! will you not join our hands?" cried he to the Friar, who with the Marquis had accompanied the surgeons. "What means thy distracted rashness?" said Jerome; "is this an hour for marriage!" "It is, it is," cried Theodore, "alas! there is no other!" "Young man, thou art too unadvised," said Frederic: "dost thou think we are to listen to thy fond transports in this hour of fate? what pretensions hast thou to the Princess?" "Those of a Prince;" said Theodore; "of the sovereign of Otranto. This reverend man, my father, has informed me who I am." "Thou ravest," said the Marquis: "there is no prince of Otranto but myself, now Manfred by murder, by sacrilegious murder, has forfeited all pretensions." "My Lord," said Jerome, assuming an air of command, "he tells you true. It was not my purpose the secret should have been divulged so soon; but fate presses onward to its work. What his hot headed passion has revealed, my tongue confirms. Know, Prince, that when Alfonso set sail for the Holy Land"—"Is this a season for explanation?" cried Theodore. "Father, come and unite me to the Princess; she shall be mine—in every other thing I will dutifully obey you. My life! my adored Matilda!" continued Theodore, rushing back into the inner chamber, "will you not be mine? will you not bless your"— Isabella made signs to him to be silent, apprehending the Princess was near her end. "What is she dead?" cried Theodore; "is it possible?" The violence of his exclamations brought Matilda to herself. Lifting up her eyes, she looked round for her mother—"Life of my soul! I am here," cried Hippolita; "think not I will quit thee!" "Oh! you are too good;" said Matilda—"but weep not for me, my mother! I am going where sorrow never dwells"—"Isabella, thou hast loved me; wo't thou not supply my fondness to this dear, dear woman?—indeed I am faint!" "Oh! my child! my child!" said Hippolita in a flood of tears, "can I not withhold thee a moment!"—"It will not be;" said Matilda— "commend me to heaven—where is my father? forgive him, dearest mother—forgive him my death; it was an error—Oh! I had forgotten—dearest mother, I vowed never to see Theodore more—perhaps that has drawn down this calamity— but it was not intentional—can you pardon me?"—"Oh! wound not my agonizing soul!" said Hippolita; "thou never couldst offend me—alas! she faints! help! help!"—"I would say something more," said Matilda struggling, "but it won- not be—Isabella—Theodore—for my sake—Oh!"—she expired. Isabella and her women tore Hippolita from the corse; but Theodore threatened destruction to all who attempted to remove him from it. He printed a thousand kisses on her clay-cold hands, and uttered every expression that despairing love could dictate.

Isabella, in the mean time, was accompanying the afflicted Hippolita to her apartment; but, in the middle of the court, they were met by Manfred, who, distracted with his own thoughts, and anxious once more to behold his daughter, was advancing to the chamber where she lay. As the moon was now at its height, he read in the countenances of this unhappy company the event he dreaded. "What! is she dead!" cried he in wild confusion—a clap of thunder at that instant shook the castle to its foundations; the earth rocked, and the clank of more than mortal armour was heard behind. Frederic and Jerome thought the last day was at hand. The latter, forcing Theodore along with them, rushed into the court. The moment Theodore appeared, the walls of the castle behind Manfred were thrown down with a mighty force, and the form of Alfonso, dilated to an immense magnitude, appeared in the center of the ruins. "Behold in Theodore the true heir of Alfonso!" said the vision: And having pronounced those words, accompanied by a clap of thunder, it ascended solemnly towards heaven, where the clouds parting asunder, the form of St. Nicholas was seen, and receiving Alfonso's shade, they were soon wrapt from mortal eyes in a blaze of glory.

The beholders fell prostrate on their faces, acknowledging the divine will. The first that broke silence was Hippolita. "My Lord," said she to the desponding Manfred, "behold the vanity of human greatness! Conrad is gone! Matilda is no more! in Theodore we view the true Prince of Otranto. By what miracle he is so, I know not—suffice it to us, our doom is pronounced! shall we not, can we but dedicate the few deplorable hours we have to live, in deprecating the farther wrath of heaven? heaven ejects us— whither can we fly, but to yon holy cells that yet offer us a retreat?"—"Thou guiltless but unhappy woman! unhappy by my crimes!" replied Manfred, "my heart at last is open to thy devout admonitions. Oh! could—but it cannot be—ye are lost in wonder—let me at last do justice on myself! To heap shame on my head is all the satisfaction I have left to offer to offended heaven. My story has drawn down these judgments: Let my confession atone—but ah! what can atone for usurpation and a murdered child! a child murdered in a consecrated place!—List, Sirs, and may this bloody record be a warning to future tyrants!

"Alfonso, ye all know, died in the holy land—ye would interrupt me; ye would say he came not fairly to his end—it is most true—why else this bitter cup which Manfred must drink to the dregs? Ricardo, my grandfather, was his chamberlain—I would draw a veil over my ancestor's crimes—but it is in vain! Alfonso died by poison. A fictitious will declared Ricardo his heir. His crimes pursued him—yet he lost no Conrad, no Matilda! I pay the price of usurpation for all! A storm overtook him. Haunted by his guilt, he vowed to St. Nicholas to found a church and two convents, if he lived to reach Otranto. The sacrifice was accepted: the saint appeared to him in a dream, and promised that Ricardo's posterity should reign in Otranto, until the rightful owner should be grown too large to inhabit the castle, and as long as issue-male from Ricardo's loins should remain to enjoy it—Alas! alas! nor male nor female, except myself, remains of all his wretched race!—I have done—the woes of these three days speak the rest. How this young man can be Alfonso's heir, I know not—yet I do not doubt it. His are these dominions; I resign them—yet I knew not Alfonso had an heir—I question not the will of heaven—poverty and prayer must fill up the woeful space, until Manfred shall be summoned to Ricardo.

"What remains, is my part to declare," said Jerome, "when Alfonso set sail for the holy land he was driven by a storm to the coast of Cicily. The other vessel, which bore Ricardo and his train, as your Lordship must have heard, was separated from him." "It is most true," said Manfred; "and the title you give me is more than an outcast can claim—well! be it so—proceed." Jerome blushed, and continued. "For three months Lord Alfonso was wind-bound in Cicily. There he became enamoured of a fair virgin named Victoria. He was too pious to tempt her to forbidden pleasures. They were married. Yet deeming this amour incongruous with the holy vow of arms by which he was bound, he determined to conceal their nuptials, until his return from the Crusado, when he purposed to seek and acknowledge her for his lawful wife. He left her pregnant. During his absence she was delivered of a daughter: But scarce had she felt a mother's pangs, ere she heard the fatal rumour of her Lord's death, and the succession of Ricardo. What could a friendless, helpless woman do? would her testimony avail? —yet, my Lord, I have an authentic writing"—"It needs not;" said Manfred; "the horrors of these days, the vision we have but now seen, all corroborate thy evidence beyond a thousand parchments. Matilda's death and my expulsion"— "Be composed, my Lord," said Hippolita; "this holy man did not mean to recall your griefs." Jerome proceeded.

"I shall not dwell on what is needless. The daughter of which Victoria was delivered, was at her maturity bestowed in marriage on me. Victoria died; and the secret remained locked in my breast. Theodore's narrative has told the rest."

The Friar ceased. The disconsolate company retired to the remaining part of the castle. In the morning Manfred signed his abdication of the principality, with the approbation of Hippolita, and each took on them the habit of religion in the neighbouring convents. Frederic offered his daughter to the new Prince, which Hippolita's tenderness for Isabella concurred to promote: But Theodore's grief was too fresh to admit the thought of another love; and it was not until after frequent discourses with Isabella of his dear Matilda, that he was persuaded he could know no happiness but in the society of one with whom he could for ever indulge the melancholy that had taken possession of his soul.

The Mysteries of Udolpho

BY

ANN RADCLIFFE

THE

MYSTERIES OF UDOLPHO,

A

ROMANCE;

INTERSPERSED WITH SOME PIECES OF POETRY.

BY

ANN RADCLIFFE,

AUTHOR OF THE ROMANCE OF THE FOREST, ETC.

IN FOUR VOLUMES.

Fate fits on thefe dark battlements, and frowns,
And, as the portals open to receive me,
Her voice, in fullen echoes through the courts,
Tells of a namelefs deed.

———————

VOL. I.

———————

LONDON:
PRINTED FOR G. G. AND J. ROBINSON,
PATERNOSTER-ROW,
1794.

Volume One

CHAPTER I

"————home is the resort
Of love, of joy, of peace and plenty, where,
Supporting and supported, polish'd friends
And dear relations mingle into bliss."

THOMPSON

On the pleasant banks of the Garonne, in the province of
Gascony, stood, in the year 1584, the chateau of Monsieur
St. Aubert. From its windows were seen the pastoral landscapes of Guienne and Gascony, stretching along the river,
gay with luxuriant woods and vines, and plantations of
olives. To the south, the view was bounded by the majestic
Pyrenées, whose summits, veiled in clouds, or exhibiting awful forms, seen, and lost again, as the partial vapours rolled
along, were sometimes barren, and gleamed through the
blue tinge of air, and sometimes frowned with forests of
gloomy pine, that swept downward to their base. These
tremendous precipices were contrasted by the soft green of
the pastures and woods that hung upon their skirts; among
whose flocks, and herds, and simple cottages, the eye, after
having scaled the cliffs above, delighted to repose. To the
north, and to the east, the plains of Guienne and Languedoc were lost in the mist of distance; on the west, Gascony
was bounded by the waters of Biscay.

M. St. Aubert loved to wander, with his wife and daughter, on the margin of the Garonne, and to listen to the

music that floated on its waves. He had known life in other forms than those of pastoral simplicity, having mingled in the gay and in the busy scenes of the world; but the flattering portrait of mankind, which his heart had delineated in early youth, his experience had too sorrowfully corrected. Yet, amidst the changing visions of life, his principles remained unshaken, his benevolence unchilled; and he retired from the multitude "more in *pity* than in anger," to scenes of simple nature, to the pure delights of literature, and to the exercise of domestic virtues.

He was a descendant from the younger branch of an illustrious family, and it was designed, that the deficiency of his patrimonial wealth should be supplied either by a splendid alliance in marriage, or by success in the intrigues of public affairs. But St. Aubert had too nice a sense of honour to fulfill the latter hope, and too small a portion of ambition to sacrifice what he called happiness, to the attainment of wealth. After the death of his father he married a very amiable woman, his equal in birth, and not his superior in fortune. The late Monsieur St. Aubert's liberality, or extravagance, had so much involved his affairs, that his son found it necessary to dispose of a part of the family domain, and, some years after his marriage, he sold it to Monsieur Quesnel, the brother of his wife, and retired to a small estate in Gascony, where conjugal felicity, and parental duties, divided his attention with the treasures of knowledge and the illuminations of genius.

To this spot he had been attached from his infancy. He had often made excursions to it when a boy, and the impressions of delight given to his mind by the homely kindness of the grey-headed peasant, to whom it was intrusted, and whose fruit and cream never failed, had not been obliterated by succeeding circumstances. The green pastures along which he had so often bounded in the exultation of health, and youthful freedom—the woods, under whose refreshing shade he had first indulged that pensive melancholy, which afterwards made a strong feature of his character—the wild walks of the mountains, the river, on whose waves he had floated, and the distant plains, which seemed boundless as his early hopes—were never after remembered by St. Aubert but with enthusiasm and regret. At length he disengaged himself from the world, and retired hither, to realize the wishes of many years.

The building, as it then stood, was merely a summer cottage, rendered interesting to a stranger by its neat simplicity, or the beauty of the surrounding scene; and considerable additions were necessary to make it a comfortable family residence. St. Aubert felt a kind of affection for every part of the fabric, which he remembered in his youth, and would not suffer a stone of it to be removed, so that the new building, adapted to the style of the old one, formed with it only a simple and elegant residence. The taste of Madame St. Aubert was conspicuous in its internal finishing, where the same chaste simplicity was observable in the furniture, and in the few ornaments of the apartments, that characterized the manners of its inhabitants.

The library occupied the west side of the chateau, and was enriched by a collection of the best books in the ancient and modern languages. This room opened upon a grove, which stood on the brow of a gentle declivity, that fell towards the river, and the tall trees gave it a melancholy and pleasing shade; while from the windows the eye caught, beneath the spreading branches, the gay and luxuriant landscape stretching to the west, and overlooked on the left by the bold precipices of the Pyrenées. Adjoining the library was a greenhouse, stored with scarce and beautiful plants; for one of the amusements of St. Aubert was the study of botany, and among the neighbouring mountains, which afforded a luxurious feast to the mind of the naturalist, he often passed the day in the pursuits of his favourite science.

He was sometimes accompanied in these little excursions by Madame St. Aubert, and frequently by his daughter; when, with a small osier basket to receive plants, and another filled with cold refreshments, such as the cabin of the shepherd did not afford, they wandered away among the most romantic and magnificent scenes, nor suffered the charms of Nature's lowly children to abstract them from the observance of her stupendous works. When weary of sauntering among cliffs that seemed scarcely accessible but to the steps of the enthusiast, and where no track appeared on the vegetation, but what the foot of the izard had left; they would seek one of those green recesses, which so beautifully adorn the bosom of these mountains, where, under the shade of the lofty larch, or cedar, they enjoyed their simple repast, made sweeter by the waters of the cool stream, that crept along the turf, and by the breath of wild flowers and aromatic plants, that fringed the rocks, and inlaid the grass.

Adjoining the eastern side of the greenhouse, looking towards the plains of Languedoc, was a room, which Emily called hers, and which contained her books, her drawings, her musical instruments, with some favourite birds and plants. Here she usually exercised herself in elegant arts, cultivated only because they were congenial to her taste, and in which native genius, assisted by the instructions of Monsieur and Madame St. Aubert, made her an early proficient. The windows of this room were particularly pleasant; they descended to the floor, and, opening upon the little lawn that surrounded the house, the eye was led between groves of almond, palm-trees, flowering-ash, and myrtle, to the distant landscape, where the Garonne wandered.

The peasants of this gay climate were often seen on an evening, when the day's labour was done, dancing in groups on the margin of the river. Their sprightly melodies, *debonnaire* steps, the fanciful figure of their dances, with the tasteful and capricious manner in which the girls adjusted their simple dress, gave a character to the scene entirely French.

The front of the chateau, which, having a southern aspect, opened upon the grandeur of the mountains, was occupied on the ground floor by a rustic hall, and two excellent sitting rooms. The first floor, for the cottage had no second story, was laid out in bed-chambers, except one apartment that opened to a balcony, and which was generally used for a breakfast-room.

In the surrounding ground, St. Aubert had made very tasteful improvements; yet, such was his attachment to objects he had remembered from his boyish days, that he had in some instances sacrificed taste to sentiment. There were two old larches that shaded the building, and interrupted the prospect; St. Aubert had sometimes declared that he believed he should have been weak enough to have wept at their fall. In addition to these larches he planted a little grove of beech, pine, and mountain-ash. On a lofty terrace, formed by the swelling bank of the river, rose a plantation of orange, lemon and palm-trees, whose fruit, in the coolness of evening, breathed delicious fragrance. With these were mingled a few trees of other species. Here, under the ample shade of a plane-tree, that spread its majestic canopy towards the river, St. Aubert loved to sit in the fine evenings of summer, with his wife and children, watching, beneath its foliage, the setting-sun, the mild splendour of its light fading from the distant landscape, till the shadows of twilight melted its various features into one tint of sober gray. Here, too, he loved to read, and to converse with Madame St. Aubert; or to play with his children, resigning himself to the influence of those sweet affections, which are ever attendant on simplicity and nature. He has often said, while tears of pleasure trembled in his eyes, that these were moments infinitely more delightful than any passed amid the brilliant and tumultuous scenes that are courted by the world. His heart was occupied; it had, what can be so rarely said, no wish for a happiness beyond what it experienced. The consciousness of acting right diffused a serenity over his manners, which nothing else could impart to a man of moral perceptions like his, and which refined his sense of every surrounding blessing.

The deepest shade of twilight did not send him from his favourite plane-tree. He loved the soothing hour, when the last tints of light die away; when the stars, one by one, tremble through æther, and are reflected on the dark mirror of the waters; that hour, which, of all others, inspires the mind with pensive tenderness, and often elevates it to sublime contemplation. When the moon shed her soft rays among the foliage, he still lingered, and his pastoral supper of cream and fruits was often spread beneath it. Then, on the stillness of night, came the song of the nightingale, breathing sweetness, and awakening melancholy.

The first interruptions to the happiness he had known since his retirement, were occasioned by the death of his two sons. He lost them at that age when infantine simplicity is so fascinating; and though, in consideration of Madame St. Aubert's distress, he restrained the expression of his own, and endeavoured to bear it, as he meant, with philosophy, he had, in truth, no philosophy that could render him calm to such losses. One daughter was now his only surviving child; and, while he watched the unfolding of her infant character, with anxious fondness, he endeavoured, with unremitting effort, to counteract those traits in her disposition, which might hereafter lead her from happiness. She had discovered in her early years uncommon delicacy of mind, warm affections, and ready benevolence; but with these was observable a degree of susceptibility too exquisite to admit of lasting peace. As she advanced in youth, this sensibility gave a pensive tone to her spirits, and a softness to her manner, which added grace to beauty, and rendered

her a very interesting object to persons of a congenial disposition. But St. Aubert had too much good sense to prefer
a charm to a virtue; and had penetration enough to see,
that this charm was too dangerous to its possessor to be
allowed the character of a blessing. He endeavoured, therefore, to strengthen her mind; to enure her to habits of self-
command; to teach her to reject the first impulse of her
feelings, and to look, with cool examination, upon the disappointments he sometimes threw in her way. While he
instructed her to resist first impressions, and to acquire that
steady dignity of mind, that can alone counterbalance the
passions, and bear us, as far as is compatible with our
nature, above the reach of circumstances, he taught himself
a lesson of fortitude; for he was often obliged to witness,
with seeming indifference, the tears and struggles which his
caution occasioned her.

In person, Emily resembled her mother; having the same
elegant symmetry of form, the same delicacy of features, and
the same blue eyes, full of tender sweetness. But, lovely as
was her person, it was the varied expression of her countenance, as conversation awakened the nicer emotions of her
mind, that threw such a captivating grace around her:

> "Those tend'rer tints, that shun the careless eye,
> And, in the world's contagious circle, die."

St. Aubert cultivated her understanding with the most
scrupulous care. He gave her a general view of the sciences,
and an exact acquaintance with every part of elegant literature. He taught her Latin and English, chiefly that she
might understand the sublimity of their best poets. She discovered in her early years a taste for works of genius; and
it was St. Aubert's principle, as well as his inclination, to
promote every innocent means of happiness. "A well-informed mind," he would say, "is the best security against
the contagion of folly and of vice. The vacant mind is ever

on the watch for relief, and ready to plunge into error, to escape from the languor of idleness. Store it with ideas, teach it the pleasure of thinking; and the temptations of the world without, will be counteracted by the gratifications derived from the world within. Thought, and cultivation, are necessary equally to the happiness of a country and a city life; in the first they prevent the uneasy sensations of indolence, and afford a sublime pleasure in the taste they create for the beautiful, and the grand; in the latter, they make dissipation less an object of necessity, and consequently of interest."

It was one of Emily's earliest pleasures to ramble among the scenes of nature; nor was it in the soft and glowing landscape that she most delighted; she loved more the wild wood-walks, that skirted the mountain; and still more the mountain's stupendous recesses, where the silence and grandeur of solitude impressed a sacred awe upon her heart, and lifted her thoughts to the GOD OF HEAVEN AND EARTH. In scenes like these she would often linger alone, wrapt in a melancholy charm, till the last gleam of day faded from the west; till the lonely sound of a sheep-bell, or the distant bark of a watch-dog, were all that broke on the stillness of the evening. Then, the gloom of the woods; the trembling of their leaves, at intervals, in the breeze; the bat, flitting on the twilight; the cottage-lights, now seen, and now lost— were circumstances that awakened her mind into effort, and led to enthusiasm and poetry.

Her favourite walk was to a little fishing-house, belonging to St. Aubert, in a woody glen, on the margin of a rivulet that descended from the Pyrenées, and, after foaming among their rocks, wound its silent way beneath the shades it reflected. Above the woods, that screened this glen, rose the lofty summits of the Pyrenées, which often burst boldly on the eye through the glades below. Sometimes the shattered face of a rock only was seen, crowned with wild shrubs; or a shepherd's cabin seated on a cliff, overshadowed by dark cypress, or waving ash. Emerging from the deep recesses of the woods, the glade opened to the distant landscape, where the rich pastures and vine-covered slopes of Gascony gradually declined to the plains; and there, on the winding shores of the Garonne, groves, and hamlets, and villas,—their outlines softened by distance, melted from the eye into one rich harmonious tint.

This, too, was the favourite retreat of St. Aubert, to which he frequently withdrew from the fervour of noon, with his wife, his daughter, and his books; or came at the sweet evening hour to welcome the silent dusk, or to listen for the music of the nightingale. Sometimes, too, he brought music of his own, and awakened every fairy echo with the tender accents of his oboe; and often have the tones of Emily's voice drawn sweetness from the waves, over which they trembled.

It was in one of her excursions to this spot, that she observed the following lines written with a pencil on a part of the wainscot:

SONNET.

Go, pencil! faithful to thy master's sighs!
Go—tell the Goddess of this fairy scene,
When next her light steps wind these wood-walks green,
Whence all his tears, his tender sorrows, rise:
Ah! paint her form, her soul-illumin'd eyes,
The sweet expression of her pensive face,
The light'ning smile, the animated grace—
The portrait well the lover's voice supplies;
Speaks all his heart must feel, his tongue would say:
Yet ah! not all his heart must sadly feel!
How oft the flow'ret's silken leaves conceal
The drug that steals the vital spark away!
And who that gazes on that angel-smile,
Would fear its charm, or think it could beguile!

These lines were not inscribed to any person; Emily therefore could not apply them to herself, though she was undoubtedly the nymph of these shades. Having glanced round the little circle of her acquaintance without being detained by a suspicion as to whom they could be addressed, she was compelled to rest in uncertainty; an uncertainty which would have been more painful to an idle mind than it was to hers. She had no leisure to suffer this circumstance, trifling at first, to swell into importance by frequent remembrance. The little vanity it had excited (for the incertitude which forbade her to presume upon having inspired the sonnet, forbade her also to disbelieve it) passed away, and the incident was dismissed from her thoughts amid her books, her studies, and the exercise of social charities.

Soon after this period, her anxiety was awakened by the indisposition of her father, who was attacked with a fever; which, though not thought to be of a dangerous kind, gave a severe shock to his constitution. Madame St. Aubert and Emily attended him with unremitting care; but his recovery was very slow, and, as he advanced towards health, Madame seemed to decline.

The first scene he visited, after he was well enough to take the air, was his favourite fishing-house. A basket of provisions was sent thither, with books, and Emily's lute; for fishing-tackle he had no use, for he never could find amusement in torturing or destroying.

After employing himself, for about an hour, in botanizing, dinner was served. It was a repast, to which gratitude, for being again permitted to visit this spot, gave sweetness; and family happiness once more smiled beneath these shades. Monsieur St. Aubert conversed with unusual cheerfulness; every object delighted his senses. The refreshing pleasure from the first view of nature, after the pain of illness, and the confinement of a sick-chamber, is above the conceptions, as well as the descriptions, of those in health.

The green woods and pastures; the flowery turf; the blue concave of the heavens; the balmy air; the murmur of the limpid stream; and even the hum of every little insect of the shade, seem to revivify the soul, and make mere existence bliss.

Madame St. Aubert, reanimated by the cheerfulness and recovery of her husband, was no longer sensible of the indisposition which had lately oppressed her; and, as she sauntered along the wood-walks of this romantic glen, and conversed with him, and with her daughter, she often looked at them alternately with a degree of tenderness, that filled her eyes with tears. St. Aubert observed this more than once, and gently reproved her for the emotion; but she could only smile, clasp his hand, and that of Emily, and weep the more. He felt the tender enthusiasm stealing upon himself in a degree that became almost painful; his features assumed a serious air, and he could not forbear secretly sighing—"Perhaps I shall some time look back to these moments, as to the summit of my happiness, with hopeless regret. But let me not misuse them by useless anticipation; let me hope I shall not live to mourn the loss of those who are dearer to me than life."

To relieve, or perhaps to indulge, the pensive temper of his mind, he bade Emily fetch the lute she knew how to touch with such sweet pathos. As she drew near the fishing-house, she was surprised to hear the tones of the instrument, which were awakened by the hand of taste, and uttered a plaintive air, whose exquisite melody engaged all her attention. She listened in profound silence, afraid to move from the spot, lest the sound of her steps should occasion her to lose a note of the music, or should disturb the musician. Every thing without the building was still, and no person appeared. She continued to listen, till timidity succeeded to surprise and delight; a timidity, increased by a remembrance of the pencilled lines she had formerly seen, and she hesitated whether to proceed, or to return.

While she paused, the music ceased; and, after a momentary hesitation, she recollected courage to advance to the fishing-house, which she entered with faltering steps, and found unoccupied! Her lute lay on the table; every thing seemed undisturbed, and she began to believe it was another instrument she had heard, till she remembered, that, when she followed M. and Madame St. Aubert from this spot, her lute was left on a window seat. She felt alarmed, yet knew not wherefore; the melancholy gloom of evening, and the profound stillness of the place, interrupted only by the light trembling of leaves, heightened her fanciful apprehensions, and she was desirous of quitting the building, but perceived herself grow faint, and sat down. As she tried to recover herself, the pencilled lines on the wainscot met her eyes; she started, as if she had seen a stranger; but, endeavouring to conquer the tremour of her spirits, rose, and went to the window. To the lines before noticed she now perceived that others were added, in which her name appeared.

Though no longer suffered to doubt that they were addressed to herself, she was as ignorant, as before, by whom they could be written. While she mused, she thought she heard the sound of a step without the building, and again alarmed, she caught up her lute, and hurried away. Monsieur and Madame St. Aubert she found in a little path that wound along the sides of the glen.

Having reached a green summit, shadowed by palm-trees, and overlooking the vallies and plains of Gascony, they seated themselves on the turf; and while their eyes wandered over the glorious scene, and they inhaled the sweet breath of flowers and herbs that enriched the grass, Emily played and sung several of their favourite airs, with the delicacy of expression in which she so much excelled.

Music and conversation detained them in this enchanting spot, till the sun's last light slept upon the plains; till the white sails that glided beneath the mountains, where the Garonne wandered, became dim, and the gloom of evening stole over the landscape. It was a melancholy but not unpleasing gloom. St. Aubert and his family rose, and left the place with regret; alas! Madame St. Aubert knew not that she left it for ever.

When they reached the fishing-house she missed her bracelet, and recollected that she had taken it from her arm after dinner, and had left it on the table when she went to walk. After a long search, in which Emily was very active, she was compelled to resign herself to the loss of it. What made this bracelet valuable to her was a miniature of her daughter to which it was attached, esteemed a striking resemblance, and which had been painted only a few months before. When Emily was convinced that the bracelet was really gone, she blushed, and became thoughtful. That some stranger had been in the fishing-house, during her absence, her lute, and the additional lines of a pencil, had already informed her: from the purport of these lines it was not unreasonable to believe, that the poet, the musician, and the thief were the same person. But though the music she had heard, the written lines she had seen, and the disappearance of the picture, formed a combination of circumstances very remarkable, she was irresistibly restrained from mentioning them; secretly determining, however, never again to visit the fishing-house without Monsieur or Madame St. Aubert.

They returned pensively to the chateau, Emily musing on the incident which had just occurred; St. Aubert reflecting, with placid gratitude, on the blessings he possessed; and Madame St. Aubert somewhat disturbed, and perplexed, by the loss of her daughter's picture. As they drew near the house, they observed an unusual bustle about it; the sound of voices was distinctly heard, servants and horses were seen passing between the trees, and, at length, the wheels of a carriage rolled along. Having come within view of the front of the chateau, a landau, with smoking horses, appeared on the little lawn before it. St. Aubert perceived the liveries of his brother-in-law, and in the parlour he found Monsieur and Madame Quesnel already entered. They had left Paris some days before, and were on the way to their estate, only ten leagues distant from La Vallée, and which Monsieur Quesnel had purchased several years before of St. Aubert. This gentleman was the only brother of Madame St. Aubert; but the ties of relationship having never been strengthened by congeniality of character, the intercourse between them had not been frequent. M. Quesnel had lived altogether in the world; his aim had been consequence; splendour was the object of his taste; and his address and knowledge of character had carried him forward to the attainment of almost all that he had courted. By a man of such a disposition, it is not surprising that the virtues of St. Aubert should be overlooked; or that his pure taste, simplicity, and moderated wishes, were considered as marks of a weak intellect, and of confined views. The marriage of his sister with St. Aubert had been mortifying to his ambition, for he had designed that the matrimonial connection she formed should assist him to attain the consequence which he so much desired; and some offers were made her by persons whose rank and fortune flattered his warmest hope. But his sister, who was then addressed also by St. Aubert, perceived, or thought she perceived, that happiness and splendour were not the same, and she did not hesitate to forego the last for the attainment of the former. Whether Monsieur Quesnel thought them the same, or not, he would readily have sacrificed his sister's peace to the gratification of his own ambition; and, on her marriage with St. Aubert, expressed in private his contempt of her spiritless conduct, and of the connection which it permitted. Madame St. Aubert, though she concealed this insult from her husband, felt, perhaps, for the first time, resentment lighted in her heart; and, though a regard for her own dignity, united with considerations of prudence, restrained her expression of this resentment, there was ever after a mild reserve in her manner towards M. Quesnel, which he both understood and felt.

In his own marriage he did not follow his sister's example. His lady was an Italian, and an heiress by birth; and, by nature and education, was a vain and frivolous woman.

They now determined to pass the night with St. Aubert; and as the chateau was not large enough to accommodate their servants, the latter were dismissed to the neighbouring village. When the first compliments were over, and the arrangements for the night made, M. Quesnel began the display of his intelligence and his connections; while St. Aubert, who had been long enough in retirement to find these topics recommended by their novelty, listened, with a degree of patience and attention, which his guest mistook for the humility of wonder. The latter, indeed, described the few festivities which the turbulence of that period permitted to the court of Henry the Third, with a minuteness, that somewhat recompensed for his ostentation; but, when he came to speak of the character of the Duke de Joyeuse, of a secret treaty, which he knew to be negotiating with the Porte, and of the light in which Henry of Navarre was received, M. St. Aubert recollected enough of his former experience to be assured, that his guest could be only of an inferior class of politicians; and that, from the importance of the subjects upon which he committed himself, he could not be of the rank to which he pretended to belong. The opinions delivered by M. Quesnel, were such as St. Aubert forbore to reply to, for he knew that his guest had neither humanity to feel, nor discernment to perceive, what is just

Madame Quesnel, meanwhile, was expressing to Madame St. Aubert her astonishment, that she could bear to pass her life in this remote corner of the world, as she called it, and describing, from a wish, probably, of exciting envy, the splendour of the balls, banquets, and processions which had just been given by the court, in honour of the nuptials of the Duke de Joyeuse with Margaretta of Lorrain, the sister of the Queen. She described with equal minuteness the magnificence she had seen, and that from which she had been excluded; while Emily's vivid fancy, as she listened with the ardent curiosity of youth, heightened the scenes she heard of; and Madame St. Aubert, looking on her family, felt, as a tear stole to her eye, that though splendour may grace happiness, virtue only can bestow it.

"It is now twelve years, St. Aubert," said M. Quesnel, "since I purchased your family estate."—"Somewhere thereabout," replied St. Aubert, suppressing a sigh. "It is near five years since I have been there," resumed Quesnel; "for Paris and its neighbourhood is the only place in the world to live in, and I am so immersed in politics, and have so many affairs of moment on my hands, that I find it difficult to steal away even for a month or two." St. Aubert remaining silent, M. Quesnel proceeded: "I have sometimes wondered how you, who have lived in the capital, and have been accustomed to company, can exist elsewhere;—especially in so remote a country as this, where you can neither hear nor see any thing, and can in short be scarcely conscious of life."

"I live for my family and myself," said St. Aubert; "I am now contented to know only happiness;—formerly I knew life."

"I mean to expend thirty or forty thousand livres on improvements," said M. Quesnel, without seeming to notice the words of St. Aubert; "for I design, next summer, to bring here my friends, the Duke de Durefort and the Marquis Ra-

mont, to pass a month or two with me." To St. Aubert's
enquiry, as to these intended improvements, he replied, that
he should take down the old east wing of the chateau, and
raise upon the site a set of stables. "Then I shall build," said
he, "a *salle à manger,* a *salon,* a *salle au commune,* and a
number of rooms for servants; for at present there is not
accommodation for a third part of my own people."

"It accommodated our father's household," said St. Aubert, grieved that the old mansion was to be thus improved,
"and that was not a small one."

"Our notions are somewhat enlarged since those days,"
said M. Quesnel;—"what was then thought a decent style
of living would not now be endured." Even the calm St.
Aubert blushed at these words, but his anger soon yielded
to contempt. "The ground about the chateau is encumbered
with trees; I mean to cut some of them down."

"Cut down the trees too!" said St. Aubert.

"Certainly. Why should I not? they interrupt my prospects. There is a chestnut which spreads its branches before
the whole south side of the chateau, and which is so ancient
that they tell me the hollow of its trunk will hold a dozen
men. Your enthusiasm will scarcely contend that there can
be either use, or beauty, in such a sapless old tree as this."

"Good God!" exclaimed St. Aubert, "you surely will not
destroy that noble chestnut, which has flourished for cen-
turies, the glory of the estate! It was in its maturity when
the present mansion was built. How often, in my youth, I
have climbed among its broad branches, and sat embowered
amidst a world of leaves, while the heavy shower has pat-
tered above, and not a rain drop reached me! How often I
have sat with a book in my hand, sometimes reading, and
sometimes looking out between the branches upon the wide
landscape, and the setting sun, till twilight came, and
brought the birds home to their little nests among the
leaves! How often—but pardon me," added St. Aubert,

recollecting that he was speaking to a man who could neither comprehend, nor allow for his feelings. "I am talking of times and feelings as old-fashioned as the taste that would spare that venerable tree."

"It will certainly come down," said M. Quesnel; "I believe I shall plant some Lombardy poplars among the clumps of chestnut, that I shall leave on the avenue. Madame Quesnel is partial to the poplar, and tells me how much it adorns a villa of her uncle, not far from Venice."

"On the banks of the Brenta, indeed," continued St. Aubert, "where its spiry form is intermingled with the pine, and the cypress, and where it plays over light and elegant porticos and colonnades, it, unquestionably, adorns the scene; but among the giants of the forest, and near a heavy gothic mansion—"

"Well, my good sir," said M. Quesnel, "I will not dispute with you. You must return to Paris before our ideas can at all agree. But à-propos of Venice; I have some thoughts of going thither, next summer; events may call me to take possession of that same villa, too, which they tell me is the most charming that can be imagined. In that case I shall leave the improvements I mention to another year, and I may, perhaps, be tempted to stay some time in Italy."

Emily was somewhat surprised to hear him talk of being tempted to remain abroad, after he had mentioned his presence to be so necessary at Paris, that it was with difficulty he could steal away for a month or two; but St. Aubert understood the self-importance of the man too well to wonder at this trait; and the possibility, that these projected improvements might be deferred, gave him a hope, that they might never take place.

Before they separated for the night, M. Quesnel desired to speak with St. Aubert alone, and they retired to another room, where they remained a considerable time. The subject of this conversation was not known; but, whatever it might be, St. Aubert, when he returned to the supper-room, seemed much disturbed, and a shade of sorrow sometimes fell upon his features, that alarmed Madame St. Aubert. When they were alone she was tempted to enquire the occasion of it, but the delicacy of mind, which had ever appeared in his conduct, restrained her: she considered that, if St. Aubert wished her to be acquainted with the subject of his concern, he would not wait for her enquiries.

On the following day, before M. Quesnel departed, he had a second conference with St. Aubert.

The guests, after dining at the chateau, set out in the cool of the day for Epourville, whither they gave him and Madame St. Aubert a pressing invitation, prompted rather by the vanity of displaying their splendour, than by a wish to make their friends happy.

Emily returned, with delight, to the liberty which their presence had restrained, to her books, her walks, and the rational conversation of M. and Madame St. Aubert, who seemed to rejoice, no less, that they were delivered from the shackles, which arrogance and frivolity had imposed.

Madame St. Aubert excused herself from sharing their usual evening walk, complaining that she was not quite well, and St. Aubert and Emily went out together.

They chose a walk towards the mountains, intending to visit some old pensioners of St. Aubert, which, from his very moderate income, he contrived to support, though it is probable M. Quesnel, with his very large one, could not have afforded this.

After distributing to his pensioners their weekly stipends, listening patiently to the complaints of some, redressing the grievances of others, and softening the discontents of all, by the look of sympathy, and the smile of benevolence, St. Aubert returned home through the woods,

———"where
At fall of eve the fairy-people throng,
In various games and revelry to pass
The summer night, as village stories tell."

THOMPSON

"The evening gloom of woods was always delightful to me," said St. Aubert, whose mind now experienced the sweet calm, which results from the consciousness of having done a beneficent action, and which disposes it to receive pleasure from every surrounding object. "I remember that in my youth this gloom used to call forth to my fancy a thousand fairy visions, and romantic images; and, I own, I am not yet wholly insensible of that high enthusiasm, which wakes the poet's dream. I can linger, with solemn steps, under the deep shades, send forward a transforming eye into the distant obscurity, and listen with thrilling delight to the mystic murmuring of the woods."

"O my dear father," said Emily, while a sudden tear started to her eye, "how exactly you describe what I have felt so often, and which I thought nobody had ever felt but myself! But hark! here comes the sweeping sound over the wood-tops;—now it dies away;—how solemn the stillness that succeeds! Now the breeze swells again. It is like the voice of some supernatural being—the voice of the spirit of the woods, that watches over them by night. Ah! what light is yonder? But it is gone. And now it gleams again, near the root of that large chestnut: look, sir!"

"Are you such an admirer of nature," said St. Aubert, "and so little acquainted with her appearances as not to know that for the glow-worm? But come," added he gaily, "step a little further, and we shall see fairies, perhaps; they are often companions. The glow-worm lends his light, and they in return charm him with music, and the dance. Do you see nothing tripping yonder?"

Emily laughed. "Well, my dear sir," said she, "since you

allow of this alliance, I may venture to own I have anticipated you; and almost dare venture to repeat some verses I
made one evening in these very woods."

"Nay," replied St. Aubert, "dismiss the *almost,* and venture quite; let us hear what vagaries fancy has been playing
in your mind. If she has given you one of her spells, you
need not envy those of the fairies."

"If it is strong enough to enchant your judgment, sir,"
said Emily, "while I disclose her images, I need *not* envy
them. The lines go in a sort of tripping measure, which I
thought might suit the subject well enough, but I fear they
are too irregular.

THE GLOW-WORM

How pleasant is the green-wood's deep-matted shade
On a mid-summer's eve; when the fresh rain is o'er;
When the yellow beams slope, and sparkle thro' the glade,
And swiftly in the thin air the light swallows soar!

But sweeter, sweeter still, when the sun sinks to rest,
And twilight comes on, with the fairies so gay
Tripping through the forest-walk, where flow'rs, unprest,
Bow not their tall heads beneath their frolic play.

To music's softest sounds they dance away the hour,
Till moon-light steals down among the trembling leaves,
And checquers all the ground, and guides them to the bow'r,
The long haunted bow'r, where the nightingale grieves.

Then no more they dance, till her sad song is done,
But, silent as the night, to her mourning attend;
And often as her dying notes their pity have won,
They vow all her sacred haunts from mortals to defend.

When, down among the mountains, sinks the ev'ning star,
And the changing moon forsakes this shadowy sphere,
How cheerless would they be, tho' they fairies are,
If I, with my pale light, came not near!

Yet cheerless tho' they'd be, they're ungrateful to my love!
For, often when the traveller's benighted on his way,
And I glimmer in his path, and would guide him thro' the grove,
They bind me in their magic spells to lead him far astray;

And in the mire to leave him, till the stars are all burnt out,
While, in strange-looking shapes, they frisk about the ground,
And, afar in the woods, they raise a dismal shout,
Till I shrink into my cell again for terror of the sound!

But, see where all the tiny elves come dancing in a ring,
With the merry, merry pipe, and the tabor, and the horn,
And the timbrel so clear, and the lute with dulcet string;
Then round about the oak they go till peeping of the morn.

Down yonder glade two lovers steal, to shun the fairy-queen,
Who frowns upon their plighted vows, and jealous is of me,
That yester-eve I lighted them, along the dewy green,
To seek the purple flow'r, whose juice from all her spells can free.

And now, to punish me, she keeps afar her jocund band,
With the merry, merry pipe, and the tabor, and the lute;
If I creep near yonder oak she will wave her fairy wand,
And to me the dance will cease, and the music all be mute.

O! had I but that purple flow'r whose leaves her charms can foil,
And knew like fays to draw the juice, and throw it on the wind,
I'd be her slave no longer, nor the traveller beguile,
And help all faithful lovers, nor fear the fairy kind!

But soon the *vapour of the woods* will wander afar,
And the fickle moon will fade, and the stars disappear,
Then, cheerless will they be, tho' they fairies are,
If I, with my pale light, come not near!

Whatever St. Aubert might think of the stanzas, he
would not deny his daughter the pleasure of believing that
he approved them; and, having given his commendation, he
sunk into a reverie, and they walked on in silence.

"———A faint erroneous ray
Glanc'd from th' imperfect surfaces of things,
Flung half an image on the straining eye;
While waving woods, and villages, and streams,
And rocks, and mountain-tops, that long retain
The ascending gleam, are all one swimming scene,
Uncertain if beheld."

THOMPSON

St. Aubert continued silent till he reached the chateau, where his wife had retired to her chamber. The languor and dejection, that had lately oppressed her, and which the exertion called forth by the arrival of her guests had suspended, now returned with increased effect. On the following day, symptoms of fever appeared, and St. Aubert, having sent for medical advice, learned, that her disorder was a fever of the same nature as that, from which he had lately recovered. She had, indeed, taken the infection, during her attendance upon him, and, her constitution being too weak to throw out the disease immediately, it had lurked in her veins, and occasioned the heavy languor of which she had complained. St. Aubert, whose anxiety for his wife overcame every other consideration, detained the physician in his house. He remembered the feelings and the reflections that had called a momentary gloom upon his mind, on the day when he had last visited the fishing-house, in company with Madame St. Aubert, and he now admitted a presentiment, that this illness would be a fatal one. But he effectually concealed this from her, and from his daughter, whom he endeavoured to re-animate with hopes that her constant assiduities would not be unavailing. The physician, when asked by St. Aubert for his opinion of the disorder, replied, that the event of it depended upon circumstances which he could not ascertain. Madame St. Aubert seemed to have formed a more decided one; but her eyes only gave hints of this. She frequently fixed them upon her anxious friends

with an expression of pity, and of tenderness, as if she anticipated the sorrow that awaited them, and that seemed to say,
it was for their sakes only, for their sufferings, that she regretted life. On the seventh day, the disorder was at its
crisis. The physician assumed a graver manner, which she
observed, and took occasion, when her family had once
quitted the chamber, to tell him, that she perceived her
death was approaching. "Do not attempt to deceive me,"
said she, "I feel that I cannot long survive. I am prepared
for the event, I have long, I hope, been preparing for it.
Since I have not long to live, do not suffer a mistaken compassion to induce you to flatter my family with false hopes.
If you do, their affliction will only be the heavier when it
arrives: I will endeavour to teach them resignation by my
example."

The physician was affected; he promised to obey her,
and told St. Aubert, somewhat abruptly, that there was
nothing to expect. The latter was not philosopher enough
to restrain his feelings when he received this information;
but a consideration of the increased affliction which the
observance of his grief would occasion his wife, enabled
him, after some time, to command himself in her presence.
Emily was at first overwhelmed with the intelligence; then,
deluded by the strength of her wishes, a hope sprung up in
her mind that her mother would yet recover, and to this she
pertinaciously adhered almost to the last hour.

The progress of this disorder was marked, on the side of
Madame St. Aubert, by patient suffering, and subjected
wishes. The composure, with which she awaited her death,
could be derived only from the retrospect of a life gov-
erned, as far as human frailty permits, by a consciousness
of being always in the presence of the Deity, and by the
hope of an higher world. But her piety could not entirely
subdue the grief of parting from those whom she so dearly
loved. During these her last hours, she conversed much with

St. Aubert and Emily, on the prospect of futurity, and on other religious topics. The resignation she expressed, with the firm hope of meeting in a future world the friends she left in this, and the effort which sometimes appeared to conceal her sorrow at this temporary separation, frequently affected St. Aubert so much as to oblige him to leave the room. Having indulged his tears awhile, he would dry them and return to the chamber with a countenance composed by an endeavour which did but increase his grief.

Never had Emily felt the importance of the lessons, which had taught her to restrain her sensibility, so much as in these moments, and never had she practised them with a triumph so complete. But when the last was over, she sunk at once under the pressure of her sorrow, and then perceived that it was hope, as well as fortitude, which had hitherto supported her. St. Aubert was for a time too devoid of comfort himself to bestow any on his daughter.

CHAPTER II

"I could a tale unfold, whose lightest word
Would harrow up thy soul."

SHAKESPEARE

Madame St. Aubert was interred in the neighbouring village church; her husband and daughter attended her to the grave, followed by a long train of the peasantry, who were sincere mourners of this excellent woman.

On his return from the funeral, St. Aubert shut himself in his chamber. When he came forth, it was with a serene countenance, though pale in sorrow. He gave orders that his family should attend him. Emily only was absent; who, overcome with the scene she had just witnessed, had retired to her closet to weep alone. St. Aubert followed her thither: he took her hand in silence, while she continued to weep; and it was some moments before he could so far command his voice as to speak. It trembled while he said, "My Emily, I am going to prayers with my family; you will join us. We must ask support from above. Where else ought we to seek it—where else can we find it?"

Emily checked her tears, and followed her father to the parlour, where, the servants being assembled, St. Aubert read, in a low and solemn voice, the evening service, and added a prayer for the soul of the departed. During this, his voice often faltered, his tears fell upon the book, and at length he paused. But the sublime emotions of pure devotion gradually elevated his views above this world, and finally brought comfort to his heart.

When the service was ended, and the servants were withdrawn, he tenderly kissed Emily, and said, "I have endeavoured to teach you, from your earliest youth, the duty of self-command; I have pointed out to you the great importance of it through life, not only as it preserves us in the various and dangerous temptations that call us from rectitude and virtue, but as it limits the indulgences which are termed virtuous, yet which, extended beyond a certain boundary, are vicious, for their consequence is evil. All excess is vicious; even that sorrow, which is amiable in its origin, becomes a selfish and unjust passion, if indulged at the expence of our duties—by our duties I mean what we owe to ourselves, as well as to others. The indulgence of excessive grief enervates the mind, and almost incapacitates it for again partaking of those various innocent enjoyments which a benevolent God designed to be the sun-shine of our lives. My dear Emily, recollect and practise the precepts I have so often given you, and which your own experience has so often shewn you to be wise.

"Your sorrow is useless. Do not receive this as merely a common-place remark, but let reason *therefore* restrain sorrow. I would not annihilate your feelings, my child, I would only teach you to command them; for whatever may be the evils resulting from a too susceptible heart, nothing can be hoped from an insensible one; that, on the other hand, is all vice—vice, of which the deformity is not softened, or the effect consoled for, by any semblance or possibility of good. You know my sufferings, and are, therefore, convinced that mine are not the light words which, on these occasions, are so often repeated to destroy even the sources of honest emotion, or which merely display the selfish ostentation of a false philosophy. I will shew my Emily, that I can practise what I advise. I have said thus much, because I cannot bear to see you wasting in useless sorrow, for want of that resistance which is due from mind; and I have not said it till now, because there is a period when all reasoning must yield to nature; that is past: and another, when excessive indulgence, having sunk into habit, weighs down the elasticity of the spirits so as to render conquest nearly impossible; this is to come. You, my Emily, will shew that you are willing to avoid it."

Emily smiled through her tears upon her father: "Dear Sir," said she, and her voice trembled; she would have added, "I will shew myself worthy of being your daughter;" but a mingled emotion of gratitude, affection, and grief overcame her. St. Aubert suffered her to weep without interruption, and then began to talk on common topics.

The first person who came to condole with St. Aubert was an M. Barreaux, an austere and seemingly unfeeling man. A taste for botany had introduced them to each other, for they had frequently met in their wanderings among the mountains. M. Barreaux had retired from the world, and almost from society, to live in a pleasant chateau, on the skirts of the woods, near La Vallée. He also had been disappointed in his opinion of mankind; but he did not, like St. Aubert, pity and mourn for them; he felt more indignation at their vices, than compassion for their weaknesses.

St. Aubert was somewhat surprised to see him; for, though he had often pressed him to come to the chateau, he had never till now accepted the invitation; and now he came without ceremony or reserve, entering the parlour as an old friend. The claims of misfortune appeared to have softened down all the ruggedness and prejudices of his heart. St. Aubert unhappy, seemed to be the sole idea that occupied his mind. It was in manners, more than in words, that he appeared to sympathize with his friends: he spoke little on the subject of their grief; but the minute attention he gave them, and the modulated voice, and softened look that accompanied it, came from his heart, and spoke to theirs.

At this melancholy period, St. Aubert was likewise visited by Madame Cheron, his only surviving sister, who had been some years a widow, and now resided on her own estate near Tholouse. The intercourse between them had not been very frequent. In her condolements, words were not wanting; she understood not the magic of the look that speaks at once to the soul, or the voice that sinks like balm to the heart: but she assured St. Aubert that she sincerely sympathized with him, praised the virtues of his late wife, and then offered what she considered to be consolation. Emily wept unceasingly while she spoke; St. Aubert was tranquil, listened to what she said in silence, and then turned the discourse upon another subject.

At parting she pressed him and her niece to make her an early visit. "Change of place will amuse you," said she, "and it is wrong to give way to grief." St. Aubert acknowledged the truth of these words of course; but, at the same time, felt more reluctant than ever to quit the spot which his past happiness had consecrated. The presence of his wife had sanctified every surrounding scene, and, each day, as it gradually softened the acuteness of his suffering, assisted the tender enchantment that bound him to home.

But there were calls which must be complied with, and of this kind was the visit he paid to his brother-in-law M. Quesnel. An affair of an interesting nature made it necessary that he should delay this visit no longer, and, wishing to rouse Emily from her dejection, he took her with him to Epourville.

As the carriage entered upon the forest that adjoined his paternal domain, his eyes once more caught, between the chestnut avenue, the turreted corners of the chateau. He sighed to think of what had passed since he was last there, and that it was now the property of a man who neither revered nor valued it. At length he entered the avenue, whose lofty trees had so often delighted him when a boy, and whose melancholy shade was now so congenial with the tone of his spirits. Every feature of the edifice, distinguished by an air of heavy grandeur, appeared successively between the branches of the trees—the broad turret, the arched gateway that led into the courts, the draw-bridge, and the dry fosse which surrounded the whole.

The sound of carriage wheels, brought a troop of servants to the great gate, where St. Aubert alighted, and from which he led Emily into the gothic hall, now no longer hung with the arms and ancient banners of the family. These were displaced, and the oak wainscoting, and beams that crossed the roof, were painted white. The large table, too, that used to stretch along the upper end of the hall, where the master of the mansion loved to display his hospitality, and whence the peal of laughter, and the song of conviviality, had so often resounded, was now removed; even the benches that had surrounded the hall were no longer there. The heavy walls were hung with frivolous ornaments, and every thing that appeared denoted the false taste and corrupted sentiments of the present owner.

St. Aubert followed a gay Parisian servant to a parlour, where sat Mons. and Madame Quesnel, who received him with a stately politeness, and, after a few formal words of condolement, seemed to have forgotten that they ever had a sister.

Emily felt tears swell into her eyes, and then resentment checked them. St. Aubert, calm and deliberate, preserved his dignity without assuming importance, and Quesnel was depressed by his presence without exactly knowing wherefore.

After some general conversation, St. Aubert requested to speak with him alone; and Emily, being left with Madame Quesnel, soon learned that a large party was invited to dine at the chateau, and was compelled to hear that nothing which was past and irremediable ought to prevent the festivity of the present hour.

St. Aubert, when he was told that company were expected, felt a mixed emotion of disgust and indignation against the insensibility of Quesnel, which prompted him to return home immediately. But he was informed, that Madame Cheron had been asked to meet him; and, when he looked at Emily, and considered that a time might come when the enmity of her uncle would be prejudicial to her, he determined not to incur it himself, by conduct which would be resented as indecorous, by the very persons who now shewed so little sense of decorum.

Among the visitors assembled at dinner were two Italian gentlemen, of whom one was named Montoni, a distant relation of Madame Quesnel, a man about forty, of an uncommonly handsome person, with features manly and expressive, but whose countenance exhibited, upon the whole, more of the haughtiness of command, and the quickness of discernment, than of any other character.

Signor Cavigni, his friend, appeared to be about thirty—his inferior in dignity, but equal to him in penetration of countenance, and superior in insinuation of manner.

Emily was shocked by the salutation with which Madame Cheron met her father—"Dear brother," said she, "I am concerned to see you look so very ill; do, pray, have advice!" St. Aubert answered, with a melancholy smile, that he felt himself much as usual; but Emily's fears made her now fancy that her father looked worse than he really did.

Emily would have been amused by the new characters she saw, and the varied conversation that passed during dinner, which was served in a style of splendour she had seldom seen before, had her spirits been less oppressed. Of the guests, Signor Montoni was lately come from Italy, and he spoke of the commotions which at that period agitated the country; talked of party differences with warmth, and then lamented the probable consequences of the tumults. His friend spoke with equal ardour, of the politics of his country; praised the government and prosperity of Venice, and boasted of its decided superiority over all the other Italian states. He then turned to the ladies, and talked with the same eloquence, of Parisian fashions, the French opera, and French manners; and on the latter subject he did not fail to mingle what is so particularly agreeable to French taste. The flattery was not detected by those to whom it was addressed, though its effect, in producing submissive attention, did not escape his observation. When he could disengage himself from the assiduities of the other ladies, he sometimes addressed Emily: but she knew nothing of Parisian fashions, or Parisian operas; and her modesty, simplicity, and correct manners formed a decided contrast to those of her female companions.

After dinner, St. Aubert stole from the room to view once more the old chestnut which Quesnel talked of cutting down. As he stood under its shade, and looked up among its branches, still luxuriant, and saw here and there the blue sky trembling between them; the pursuits and events of his early days crowded fast to his mind, with the figures and characters of friends—long since gone from the earth; and he now felt himself to be almost an insulated being, with nobody but his Emily for his heart to turn to.

He stood lost amid the scenes of years which fancy called up, till the succession closed with the picture of his dying wife, and he started away, to forget it, if possible, at the social board.

St. Aubert ordered his carriage at an early hour, and Emily observed, that he was more than unusually silent and dejected on the way home; but she considered this to be the effect of his visit to a place which spoke so eloquently of former times, nor suspected that he had a cause of grief which he concealed from her.

On entering the chateau she felt more depressed than ever, for she more than ever missed the presence of that dear parent, who, whenever she had been from home, used to welcome her return with smiles and fondness; now, all was silent and forsaken.

But what reason and effort may fail to do, time effects. Week after week passed away, and each, as it passed, stole something from the harshness of her affliction, till it was mellowed to that tenderness which the feeling heart cherishes as sacred. St. Aubert, on the contrary, visibly declined in health; though Emily, who had been so constantly with him, was almost the last person who observed it. His constitution had never recovered from the late attack of the fever, and the succeeding shock it had received from Madame St. Aubert's death had produced its present infirmity. His physician now ordered him to travel; for it was perceptible that sorrow had seized upon his nerves, weakened as they had been by the preceding illness; and variety of scene, it was probable, would, by amusing his mind, restore them to their proper tone.

For some days Emily was occupied in preparations to attend him; and he, by endeavours to diminish his expences at home during the journey—a purpose which determined him at length to dismiss his domestics. Emily seldom opposed her father's wishes by questions or remonstrances, or she would now have asked why he did not take a servant, and have represented that his infirm health made one almost necessary. But when, on the eve of their departure, she found that he had dismissed Jacques, Francis, and Mary, and detained only Theresa the old housekeeper, she was extremely surprised, and ventured to ask his reason for having done so. "To save expences, my dear," he replied—"we are going on an expensive excursion."

The physician had prescribed the air of Languedoc and Provence; and St. Aubert determined, therefore, to travel leisurely along the shores of the Mediterranean, towards Provence.

They retired early to their chamber on the night before their departure; but Emily had a few books and other things to collect, and the clock had struck twelve before she had finished, or had remembered that some of her drawing instruments, which she meant to take with her, were in the parlour below. As she went to fetch these, she passed her father's room, and, perceiving the door half open, con-cluded that he was in his study—for, since the death of Madame St. Aubert, it had been frequently his custom to rise from his restless bed, and go thither to compose his mind. When she was below stairs she looked into this room, but without finding him; and as she returned to her cham-ber, she tapped at his door, and receiving no answer, stepped softly in, to be certain whether he was there.

The room was dark, but a light glimmered through some panes of glass that were placed in the upper part of a closet-door. Emily believed her father to be in the closet, and, surprised that he was up at so late an hour, appre-hended he was unwell, and was going to enquire; but, con-sidering that her sudden appearance at this hour might alarm him, she removed her light to the stair-case, and then stepped softly to the closet. On looking through the panes of glass, she saw him seated at a small table, with papers before him, some of which he was reading with deep atten-tion and interest, during which he often wept, and sobbed aloud. Emily, who had come to the door to learn whether her father was ill, was now detained there by a mixture of curiosity and tenderness. She could not witness his sorrow, without being anxious to know the subject of it; and she therefore continued to observe him in silence, concluding that those papers were letters of her late mother. Presently he knelt down, and with a look so solemn as she had seldom seen him assume, and which was mingled with a certain wild expression, that partook more of horror than of any other character, he prayed silently for a considerable time.

When he rose, a ghastly paleness was on his countenance. Emily was hastily retiring; but she saw him turn again to the papers, and she stopped. He took from among them a small case, and from thence a miniature picture. The rays of light fell strongly upon it, and she perceived it to be that of a lady, but not of her mother.

St. Aubert gazed earnestly and tenderly upon this portrait, put it to his lips, and then to his heart, and sighed with a convulsive force. Emily could scarcely believe what she saw to be real. She never knew till now that he had a picture of any other lady than her mother, much less that he had one which he evidently valued so highly; but having looked repeatedly, to be certain that it was not the resemblance of Madame St. Aubert, she became entirely convinced that it was designed for that of some other person.

At length St. Aubert returned the picture into its case; and Emily, recollecting that she was intruding upon his private sorrows, softly withdrew from the chamber.

CHAPTER III

"O how canst thou renounce the boundless store
Of charms which nature to her vot'ry yields!
The warbling woodland, the resounding shore,
The pomp of groves, and garniture of fields;
All that the genial ray of morning gilds,
And all that echoes to the song of even;
All that the mountain's shelt'ring bosom shields,
And all the dread magnificence of heaven;
O how canst thou renounce, and hope to be forgiven!"
. . . .
"These charms shall work thy soul's eternal health,
And love, and gentleness, and joy impart."

THE MINSTREL

St. Aubert, instead of taking the more direct road, that ran along the feet of the Pyrenées to Languedoc, chose one that, winding over the heights, afforded more extensive views and greater variety of romantic scenery. He turned a little out of his way to take leave of M. Barreaux, whom he found botanizing in the wood near his chateau, and who, when he was told the purpose of St. Aubert's visit, expressed a degree of concern, such as his friend had thought it was scarcely possible for him to feel on any similar occasion. They parted with mutual regret.

"If any thing could have tempted me from my retirement," said M. Barreaux, "it would have been the pleasure of accompanying you on this little tour. I do not often offer compliments; you may, therefore, believe me, when I say, that I shall look for your return with impatience."

The travellers proceeded on their journey. As they ascended the heights, St. Aubert often looked back upon his chateau, in the plain below; tender images crowded to his mind; his melancholy imagination suggested that he should return no more; and though he checked this wandering thought, still he continued to look, till the haziness of distance blended his home with the general landscape, and St. Aubert seemed to

"Drag at each remove a lengthening chain."

He and Emily continued sunk in musing silence for some leagues, from which melancholy reverie Emily first awoke, and her young fancy, struck with the grandeur of the objects around, gradually yielded to delightful impressions. The road now descended into glens, confined by stupendous walls of rock, grey and barren, except where shrubs fringed their summits, or patches of meagre vegetation tinted their recesses, in which the wild goat was frequently browsing. And now, the way led to the lofty cliffs, from whence the landscape was seen extending in all its magnificence.

Emily could not restrain her transport as she looked over the pine forests of the mountains upon the vast plains, that, enriched with woods, towns, blushing vines, and plantations of almonds, palms and olives, stretched along, till their various colours melted in distance into one harmonious hue, that seemed to unite earth with heaven. Through the whole of this glorious scene the majestic Garonne wandered; descending from its source among the Pyrenées, and winding its blue waves towards the Bay of Biscay.

The ruggedness of the unfrequented road often obliged the wanderers to alight from their little carriage, but they thought themselves amply repaid for this inconvenience by the grandeur of the scenes; and, while the muleteer led his animals slowly over the broken ground, the travellers had leisure to linger amid these solitudes, and to indulge the sublime reflections, which soften, while they elevate, the heart, and fill it with the certainty of a present God! Still the enjoyment of St. Aubert was touched with that pensive melancholy, which gives to every object a mellower tint, and breathes a sacred charm over all around.

They had provided against part of the evil to be encountered from a want of convenient inns, by carrying a stock of provisions in the carriage, so that they might take refreshment on any pleasant spot, in the open air, and pass the nights wherever they should happen to meet with a comfortable cottage. For the mind, also, they had provided, by a work on botany, written by M. Barreaux, and by several of the Latin and Italian poets; while Emily's pencil enabled her to preserve some of those combinations of forms, which charmed her at every step.

The loneliness of the road, where, only now and then, a peasant was seen driving his mule, or some mountaineer-children at play among the rocks, heightened the effect of the scenery. St. Aubert was so much struck with it, that he determined, if he could hear of a road, to penetrate further among the mountains, and, bending his way rather more to the south, to emerge into Rousillon, and coast the Mediterranean along part of that country to Languedoc.

Soon after mid-day, they reached the summit of one of those cliffs, which, bright with the verdure of palm trees, adorn, like gems, the tremendous walls of the rocks, and which overlooked the greater part of Gascony, and part of Languedoc. Here was shade, and the fresh water of a spring, that, gliding among the turf, under the trees, thence precipitated itself from rock to rock, till its dashing murmurs were lost in the abyss, though its white foam was long seen amid the darkness of the pines below.

This was a spot well suited for rest, and the travellers

alighted to dine, while the mules were unharnessed to browse on the savoury herbs that enriched this summit.

It was some time before St. Aubert or Emily could withdraw their attention from the surrounding objects, so as to partake of their little repast. Seated in the shade of the palms, St. Aubert pointed out to her observation the course of the rivers, the situation of great towns, and the boundaries of provinces, which science, rather than the eye, enabled him to describe. Notwithstanding this occupation, when he talked awhile he suddenly became silent, thoughtful, and tears often swelled to his eyes, which Emily observed, and the sympathy of her own heart told her their cause. The scene before them bore some resemblance, though it was on a much grander scale, to a favourite one of the late Madame St. Aubert, within view of the fishing-house. They both observed this, and thought how delighted she would have been with the present landscape, while they knew that her eyes must never, never more open upon this world. St. Aubert remembered the last time of his visiting that spot in company with her, and also the mournfully presaging thoughts which had then arisen in his mind, and were now, even thus soon, realized! The recollections subdued him, and he abruptly rose from his seat, and walked away to where no eye could observe his grief.

When he returned, his countenance had recovered its usual serenity; he took Emily's hand, pressed it affectionately, without speaking, and soon after called to the muleteer, who sat at a little distance, concerning a road among the mountains towards Rousillon. Michael said, there were several that way, but he did not know how far they extended, or even whether they were passable; and St. Aubert, who did not intend to travel after sun set, asked what village they could reach about that time. The muleteer calculated, that they could easily reach Mateau, which was in their present road; but that, if they took a road that sloped more to the south, towards Rousillon, there was a hamlet, which he thought they could gain before the evening shut in.

St. Aubert, after some hesitation, determined to take the latter course, and Michael, having finished his meal, and harnessed his mules, again set forward, but soon stopped; and St. Aubert saw him doing homage to a cross, that stood on a rock impending over their way. Having concluded his devotions, he smacked his whip in the air, and, in spite of the rough road, and the pain of his poor mules, which he had been lately lamenting, rattled, in a full gallop, along the edge of a precipice, which it made the eye dizzy to look down. Emily was terrified almost to fainting; and St. Aubert, apprehending still greater danger from suddenly stopping the driver, was compelled to sit quietly, and trust his fate to the strength and discretion of the mules, who seemed to possess a greater portion of the latter quality than their master; for they carried the travellers safely into the valley, and there stopped upon the brink of the rivulet that watered it.

Leaving the splendour of extensive prospects, they now entered this narrow valley screened by

> Rocks on rocks piled, as if by magic spell,
> Here scorch'd by lightnings, there with ivy green.

The scene of barrenness was here and there interrupted by the spreading branches of the larch and cedar, which threw their gloom over the cliff, or athwart the torrent that rolled in the vale. No living creature appeared, except the izard, scrambling among the rocks, and often hanging upon points so dangerous, that fancy shrunk from the view of them. This was such a scene as *Salvator* would have chosen, had he then existed, for his canvass; St. Aubert, impressed by the romantic character of the place, almost expected to see banditti start from behind some projecting rock, and he kept his hand upon the arms with which he always travelled.

As they advanced, the valley opened; its savage features gradually softened, and, towards evening, they were among heathy mountains, stretched in far perspective, along which the solitary sheep-bell was heard, and the voice of the shepherd calling his wandering flocks to the nightly fold. His cabin, partly shadowed by the cork-tree and the ilex, which St. Aubert observed to flourish in higher regions of the air than any other trees, except the fir, was all the human habitation that yet appeared. Along the bottom of this valley the most vivid verdure was spread; and, in the little hollow recesses of the mountains, under the shade of the oak and chestnut, herds of cattle were grazing. Groups of them, too, were often seen reposing on the banks of the rivulet, or laving their sides in the cool stream, and sipping its wave.

The sun was now setting upon the valley; its last light gleamed upon the water, and heightened the rich yellow and purple tints of the heath and broom, that overspread the mountains. St. Aubert enquired of Michael the distance to the hamlet he had mentioned, but the man could not with certainty tell; and Emily began to fear that he had mistaken the road. Here was no human being to assist, or direct them; they had left the shepherd and his cabin far behind, and the scene became so obscured in twilight, that the eye could not follow the distant perspective of the valley in search of a cottage, or a hamlet. A glow of the horizon still marked the west, and this was of some little use to the travellers. Michael seemed endeavouring to keep up his courage by singing; his music, however, was not of a kind to disperse melancholy; he sung, in a sort of chant, one of the most dismal ditties his present auditors had ever heard, and St. Aubert at length discovered it to be a vesper-hymn to his favourite saint.

They travelled on, sunk in that thoughtful melancholy, with which twilight and solitude impress the mind. Michael had now ended his ditty, and nothing was heard but the drowsy murmur of the breeze among the woods, and its light flutter, as it blew freshly into the carriage. They were at length roused by the sound of fire-arms. St. Aubert called to the muleteer to stop, and they listened. The noise was not repeated; but presently they heard a rustling among the brakes. St. Aubert drew forth a pistol, and ordered Michael to proceed as fast as possible; who had not long obeyed, before a horn sounded, that made the mountains ring. He looked again from the window, and then saw a young man spring from the bushes into the road, followed by a couple of dogs. The stranger was in a hunter's dress. His gun was slung across his shoulders, the hunter's horn hung from his belt, and in his hand was a small pike, which, as he held it, added to the manly grace of his figure, and assisted the agility of his steps.

After a moment's hesitation, St. Aubert again stopped the carriage, and waited till he came up, that they might en-quire concerning the hamlet they were in search of. The stranger informed him, that it was only half a league dis-tant, that he was going thither himself, and would readily shew the way. St. Aubert thanked him for the offer, and, pleased with his chevalier-like air and open countenance, asked him to take a seat in the carriage; which the stranger, with an acknowledgment, declined, adding that he would keep pace with the mules. "But I fear you will be wretch-edly accommodated," said he: "the inhabitants of these mountains are a simple people, who are not only without the luxuries of life, but almost destitute of what in other places are held to be its necessaries."

"I perceive you are not one of its inhabitants, sir," said St. Aubert.

"No, sir, I am only a wanderer here."

The carriage drove on, and the increasing dusk made the travellers very thankful that they had a guide; the frequent glens, too, that now opened among the mountains, would likewise have added to their perplexity. Emily, as she looked up one of these, saw something at a great distance like a bright cloud in the air. "What light is yonder, sir?" said she. St. Aubert looked, and perceived that it was the snowy summit of a mountain, so much higher than any around it, that it still reflected the sun's rays, while those below lay in deep shade.

At length, village lights were seen to twinkle through the dusk, and, soon after, some cottages were discovered in the valley, or rather were seen by reflection in the stream, on whose margin they stood, and which still gleamed with the evening light.

The stranger now came up, and St. Aubert, on further enquiry, found not only that there was no inn in the place, but not any sort of house of public reception. The stranger, however, offered to walk on, and enquire for a cottage to accommodate them; for which further civility St. Aubert returned his thanks, and said, that, as the village was so near, he would alight, and walk with him. Emily followed slowly in the carriage.

On the way, St. Aubert asked his companion what success he had had in the chase. "Not much, sir," he replied, "nor do I aim at it. I am pleased with the country, and mean to saunter away a few weeks among its scenes. My dogs I take with me more for companionship than for game. This dress, too, gives me an ostensible business, and procures me that respect from the people, which would, perhaps, be refused to a lonely stranger, who had no visible motive for coming among them."

"I admire your taste," said St. Aubert, "and, if I was a younger man, should like to pass a few weeks in your way exceedingly. I, too, am a wanderer, but neither my plan nor pursuits are exactly like yours—I go in search of health, as much as of amusement." St. Aubert sighed, and paused; and then, seeming to recollect himself, he resumed: "If I can hear of a tolerable road, that shall afford decent accommodation, it is my intention to pass into Rousillon, and along the sea-shore to Languedoc. You, sir, seem to be acquainted with the country, and can, perhaps, give me information on the subject."

The stranger said, that what information he could give was entirely at his service; and then mentioned a road rather more to the east, which led to a town, whence it would be easy to proceed into Rousillon.

They now arrived at the village, and commenced their search for a cottage, that would afford a night's lodging. In several, which they entered, ignorance, poverty, and mirth seemed equally to prevail; and the owners eyed St. Aubert with a mixture of curiosity and timidity. Nothing like a bed could be found, and he had ceased to enquire for one, when Emily joined him, who observed the languor of her father's countenance, and lamented, that he had taken a road so ill provided with the comforts necessary for an invalid. Other cottages, which they examined, seemed somewhat less savage than the former, consisting of two rooms, if such they could be called; the first of these occupied by mules and pigs, the second by the family, which generally consisted of six or eight children, with their parents, who slept on beds of skins and dried beech leaves, spread upon a mud floor. Here, light was admitted, and smoke discharged, through an aperture in the roof; and here the scent of spirits (for the travelling smugglers, who haunted the Pyrénées, had made this rude people familiar with the use of liquors) was generally perceptible enough. Emily turned from such scenes, and looked at her father with anxious tenderness, which the young stranger seemed to observe; for, drawing St. Aubert aside, he made him an offer of his own bed. "It is a decent one," said he, "when compared with what we have just seen, yet such as in other circumstances I should be ashamed to offer you." St. Aubert acknowledged how much he felt himself obliged by this kindness, but refused to accept it, till the young stranger would take no denial. "Do not give me the pain of knowing, sir," said he, "that an invalid, like you, lies on hard skins, while I sleep in a bed. Besides, sir, your refusal wounds my pride; I must believe you think my offer unworthy your acceptance. Let me shew you the way. I have no doubt my landlady can accommodate this young lady also."

St. Aubert, at length, consented, that, if this could be done, he would accept his kindness, though he felt rather surprised, that the stranger had proved himself so deficient in gallantry, as to administer to the repose of an infirm man, rather than to that of a very lovely young woman, for he had not once offered the room for Emily. But she thought not of herself, and the animated smile she gave him, told how much she felt herself obliged for the preference of her father.

On their way, the stranger, whose name was Valancourt, stepped on first to speak to his hostess, and she came out to welcome St. Aubert into a cottage, much superior to any he had seen. This good woman seemed very willing to accommodate the strangers, who were soon compelled to accept the only two beds in the place. Eggs and milk were the only food the cottage afforded; but against scarcity of provisions St. Aubert had provided, and he requested Valancourt to stay, and partake with him of less homely fare; an invitation, which was readily accepted, and they passed an hour in intelligent conversation. St. Aubert was much pleased with the manly frankness, simplicity, and keen susceptibility to the grandeur of nature, which his new acquaintance discovered; and, indeed, he had often been heard to say, that, without a certain simplicity of heart, this taste could not exist in any strong degree.

The conversation was interrupted by a violent uproar

without, in which the voice of the muleteer was heard above every other sound. Valancourt started from his seat, and went to enquire the occasion; but the dispute continued so long afterwards, that St. Aubert went himself, and found Michael quarrelling with the hostess, because she had refused to let his mules lie in a little room where he and three of her sons were to pass the night. The place was wretched enough, but there was no other for these people to sleep in; and, with somewhat more of delicacy than was usual among the inhabitants of this wild tract of country, she persisted in refusing to let the animals have the same *bed-chamber* with her children. This was a tender point with the muleteer; his honour was wounded when his mules were treated with disrespect, and he would have received a blow, perhaps, with more meekness. He declared that his beasts were as honest beasts, and as good beasts, as any in the whole province; and that they had a right to be well treated wherever they went. "They are as harmless as lambs," said he, "if people don't affront them. I never knew them behave themselves amiss above once or twice in my life, and then they had good reason for doing so. Once, indeed, they kicked at a boy's leg that lay asleep in the stable, and broke it; but I told them they were out there, and by Saint Anthony! I believe they understood me, for they never did so again."

He concluded this eloquent harangue with protesting, that they should share with him, go where he would.

The dispute was at length settled by Valancourt, who drew the hostess aside, and desired she would let the muleteer and his beasts have the place in question to themselves, while her sons should have the bed of skins designed for him, for that he would wrap himself in his cloak, and sleep on the bench by the cottage door. But this she thought it her duty to oppose, and she felt it to be her inclination to disappoint the muleteer. Valancourt, however, was positive, and the tedious affair was at length settled.

It was late when St. Aubert and Emily retired to their rooms, and Valancourt to his station at the door, which, at this mild season, he preferred to a close cabin and a bed of skins. St. Aubert was somewhat surprised to find in his room volumes of Homer, Horace, and Petrarch; but the name of Valancourt, written in them, told him to whom they belonged.

CHAPTER IV

"In truth he was a strange and wayward wight,
Fond of each gentle, and each dreadful scene,
In darkness, and in storm he found delight;
Nor less than when on ocean-wave serene
The southern sun diffus'd his dazzling sheen.
Even sad vicissitude amus'd his soul;
And if a sigh would sometimes intervene,
And down his cheek a tear of pity roll,
A sigh, a tear, so sweet, he wish'd not to control."

THE MINSTREL

St. Aubert awoke at an early hour, refreshed by sleep, and
desirous to set forward. He invited the stranger to breakfast
with him; and, talking again of the road, Valancourt said,
that, some months past, he had traveled as far as Beaujeu,
which was a town of some consequence on the way to Rousillon. He recommended it to St. Aubert to take that route,
and the latter determined to do so.

"The road from this hamlet," said Valancourt, "and that
to Beaujeu, part at the distance of about a league and an
half from hence; if you will give me leave, I will direct your
muleteer so far. I must wander somewhere, and your company would make this a pleasanter ramble than any other
I could take."

St. Aubert thankfully accepted his offer, and they set out

together, the young stranger on foot, for he refused the invitation of St. Aubert to take a seat in his little carriage.

The road wound along the feet of the mountains through a pastoral valley, bright with verdure, and varied with groves of dwarf oak, beech, and sycamore, under whose branches herds of cattle reposed. The mountain-ash too, and the weeping birch, often threw their pendant foliage over the steeps above, where the scanty soil scarcely concealed their roots, and where their light branches waved to every breeze that fluttered from the mountains.

The travellers were frequently met at this early hour, for the sun had not yet risen upon the valley, by shepherds driving immense flocks from their folds to feed upon the hills. St. Aubert had set out thus early, not only that he might enjoy the first appearance of sun-rise, but that he might inhale the first pure breath of morning, which above all things is refreshing to the spirits of the invalid. In these regions it was particularly so, where an abundance of wild flowers and aromatic herbs breathed forth their essence on the air.

The dawn, which softened the scenery with its peculiar grey tint, now dispersed, and Emily watched the progress of the day, first trembling on the tops of the highest cliffs, then touching them with splendid light, while their sides and the vale below were still wrapt in dewy mist. Meanwhile, the sullen grey of the eastern clouds began to blush, then to redden, and then to glow with a thousand colours, till the golden light darted over all the air, touched the lower points of the mountain's brow, and glanced in long sloping beams upon the valley and its stream. All nature seemed to have awakened from death into life; the spirit of St. Aubert was renovated. His heart was full; he wept, and his thoughts ascended to the Great Creator.

Emily wished to trip along the turf, so green and bright with dew, and to taste the full delight of that liberty, which the izard seemed to enjoy as he bounded along the brow of the cliffs; while Valancourt often stopped to speak with the travellers, and with social feeling to point out to them the peculiar objects of his admiration. St. Aubert was pleased with him: "Here is the real ingenuousness and ardour of youth," said he to himself; "this young man has never been at Paris."

He was sorry when they came to the spot where the roads parted, and his heart took a more affectionate leave of him than is usual after so short an acquaintance. Valancourt talked long by the side of the carriage; seemed more than once to be going, but still lingered, and appeared to search anxiously for topics of conversation to account for his delay. At length he took leave. As he went, St. Aubert observed him look with an earnest and pensive eye at Emily, who bowed to him with a countenance full of timid sweetness, while the carriage drove on. St. Aubert, for whatever reason, soon after looked from the window, and saw Valancourt standing upon the bank of the road, resting on his pike with folded arms, and following the carriage with his eyes. He waved his hand, and Valancourt, seeming to awake from his reverie, returned the salute, and started away.

The aspect of the country now began to change, and the travellers soon found themselves among mountains covered from their base nearly to their summits with forests of gloomy pine, except where a rock of granite shot up from the vale, and lost its snowy top in the clouds. The rivulet, which had hitherto accompanied them, now expanded into a river; and, flowing deeply and silently along, reflected, as in a mirror, the blackness of the impending shades. Sometimes a cliff was seen lifting its bold head above the woods and the vapours, that floated mid-way down the mountains; and sometimes a face of perpendicular marble rose from the water's edge, over which the larch threw his gigantic arms, here scathed with lightning, and there floating in luxuriant foliage.

They continued to travel over a rough and unfrequented road, seeing now and then at a distance the solitary shepherd, with his dog, stalking along the valley, and hearing only the dashing of torrents, which the woods concealed from the eye, the long sullen murmur of the breeze, as it swept over the pines, or the notes of the eagle and the vulture, which were seen towering round the beetling cliff.

Often, as the carriage moved slowly over uneven ground, St. Aubert alighted, and amused himself with examining the curious plants that grew on the banks of the road, and with which these regions abound; while Emily, wrapt in high enthusiasm, wandered away under the shades, listening in deep silence to the lonely murmur of the woods.

Neither village nor hamlet was seen for many leagues; the goat-herd's or the hunter's cabin, perched among the cliffs of the rocks, were the only human habitations that appeared.

The travellers again took their dinner in the open air, on a pleasant spot in the valley, under the spreading shade of cedars; and then set forward towards Beaujeu.

The road now began to ascend, and, leaving the pine forests behind, wound among rocky precipices. The evening twilight again fell over the scene, and the travellers were ignorant how far they might yet be from Beaujeu. St. Aubert, however, conjectured that the distance could not be very great, and comforted himself with the prospect of travelling on a more frequented road after reaching that town, where he designed to pass the night. Mingled woods, and rocks, and heathy mountains were now seen obscurely through the dusk; but soon even these imperfect images faded in darkness. Michael proceeded with caution, for he could scarcely distinguish the road; his mules, however, seemed to have more sagacity, and their steps were sure.

On turning the angle of a mountain, a light appeared at a distance, that illumined the rocks, and the horizon to a

great extent. It was evidently a large fire, but whether accidental, or otherwise, there were no means of knowing. St.
Aubert thought it was probably kindled by some of the
numerous banditti, that infested the Pyrenées, and he became watchful and anxious to know whether the road
passed near this fire. He had arms with him, which, on an
emergency, might afford some protection, though certainly
a very unequal one, against a band of robbers, so desperate
too as those usually were who haunted these wild regions.
While many reflections rose upon his mind, he heard a voice
shouting from the road behind, and ordering the muleteer
to stop. St. Aubert bade him proceed as fast as possible; but
either Michael, or his mules were obstinate, for they did not
quit the old pace. Horses' feet were now heard; a man rode
up to the carriage, still ordering the driver to stop; and St.
Aubert, who could no longer doubt his purpose, was with
difficulty able to prepare a pistol for his defence, when his
hand was upon the door of the chaise. The man staggered
on his horse, the report of the pistol was followed by a
groan, and St. Aubert's horror may be imagined, when in
the next instant he thought he heard the faint voice of Valancourt. He now himself bade the muleteer stop; and, pro-
nouncing the name of Valancourt, was answered in a voice,
that no longer suffered him to doubt. St. Aubert, who instantly alighted and went to his assistance, found him still
sitting on his horse, but bleeding profusely, and appearing
to be in great pain, though he endeavoured to soften the
terror of St. Aubert by assurances that he was not materially
hurt, the wound being only in his arm. St. Aubert, with the
muleteer, assisted him to dismount, and he sat down on the
bank of the road, where St. Aubert tried to bind up his arm,
but his hands trembled so excessively that he could not
accomplish it; and, Michael being now gone in pursuit of
the horse, which, on being disengaged from his rider, had
galloped off, he called Emily to his assistance. Receiving no

answer, he went to the carriage, and found her sunk on the seat in a fainting fit. Between the distress of this circumstance and that of leaving Valancourt bleeding, he scarcely knew what he did; he endeavoured, however, to raise her, and called to Michael to fetch water from the rivulet that flowed by the road, but Michael was gone beyond the reach of his voice. Valancourt, who heard these calls, and also the repeated name of Emily, instantly understood the subject of his distress; and, almost forgetting his own condition, he hastened to her relief. She was reviving when he reached the carriage; and then, understanding that anxiety for him had occasioned her indisposition, he assured her, in a voice that trembled, but not from anguish, that his wound was of no consequence. While he said this St. Aubert turned round, and perceiving that he was still bleeding, the subject of his alarm changed again, and he hastily formed some handkerchiefs into a bandage. This stopped the effusion of the blood; but St. Aubert, dreading the consequence of the wound, enquired repeatedly how far they were from Beaujeu; when, learning that it was at two leagues distance, his distress increased, since he knew not how Valancourt, in his present state, would bear the motion of the carriage, and perceived that he was already faint from loss of blood. When he mentioned the subject of his anxiety, Valancourt entreated that he would not suffer himself to be thus alarmed on his account, for that he had no doubt he should be able to support himself very well; and then he talked of the accident as a slight one. The muleteer being now returned with Valancourt's horse, assisted him into the chaise; and, as Emily was now revived, they moved slowly on towards Beaujeu.

St. Aubert, when he had recovered from the terror occasioned him by this accident, expressed surprise on seeing Valancourt, who explained his unexpected appearance by saying, "You, Sir, renewed my taste for society; when you had left the hamlet, it did indeed appear a solitude. I determined, therefore, since my object was merely amusement, to change the scene; and I took this road, because I knew it led through a more romantic tract of mountains than the spot I have left. Besides," added he, hesitating for an instant, "I will own, and why should I not? that I had some hope of overtaking you."

"And I have made you a very unexpected return for the compliment," said St. Aubert, who lamented again the rashness which had produced the accident, and explained the cause of his late alarm. But Valancourt seemed anxious only to remove from the minds of his companions every unpleasant feeling relative to himself; and, for that purpose, still struggled against a sense of pain, and tried to converse with gaiety. Emily meanwhile was silent, except when Valancourt particularly addressed her, and there was at those times a tremulous tone in his voice that spoke much.

They were now so near the fire, which had long flamed at a distance on the blackness of night, that it gleamed upon the road, and they could distinguish figures moving about the blaze. The way winding still nearer, they perceived in the valley one of those numerous bands of gipsies, which at that period particularly haunted the wilds of the Pyrenées, and lived partly by plundering the traveller. Emily looked with some degree of terror on the savage countenances of these people, shewn by the fire, which heightened the romantic effect of the scenery, as it threw a red dusky gleam upon the rocks and on the foliage of the trees, leaving heavy masses of shade and regions of obscurity, which the eye feared to penetrate.

They were preparing their supper; a large pot stood by the fire, over which several figures were busy. The blaze discovered a rude kind of tent, round which many children and dogs were playing, and the whole formed a picture highly grotesque. The travellers saw plainly their danger.

Valancourt was silent, but laid his hand on one of St. Aubert's pistols; St. Aubert drew forth another, and Michael was ordered to proceed as fast as possible. They passed the place, however, without being attacked; the rovers being probably unprepared for the opportunity, and too busy about their supper to feel much interest, at the moment, in any thing besides.

After a league and a half more, passed in darkness, the travellers arrived at Beaujeu, and drove up to the only inn the place afforded; which, though superior to any they had seen since they entered the mountains, was bad enough.

The surgeon of the town was immediately sent for, if a surgeon he could be called, who prescribed for horses as well as for men, and shaved faces at least as dexterously as he set bones. After examining Valancourt's arm, and perceiving that the bullet had passed through the flesh without touching the bone, he dressed it, and left him with a solemn prescription of quiet, which his patient was not inclined to obey. The delight of ease had now succeeded to pain; for ease may be allowed to assume a positive quality when contrasted with anguish; and, his spirits thus re-animated, he wished to partake of the conversation of St. Aubert and Emily, who, released from so many apprehensions, were uncommonly cheerful. Late as it was, however, St. Aubert was obliged to go out with the landlord to buy meat for supper; and Emily, who, during this interval, had been absent as long as she could, upon excuses of looking to their accommodation, which she found rather better than she expected, was compelled to return, and converse with Valancourt alone. They talked of the character of the scenes they had passed, of the natural history of the country, of poetry, and of St. Aubert; a subject on which Emily always spoke and listened to with peculiar pleasure.

The travellers passed an agreeable evening, but St. Aubert was fatigued with his journey; and, as Valancourt seemed again sensible of pain, they separated soon after supper.

In the morning St. Aubert found that Valancourt had passed a restless night; that he was feverish, and his wound very painful. The surgeon, when he dressed it, advised him to remain quietly at Beaujeu; advice which was too reasonable to be rejected. St. Aubert, however, had no favourable opinion of this practitioner, and was anxious to commit Valancourt into more skilful hands; but learning, upon enquiry, that there was no town within several leagues which seemed more likely to afford better advice, he altered the plan of his journey, and determined to await the recovery of Valancourt, who, with somewhat more ceremony than sincerity, made many objections to this delay.

By order of his surgeon, Valancourt did not go out of the house that day; but St. Aubert and Emily surveyed with delight the environs of the town, situated at the feet of the Pyrenean Alps, that rose, some in abrupt precipices, and others swelling with woods of cedar, fir, and cypress, which stretched nearly to their highest summits. The cheerful green of the beech and mountain-ash was sometimes seen, like a gleam of light, amidst the dark verdure of the forest; and sometimes a torrent poured its sparkling flood, high among the woods.

Valancourt's indisposition detained the travellers at Beaujeu several days, during which interval St. Aubert had observed his disposition and his talents with the philosophic enquiry so natural to him. He saw a frank and generous nature, full of ardour, highly susceptible of whatever is grand and beautiful, but impetuous, wild, and somewhat romantic. Valancourt had known little of the world. His perceptions were clear, and his feelings just; his indignation of an unworthy, or his admiration of a generous action, were expressed in terms of equal vehemence. St. Aubert sometimes smiled at his warmth, but seldom checked it, and often repeated to himself, "This young man has never been at Paris." A sigh sometimes followed this silent ejaculation. He determined not to leave Valanacourt till he should be perfectly recovered; and, as he was now well enough to travel, though not able to manage his horse, St. Aubert invited him to accompany him for a few days in the carriage. This he the more readily did, since he had discovered that Valancourt was of a family of the same name in Gascony, with whose respectability he was well acquainted. The latter accepted the offer with great pleasure, and they again set forward among these romantic wilds towards Rousillon.

They travelled leisurely; stopping wherever a scene uncommonly grand appeared; frequently alighting to walk to an eminence, whither the mules could not go, from which the prospect opened in greater magnificence; and often sauntering over hillocks covered with lavender, wild thyme, juniper, and tamarisc; and under the shades of woods, between whose boles they caught the long mountain-vista, sublime beyond any thing that Emily had ever imagined.

St. Aubert sometimes amused himself with botanizing, while Valancourt and Emily strolled on; he pointing out to her notice the objects that particularly charmed him, and reciting beautiful passages from such of the Latin and Italian poets as he had heard her admire. In the pauses of conversation, when he thought himself not observed, he frequently fixed his eyes pensively on her countenance, which expressed with so much animation the taste and energy of her mind; and when he spoke again, there was a peculiar tenderness in the tone of his voice, that defeated any attempt to conceal his sentiments. By degrees these silent pauses became more frequent; till Emily, only, betrayed an anxiety to interrupt them; and she, who had been hitherto reserved, would now talk again, and again, of the woods and the vallies and the mountains, to avoid the danger of sympathy and silence.

From Beaujeu the road had constantly ascended, conducting the travellers into the higher regions of the air, where immense glaciers exhibited their frozen horrors, and eternal snow whitened the summits of the mountains. They often paused to contemplate these stupendous scenes, and, seated on some wild cliff, where only the ilex or the larch could flourish, looked over dark forests of fir, and precipices where human foot had never wandered, into the glen—so deep, that the thunder of the torrent, which was seen to foam along the bottom, was scarcely heard to murmur. Over these crags rose others of stupendous height, and fantastic shape; some shooting into cones; others impending far over their base, in huge masses of granite, along whose broken ridges was often lodged a weight of snow, that, trembling even to the vibration of a sound, threatened to bear destruction in its course to the vale. Around, on every side, far as the eye could penetrate, were seen only forms of grandeur—the long perspective of mountain-tops, tinged with ethereal blue, or white with snow; valleys of ice, and forests of gloomy fir. The serenity and clearness of the air in these high regions were particularly delightful to the travellers; it seemed to inspire them with a finer spirit, and diffused an indescribable complacency over their minds. They had no words to express the sublime emotions they felt. A solemn expression characterized the feelings of St. Aubert; tears often came to his eyes, and he frequently walked away from his companions. Valancourt now and then spoke, to point to Emily's notice some feature of the scene. The thinness of the atmosphere, through which every object came so distinctly to the eye, surprised and deluded her; who could scarcely believe that objects, which appeared so near, were, in reality, so distant. The deep silence of these solitudes was broken only at intervals by the scream of the vultures, seen cowering round some cliff below, or by the cry of the eagle sailing high in the air; except when the travellers listened to the hollow thunder that sometimes muttered at their feet. While, above, the deep blue of the heavens was unobscured by the lightest cloud, half way down the mountains, long billows of vapour were frequently seen rolling, now wholly excluding the country below, and now opening, and partially revealing its features. Emily delighted to observe the grandeur of these clouds as they changed in shape and tints, and to watch their various effect on the lower world, whose features, partly veiled, were continually assuming new forms of sublimity.

After traversing these regions for many leagues, they began to descend towards Rousillon, and features of beauty then mingled with the scene. Yet the travellers did not look back without some regret to the sublime objects they had quitted; though the eye, fatigued with the extension of its powers, was glad to repose on the verdure of woods and pastures, that now hung on the margin of the river below; to view again the humble cottage shaded by cedars, the playful group of mountaineer-children, and the flowery nooks that appeared among the hills.

As they descended, they saw at a distance, on the right, one of the grand passes of the Pyrenées into Spain, gleaming with its battlements and towers to the splendour of the setting rays, yellow tops of woods colouring the steeps below, while far above aspired the snowy points of the mountains, still reflecting a rosy hue.

St. Aubert began to look out for the little town he had been directed to by the people of Beaujeu, and where he meant to pass the night; but no habitation yet appeared. Of its distance Valancourt could not assist him to judge, for he had never been so far along this chain of Alps before. There was, however, a road to guide them; and there could be little doubt that it was the right one; for, since they had left Beaujeu, there had been no variety of tracks to perplex or mislead.

The sun now gave his last light, and St. Aubert bade the muleteer proceed with all possible dispatch. He found, indeed, the lassitude of illness return upon him, after a day of uncommon fatigue, both of body and mind, and he longed for repose. His anxiety was not soothed by observing a numerous train, consisting of men, horses, and loaded mules, winding down the steeps of an opposite mountain, appearing and disappearing at intervals among the woods, so that its numbers could not be judged of. Something bright, like arms, glanced in the setting ray, and the military dress was distinguishable upon the men who were in the van, and on others scattered among the troop that followed. As these wound into the vale, the rear of the party emerged from the woods, and exhibited a band of soldiers. St. Aubert's apprehensions now subsided; he had no doubt that the train before him consisted of smugglers, who, in conveying prohibited goods over the Pyrenées, had been encountered, and conquered by a party of troops.

The travellers had lingered so long among the sublimer scenes of these mountains, that they found themselves entirely mistaken in their calculation that they could reach Montigny at sun-set; but, as they wound along the valley, they saw, on a rude Alpine bridge, that united two lofty crags of the glen, a group of mountaineer-children, amusing themselves with dropping pebbles into a torrent below, and watching the stones plunge into the water, that threw up its white spray high in the air as it received them, and returned a sullen sound, which the echoes of the mountains prolonged. Under the bridge was seen a perspective of the valley, with its cataract descending among the rocks, and a cottage on a cliff, overshadowed with pines. It appeared, that they could not be far from some small town. St. Aubert bade the muleteer stop, and then called to the children to enquire if he was near Montigny; but the distance, and the roaring of the waters, would not suffer his voice to be heard; and the crags, adjoining the bridge, were of such tremendous height and steepness, that to have climbed either would have been scarcely practicable to a person unacquainted with the ascent. St. Aubert, therefore, did not waste more moments in delay. They continued to travel long after twilight had obscured the road, which was so broken, that, now thinking it safer to walk than to ride, they all alighted. The moon was rising, but her light was yet too feeble to assist them. While they stepped carefully on, they heard the vesper-bell of a convent. The twilight would not permit them to distinguish any thing like a building, but the sounds seemed to come from some woods, that overhung an acclivity to the right. Valancourt proposed to go in search of this convent. "If they will not accommodate us with a night's lodging," said he, "they may certainly inform us how far we are from Montigny, and direct us towards it." He was bounding forward, without waiting St. Aubert's reply, when the latter stopped him. "I am very weary," said St. Aubert, "and wish for nothing so much as for immediate rest. We will all go to the convent; your good looks would defeat our purpose; but when they see mine and Emily's exhausted countenances, they will scarcely deny us repose."

As he said this, he took Emily's arm within his, and, telling Michael to wait a while in the road with the carriage, they began to ascend towards the woods, guided by the bell of the convent. His steps were feeble, and Valancourt offered him his arm, which he accepted. The moon now threw a faint light over their path, and, soon after, enabled them to distinguish some towers rising above the tops of the woods. Still following the note of the bell, they entered the shade of those woods, lighted only by the moonbeams, that glided down between the leaves, and threw a tremulous uncertain gleam upon the steep track they were winding. The gloom and the silence that prevailed, except when the bell returned upon the air, together with the wildness of the surrounding scene, struck Emily with a degree of fear, which, however, the voice and conversation of Valancourt somewhat repressed. When they had been some time ascending, St. Aubert complained of weariness, and they stopped to rest upon a little green summit, where the trees opened, and admitted the moon-light. He sat down upon the turf, between Emily and Valancourt. The bell had now ceased, and the deep repose of the scene was undisturbed by any sound, for the low dull murmur of some distant torrents might be said to sooth, rather than to interrupt, the silence.

Before them, extended the valley they had quitted; its rocks, and woods to the left, just silvered by the rays, formed a contrast to the deep shadow, that involved the opposite cliffs, whose fringed summits only were tipped with light; while the distant perspective of the valley was lost in the yellow mist of moon-light. The travellers sat for some time wrapt in the complacency which such scenes inspire.

"These scenes," said Valancourt, at length, "soften the heart, like the notes of sweet music, and inspire that delicious melancholy which no person, who had felt it once, would resign for the gayest pleasures. They waken our best and purest feelings, disposing us to benevolence, pity, and friendship. Those whom I love—I always seem to love more in such an hour as this." His voice trembled, and he paused.

St. Aubert was silent; Emily perceived a warm tear fall upon the hand he held; she knew the object of his thoughts; hers too had, for some time, been occupied by the remembrance of her mother. He seemed by an effort to rouse himself. "Yes," said he, with an half-suppressed sigh, "the memory of those we love—of times for ever past! in such an hour as this steals upon the mind, like a strain of distant music in the stillness of night;—all tender and harmonious as this landscape, sleeping in the mellow moon-light." After the pause of a moment, St. Aubert added, "I have always fancied, that I thought with more clearness, and precision, at such an hour than at any other, and that heart must be insensible in a great degree, that does not soften to its influence. But many such there are."

Valancourt sighed.

"Are there, indeed, many such?" said Emily.

"A few years hence, my Emily," replied St. Aubert, "and you may smile at the recollection of that question—if you do not weep to it. But come, I am somewhat refreshed, let us proceed."

Having emerged from the woods, they saw, upon a turfy hillock above, the convent of which they were in search. An high wall, that surrounded it, led them to an ancient gate, at which they knocked; and the poor monk, who opened it, conducted them into a small adjoining room, where he desired they would wait while he informed the superior of their request. In this interval, several friars came in separately to look at them; and at length the first monk returned, and they followed him to a room, where the superior was sitting in an arm chair, with a large folio volume, printed in black letter, open on a desk before him. He received them with courtesy, though he did not rise from his seat; and, having asked them a few questions, granted their request. After a short conversation, formal and solemn on the part of the superior, they withdrew to the apartment where they were to sup, and Valancourt, whom one of the inferior friars civilly desired to accompany, went to seek Michael and his mules. They had not descended half way down the cliffs, before they heard the voice of the muleteer echoing far and wide. Sometimes he called on St. Aubert, and sometimes on Valancourt; who having, at length, convinced him that he had nothing to fear either for himself,

or his master; and having disposed of him, for the night, in
a cottage on the skirts of the woods, returned to sup with
his friends, on such sober fare as the monks thought it prudent to set before them. While St. Aubert was too much
indisposed to share it, Emily, in her anxiety for her father,
forgot herself; and Valancourt, silent and thoughtful, yet
never inattentive to them, appeared particularly solicitous
to accommodate and relieve St. Aubert, who often observed,
while his daughter was pressing him to eat, or adjusting
the pillow she had placed in the back of his arm-chair, that
Valancourt fixed on her a look of pensive tenderness, which
he was not displeased to understand.

They separated at an early hour, and retired to their
respective apartments. Emily was shown to hers by a nun of
the convent, whom she was glad to dismiss, for her heart
was melancholy, and her attention so much abstracted, that
conversation with a stranger was painful. She thought her
father daily declining, and attributed his present fatigue
more to the feeble state of his frame, than to the difficulty of
the journey. A train of gloomy ideas haunted her mind, till
she fell asleep.

In about two hours after, she was awakened by the chim-
ing of a bell, and then heard quick steps pass along the
gallery, into which her chamber opened. She was so little
accustomed to the manners of a convent, as to be alarmed
by this circumstance; her fears, ever alive for her father,
suggested that he was very ill, and she rose in haste to go to
him. Having paused, however, to let the persons in the gallery pass before she opened her door, her thoughts, in the
mean time, recovered from the confusion of sleep, and she
understood that the bell was the call of the monks to
prayers. It had now ceased, and, all being again still, she
forbore to go to St. Aubert's room. Her mind was not disposed for immediate sleep, and the moon-light, that shone
into her chamber, invited her to open the casement, and
look out upon the country.

It was a still and beautiful night, the sky was unobscured by any cloud, and scarce a leaf of the woods beneath trembled in the air. As she listened, the mid-night hymn of the monks rose softly from a chapel, that stood on one of the lower cliffs, an holy strain, that seemed to ascend through the silence of night to heaven, and her thoughts ascended with it. From the consideration of his works, her mind arose to the adoration of the Deity, in his goodness and power; wherever she turned her view, whether on the sleeping earth, or to the vast regions of space, glowing with worlds beyond the reach of human thought, the sublimity of God, and the majesty of his presence appeared. Her eyes were filled with tears of awful love and admiration; and she felt that pure devotion, superior to all the distinctions of human system, which lifts the soul above this world, and seems to expand it into a nobler nature; such devotion as can, perhaps, only be experienced, when the mind, rescued, for a moment, from the humbleness of earthly considerations, aspires to contemplate His power in the sublimity of His works, and His goodness in the infinity of His blessings.

> ———"Is it not now the hour,
> The holy hour, when to the cloudless height
> Of yon starred concave climbs the full-orbed moon,
> And to this nether world in solemn stillness
> Gives sign, that to the list'ning ear of Heaven
> Religion's voice should plead? The very babe
> Knows this, and, 'chance awak'd, his little hands
> Lifts to the gods, and on his innocent couch
> Calls down a blessing."
>
> CARACTACUS

The midnight chant of the monks soon after dropped into silence; but Emily remained at the casement, watching the setting moon, and the valley sinking into deep shade, and willing to prolong her present state of mind. At length she retired to her mattress, and sunk into tranquil slumber.

* * *

Volume Two

CHAPTER V

"Dark power! with shudd'ring, meek submitted thought
Be mine to read the visions old
Which thy awak'ning bards have told,
And, lest they meet my blasted view,
Hold each strange tale devoutly true."

COLLINS' ODE TO FEAR

Emily was recalled from a kind of slumber, into which she had, at length, sunk, by a quick knocking at her chamber door. She started up in terror, for Montoni and Count Morano instantly came to her mind;* but, having listened in silence for some time, and recognising the voice of Annette, she rose and opened the door. "What brings you hither so early?" said Emily, trembling excessively. She was unable to support herself, and sat down on the bed.

"Dear ma'amselle!" said Annette, "do not look so pale. I am quite frightened to see you. Here is a fine bustle below stairs, all the servants running to and fro, and none of them fast enough! Here is a bustle, indeed, all of a sudden, and nobody knows for what!"

"Who is below besides them?" said Emily, "Annette, do not trifle with me!"

* He has made persistent addresses to Emily despite her rebuffs.—ED.

"Not for the world, ma'amselle, I would not trifle for the world; but one cannot help making one's remarks, and there is the Signor in such a bustle, as I never saw him before; and he has sent me to tell you, ma'am, to get ready immediately."

"Good God support me!" cried Emily, almost fainting, "Count Morano is below, then!"

"No, ma'amselle, he is not below that I know of," replied Annette, "only his *Excellenza* sent me to desire you would get ready directly to leave Venice, for that the gondolas would be at the steps of the canal in a few minutes: but I must hurry back to my lady, who is just at her wits end, and knows not which way to turn for haste."

"Explain, Annette, explain the meaning of all this before you go," said Emily, so overcome with surprise and timid hope, that she had scarcely breath to speak.

"Nay, ma'amselle, that is more than I can do. I only know that the Signor is just come home in a very ill humour, that he has had us all called out of our beds, and tells us we are all to leave Venice immediately."

"Is Count Morano to go with the Signor?" said Emily, "and whither are we going?"

"I know neither, ma'am, for certain; but I heard Ludovico say something about going, after we got to *Terra-firma,* to the Signor's castle among some mountains, that he talked of."

"The Apennines!" said Emily, eagerly, "O! then I have little to hope!"

"That is the very place, ma'am. But cheer up, and do not take it so much to heart, and think what a little time you have to get ready in, and how impatient the Signor is. Holy St. Mark! I hear the oars on the canal; and now they come nearer, and now they are dashing at the steps below; it is the gondola, sure enough."

Annette hastened from the room; and Emily prepared for this unexpected flight as fast as her trembling hands would permit, not perceiving, that any change in her situation could possibly be for the worse. She had scarcely thrown her books and clothes into her travelling trunk, when, receiving a second summons, she went down to her aunt's dressing-room, where she found Montoni impatiently reproving his wife for delay.* He went out, soon after, to give some further orders to his people, and Emily then enquired the occasion of this hasty journey; but her aunt appeared to be as ignorant as herself, and to undertake the journey with more reluctance.

The family at length embarked, but neither Count Morano, or Cavigni, was of the party. Somewhat revived by observing this, Emily, when the gondolieri dashed their oars in the water, and put off from the steps of the portico, felt like a criminal, who receives a short reprieve. Her heart beat yet lighter, when they emerged from the canal into the ocean, and lighter still, when they skimmed past the walls of St. Mark, without having stopped to take up Count Morano.

The dawn now began to tint the horizon, and to break upon the shores of the Adriatic. Emily did not venture to ask any questions of Montoni, who sat, for some time, in gloomy silence, and then rolled himself up in his cloak, as if to sleep, while Madame Montoni did the same; but Emily, who could not sleep, undrew one of the little curtains of the gondola, and looked out upon the sea. The rising dawn now enlightened the mountain-tops of Friuli, but their lower sides, and the distant waves, that rolled at their feet, were still in deep shadow. Emily, sunk in tranquil melancholy, watched the strengthening light spreading upon the ocean, shewing successively Venice and her islets,

---

* Montoni is now married to Madame Cheron, St. Aubert's sister.—ED.

and the shores of Italy, along which boats, with their pointed latin sails, began to move.

The gondolieri were frequently hailed, at this early hour, by the market-people, as they glided by towards Venice, and the *Lagune* soon displayed a gay scene of innumerable little barks, passing from *Terra-firma* with provisions. Emily gave a last look to that splendid city, but her mind was then occupied by considering the probable events, that awaited her, in the scenes, to which she was removing, and with conjectures, concerning the motive of this sudden journey. It appeared, upon calmer consideration, that Montoni was removing her to his secluded castle, because he could there, with more probability of success, attempt to terrify her into obedience; or, that, should its gloomy and sequestered scenes fail of this effect, her forced marriage with the Count could there be solemnized with the secrecy, which was necessary to the honour of Montoni. The little spirit, which this reprieve had recalled, now began to fail, and, when Emily reached the shore, her mind had sunk into all its former depression.

Montoni did not embark on the Brenta, but pursued his way in carriages across the country, towards the Apennine; during which journey, his manner to Emily was so particularly severe, that this alone would have confirmed her late conjecture, had any such confirmation been necessary. Her senses were now dead to the beautiful country, through which she travelled. Sometimes she was compelled to smile at the *naïveté* of Annette, in her remarks on what she saw, and sometimes to sigh, as a scene of peculiar beauty recalled Valancourt to her thoughts, who was indeed seldom absent from them, and of whom she could never hope to hear in the solitude, to which she was hastening.

At length, the travellers began to ascend among the Apennines. The immense pine forests, which, at that period, overhung these mountains, and between which the road wound, excluded all view but of the cliffs aspiring above, except, that, now and then, an opening through the dark woods allowed the eye a momentary glimpse of the country below. The gloom of these shades, their solitary silence, except when the breeze swept over their summits, the tremendous precipices of the mountains, that came partially to the eye, each assisted to raise the solemnity of Emily's feelings into awe; she saw only images of gloomy grandeur, or of dreadful sublimity, around her; other images, equally gloomy and equally terrible, gleamed on her imagination. She was going she scarcely knew whither, under the dominion of a person, from whose arbitrary disposition she had already suffered so much, to marry, perhaps, a man who possessed neither her affection, or esteem; or to endure, beyond the hope of succour, whatever punishment revenge, and that Italian revenge, might dictate.—The more she considered what might be the motive of the journey, the more she became convinced, that it was for the purpose of concluding her nuptials with Count Morano, with that secrecy which her resolute resistance had made necessary to the honour, if not to the safety, of Montoni. From the deep solitudes, into which she was immerging, and from the gloomy castle, of which she had heard some mysterious hints, her sick heart recoiled in despair, and she experienced, that, though her mind was already occupied by peculiar distress, it was still alive to the influence of new and local circumstance; why else did she shudder at the idea of this desolate castle?

As the travellers still ascended among the pine forests, steep rose over steep, the mountains seemed to multiply, as they went, and what was the summit of one eminence proved to be only the base of another. At length, they reached a little plain, where the drivers stopped to rest the mules, whence a scene of such extent and magnificence opened below, as drew even from Madame Montoni a note of admiration. Emily lost, for a moment, her sorrows, in the immensity of nature. Beyond the amphi-theatre of mountains, that stretched below, whose tops appeared as numerous almost, as the waves of the sea, and whose feet were concealed by the forests—extended the *Campagna* of Italy, where cities and rivers, and woods and all the glow of cultivation were mingled in gay confusion. The Adriatic bounded the horizon, into which the Po and the Brenta, after winding through the whole extent of the landscape, poured their fruitful waves. Emily gazed long on the splendours of the world she was quitting, of which the whole magnificence seemed thus given to her sight only to increase her regret on leaving it; for her, Valancourt alone was in that world; to him alone her heart turned, and for him alone fell her bitter tears.

From this sublime scene the travellers continued to ascend among the pines, till they entered a narrow pass of the mountains, which shut out every feature of the distant country, and, in its stead, exhibited only tremendous crags, impending over the road, where no vestige of humanity, or even of vegetation, appeared, except here and there the trunk and scathed branches of an oak, that hung nearly headlong from the rock, into which its strong roots had fastened. This pass, which led into the heart of the Apennine, at length opened to day, and a scene of mountains stretched in long perspective, as wild as any the travellers had yet passed. Still vast pine forests hung upon their base, and crowned the ridgy precipice, that rose perpendicularly from the vale, while, above, the rolling mists caught the sunbeams, and touched their cliffs with all the magical colouring of light and shade. The scene seemed perpetually changing, and its features to assume new forms, as the winding road brought them to the eye in different attitudes; while the shifting vapours, now partially concealing their minuter beauties and now illuminating them with splendid tints, assisted the illusions of the sight.

Though the deep valleys between these mountains were, for the most part, clothed with pines, sometimes an abrupt opening presented a perspective of only barren rocks, with a cataract flashing from their summit among broken cliffs, till its waters, reaching the bottom, foamed along with unceasing fury; and sometimes pastoral scenes exhibited their "green delights" in the narrow vales, smiling amid surrounding horror. There herds and flocks of goats and sheep, browsing under the shade of hanging woods, and the shepherd's little cabin, reared on the margin of a clear stream, presented a sweet picture of repose.

Wild and romantic as were these scenes, their character had far less of the sublime, than had those of the Alps, which guard the entrance of Italy. Emily was often elevated, but seldom felt those emotions of indescribable awe, which she had so continually experienced, in her passage over the Alps.

Towards the close of day, the road wound into a deep valley. Mountains, whose shaggy steeps appeared to be inaccessible, almost surrounded it. To the east, a vista opened, that exhibited the Apennines in their darkest horrors; and the long perspective of retiring summits, rising over each other, their ridges clothed with pines, exhibited a stronger image of grandeur, than any that Emily had yet seen. The sun had just sunk below the top of the mountains she was descending, whose long shadow stretched athwart the valley, but his sloping rays, shooting through an opening of the cliffs, touched with a yellow gleam the summits of the forest, that hung upon the opposite steeps, and streamed in full splendour upon the towers and battlements of a castle, that spread its extensive ramparts along the brow of a precipice above. The splendour of these illumined objects was heightened by the contrasted shade, which involved the valley below.

"There," said Montoni, speaking for the first time in several hours, "is Udolpho."

Emily gazed with melancholy awe upon the castle, which she understood to be Montoni's; for, though it was now lighted up by the setting sun, the gothic greatness of its features, and its mouldering walls of dark grey stone, rendered it a gloomy and sublime object. As she gazed, the light died away on its walls, leaving a melancholy purple tint, which spread deeper and deeper, as the thin vapour crept up the mountain, while the battlements above were still tipped with splendour. From those too, the rays soon faded, and the whole edifice was invested with the solemn duskiness of evening. Silent, lonely and sublime, it seemed to stand the sovereign of the scene, and to frown defiance on all, who dared to invade its solitary reign. As the twilight deepened, its features became more awful in obscurity, and Emily continued to gaze, till its clustering towers were alone seen, rising over the tops of the woods, beneath whose thick shade the carriages soon after began to ascend.

The extent and darkness of these tall woods awakened terrific images in her mind, and she almost expected to see banditti start up from under the trees. At length, the carriages emerged upon a healthy rock, and, soon after, reached the castle gates, where the deep tone of the portal bell, which was struck upon to give notice of their arrival, increased the fearful emotions, that had assailed Emily. While they waited till the servant within should come to open the gates, she anxiously surveyed the edifice: but the gloom, that overspread it, allowed her to distinguish little more than a part of its outline, with the massy walls of the ramparts, and to know, that it was vast, ancient and dreary. From the parts she saw, she judged of the heavy strength and extent of the whole. The gateway before her, leading into the courts, was of gigantic size, and was defended by two round towers, crowned by overhanging turrets, embattled, where, instead of banners, now waved long grass and wild plants, that had taken root among the mouldering stones, and which seemed to sigh, as the breeze rolled past, over the desolation around them. The towers were united by a curtain, pierced and embattled also, below which appeared the pointed arch of an huge portcullis, surmounting the gates: from these, the walls of the ramparts extended to other towers, overlooking the precipice, whose shattered outline, appearing on a gleam, that lingered in the west, told of the ravages of war.—Beyond these all was lost in the obscurity of evening.

While Emily gazed with awe upon the scene, footsteps were heard within the gates, and the undrawing of bolts; after which an ancient servant of the castle appeared, forcing back the huge folds of the portal, to admit his lord. As the carriage-wheels rolled heavily under the portcullis, Emily's heart sunk, and she seemed, as if she was going into her prison; the gloomy court, into which she passed, served to confirm the idea, and her imagination, ever awake to circumstance, suggested even more terrors, than her reason could justify.

Another gate delivered them into the second court, grass-grown, and more wild than the first, where, as she surveyed through the twilight its desolation—its lofty walls, overtopt with briony, moss and night-shade, and the embattled towers that rose above,—long-suffering and murder came to her thoughts. One of those instantaneous and unaccountable convictions, which sometimes conquer even strong minds, impressed her with its horror. The sentiment was not diminished, when she entered an extensive gothic hall, obscured by the gloom of evening, which a light, glimmering at a distance through a long perspective of arches, only rendered more striking. As a servant brought the lamp nearer, partial gleams fell upon the pillars and the pointed arches, forming a strong contrast with their shadows, that stretched along the pavement and the walls.

The sudden journey of Montoni had prevented his people from making any other preparations for his reception, than could be had in the short interval, since the arrival of the servant, who had been sent forward from Venice; and this, in some measure, may account for the air of extreme desolation, that every where appeared.

The servant, who came to light Montoni, bowed in silence, and the muscles of his countenance relaxed with no symptom of joy.—Montoni noticed the salutation by a slight motion of his hand, and passed on, while his lady, following, and looking round with a degree of surprise and discontent, which she seemed fearful of expressing, and Emily, surveying the extent and grandeur of the hall in timid wonder, approached a marble stair-case. The arches here opened to a lofty vault, from the centre of which hung a tripod lamp, which a servant was hastily lighting; and the rich fret-work of the roof, a corridor, leading into several upper apartments, and a painted window, stretching nearly from the pavement to the ceiling of the hall, became gradually visible.

Having crossed the foot of the stair-case, and passed through an anti-room, they entered a spacious apartment, whose walls, wainscoted with black larch-wood, the growth of the neighbouring mountains, were scarcely distinguishable from darkness itself. "Bring more light," said Montoni, as he entered. The servant, setting down his lamp, was withdrawing to obey him, when Madame Montoni observing, that the evening air of this mountainous region was cold, and that she should like a fire, Montoni ordered that wood might be brought.

While he paced the room with thoughtful steps, and Madame Montoni sat silently on a couch, at the upper end of it, waiting till the servant returned, Emily was observing the singular solemnity and desolation of the apartment, viewed, as it now was, by the glimmer of the single lamp, placed near a large Venetian mirror, that duskily reflected the scene, with the tall figure of Montoni passing slowly along, his arms folded, and his countenance shaded by the plume, that waved in his hat.

From the contemplation of this scene, Emily's mind proceeded to the apprehension of what she might suffer in it, till the remembrance of Valancourt, far, far distant! came to her heart, and softened it into sorrow. A heavy sigh escaped her: but, trying to conceal her tears, she walked away to one of the high windows, that opened upon the ramparts, below which, spread the woods she had passed in her approach to the castle. But the night-shade sat deeply on the mountains beyond, and their indented outline alone could be faintly traced on the horizon, where a red streak yet glimmered in the west. The valley between was sunk in darkness.

The scene within, upon which Emily turned on the opening of the door, was scarcely less gloomy. The old servant, who had received them at the gates, now entered, bending under a load of pine-branches, while two of Montoni's Venetian servants followed with lights.

"Your *Excellenza* is welcome to the castle," said the old man, as he raised himself from the hearth, where he had laid the wood: "it has been a lonely place a long while; but you will excuse it, Signor, knowing we had but short notice. It is near two years, come next feast of St. Mark, since your *Excellenza* was within these walls."

"You have a good memory, old Carlo," said Montoni: "it is thereabout; and how hast thou contrived to live so long?"

"A-well-a-day, sir, with much ado; the cold winds, that blow through the castle in winter, are almost too much for me; and I thought sometimes of asking your *Excellenza* to let me leave the mountains, and go down into the lowlands. But I don't know how it is—I am loth to quit these old walls I have lived in so long."

"Well, how have you gone on in the castle, since I left it?" said Montoni.

"Why much as usual, Signor, only it wants a good deal of repairing. There is the north tower—some of the battlements have tumbled down, and had liked one day to have knocked my poor wife (God rest her soul!) on the head. Your *Excellenza* must know"—

"Well, but the repairs," interrupted Montoni.

"Aye, the repairs," said Carlo: "a part of the roof of the great hall has fallen in, and all the winds from the mountains rushed through it last winter, and whistled through the whole castle so, that there was no keeping one's self warm, be where one would. There, my wife and I used to sit shivering over a great fire in one corner of the little hall, ready to die with cold, and"—

"But there are no more repairs wanted," said Montoni, impatiently.

"O Lord! your *Excellenza*, yes—the wall of the rampart has tumbled down in three places; then, the stairs, that lead to the west gallery, have been a long time so bad, that it is dangerous to go up them; and the passage leading to the great oak chamber, that overhangs the north rampart—one night last winter I ventured to go there by myself, and your *Excellenza*"—

"Well, well, enough of this," said Montoni, with quickness: "I will talk more with thee to-morrow."

The fire was now lighted; Carlo swept the hearth, placed chairs, wiped the dust from a large marble table that stood near it, and then left the room.

Montoni and his family drew round the fire. Madame Montoni made several attempts at conversation, but his sullen answers repulsed her, while Emily sat endeavouring to acquire courage enough to speak to him. At length, in a tremulous voice, she said, "May I ask, sir, the motive of this sudden journey?"—After a long pause, she recovered sufficient courage to repeat the question.

"It does not suit me to answer enquiries," said Montoni, "nor does it become you to make them; time may unfold them all: but I desire I may be no further harassed, and I recommend it to you to retire to your chamber, and to endeavour to adopt a more rational conduct, than that of yielding to fancies, and to a sensibility, which, to call it by the gentlest name, is only a weakness."

Emily rose to withdraw. "Good night, madam," said she to her aunt, with an assumed composure, that could not disguise her emotion.

"Good night, my dear," said Madame Montoni, in a tone of kindness, which her niece had never before heard from her; and the unexpected endearment brought tears to Emily's eyes. She curtsied to Montoni, and was retiring; "But you do not know the way to your chamber," said her aunt. Montoni called the servant, who waited in the antiroom, and bade him send Madame Montoni's woman, with whom, in a few minutes, Emily withdrew.

"Do you know which is my room?" said she to Annette, as they crossed the hall.

"Yes, I believe I do, ma'amselle; but this is such a strange rambling place! I have been lost in it already: they call it the double chamber, over the fourth rampart, and I went up this great stair-case to it. My lady's room is at the other end of the castle."

Emily ascended the marble stair-case, and came to the corridor, as they passed through which, Annette resumed her chat—"What a wild lonely place this is, ma'am! I shall be quite frightened to live in it. How often, and often I have wished myself in France again! I little thought, when I came with my lady to see the world, that I should ever be shut up in such a place as this, or I would never have left my own country! This way, ma'amselle, down this turning. I can almost believe in giants again, and such like, for this is just like one of their castles; and, some night or other; I suppose I shall see fairies too, hopping about in that great old hall, that looks more like a church, with its huge pillars, than any thing else."

"Yes," said Emily, smiling, and glad to escape from more serious thought, "if we come to the corridor, about midnight, and look down into the hall, we shall certainly see it illuminated with a thousand lamps, and the fairies tripping in gay circles to the sound of delicious music; for it is in such places as this, you know, that they come to hold their revels. But I am afraid, Annette, you will not be able to pay the necessary penance for such a sight: and, if once they hear your voice, the whole scene will vanish in an instant."

"O! if you will bear me company, ma'amselle, I will come to the corridor, this very night, and I promise you I will hold my tongue; it shall not be my fault if the show vanishes.—But do you think they will come?"

"I cannot promise that with certainty, but I will venture to say, it will not be your fault if the enchantment should vanish."

"Well, ma'amselle, that is saying more than I expected of you: but I am not so much afraid of fairies, as of ghosts, and they say there are a plentiful many of them about the castle: now I should be frightened to death, if I should chance to see any of them. But hush! ma'amselle, walk softly! I have thought, several times, something passed by me."

"Ridiculous!" said Emily, "you must not indulge such fancies."

"O ma'am! they are not fancies, for aught I know; Benedetto says these dismal galleries and halls are fit for nothing but ghosts to live in; and I verily believe, if I *live* long in them I shall turn to one myself!"

"I hope," said Emily, "you will not suffer Signor Montoni to hear of these weak fears; they would highly displease him."

"What, you know then, ma'amselle, all about it!" rejoined Annette. "No, no, I do know better than to do so; though, if the Signor can sleep sound, nobody else in the castle has any right to lie awake, I am sure." Emily did not appear to notice this remark.

"Down this passage, ma'amselle; this leads to a back staircase. O! if I see any thing, I shall be frightened out of my wits!"

"That will scarcely be possible," said Emily, smiling, as she followed the winding of the passage, which opened into another gallery: and then Annette, perceiving that she had missed her way, while she had been so eloquently haranguing on ghosts and fairies, wandered about through other passages and galleries, till, at length, frightened by their intricacies and desolation, she called aloud for assistance: but they were beyond the hearing of the servants, who were on the other side of the castle, and Emily now opened the door of a chamber on the left.

"O! do not go in there, ma'amselle," said Annette, "you will only lose yourself further."

"Bring the light forward," said Emily, "we may possibly find our way through these rooms."

Annette stood at the door, in an attitude of hesitation, with the light held up to shew the chamber, but the feeble rays spread through not half of it. "Why do you hesitate?" said Emily, "let me see whither this room leads."

Annette advanced reluctantly. It opened into a suite of spacious and ancient apartments, some of which were hung with tapestry, and others wainscoted with cedar and black larch-wood. What furniture there was, seemed to be almost as old as the rooms, and retained an appearance of grandeur, though covered with dust, and dropping to pieces with the damps, and with age.

"How cold these rooms are, ma'amselle!" said Annette: "nobody has lived in them for many, many years, they say. Do let us go."

"They may open upon the great stair-case, perhaps," said Emily, passing on till she came to a chamber, hung with pictures, and took the light to examine that of a soldier on horseback in a field of battle.—He was darting his spear upon a man, who lay under the feet of the horse, and who held up one hand in a supplicating attitude. The soldier, whose beaver was up, regarded him with a look of vengeance, and the countenance, with that expression, struck Emily as resembling Montoni. She shuddered, and turned from it. Passing the light hastily over several other pictures, she came to one concealed by a veil of black silk. The singularity of the circumstance struck her, and she stopped before it, wishing to remove the veil, and examine what could thus carefully be concealed, but somewhat wanting courage. "Holy Virgin! what can this mean?" exclaimed Annette. "This is surely the picture they told me of at Venice."

"What picture?" said Emily. "Why a picture—a picture," replied Annette, hesitatingly—"but I never could make out exactly what it was about, either."

"Remove the veil, Annette."

"What! I, ma'amselle!—I! not for the world!" Emily, turning round, saw Annette's countenance grow pale. "And pray, what have you heard of this picture, to terrify you so, my good girl?" said she. "Nothing, ma'amselle: I have heard nothing, only let us find our way out."

"Certainly: but I wish first to examine the picture; take the light, Annette, while I lift the veil." Annette took the light, and immediately walked away with it, disregarding Emily's calls to stay, who, not choosing to be left alone in the dark chamber, at length followed her. "What is the reason of this, Annette?" said Emily, when she overtook her, "what have you heard concerning that picture, which makes you so unwilling to stay when I bid you?"

"I don't know what is the reason, ma'amselle," replied Annette, "nor any thing about the picture, only I have heard there is something very dreadful belonging to it—and that it has been covered up in black *ever since*—and that nobody has looked at it for a great many years—and it somehow has to do with the owner of this castle before Signor Montoni came to the possession of it—and"—

"Well, Annette," said Emily, smiling, "I perceive it is as you say—that you know nothing about the picture."

"No, nothing, indeed, ma'amselle, for they made me promise never to tell: but"—

"Well," rejoined Emily, who observed that she was struggling between her inclination to reveal a secret, and her apprehension for the consequence, "I will enquire no further"—

"No, pray, ma'am, do not."

"Lest you should tell all," interrupted Emily.

Annette blushed, and Emily smiled, and they passed on to the extremity of this suite of apartments, and found themselves after some farther perplexity, once more at the top of the marble stair-case, where Annette left Emily, while she went to call one of the servants of the castle to shew them to the chamber, for which they had been seeking.

While she was absent, Emily's thoughts returned to the picture; an unwillingness to tamper with the integrity of a servant, had checked her enquiries on this subject, as well as concerning some alarming hints, which Annette had dropped respecting Montoni; though her curiosity was entirely awakened, and she had perceived, that her questions might easily be answered. She was now, however, inclined to go back to the apartment and examine the picture; but the loneliness of the hour and of the place, with the melancholy silence that reigned around her, conspired with a certain degree of awe, excited by the mystery attending this picture, to prevent her. She determined, however, when daylight should have re-animated her spirits, to go thither and remove the veil. As she leaned from the corridor, over the stair-case, and her eyes wandered round, she again observed, with wonder, the vast strength of the walls, now somewhat decayed, and the pillars of solid marble, that rose from the hall, and supported the roof.

A servant now appeared with Annette, and conducted Emily to her chamber, which was in a remote part of the castle, and at the end of the very corridor, from whence the suite of apartments opened, through which they had been wandering. The lonely aspect of her room made Emily unwilling that Annette should leave her immediately, and the dampness of it chilled her with more than fear. She begged Caterina, the servant of the castle, to bring some wood and light a fire.

"Aye, lady, it's many a year since a fire was lighted here," said Caterina.

"You need not tell us that, good woman," said Annette; "every room in the castle feels like a well. I wonder how you contrive to live here; for my part, I wish myself at Venice again." Emily waved her hand for Caterina to fetch the wood.

"I wonder, ma'am, why they call this the double chamber?" said Annette, while Emily surveyed it in silence and saw that it was lofty and spacious, like the others she had seen, and, like many of them, too, had its walls lined with dark larch-wood. The bed and other furniture was very ancient, and had an air of gloomy grandeur, like all that she had seen in the castle. One of the high casements, which she opened, overlooked a rampart, but the view beyond was hid in darkness.

In the presence of Annette, Emily tried to support her spirits, and to restrain the tears, which, every now and then, came to her eyes. She wished much to enquire when Count Morano was expected at the castle, but an unwillingness to ask unnecessary questions, and to mention family concerns to a servant, withheld her. Meanwhile, Annette's thoughts were engaged upon another subject: she dearly loved the marvellous, and had heard of a circumstance, connected with the castle, that highly gratified this taste. Having been enjoined not to mention it, her inclination to tell it was so strong, that she was every instant on the point of speaking what she had heard. Such a strange circumstance, too, and to be obliged to conceal it, was a severe punishment; but she knew, that Montoni might impose one much severer, and she feared to incur it by offending him.

Caterina now brought the wood, and its bright blaze dispelled, for a while, the gloom of the chamber. She told Annette, that her lady had enquired for her, and Emily was once again left to her own sad reflections. Her heart was not yet hardened against the stern manners of Montoni, and she was nearly as much shocked now, as she had been when she first witnessed them. The tenderness and affection, to which she had been accustomed, till she lost her parents, had made her particularly sensible to any degree of unkindness, and such a reverse as this no apprehension had prepared her to support.

To call off her attention from subjects, that pressed heavily upon her spirits, she rose and again examined her room and its furniture. As she walked round it, she passed a door, that was not quite shut, and, perceiving, that it was not the one, through which she entered, she brought the light forward to discover whither it led. She opened it, and, going forward, had nearly fallen down a steep, narrow stair-case, that wound from it, between two stone walls. She wished to know to what it led, and was the more anxious, since it communicated so immediately with her apartment; but, in the present state of her spirits, she wanted courage to venture into the darkness alone. Closing the door, therefore, she endeavoured to fasten it, but, upon further examination, perceived, that it had no bolts on the chamber side, though it had two on the other. By placing a heavy chair against it, she in some measure remedied the defect; yet she was still alarmed at the thought of sleeping in this remote room alone, with a door opening she knew not whither, and which could not be perfectly fastened on the inside. Sometimes she wished to entreat of Madame Montoni, that Annette might have leave to remain with her all night, but was deterred by an apprehension of betraying what would be thought childish fears, and by an unwillingness to increase the apt terrors of Annette.

Her gloomy reflections were, soon after, interrupted by a footstep in the corridor, and she was glad to see Annette enter with some supper, sent by Madame Montoni. Having a table near the fire, she made the good girl sit down and sup with her; and, when their little repast was over, Annette, encouraged by her kindness and stirring the wood into a blaze, drew her chair upon the hearth, nearer to Emily, and said,—"Did you ever hear, ma'amselle, of the strange accident, that made the Signor lord of this castle?"

"What wonderful story have you now to tell?" said Emily, concealing the curiosity, occasioned by the mysterious hints she had formerly heard on that subject.

"I have heard all about it, ma'amselle," said Annette, looking round the chamber and drawing closer to Emily; "Benedetto told it me as we travelled together: says he, 'Annette, you don't know about this castle here, that we are going to?' No, says I, Mr. Benedetto, pray what do you know? But, ma'amselle, you can keep a secret, or I would not tell it you for the world; for I promised never to tell, and they say, that the Signor does not like to have it talked of."

"If you promised to keep this secret," said Emily, "you do right not to mention it."

Annette paused a moment, and then said, "O, but to you, ma'amselle, to you I may tell it safely, I know."

Emily smiled, "I certainly shall keep it as faithfully as yourself, Annette."

Annette replied very gravely, that would do, and proceeded—"This castle, you must know, ma'amselle, is very old, and very strong, and has stood out many sieges, as they say. Now it was not Signor Montoni's always, nor his father's; no; but, by some law or other, it was to come to the Signor, if the lady died unmarried."

"What lady?" said Emily.

"I am not come to that yet," replied Annette, "it is the lady I am going to tell you about, ma'amselle: but, as I was saying, this lady lived in the castle, and had every thing very grand about her, as you may suppose, ma'amselle. The Signor used often to come to see her, and was in love with her, and offered to marry her; for, though he was somehow related, that did not signify. But she was in love with somebody else, and would not have him, which made him very angry, as they say, and you know, ma'amselle, what an ill-looking gentleman he is, when he is angry. Perhaps she saw him in a passion, and therefore would not have him. But, as I was saying, she was very melancholy and unhappy, and all that, for a long while, and—Holy Virgin! what noise is that? did not you hear a sound, ma'amselle?"

"It was only the wind," said Emily, "but do come to the end of your story."

"As I was saying—O, where was I?—as I was saying—she was very melancholy and unhappy a long while, and used to walk about upon the terrace, there, under the windows, by herself, and cry so! it would have done your heart good to hear her. That is—I don't mean good, but it would have made you cry too, as they tell me."

"Well, but, Annette, do tell me the substance of your tale."

"All in good time, ma'am; all this I heard before at Venice, but what is to come I never heard till to-day. This happened a great many years ago, when Signor Montoni was quite a young man. The lady—they called her Signora Laurentini, was very handsome, but she used to be in great passions, too, sometimes, as well as the Signor. Finding he could not make her listen to him—what does he do, but leave the castle, and never comes near it for a long time! but it was all one to her; she was just as unhappy whether he was here or not, till one evening, Holy St. Peter! ma'am-selle," cried Annette, "look at that lamp, see how blue it burns!" She looked fearfully round the chamber. "Ridiculous girl!" said Emily, "why will you indulge those fancies? Pray let me hear the end of your story, I am weary."

Annette still kept her eyes on the lamp, and proceeded in a lower voice. "It was one evening, they say, at the latter end of the year, it might be about the middle of September, I suppose, or the beginning of October; nay, for that matter, it might be November, for that, too, is the latter end of the year, but that I cannot say for certain, because they did not tell me for certain themselves. However, it was at the latter end of the year, this grand lady walked out of the castle into the woods below, as she had often done before, all alone, only her maid was with her. The wind blew cold, and strewed the leaves about, and whistled dismally among those great old chestnut trees, that we passed, ma'amselle, as we came to the castle—for Benedetto shewed me the trees as he was talking—the wind blew cold, and her woman would have persuaded her to return: but all would not do, for she was fond of walking in the woods, at evening time, and, if the leaves were falling about her, so much the better.

"Well, they saw her go down among the woods, but night came, and she did not return; ten o'clock, eleven o'clock, twelve o'clock came, and no lady! Well, the servants thought to be sure, some accident had befallen her, and they went out to seek her. They searched all night long, but could not find her, or any trace of her; and, from that day to this, ma'amselle, she has never been heard of."

"Is this true, Annette?" said Emily, in much surprise.

"True, ma'am!" said Annette, with a look of horror, "yes, it is true, indeed. But they do say," she added, lowering her voice, "they do say, that the Signora has been seen, several times since, walking in the woods and about the castle in the night: several of the old servants, who remained here some time after, declare they saw her; and, since then, she has been seen by some of the vassals, who have happened to be in the castle, at night. Carlo, the old steward, could tell such things, they say, if he would."

"How contradictory is this, Annette!" said Emily, "you say nothing has been since known of her, and yet she has been seen!"

"But all this was told me for a great secret," rejoined Annette, without noticing the remark, "and I am sure, ma'am, you would not hurt either me or Benedetto, so much as to go and tell it again." Emily remained silent, and Annette repeated her last sentence.

"You have nothing to fear from my indiscretion," replied Emily, "and let me advise you, my good Annette, be discreet yourself, and never mention what you have just told me to any other person. Signor Montoni, as you say, may be angry if he hears of it. But what enquiries were made concerning the lady?"

"O! a great deal, indeed, ma'amselle, for the Signor laid claim to the castle directly, as being the next heir, and they said, that is the judges, or the senators, or somebody of that sort, said, he could not take possession of it till so many years were gone by, and then, if, after all, the lady could not be found, why she would be as good as dead, and the castle would be his own; and so it is his own. But the story went round, and many strange reports were spread, so very strange, ma'amselle, that I shall not tell them."

"That is stranger still, Annette," said Emily, smiling, and rousing herself from her reverie. "But, when Signora Laurentini was afterwards seen in the castle, did nobody speak to her?"

"Speak—speak to her!" cried Annette, with a look of terror; "no, to be sure."

"And why not?" rejoined Emily, willing to hear further.

"Holy Mother! speak to a spirit!"

"But what reason had they to conclude it was a spirit, unless they had approached, and spoken to it?"

"O ma'amselle, I cannot tell. How can you ask such shocking questions? But nobody ever saw it come in, or go out of the castle; and it was in one place now, and then the next minute in quite another part of the castle; and then it never spoke, and, if it was alive, what should it do in the castle if it never spoke? Several parts of the castle have never been gone into since, they say, for that very reason."

"What, because it never spoke?" said Emily, trying to laugh away the fears, that began to steal upon her.—"No, ma'amselle, no;" replied Annette, rather angrily, "but because something has been seen there. They say, too, there is an old chapel adjoining the west side of the castle, where, any time at midnight, you may hear such groans!—it makes one shudder to think of them!—and strange sights have been seen there—"

"Pr'ythee, Annette, no more of these silly tales," said Emily.

"Silly tales, ma'amselle! O, but I will tell you one story about this, if you please, that Caterina told me. It was one cold winter's night that Caterina (she often came to the castle then, she says, to keep old Carlo and his wife company, and so he recommended her afterwards to the Signor, and she has lived here ever since) Caterina was sitting with them in the little hall, says Carlo, 'I wish we had some of those figs to roast, that lie in the store-closet, but it is a long way off, and I am loth to fetch them; do, Caterina,' says he, 'for you are young and nimble, do bring us some, the fire is in a nice trim for roasting them; they lie,' says he, 'in such a corner of the store-room, at the end of the north-gallery; here, take the lamp,' says he, 'and mind, as you go up the great stair-case, that the wind, through the roof, does not blow it out.' So, with that, Caterina took the lamp—Hush! ma'amselle, I surely heard a noise!"

Emily, whom Annette had now infected with her own terrors, listened attentively; but every thing was still, and Annette proceeded:

"Caterina went to the north-gallery, that is the wide gallery we passed, ma'am, before we came to the corridor, here. As she went with the lamp in her hand, thinking of nothing at all—There, again!" cried Annette, suddenly—"I heard it again!—it was not fancy, ma'amselle!"

"Hush!" said Emily, trembling. They listened, and, continuing to sit quite still, Emily heard a low knocking against the wall. It came repeatedly. Annette then screamed loudly, and the chamber door slowly opened.—It was Caterina, come to tell Annette, that her lady wanted her. Emily, though she now perceived who it was, could not immediately overcome her terror; while Annette, half laughing, half crying, scolded Caterina heartily for thus alarming them; and was also terrified lest what she had told had been overheard.—Emily, whose mind was deeply impressed by the chief circumstance of Annette's relation, was unwilling to be left alone, in the present state of her spirits; but, to avoid offending Madame Montoni, and betraying her own weakness, she struggled to overcome the illusions of fear, and dismissed Annette for the night.

When she was alone, her thoughts recurred to the strange history of Signora Laurentini and then to her own strange situation, in the wild and solitary mountains of a foreign country, in the castle, and the power of a man, to whom, only a few preceding months, she was an entire stranger; who had already exercised an usurped authority over her, and whose character she now regarded, with a degree of terror, apparently justified by the fears of others. She knew, that he had invention equal to the conception and talents to the execution of any project, and she greatly feared he had a heart too void of feeling to oppose the perpetration of whatever his interest might suggest. She had long observed the unhappiness of Madame Montoni, and had often been witness to the stern and contemptuous behaviour she received from her husband. To these circumstances, which conspired to give her just cause for alarm, were now added those thousand nameless terrors, which exist only in active imaginations, and which set reason and examination equally at defiance.

Emily remembered all that Valancourt had told her, on the eve of her departure from Languedoc, respecting Montoni, and all that he had said to dissuade her from venturing on the journey. His fears had often since appeared to her prophetic—now they seemed confirmed. Her heart, as it gave her back the image of Valancourt, mourned in vain regret, but reason soon came with a consolation, which, though feeble at first, acquired vigour from reflection. She considered, that, whatever might be her sufferings, she had withheld from involving him in misfortune, and that, whatever her future sorrows could be, she was, at least, free from self-reproach.

Her melancholy was assisted by the hollow sighings of the wind along the corridor and round the castle. The cheerful blaze of the wood had long been extinguished, and she sat with her eyes fixed on the dying embers, till a loud gust, that swept through the corridor, and shook the doors and casements, alarmed her, for its violence had moved the chair she had placed as a fastening, and the door, leading to the private stair-case, stood half open. Her curiosity and her fears were again awakened. She took the lamp to the top of the steps, and stood hesitating whether to go down; but again the profound stillness and the gloom of the place awed her, and, determining to enquire further, when day-light might assist the search, she closed the door, and placed against it a stronger guard.

She now retired to her bed, leaving the lamp burning on the table; but its gloomy light, instead of dispelling her fear, assisted it; for, by its uncertain rays, she almost fancied she saw shapes flit past her curtains and glide into the remote obscurity of her chamber.—The castle clock struck one before she closed her eyes to sleep.

[from] CHAPTER VI

"I think it is the weakness of mine eyes,
That shapes this monstrous apparition.
It comes upon me!"

JULIUS CÆSAR

———————

Daylight dispelled from Emily's mind the glooms of superstition, but not those of apprehension. The Count Morano
was the first image, that occurred to her waking thoughts,
and then came a train of anticipated evils, which she could
neither conquer, or avoid. She rose, and, to relieve her mind
from the busy ideas, that tormented it, compelled herself to
notice external objects. From her casement she looked out
upon the wild grandeur of the scene, closed nearly on all
sides by alpine steeps, whose tops, peeping over each other,
faded from the eye in misty hues, while the promontories
below were dark with woods, that swept down to their base,
and stretched along the narrow valleys. The rich pomp of
these woods was particularly delightful to Emily; and she
viewed with astonishment the fortifications of the castle
spreading along a vast extent of rock, and now partly in decay, the grandeur of the ramparts below, and the towers and
battlements and various features of the fabric above. From
these her sight wandered over the cliffs and woods into the
valley, along which foamed a broad and rapid stream, seen
falling among the crags of an opposite mountain, now flashing in the sun-beams, and now shadowed by over-arching
pines, till it was entirely concealed by their thick foliage.

Again it burst from beneath this darkness in one broad sheet of foam, and fell thundering into the vale. Nearer, towards the west, opened the mountain-vista, which Emily had viewed with such sublime emotion, on her approach to the castle: a thin dusky vapour, that rose from the valley, overspread its features with a sweet obscurity. As this ascended and caught the sun-beams, it kindled into a crimson tint, and touched with exquisite beauty the woods and cliffs, over which it passed to the summit of the mountains; then, as the veil drew up, it was delightful to watch the gleaming objects, that progressively disclosed themselves in the valley—the green turf—dark woods—little rocky recesses—a few peasants' huts—the foaming stream—a herd of cattle, and various images of pastoral beauty. Then, the pine-forests brightened, and then the broad breast of the mountains, till, at length, the mist settled round their summit, touching them with a ruddy glow. The features of the vista now appeared distinctly, and the broad deep shadows, that fell from the lower cliffs, gave strong effect to the streaming splendour above; while the mountains, gradually sinking in the perspective, appeared to shelve into the Adriatic sea, for such Emily imagined to be the gleam of blueish light, that terminated the view.

Thus she endeavoured to amuse her fancy, and was not unsuccessful. The breezy freshness of the morning, too, revived her. She raised her thoughts in prayer, which she felt always most disposed to do, when viewing the sublimity of nature, and her mind recovered its strength.

When she turned from the casement, her eyes glanced upon the door she had so carefully guarded, on the preceding night, and she now determined to examine whither it led; but, on advancing to remove the chairs, she perceived, that they were already moved a little way. Her surprise cannot easily be imagined, when, in the next minute, she perceived that the door was fastened.—She felt, as if she had seen an apparition. The door of the corridor was locked as she had left it, but this door, which could be secured only on the outside, must have been bolted, during the night. She became seriously uneasy at the thought of sleeping again in a chamber, thus liable to intrusion, so remote, too, as it was from the family, and she determined to mention the circumstance to Madame Montoni, and to request a change.

After some perplexity she found her way into the great hall, and to the room, which she had left, on the preceding night, where breakfast was spread, and her aunt was alone, for Montoni had been walking over the environs of the castle, examining the condition of its fortifications, and talking for some time with Carlo. Emily observed, that her aunt had been weeping, and her heart softened towards her, with an affection, that shewed itself in her manner, rather than in words, while she carefully avoided the appearance of having noticed, that she was unhappy. She seized the opportunity of Montoni's absence to mention the circumstance of the door, to request that she might be allowed another apartment, and to enquire again, concerning the occasion of their sudden journey. On the first subject her aunt referred her to Montoni, positively refusing to interfere in the affair; on the last, she professed utter ignorance.

Emily, then, with a wish of making her aunt more reconciled to her situation, praised the grandeur of the castle and the surrounding scenery, and endeavoured to soften every unpleasing circumstance attending it. But, though misfortune had somewhat conquered the asperities of Madame Montoni's temper, and, by increasing her cares for herself, had taught her to feel in some degree for others, the capricious love of rule, which nature had planted and habit had nourished in her heart, was not subdued. She could not now deny herself the gratification of tyrannizing over the innocent and helpless Emily, by attempting to ridicule the taste she could not feel.

Her satirical discourse was, however, interrupted by the entrance of Montoni, and her countenance immediately assumed a mingled expression of fear and resentment, while he seated himself at the breakfast-table, as if unconscious of there being any person but himself in the room.

Emily, as she observed him in silence, saw, that his countenance was darker and sterner than usual. "O could I know," said she to herself, "what passes in that mind; could I know the thoughts, that are known there, I should no longer be condemned to this torturing suspense!" Their breakfast passed in silence, till Emily ventured to request, that another apartment might be allotted to her, and related the circumstance which made her wish it.

"I have no time to attend to these idle whims," said Montoni, "that chamber was prepared for you, and you must rest contented with it. It is not probable, that any person would take the trouble of going to that remote staircase, for the purpose of fastening a door. If it was not fastened, when you entered the chamber, the wind, perhaps, shook the door and made the bolts slide. But I know not why I should undertake to account for so trifling an occurrence."

This explanation was by no means satisfactory to Emily, who had observed, that the bolts were rusted, and consequently could not be thus easily moved; but she forbore to say so, and repeated her request.

"If you will not release yourself from the slavery of these fears," said Montoni, sternly, "at least forbear to torment others by the mention of them. Conquer such whims, and endeavour to strengthen your mind. No existence is more contemptible than that, which is embittered by fear." As he said this, his eye glanced upon Madame Montoni, who coloured highly, but was still silent. Emily, wounded and disappointed, thought her fears were, in this instance, too reasonable to deserve ridicule; but, perceiving, that, however they might oppress her, she must endure them, she tried to withdraw her attention from the subject.

Carlo soon after entered with some fruit: "Your *Excellenza* is tired after your long ramble," said he, as he set the fruit upon the table; "but you have more to see after breakfast. There is a place in the vaulted passage leading to"—

Montoni frowned upon him, and waved his hand for him to leave the room. Carlo stopped, looked down, and then added, as he advanced to the breakfast-table, and took up the basket of fruit, "I made bold, your *Excellenza*, to bring some cherries, here, for my honoured lady and my young mistress. Will your ladyship taste them, madam?" said Carlo, presenting the basket, "they are very fine ones, though I gathered them myself, and from an old tree, that catches all the south sun; they are as big as plums, your ladyship."

"Very well, old Carlo," said Madame Montoni; "I am obliged to you."

"And the young Signora, too, she may like some of them," rejoined Carlo, turning with the basket to Emily, "it will do me good to see her eat some."

"Thank you, Carlo," said Emily, taking some cherries, and smiling kindly.

"Come, come," said Montoni, impatiently, "enough of this. Leave the room, but be in waiting. I shall want you presently."

Carlo obeyed and Montoni, soon after, went out to examine further into the state of the castle; while Emily remained with her aunt, patiently enduring her ill humour, and endeavouring, with much sweetness, to sooth her affliction, instead of resenting its effect.

When Madame Montoni retired to her dressing-room, Emily endeavoured to amuse herself by a view of the castle.

Through a folding door, she passed from the great hall to the ramparts, which extended along the brow of the precipice, round three sides of the edifice; the fourth was guarded by the high walls of the courts, and by the gate-way, through which she had passed, on the preceding evening. The grandeur of the broad ramparts, and the changing scenery they overlooked, excited her high admiration; for the extent of the terraces allowed the features of the country to be seen in such various points of view, that they appeared to form new landscapes. She often paused to examine the gothic magnificence of Udolpho, its proud irregularity, its lofty towers and battlements, its high-arched casements, and its slender watch-towers, perched upon the corners of turrets. Then she would lean on the wall of the terrace, and, shuddering, measure with her eye the precipice below, till the dark summits of the woods arrested it. Wherever she turned, appeared mountain-tops, forests of pine and narrow glens, opening among the Apennines and retiring from the sight into inaccessible regions.

While she thus leaned, Montoni, followed by two men, appeared, ascending a winding path, cut in the rock below. He stopped upon a cliff, and, pointing to the ramparts, turned to his followers, and talked with much eagerness of gesticulation.—Emily perceived, that one of these men was Carlo; the other was in the dress of a peasant, and he alone seemed to be receiving the directions of Montoni.

She withdrew from the walls, and pursued her walk, till she heard at a distance the sound of carriage wheels, and then the loud bell of the portal, when it instantly occurred to her, that Count Morano was arrived. As she hastily passed the folding doors from the terrace, towards her own apartment, several persons entered the hall by an opposite door. She saw them at the extremity of the arcades, and immediately retreated; but the agitation of her spirits, and the extent and duskiness of the hall, had prevented her from distinguishing the persons of the strangers. Her fears, how-ever, had but one object, and they had called up that object to her fancy;—she believed that she had seen Count Morano.

When she thought that they had passed the hall, she ventured again to the door, and proceeded, unobserved, to her room, where she remained, agitated with apprehensions, and listening to every distant sound. At length, hearing voices on the rampart, she hastened to her window, and ob-served Montoni, with Signor Cavigni, walking below, con-versing earnestly, and often stopping and turning towards each other, at which times their discourse seemed to be un-commonly interesting.

Of the several persons who had appeared in the hall, here was Cavigni alone: but Emily's alarm was soon after height-ened by the steps of some one in the corridor, who, she ap-prehended, brought a message from the Count. In the next moment, Annette appeared.

"Ah! ma'amselle," said she, "here is the Signor Cavigni arrived! I am sure I rejoiced to see a christian person in this place; and then he is so good-natured too, he always takes so much notice of me!—And here is also Signor Verezzi, and who do you think besides, ma'amselle?"

"I cannot guess, Annette; tell me quickly."

"Nay, ma'am, do guess once."

"Well, then," said Emily, with assumed composure, "it is —Count Morano, I suppose."

"Holy Virgin!" cried Annette, "are you ill, ma'amselle? you are going to faint! let me get some water."

Emily sunk into a chair; "Stay, Annette," said she, feebly, "do not leave me—I shall soon be better; open the casement. —The Count, you say—he is come then?"

"Who, I!—the Count! No, ma'amselle, I did not say so."

"He is *not* come then?" said Emily, eagerly. "No, ma'am-selle."

"You are sure of it?"

"Lord bless me!" said Annette, "you recover very suddenly, ma'am! why, I thought you was dying, just now."

"But the Count—you are sure, is not come?"

"O yes, quite sure of that, ma'amselle. Why, I was looking out through the grate in the north turret, when the carriages drove into the court-yard, and I never expected to see such a goodly sight in this dismal old castle! but here are masters and servants, too, enough to make the place ring again. O! I was ready to leap through the rusty old bars, for joy!—O! who would ever have thought of seeing a christian face in this huge dreary house? I could have kissed the very horses that brought them."

"Well, Annette, well, I am better now."

"Yes, ma'amselle, I see you are. O! all the servants will lead merry lives here, now; we shall have singing and dancing in the little hall, for the Signor cannot hear us there—and droll stories—Ludovico's come, ma'am; yes, there is Ludovico come with them! You remember Ludovico, ma'am —a tall, handsome, young man—Signor Cavigni's lacquey— who always wears his cloak with such a grace, thrown round his left arm, and his hat set on so smartly, all on one side, and—"

"No," said Emily, who was wearied by her loquacity.

"What, ma'amselle! don't you remember Ludovico—who rowed the Cavaliero's gondola, at the last regatta, and won the prize? And who used to sing such sweet verses about Orlandos and about the Black-a-moors, too; and Charly— Charly—magne, yes, that was the name, all under my lattice, in the west portico, on the moon-light nights at Venice? O! I have listened to him!"—

"I fear, to thy peril, my good Annette," said Emily; "for it seems his verses have stolen thy heart. But let me advise you; if it is so, keep the secret; never let him know it."

"Ah—ma'amselle!—how can one keep such a secret as that?"

"Well, Annette, I am now so much better, that you may leave me."

"O, but, ma'amselle, I forgot to ask—how did you sleep in this dreary old chamber last night?"—"As well as usual."—"Did you hear no noises?"—"None."—"Nor see any thing?"—"Nothing."—"Well, that is surprising!"—"Not in the least: and now tell me, why you ask these questions."

"O, ma'amselle! I would not tell you for the world, nor all I have heard about this chamber, either; it would frighten you so."

"If that is all, you have frightened me already, and may therefore tell me what you know, without hurting your conscience."

"O Lord! they say the room is haunted, and has been so these many years."

"It is by a ghost, then, who can draw bolts," said Emily, endeavouring to laugh away her apprehensions; "for I left that door open, last night, and found it fastened this morning."

Annette turned pale, and said not a word.

"Do you know whether any of the servants fastened this door in the morning, before I rose?"

"No, ma'am, that I will be bound they did not; but I don't know: shall I go and ask, ma'amselle?" said Annette, moving hastily towards the corridor.

"Stay, Annette, I have other questions to ask; tell me what you have heard concerning this room, and whither that stair-case leads."

"I will go and ask it all directly, ma'am; besides, I am sure my lady wants me. I cannot stay now, indeed, ma'am."

She hurried from the room, without waiting Emily's reply, whose heart, lightened by the certainty, that Morano was not arrived, allowed her to smile at the superstitious terror, which had seized on Annette; for, though she sometimes felt its influence herself, she could smile at it, when apparent in other persons.

Montoni having refused Emily another chamber, she determined to bear with patience the evil she could not remove, and, in order to make the room as comfortable as possible, unpacked her books, her sweet delight in happier days, and her soothing resource in the hours of moderate sorrow: but there were hours when even these failed of their effect; when the genius, the taste, the enthusiasm of the sublimest writers were felt no longer.

Her little library being arranged on a high chest, part of the furniture of the room, she took out her drawing utensils, and was tranquil enough to be pleased with the thought of sketching the sublime scenes, beheld from her windows; but she suddenly checked this pleasure, remembering how often she had soothed herself by the intention of obtaining amusement of this kind, and had been prevented by some new circumstance of misfortune.

"How can I suffer myself to be deluded by hope," said she, "and, because Count Morano is not yet arrived, feel a momentary happiness? Alas! what is it to me, whether he is here to-day, or to-morrow, if he comes at all?—and that he will come—it were weakness to doubt."

To withdraw her thoughts, however, from the subject of her misfortunes, she attempted to read, but her attention wandered from the page, and, at length, she threw aside the book, and determined to explore the adjoining chambers of the castle. Her imagination was pleased with the view of ancient grandeur, and an emotion of melancholy awe awakened all its powers, as she walked through rooms, obscure and desolate, where no footsteps had passed probably for many years, and remembered the strange history of the former possessor of the edifice. This brought to her recollection the veiled picture, which had attracted her curiosity, on the preceding night, and she resolved to examine it. As she passed through the chambers, that led to this, she found herself somewhat agitated; its connection with the late lady of the castle, and the conversation of Annette, together with the circumstance of the veil, throwing a mystery over the subject, that excited a faint degree of terror. But a terror of this nature, as it occupies and expands the mind, and elevates it to high expectation, is purely sublime, and leads us, by a kind of fascination, to seek even the object, from which we appear to shrink.

Emily passed on with faltering steps, and having paused a moment at the door, before she attempted to open it, she then hastily entered the chamber, and went towards the picture, which appeared to be enclosed in a frame of uncommon size, that hung in a dark part of the room. She paused again, and then, with a timid hand, lifted the veil; but instantly let it fall—perceiving that what it had concealed was no picture, and, before she could leave the chamber, she dropped senseless on the floor.

When she recovered her recollection, the remembrance of what she had seen had nearly deprived her of it a second time. She had scarcely strength to remove from the room, and regain her own; and, when arrived there, wanted courage to remain alone. Horror occupied her mind, and excluded, for a time, all sense of past, and dread of future misfortune: she seated herself near the casement, because from thence she heard voices, though distant, on the terrace, and might see people pass, and these, trifling as they were, were reviving circumstances. When her spirits had recovered their tone, she considered, whether she should mention what she had seen to Madame Montoni, and various and important motives urged her to do so, among which the least was the hope of the relief, which an overburdened mind finds in speaking of the subject of its interest. But she was aware of the terrible consequences, which such a communication might lead to; and, dreading the indiscretion of her aunt, at length, endeavoured to arm herself with resolution to observe a profound silence, on the subject. Montoni and Verezzi soon after passed under the casement, speaking cheerfully, and their voices revived her. Presently the Signors Bertolini and Cavigni joined the party on the terrace, and Emily, supposing that Madame Montoni was then alone, went to seek her; for the solitude of her chamber, and its proximity to that where she had received so severe a shock, again affected her spirits.

She found her aunt in the dressing-room, preparing for dinner. Emily's pale and affrighted countenance alarmed even Madame Montoni; but she had sufficient strength of mind to be silent on the subject, that still made her shudder, and which was ready to burst from her lips. In her aunt's apartment she remained, till they both descended to dinner. There she met the gentlemen lately arrived, who had a kind of busy seriousness in their looks, which was somewhat unusual with them, while their thoughts seemed too much occupied by some deep interest, to suffer them to bestow much attention either on Emily, or Madame Montoni. They spoke little, and Montoni less. Emily, as she now looked on him, shuddered. The horror of the chamber rushed on her mind. Several times the colour faded from her cheeks, and she feared, that illness would betray her emotions, and compel her to leave the room; but the strength of her resolution remedied the weakness of her frame; she obliged herself to converse, and even tried to look cheerful.

Montoni evidently laboured under some vexation, such as would probably have agitated a weaker mind, or a more susceptible heart, but which appeared, from the sternness of his countenance, only to bend up his faculties to energy and fortitude.

It was a comfortless and silent meal. The gloom of the castle seemed to have spread its contagion even over the gay countenance of Cavigni, and with this gloom was mingled a fierceness, such as she had seldom seen him indicate. Count Morano was not named, and what conversation there was, turned chiefly upon the wars, which at that time agitated the Italian states, the strength of the Venetian armies, and the characters of their generals.

After dinner, when the servants had withdrawn, Emily learned, that the cavalier, who had drawn upon himself the vengeance of Orsino, had since died of his wounds, and that strict search was still making for his murderer. The intelligence seemed to disturb Montoni, who mused, and then enquired, where Orsino had concealed himself. His guests, who all, except Cavigni, were ignorant, that Montoni had himself assisted him to escape from Venice, replied, that he had fled in the night with such precipitation and secrecy, that his most intimate companions knew not whither. Montoni blamed himself for having asked the question, for a second thought convinced him, that a man of Orsino's suspicious temper was not likely to trust any of the persons present with the knowledge of his asylum. He considered himself, however, as entitled to his utmost confidence, and did not doubt, that he should soon hear of him.

Emily retired with Madame Montoni, soon after the cloth was withdrawn, and left the cavaliers to their secret councils, but not before the significant frowns of Montoni had warned his wife to depart, who passed from the hall to the ramparts, and walked, for some time, in silence, which Emily did not interrupt, for her mind was also occupied by interests of its own. It required all her resolution, to forbear communicating to Madame Montoni the terrible subject, which still thrilled her every nerve with horror; and sometimes she was on the point of doing so, merely to obtain the relief of a moment; but she knew how wholly she was in the power of Montoni, and, considering, that the indiscretion of her aunt might prove fatal to them both, she compelled herself to endure a present and an inferior evil, rather than

to tempt a future and a heavier one. A strange kind of presentiment frequently, on this day, occurred to her;—it
seemed as if her fate rested here, and was by some invisible
means connected with this castle.

"Let me not accelerate it," said she to herself: "for whatever I may be reserved, let me, at least, avoid self-reproach."

As she looked on the massy walls of the edifice, her melancholy spirits represented it to be her prison; and she started
as at a new suggestion, when she considered how far distant
she was from her native country, from her little peaceful
home, and from her only friend—how remote was her hope
of happiness, how feeble the expectation of again seeing
him! Yet the idea of Valancourt, and her confidence in his
faithful love, had hitherto been her only solace, and she
struggled hard to retain them. A few tears of agony started
to her eyes, which she turned aside to conceal.

While she afterwards leaned on the wall of the rampart,
some peasants, at a little distance, were seen examining a
breach, before which lay a heap of stones, as if to repair it,
and a rusty old cannon, that appeared to have fallen from
its station above. Madame Montoni stopped to speak to the
men, and enquired what they were going to do. "To repair
the fortifications, your ladyship," said one of them; a labour
which she was somewhat surprised, that Montoni should
think necessary, particularly since he had never spoken of
the castle, as of a place, at which he meant to reside for any
considerable time; but she passed on towards a lofty arch,
that led from the south to the east rampart, and which adjoined the castle, on one side, while, on the other, it supported a small watch-tower, that entirely commanded the
deep valley below. As she approached this arch, she saw,
beyond it, winding along the woody descent of a distant
mountain, a long troop of horse and foot, whom she knew
to be soldiers, only by the glitter of their pikes and other
arms, for the distance did not allow her to discover the

colour of their liveries. As she gazed, the vanguard issued from the woods into the valley, but the train still continued to pour over the remote summit of the mountain, in endless succession; while, in the front, the military uniform became distinguishable, and the commanders, riding first, and seeming, by their gestures, to direct the march of those that followed, at length, approached very near to the castle.

Such a spectacle, in these solitary regions, both surprised and alarmed Madame Montoni, and she hastened towards some peasants, who were employed in raising bastions before the south rampart, where the rock was less abrupt than elsewhere. These men could give no satisfactory answers to her enquiries, but, being roused by them, gazed in stupid astonishment upon the long cavalcade. Madame Montoni, then thinking it necessary to communicate farther the subject of her alarm, sent Emily to say, that she wished to speak to Montoni; an errand her niece did not approve, for she dreaded his frowns, which she knew this message would provoke; but she obeyed in silence.

As she drew near the apartment, in which he sat with his guests, she heard them in earnest and loud dispute, and she paused a moment, trembling at the displeasure, which her sudden interruption would occasion. In the next, their voices sunk all together; she then ventured to open the door, and, while Montoni turned hastily and looked at her, without speaking, she delivered her message.

"Tell Madame Montoni I am engaged," said he.

Emily then thought it proper to mention the subject of her alarm. Montoni and his companions rose instantly and went to the windows, but, these not affording them a view of the troops, they at length proceeded to the ramparts, where Cavigni conjectured it to be a legion of *Condottieri*, on their march towards Modena.

One part of the cavalcade now extended along the valley, and another wound among the mountains towards the

north, while some troops still lingered on the woody precipices, where the first had appeared, so that the great length
of the procession seemed to include an whole army. While
Montoni and his family watched its progress, they heard
the sound of trumpets and the clash of cymbals in the vale,
and then others, answering from the heights. Emily listened
with emotion to the shrill blast, that woke the echoes of the
mountains, and Montoni explained the signals, with which
he appeared to be well acquainted, and which meant nothing hostile. The uniforms of the troops, and the kind of
arms they bore, confirmed to him the conjecture of Cavigni,
and he had the satisfaction to see them pass by, without
even stopping to gaze upon his castle. He did not, however,
leave the rampart, till the bases of the mountains had shut
them from his view, and the last murmur of the trumpet
floated away on the wind. Cavigni and Verezzi were in-
spirited by this spectacle, which seemed to have roused all
the fire of their temper; Montoni turned into the castle in
thoughtful silence.

Emily's mind had not yet sufficiently recovered from its
late shock, to endure the loneliness of her chamber, and she
remained upon the ramparts; for Madame Montoni had not
invited her to her dressing-room, whither she had gone evidently in low spirits, and Emily, from her late experience,
had lost all wish to explore the gloomy and mysterious recesses of the castle. The ramparts, therefore, were almost
her only retreat, and here she lingered, till the gray haze of
evening was again spread over the scene.

The cavaliers supped by themselves, and Madame Montoni remained in her apartment, whither Emily went, before she retired to her own. She found her aunt weeping,
and in much agitation. The tenderness of Emily was naturally so soothing, that it seldom failed to give comfort to
the drooping heart: but Madame Montoni's was torn, and
the softest accents of Emily's voice were lost upon it. With

her usual delicacy, she did not appear to observe her aunt's distress, but it gave an involuntary gentleness to her manners, and an air of solicitude to her countenance, which Madame Montoni was vexed to perceive, who seemed to feel the pity of her niece to be an insult to her pride, and dismissed her as soon as she properly could. Emily did not venture to mention again the reluctance she felt to her gloomy chamber, but she requested that Annette might be permitted to remain with her till she retired to rest; and the request was somewhat reluctantly granted. Annette, however, was now with the servants, and Emily withdrew alone.

With light and hasty steps she passed through the long galleries, while the feeble glimmer of the lamp she carried only shewed the gloom around her, and the passing air threatened to extinguish it. The lonely silence, that reigned in this part of the castle, awed her; now and then, indeed, she heard a faint peal of laughter rise from a remote part of the edifice, where the servants were assembled, but it was soon lost, and a kind of breathless stillness remained. As she passed the suite of rooms which she had visited in the morning, her eyes glanced fearfully on the door, and she almost fancied she heard murmuring sounds within, but she paused not a moment to enquire.

Having reached her own apartment, where no blazing wood on the hearth dissipated the gloom, she sat down with a book, to enliven her attention, till Annette should come, and a fire could be kindled. She continued to read till her light was nearly expired, but Annette did not appear, and the solitude and obscurity of her chamber again affected her spirits, the more, because of its nearness to the scene of horror, that she had witnessed in the morning. Gloomy and fantastic images came to her mind. She looked fearfully towards the door of the stair-case, and then, examining whether it was still fastened, found that it was so. Unable to conquer the uneasiness she felt at the prospect of sleeping again in this remote and insecure apartment, which some person seemed to have entered during the preceding night, her impatience to see Annette, whom she had bidden to enquire concerning this circumstance, became extremely painful. She wished also to question her, as to the object, which had excited so much horror in her own mind, and which Annette on the preceding evening had appeared to be in part acquainted with, though her words were very remote from the truth, and it appeared plainly to Emily, that the girl had been purposely misled by a false report: above all she was surprised, that the door of the chamber, which contained it, should be left unguarded. Such an instance of negligence almost surpassed belief. But her light was now expiring; the faint flashes it threw upon the walls called up all the terrors of fancy, and she rose to find her way to the habitable part of the castle, before it was quite extinguished.

As she opened the chamber door, she heard remote voices, and, soon after, saw a light issue upon the further end of the corridor, which Annette and another servant approached. "I am glad you are come," said Emily: "what has detained you so long? Pray light me a fire immediately."

"My lady wanted me, ma'amselle," replied Annette in some confusion; "I will go and get the wood."

"No," said Caterina, "that is my business," and left the room instantly, while Annette would have followed; but, being called back, she began to talk very loud, and laugh, and seemed afraid to trust a pause of silence.

Caterina soon returned with the wood, and then, when the cheerful blaze once more animated the room, and this servant had withdrawn, Emily asked Annette, whether she had made the enquiry she bade her. "Yes, ma'amselle," said Annette, "but not a soul knows any thing about the matter: and old Carlo,—I watched him well, for they say he knows strange things—old Carlo looked so as I don't know how to tell, and he asked me again and again, if I was sure the door was ever unfastened. Lord, says I—am I sure I am alive? And as for me, ma'am, I am all astounded, as one may say, and would no more sleep in this chamber, than I would on the great cannon at the end of the east rampart." "And what objection have you to that cannon, more than to any of the rest?" said Emily smiling: "the best would be rather a hard bed."

"Yes, ma'amselle, any of them would be hard enough for that matter; but they do say, that something has been seen in the dead of night, standing beside the great cannon, as if to guard it."

"Well! my good Annette, the people who tell such stories, are happy in having you for an auditor, for I perceive you believe them all."

"Dear ma'amselle! I will shew you the very cannon; you can see it from these windows!"

"Well," said Emily, "but that does not prove, that an apparition guards it."

"What! not if I shew you the very cannon! Dear ma'am, you will believe nothing."

"Nothing probably upon this subject, but what I see," said Emily.—"Well, ma'am, but you shall see it, if you will only step this way to the casement."—Emily could not forbear laughing, and Annette looked surprised. Perceiving her extreme aptitude to credit the marvelous, Emily forbore to mention the subject she had intended, lest it should overcome her with ideal terrors, and she began to speak on a lively topic—the regattas of Venice.

"Aye, ma'amselle, those rowing matches," said Annette, "and the fine moon-light nights, are all, that are worth seeing in Venice. To be sure that moon is brighter than any I ever saw; and then to hear such sweet music, too, as Ludovico has often and often sung under the lattice by the west portico! Ma'amselle, it was Ludovico, that told me about that picture, which you wanted so to look at last night, and—"

"What picture?" said Emily, wishing Annette to explain herself.

"O! that terrible picture with the black veil over it."

"You never saw it, then?" said Emily.

"Who, I!—No, ma'amselle, I never did. But this morning," continued Annette, lowering her voice, and looking round the room, "this morning, as it was broad day-light, do you know, ma'am, I took a strange fancy to see it, as I had heard such odd hints about it, and I got as far as the door, and should have opened it, if it had not been locked!"

Emily, endeavouring to conceal the emotion this circumstance occasioned, enquired at what hour she went to the chamber, and found, that it was soon after herself had been there. She also asked further questions, and the answers convinced her, that Annette, and probably her informer, were ignorant of the terrible truth, though in Annette's account something very like the truth, now and then, mingled with the falsehood. Emily now began to fear, that her visit to the chamber had been observed, since the door had been closed, so immediately after her departure; and dreaded lest this should draw upon her the vengeance of Montoni. Her anxiety, also, was excited to know whence, and for what purpose, the delusive report, which had been imposed upon Annette, had originated, since Montoni could only have wished for silence and secrecy; but she felt, that the subject was too terrible for this lonely hour, and she compelled herself to leave it, to converse with Annette, whose chat, simple as it was, she preferred to the stillness of total solitude.

Thus they sat, till near midnight, but not without many hints from Annette, that she wished to go. The embers were now nearly burnt out; and Emily heard, at a distance, the thundering sound of the hall doors, as they were shut for the night. She, therefore, prepared for rest, but was still unwilling that Annette should leave her. At this instant, the great bell of the portal sounded. They listened in fearful expectation, when, after a long pause of silence, it sounded again. Soon after, they heard the noise of carriage wheels in the court-yard. Emily sunk almost lifeless in her chair; "It is the Count," said she.

"What, at this time of night, ma'am!" said Annette: "no, my dear lady. But, for that matter, it is a strange time of night for any body to come!"

"Nay, pr'ythee, good Annette, stay not talking," said Emily in a voice of agony—"Go, pr'ythee, go, and see who it is."

Annette left the room, and carried with her the light, leaving Emily in darkness, which a few moments before would have terrified her in this room, but was now scarcely observed by her. She listened and waited, in breathless expectation, and heard distant noises, but Annette did not return. Her patience, at length, exhausted, she tried to find her way to the corridor, but it was long before she could touch the door of the chamber, and, when she had opened it, the total darkness without made her fear to proceed. Voices were now heard, and Emily even thought she distinguished those of Count Morano, and Montoni. Soon after, she heard steps approaching, and then a ray of light streamed through the darkness, and Annette appeared, whom Emily went to meet.

"Yes, ma'amselle," said she, "you was right, it is the Count sure enough."

"It is he!" exclaimed Emily, lifting her eyes towards heaven and supporting herself by Annette's arm.

"Good Lord! my dear lady, don't be in such a *fluster*, and look so pale, we shall soon hear more."

"We shall, indeed!" said Emily, moving as fast as she was able towards her apartment. "I am not well; give me air."

Annette opened a casement, and brought water. The faintness soon left Emily, but she desired Annette would not go till she heard from Montoni.

"Dear ma'amselle! he surely will not disturb you at this time of night; why he must think you are asleep."

"Stay with me till I am so, then," said Emily, who felt temporary relief from this suggestion, which appeared probable enough, though her fears had prevented its occurring to her. Annette, with secret reluctance, consented to stay, and Emily was now composed enough to ask her some questions; among others, whether she had seen the Count.

"Yes, ma'am, I saw him alight, for I went from hence to the grate in the north turret, that overlooks the inner court-yard, you know. There I saw the Count's carriage, and the Count in it, waiting at the great door,—for the porter was just gone to bed—with several men on horseback all by the light of the torches they carried."—Emily was compelled to smile. "When the door was opened, the Count said something, that I could not make out, and then got out, and another gentleman with him. I thought, to be sure, the Signor was gone to bed, and I hastened away to my lady's dressing-room, to see what I could hear. But in the way I met Ludovico, and he told me that the Signor was up, counselling with his master and the other Signors, in the room at the end of the north gallery; and Ludovico held up his finger, and laid it on his lips, as much as to say—There is more going on, than you think of, Annette, but you must hold your tongue. And so I did hold my tongue, ma'amselle, and came away to tell you directly."

Emily enquired who the cavalier was, that accompanied the Count, and how Montoni received them; but Annette could not inform her.

"Ludovico," she added, "had just been to call Signor Montoni's valet, that he might tell him they were arrived, when I met him."

Emily sat musing, for some time, and then her anxiety was so much increased, that she desired Annette would go to the servants' hall, where it was possible she might hear something of the Count's intention, respecting his stay at the castle.

"Yes, ma'am," said Annette with readiness; "but how am I to find the way, if I leave the lamp with you?"

Emily said she would light her, and they immediately quitted the chamber. When they had reached the top of the great stair-case, Emily recollected, that she might be seen by the Count, and, to avoid the great hall, Annette conducted her through some private passages to a back stair-case, which led directly to that of the servants.

As she returned towards her chamber, Emily began to fear, that she might again lose herself in the intricacies of the castle, and again be shocked by some mysterious spectacle; and, though she was already perplexed by the numerous turnings, she feared to open one of the many doors, that offered. While she stepped thoughtfully along, she fancied, that she heard a low moaning at no great distance, and, having paused a moment, she heard it again and distinctly. Several doors appeared on the right hand of the passage. She advanced, and listened. When she came to the second, she heard a voice, apparently in complaint, within, to which she continued to listen, afraid to open the door, and unwilling to leave it. Convulsive sobs followed, and then the piercing accents of an agonizing spirit burst forth. Emily stood appalled, and looked through the gloom, that surrounded her, in fearful expectation. The lamentations continued. Pity now began to subdue terror; it was possible she might administer comfort to the sufferer, at least, by expressing sympathy, and she laid her hand on the door. While she hesitated she thought she knew this voice, disguised as it was by tones of grief. Having, therefore, set down the lamp in the passage, she gently opened the door, within which all was dark, except that from an inner apartment a partial light appeared; and she stepped softly on. Before she reached it, the appearance of Madame Montoni, leaning on her dressing-table, weeping, and with a handkerchief held to her eyes, struck her, and she paused.

Some person was seated in a chair by the fire, but who it was she could not distinguish. He spoke, now and then, in a low voice, that did not allow Emily to hear what was uttered, but she thought, that Madame Montoni, at those times, wept the more, who was too much occupied by her own distress, to observe Emily, while the latter, though anxious to know what occasioned this, and who was the person admitted at so late an hour to her aunt's dressing-room, forbore to add to her sufferings by surprising her, or to take advantage of her situation, by listening to a private discourse. She, therefore, stepped softly back, and, after some further difficulty, found the way to her own chamber, where nearer interests, at length, excluded the surprise and concern she had felt, respecting Madame Montoni.

Annette, however, returned without satisfactory intelligence, for the servants, among whom she had been, were either entirely ignorant, or affected to be so, concerning the Count's intended stay at the castle. They could talk only of the steep and broken road they had just passed, and of the numerous dangers they had escaped, and express wonder how their lord could choose to encounter all these, in the darkness of night; for they scarcely allowed, that the torches had served for any other purpose but that of shewing the dreariness of the mountains. Annette, finding she could gain no information, left them, making noisy petitions, for more wood on the fire and more supper on the table.

"And now, ma'amselle," added she, "I am so sleepy!—I am sure, if you was so sleepy, you would not desire me to sit up with you."

Emily, indeed, began to think it was cruel to wish it;

she had also waited so long, without receiving a summons
from Montoni, that it appeared he did not mean to disturb
her, at this late hour, and she determined to dismiss Annette. But, when she again looked round her gloomy chamber, and recollected certain circumstances, fear seized her
spirits, and she hesitated.

"And yet it were cruel of me to ask you to stay, till I am
asleep, Annette," said she, "for I fear it will be very long
before I forget myself in sleep."

"I dare say it will be very long, ma'amselle," said Annette.

"But, before you go," rejoined Emily, "let me ask you—
Had Signor Montoni left Count Morano, when you quitted
the hall?"

"O no, ma'am, they were alone together."

"Have you been in my aunt's dressing-room, since you
left me?"

"No, ma'amselle, I called at the door as I passed, but it
was fastened; so I thought my lady was gone to bed."

"Who, then, was with your lady just now?" said Emily,
forgetting, in surprise, her usual prudence.

"Nobody, I believe, ma'am," replied Annette, "nobody
has been with her, I believe, since I left you."

Emily took no further notice of the subject, and, after
some struggle with imaginary fears, her good nature prevailed over them so far, that she dismissed Annette for the
night. She then sat, musing upon her own circumstances
and those of Madame Montoni, till her eye rested on the
miniature picture, which she had found, after her father's
death, among the papers he had enjoined her to destroy. It
was open upon the table, before her, among some loose
drawings, having, with them, been taken out of a little box
by Emily, some hours before. The sight of it called up many
interesting reflections, but the melancholy sweetness of the
countenance soothed the emotions, which these had occasioned. It was the same style of countenance as that of her

late father, and, while she gazed on it with fondness on
this account, she even fancied a resemblance in the features.
But this tranquillity was suddenly interrupted, when she
recollected the words in the manuscript, that had been
found with this picture, and which had formerly occasioned
her so much doubt and horror. At length, she roused herself
from the deep reverie, into which this remembrance had
thrown her; but, when she rose to undress, the silence and
solitude, to which she was left, at this midnight hour, for
not even a distant sound was now heard, conspired with the
impression the subject she had been considering had given
to her mind, to appall her. Annette's hints, too, concerning
this chamber, simple as they were, had not failed to affect
her, since they followed a circumstance of peculiar horror,
which she herself had witnessed, and since the scene of this
was a chamber nearly adjoining her own.

The door of the stair-case was, perhaps, a subject of more
reasonable alarm, and she now began to apprehend, such
was the aptitude of her fears, that this stair-case had some
private communication with the apartment, which she shuddered even to remember. Determined not to undress, she lay
down to sleep in her clothes, with her late father's dog, the
faithful *Manchon,* at the foot of the bed, whom she considered as a kind of guard.

Thus circumstanced, she tried to banish reflection, but
her busy fancy would still hover over the subjects of her
interest, and she heard the clock of the castle strike two, before she closed her eyes.

From the disturbed slumber, into which she then sunk,
she was soon awakened by a noise, which seemed to arise
within her chamber; but the silence, that prevailed, as she
fearfully listened, inclined her to believe, that she had been
alarmed by such sounds as sometimes occur in dreams, and
she laid her head again upon the pillow.

A return of the noise again disturbed her; it seemed to

come from that part of the room, which communicated with the private stair-case, and she instantly remembered the odd circumstance of the door having been fastened, during the preceding night, by some unknown hand. Her late alarming suspicion, concerning its communication, also occurred to her. Her heart became faint with terror. Half raising herself from the bed, and gently drawing aside the curtain, she looked towards the door of the stair-case, but the lamp, that burnt on the hearth, spread so feeble a light through the apartment, that the remote parts of it were lost in shadow. The noise, however, which, she was convinced, came from the door, continued. It seemed like that made by the un-drawing of rusty bolts, and often ceased, and was then re-newed more gently, as if the hand, that occasioned it, was restrained by a fear of discovery. While Emily kept her eyes fixed on the spot, she saw the door move, and then slowly open, and perceived something enter the room, but the ex-treme duskiness prevented her distinguishing what it was. Almost fainting with terror, she had yet sufficient command over herself, to check the shriek, that was escaping from her lips, and, letting the curtain drop from her hand, continued to observe in silence the motions of the mysterious form she saw. It seemed to glide along the remote obscurity of the apartment, then paused, and, as it approached the hearth, she perceived, in the stronger light, what appeared to be a human figure. Certain remembrances now struck upon her heart, and almost subdued the feeble remains of her spirits; she continued, however, to watch the figure, which re-mained for some time motionless, but then, advancing slowly towards the bed, stood silently at the feet, where the curtains, being a little open, allowed her still to see it; ter-ror, however, had now deprived her of the power of discrim-ination, as well as of that of utterance.

Having continued there a moment, the form retreated towards the hearth, when it took the lamp, held it up, surveyed the chamber, for a few moments, and then again advanced towards the bed. The light at that instant awakening the dog, that had slept at Emily's feet, he barked loudly, and, jumping to the floor, flew at the stranger, who struck the animal smartly with a sheathed sword, and, springing towards the bed, Emily discovered—Count Morano!

She gazed at him for a moment in speechless affright, while he, throwing himself on his knee at the bed-side, besought her to fear nothing, and, having thrown down his sword, would have taken her hand, when the faculties, that terror had suspended, suddenly returned, and she sprung from the bed, in the dress, which surely a kind of prophetic apprehension had prevented her, on this night, from throwing aside.

Morano rose, followed her to the door, through which he had entered, and caught her hand, as she reached the top of the stair-case, but not before she had discovered, by the gleam of a lamp, another man half-way down the steps. She now screamed in despair, and, believing herself given up by Montoni, saw, indeed, no possibility of escape.

The Count, who still held her hand, led her back into the chamber.

"Why all this terror?" said he, in a tremulous voice. "Hear me, Emily: I come not to alarm you; no, by Heaven! I love you too well—too well for my own peace."

Emily looked at him for a moment, in fearful doubt.

"Then leave me, sir," said she, "leave me instantly."

"Hear me, Emily," resumed Morano, "hear me! I love, and am in despair—yes—in despair. How can I gaze upon you, and know, that it is, perhaps, for the last time, without suffering all the phrensy of despair? But it shall not be so; you shall be mine, in spite of Montoni and all his villany."

"In spite of Montoni!" cried Emily eagerly: "what is it I hear?"

"You hear, that Montoni is a villain," exclaimed Morano

with vehemence,—"a villain who would have sold you to my love!—Who—"

"And is he less, who would have bought me?" said Emily, fixing on the Count an eye of calm contempt. "Leave the room, sir, instantly," she continued in a voice, trembling between joy and fear, "or I will alarm the family, and you may receive that from Signor Montoni's vengeance, which I have vainly supplicated from his pity." But Emily knew, that she was beyond the hearing of those, who might protect her.

"You can never hope any thing from his pity," said Morano, "he has used me infamously, and my vengeance shall pursue him. And for you, Emily, for you, he has new plans more profitable than the last, no doubt." The gleam of hope, which the Count's former speech had revived, was now nearly extinguished by the latter; and, while Emily's countenance betrayed the emotions of her mind, he endeavoured to take advantage of the discovery.

"I lose time," said he: "I came not to exclaim against Montoni; I came to solicit, to plead—to Emily; to tell her all I suffer, to entreat her to save me from despair, and herself from destruction. Emily! the schemes of Montoni are insearchable, but, I warn you, they are terrible; he has no principle, when interest, or ambition leads. Can I love you, and abandon you to his power? Fly, then, fly from this gloomy prison, with a lover, who adores you! I have bribed a servant of the castle to open the gates, and, before to-morrow's dawn, you shall be far on the way to Venice."

Emily, overcome by the sudden shock she had received, at the moment, too, when she had begun to hope for better days, now thought she saw destruction surround her on every side. Unable to reply, and almost to think, she threw herself into a chair, pale and breathless. That Montoni had formerly sold her to Morano, was very probable; that he had now withdrawn his consent to the marriage, was evident from the Count's present conduct; and it was nearly certain, that a scheme of stronger interest only could have induced the selfish Montoni to forego a plan, which he had hitherto so strenuously pursued. These reflections made her tremble at the hints, which Morano had just given, which she no longer hesitated to believe; and, while she shrunk from the new scenes of misery and oppression, that might await her in the castle of Udolpho, she was compelled to observe, that almost her only means of escaping them was by submitting herself to the protection of this man, with whom evils more certain and not less terrible appeared,— evils, upon which she could not endure to pause for an instant.

Her silence, though it was that of agony, encouraged the hopes of Morano, who watched her countenance with impatience, took again the resisting hand she had withdrawn, and, as he pressed it to his heart, again conjured her to determine immediately. "Every moment we lose, will make our departure more dangerous," said he: "these few moments lost may enable Montoni to overtake us."

"I beseech you, sir, be silent," said Emily faintly: "I am indeed very wretched, and wretched I must remain. Leave me—I command you, leave me to my fate."

"Never!" cried the Count vehemently: "let me perish first! But forgive my violence! the thought of losing you is madness. You cannot be ignorant of Montoni's character, you may be ignorant of his schemes—nay, you must be so, or you would not hesitate between my love and his power."

"Nor do I hesitate," said Emily.

"Let us go, then," said Morano, eagerly kissing her hand, and rising, "my carriage waits, below the castle walls."

"You mistake me, sir," said Emily. "Allow me to thank you for the interest you express in my welfare, and to decide by my own choice. I shall remain under the protection of Signor Montoni."

"Under his protection!" exclaimed Morano, proudly, "his *protection!* Emily, why will you suffer yourself to be thus deluded? I have already told you what you have to expect from his *protection*."

"And pardon me, sir, if, in this instance, I doubt mere assertion, and, to be convinced, require something approaching to proof."

"I have now neither the time, or the means of adducing proof," replied the Count.

"Nor have I, sir, the inclination to listen to it, if you had."

"But you trifle with my patience and my distress," continued Morano. "Is a marriage with a man, who adores you, so very terrible in your eyes, that you would prefer to it all the misery, to which Montoni may condemn you in this remote prison? Some wretch must have stolen those affections, which ought to be mine, or you could not thus obstinately persist in refusing an offer, that would place you beyond the reach of oppression." Morano walked about the room, with quick steps, and a disturbed air.

"This discourse, Count Morano, sufficiently proves, that my affections ought not to be yours," said Emily, mildly, "and this conduct, that I should not be placed beyond the reach of oppression, so long as I remained in your power. If you wish me to believe otherwise, cease to oppress me any longer by your presence. If you refuse this, you will compel me to expose you to the resentment of Signor Montoni."

"Yes, let him come," cried Morano furiously, "and brave *my* resentment! Let him dare to face once more the man he has so courageously injured; danger shall teach him morality, and vengeance justice—let him come, and receive my sword in his heart!"

The vehemence, with which this was uttered, gave Emily new cause of alarm, who arose from her chair, but her trembling frame refused to support her, and she resumed her seat;—the words died on her lips, and, when she looked wistfully towards the door of the corridor, which was locked, she considered it was impossible for her to leave the apartment, before Morano would be apprised of, and able to counteract, her intention.

Without observing her agitation, he continued to pace the room in the utmost perturbation of spirits. His darkened countenance expressed all the rage of jealousy and revenge; and a person, who had seen his features under the smile of ineffable tenderness, which he so lately assumed, would now scarcely have believed them to be the same.

"Count Morano," said Emily, at length recovering her voice, "calm, I entreat you, these transports, and listen to reason, if you will not to pity. You have equally misplaced your love, and your hatred.—I never could have returned the affection, with which you honour me, and certainly have never encouraged it; neither has Signor Montoni injured you, for you must have known, that he had no right to dispose of my hand, had he even possessed the power to do so. Leave, then, leave the castle, while you may with safety. Spare yourself the dreadful consequences of an unjust revenge, and the remorse of having prolonged to me these moments of suffering."

"Is it for mine, or for Montoni's safety, that you are thus alarmed?" said Morano, coldly, and turning towards her with a look of acrimony.

"For both," replied Emily, in a trembling voice.

"Unjust revenge!" cried the Count, resuming the abrupt tones of passion. "Who, that looks upon that face, can imagine a punishment adequate to the injury he would have done me? Yes, I will leave the castle; but it shall not be alone. I have trifled too long. Since my prayers and my sufferings cannot prevail, force shall. I have people in waiting, who shall convey you to my carriage. Your voice will bring no succour; it cannot be heard from this remote part of the castle; submit, therefore, in silence to go with me."

This was an unnecessary injunction, at present; for Emily was too certain, that her call would avail her nothing; and terror had so entirely disordered her thoughts, that she knew not how to plead to Morano, but sat, mute and trembling, in her chair, till he advanced to lift her from it, when she suddenly raised herself, and, with a repulsive gesture, and a countenance of forced serenity, said, "Count Morano! I am now in your power; but you will observe, that this is not the conduct which can win the esteem you appear so solicitous to obtain, and that you are preparing for yourself a load of remorse, in the miseries of a friendless orphan, which can never leave you. Do you believe your heart to be, indeed, so hardened, that you can look without emotion on the suffering, to which you would condemn me?"—

Emily was interrupted by the growling of the dog, who now came again from the bed, and Morano looked towards the door of the stair-case, where no person appearing, he called aloud, "Cesario!"

"Emily," said the Count, "why will you reduce me to adopt this conduct? How much more willingly would I persuade, than compel you to become my wife! but, by Heaven! I will not leave you to be sold by Montoni. Yet a thought glances across my mind, that brings madness with it. I know not how to name it. It is preposterous—it cannot be.—Yet you tremble—you grow pale! It is! it is so;—you—you—love Montoni!" cried Morano, grasping Emily's wrist, and stamping his foot on the floor.

An involuntary air of surprise appeared on her countenance. "If you have indeed believed so," said she, "believe so still."

"That look, those words confirm it," exclaimed Morano, furiously. "No, no, no, Montoni had a richer prize in view, than gold. But he shall not live to triumph over me!—This very instant—"

He was interrupted by the loud barking of the dog.

"Stay, Count Morano," said Emily, terrified by his words, and by the fury expressed in his eyes, "I will save you from this error.—Of all men, Signor Montoni is not your rival; though, if I find all other means of saving myself vain, I will try whether my voice may not arouse his servants to my succour."

"Assertion," replied Morano, "at such a moment, is not to be depended upon. How could I suffer myself to doubt, even for an instant, that he could see you, and not love?— But my first care shall be to convey you from the castle. Cesario! ho,—Cesario!"

A man now appeared at the door of the stair-case, and other steps were heard ascending. Emily uttered a loud shriek, as Morano hurried her across the chamber, and, at the same moment, she heard a noise at the door, that opened upon the corridor. The Count paused an instant, as if his mind was suspended between love and the desire of vengeance; and, in that instant, the door gave way, and Montoni, followed by the old steward and several other persons, burst into the room.

"Draw!" cried Montoni to the Count, who did not pause for a second bidding, but, giving Emily into the hands of the people, that appeared from the stair-case, turned fiercely round. "This in thine heart, villain!" said he, as he made a thrust at Montoni with his sword, who parried the blow, and aimed another, while some of the persons, who had followed him into the room, endeavoured to part the combatants, and others rescued Emily from the hands of Morano's servants.

"Was it for this, Count Morano," said Montoni, in a cool sarcastic tone of voice, "that I received you under my roof, and permitted you, though my declared enemy, to remain under it for the night? Was it, that you might repay my hospitality with the treachery of a fiend, and rob me of my niece?"

"Who talks of treachery?" said Morano, in a tone of unrestrained vehemence. "Let him that does, shew an unblushing face of innocence. Montoni, you are a villain! If there is treachery in this affair, look to yourself as the author of it. *If*—do I say? *I*—whom you have wronged with unexampled baseness, whom you have injured almost beyond redress! But why do I use words?—Come on, coward, and receive justice at my hands!"

"Coward!" cried Montoni, bursting from the people who held him, and rushing on the Count, when they both retreated into the corridor, where the fight continued so desperately, that none of the spectators dared approach them, Montoni swearing, that the first, who interfered, should fall by his sword.

Jealousy and revenge lent all their fury to Morano, while the superior skill and the temperance of Montoni enabled him to wound his adversary, whom his servants now attempted to seize, but he would not be restrained, and, regardless of his wound, continued to fight. He seemed to be insensible both of pain and loss of blood, and alive only to the energy of his passions. Montoni, on the contrary, persevered in the combat, with a fierce, yet wary, valour; he received the point of Morano's sword on his arm, but, almost in the same instant, severely wounded and disarmed him. The Count then fell back into the arms of his servant, while Montoni held his sword over him, and bade him ask his life. Morano, sinking under the anguish of his wound, had scarcely replied by a gesture, and by a few words, feebly articulated, that he would not—when he fainted; and Montoni was then going to have plunged the sword into his breast, as he lay senseless, but his arm was arrested by Cavigni. To the interruption he yielded without much difficulty, but his complexion changed almost to blackness, as he looked upon his fallen adversary, and ordered, that he should be carried instantly from the castle.

In the mean time, Emily, who had been with-held from leaving the chamber during the affray, now came forward into the corridor, and pleaded a cause of common humanity, with the feelings of the warmest benevolence, when she entreated Montoni to allow Morano the assistance in the castle, which his situation required. But Montoni, who had seldom listened to pity, now seemed rapacious of vengeance, and, with a monster's cruelty, again ordered his defeated enemy to be taken from the castle, in his present state, though there were only the woods, or a solitary neighbouring cottage, to shelter him from the night.

The Count's servants having declared, that they would not move him till he revived, Montoni's stood inactive, Cavigni remonstrating, and Emily, superior to Montoni's menaces, giving water to Morano, and directing the attendants to bind up his wound. At length, Montoni had leisure to feel pain from his own hurt, and he withdrew to examine it.

The Count, meanwhile, having slowly recovered, the first object he saw, on raising his eyes, was Emily, bending over him with a countenance strongly expressive of solicitude. He surveyed her with a look of anguish.

"I have deserved this," said he, "but not from Montoni. It is from you, Emily, that I have deserved punishment, yet I receive only pity!" He paused, for he had spoken with difficulty. After a moment, he proceeded. "I must resign you, but not to Montoni. Forgive me the sufferings I have already occasioned you! But for *that* villain—his infamy shall not go unpunished. Carry me from this place," said he to his servants. "I am in no condition to travel: you must, therefore, take me to the nearest cottage, for I will not pass the night under his roof, although I may expire on the way from it."

Cesario proposed to go out, and enquire for a cottage, that might receive his master, before he attempted to remove him: but Morano was impatient to be gone; the anguish of his mind seemed to be even greater than that of his wound, and he rejected, with disdain, the offer of Cavigni to entreat Montoni, that he might be suffered to pass the night in the castle. Cesario was now going to call up the carriage to the great gate, but the Count forbade him. "I cannot bear the motion of a carriage," said he: "call some others of my people, that they may assist in bearing me in their arms."

At length, however, Morano submitted to reason, and consented, that Cesario should first prepare some cottage to receive him. Emily, now that he had recovered his senses, was about to withdraw from the corridor, when a message from Montoni commanded her to do so, and also that the Count, if he was not already gone, should quit the castle immediately. Indignation flashed from Morano's eyes, and flushed his cheeks.

"Tell Montoni," said he, "that I shall go when it suits my own convenience; that I quit the castle, he dares to call his, as I would the nest of a serpent, and that this is not the last he shall hear from me. Tell him, I will not leave *another* murder on his conscience, if I can help it."

"Count Morano! do you know what you say?" said Cavigni.

"Yes, Signor, I know well what I say, and he will understand well what I mean. His conscience will assist his understanding, on this occasion."

"Count Morano," said Verezzi, who had hitherto silently observed him, "dare again to insult my friend, and I will plunge this sword in your body."

"It would be an action worthy the friend of a villain!" said Morano, as the strong impulse of his indignation enabled him to raise himself from the arms of his servants; but the energy was momentary, and he sunk back, exhausted by the effort. Montoni's people, meanwhile, held Verezzi, who seemed inclined, even in this instant, to execute his threat; and Cavigni, who was not so depraved as to abet the cowardly malignity of Verezzi, endeavoured to withdraw him from the corridor; and Emily, whom a compassionate interest had thus long detained, was now quitting it in new terror, when the supplicating voice of Morano arrested her, and, by a feeble gesture, he beckoned her to draw nearer. She advanced with timid steps, but the fainting languor of his countenance again awakened her pity, and overcame her terror.

"I am going from hence for ever" said he: "perhaps, I shall never see you again. I would carry with me your forgiveness, Emily; nay more—I would also carry your good wishes."

"You have my forgiveness, then," said Emily, "and my sincere wishes for your recovery."

"And only for my recovery?" said Morano, with a sigh. "For your general welfare," added Emily.

"Perhaps I ought to be contented with this," he resumed; "I certainly have not deserved more; but I would ask you, Emily, sometimes to think of me, and, forgetting my offence, to remember only the passion which occasioned it. I would ask, alas! impossibilities: I would ask you to love me! At this moment, when I am about to part with you, and that, perhaps, for ever, I am scarcely myself. Emily—may you never know the torture of a passion like mine! What do I say? O, that, for me, you might be sensible of such a passion!"

Emily looked impatient to be gone. "I entreat you, Count, to consult your own safety," said she, "and linger here no longer. I tremble for the consequences of Signor Verezzi's passion, and of Montoni's resentment, should he learn that you are still here."

Morano's face was overspread with a momentary crimson, his eyes sparkled, but he seemed endeavouring to conquer his emotion, and replied in a calm voice, "Since you are interested for my safety, I will regard it, and be gone. But, before I go, let me again hear you say, that you wish me well," said he, fixing on her an earnest and mournful look.

Emily repeated her assurances. He took her hand, which she scarcely attempted to withdraw, and put it to his lips. "Farewel, Count Morano!" said Emily; and she turned to go, when a second message arrived from Montoni, and she again conjured Morano, as he valued his life, to quit the castle immediately. He regarded her in silence, with a look of fixed despair. But she had no time to enforce her compassionate entreaties, and, not daring to disobey the second command of Montoni, she left the corridor, to attend him.

He was in the cedar parlour, that adjoined the great hall, laid upon a couch, and suffering a degree of anguish from his wound, which few persons could have disguised, as he did. His countenance, which was stern, but calm, expressed the dark passion of revenge, but no symptom of pain; bodily pain, indeed, he had always despised, and had yielded only to the strong and terrible energies of the soul. He was attended by old Carlo and by Signor Bertolini, but Madame Montoni was not with him.

Emily trembled, as she approached and received his severe rebuke, for not having obeyed his first summons; and perceived, also, that he attributed her stay in the corridor to a motive, that had not even occurred to her artless mind.

"This is an instance of female caprice," said he, "which I ought to have foreseen. Count Morano, whose suit you obstinately rejected, so long as it was countenanced by me, you favour, it seems, since you find I have dismissed him."

Emily looked astonished. "I do not comprehend you, sir," said she: "You certainly do not mean to imply, that the design of the Count to visit the double-chamber, was founded upon any approbation of mine."

"To that I reply nothing," said Montoni; "but it must

certainly be a more than common interest, that made you plead so warmly in his cause, and that could detain you thus long in his presence, contrary to my express order—in the presence of a man, whom you have hitherto, on all occasions, most scrupulously shunned!"

"I fear, sir, it was a more than common interest, that detained me," said Emily calmly; "for of late I have been inclined to think, that of compassion is an uncommon one. But how could I, could *you*, sir, witness Count Morano's deplorable condition, and not wish to relieve it?"

"You add hypocrisy to caprice," said Montoni, frowning, "and an attempt at satire, to both; but, before you undertake to regulate the morals of other persons, you should learn and practise the virtues, which are indispensable to a woman—sincerity, uniformity of conduct and obedience."

Emily, who had always endeavoured to regulate her conduct by the nicest laws, and whose mind was finely sensible, not only of what is just in morals, but of whatever is beautiful in the female character, was shocked by these words; yet, in the next moment, her heart swelled with the consciousness of having deserved praise, instead of censure, and she was proudly silent. Montoni, acquainted with the delicacy of her mind, knew how keenly she would feel his rebuke; but he was a stranger to the luxury of conscious worth, and, therefore, did not foresee the energy of that sentiment, which now repelled his satire. Turning to a servant who had lately entered the room, he asked whether Morano had quitted the castle. The man answered, that his servants were then removing him, on a couch, to a neighbouring cottage. Montoni seemed somewhat appeased, on hearing this; and, when Ludovico appeared, a few moments after, and said, that Morano was gone, he told Emily she might retire to her apartment. . . .

[*from*] CHAPTER X

At length, she reached her chamber, and, having secured the door of the corridor, felt herself, for a moment, in safety. A profound stillness reigned in this remote apartment, which not even the faint murmur of the most distant sounds now reached. She sat down, near one of the casements, and, as she gazed on the mountain-view beyond, the deep repose of its beauty struck her with all the force of contrast, and she could scarcely believe herself so near a scene of savage discord. The contending elements seemed to have retired from their natural spheres, and to have collected themselves into the minds of men, for there alone the tempest now reigned.

Emily tried to tranquillize her spirits, but anxiety made her constantly listen for some sound, and often look out upon the ramparts, where all, however, was lonely and still. As a sense of her own immediate danger had decreased, her apprehension concerning Madame Montoni heightened, who, she remembered, had been fiercely threatened with confinement in the east turret, and it was possible, that her husband had satisfied his present vengeance with this punishment. She, therefore, determined, when night should return, and the inhabitants of the castle should be asleep, to explore the way to the turret, which, as the direction it stood in was mentioned, appeared not very difficult to be done. She knew, indeed, that although her aunt might be there, she could afford her no effectual assistance, but it might give her some comfort even to know, that she was discovered, and to hear the sound of her niece's voice; for herself, any certainty, concerning Madame Montoni's fate, appeared more tolerable, than this exhausting suspense.

Meanwhile, Annette did not appear, and Emily was surprised, and somewhat alarmed for her, whom, in the confusion of the late scene, various accidents might have befallen, and it was improbable, that she would have failed to come to her apartment, unless something unfortunate had happened.

Thus the hours passed in solitude, in silence, and in anxious conjecturing. Being not once disturbed by a message, or a sound, it appeared, that Montoni had wholly forgotten her, and it gave her some comfort to find, that she could be so unnoticed. She endeavoured to withdraw her thoughts from the anxiety, that preyed upon them, but they refused control; she could neither read, or draw, and the tones of her lute were so utterly discordant with the present state of her feelings, that she could not endure them for a moment.

The sun, at length, set behind the western mountains; his fiery beams faded from the clouds, and then a dun melancholy purple drew over them, and gradually involved the features of the country below. Soon after, the sentinels passed on the rampart to commence the watch.

Twilight had now spread its gloom over every object; the dismal obscurity of her chamber recalled fearful thoughts, but she remembered, that to procure a light she must pass through a great extent of the castle, and, above all, through the halls, where she had already experienced so much horror. Darkness, indeed, in the present state of her spirits, made silence and solitude terrible to her; it would also prevent the possibility of her finding her way to the turret, and condemn her to remain in suspense, concerning the fate of her aunt; yet she dared not to venture forth for a lamp.

Continuing at the casement, that she might catch the last lingering gleam of evening, a thousand vague images of fear floated on her fancy. "What if some of these ruffians," said she, "should find out the private stair-case, and in the darkness of night steal into my chamber!" Then, recollecting the mysterious inhabitant of the neighbouring apartment, her terror changed its object. "He is not a prisoner," said she, "though he remains in one chamber, for Montoni did not fasten the door, when he left it; the unknown person himself did this; it is certain, therefore, he can come out when he pleases."

She paused, for, notwithstanding the terrors of darkness, she considered it to be very improbable, whoever he was, that he could have any interest in intruding upon her retirement; and again the subject of her emotion changed, when, remembering her nearness to the chamber, where the veil had formerly disclosed a dreadful spectacle, she doubted whether some passage might not communicate between it and the insecure door of the stair-case.

It was now entirely dark, and she left the casement. As she sat with her eyes fixed on the hearth, she thought she perceived there a spark of light; it twinkled and disappeared, and then again was visible. At length, with much care, she fanned the embers of a wood fire, that had been lighted in the morning, into flame, and, having communicated it to a lamp, which always stood in her room, felt a satisfaction not to be conceived, without a review of her situation. Her first care was to guard the door of the stair-case, for which purpose she placed against it all the furniture she could move, and she was thus employed, for some time, at the end of which she had another instance how much more oppressive misfortune is to the idle, than to the busy; for, having then leisure to think over all the circumstances of her present afflictions, she imagined a thousand evils for futurity, and these real and ideal subjects of distress alike wounded her mind.

Thus heavily moved the hours till midnight, when she counted the sullen notes of the great clock, as they rolled along the rampart, unmingled with any sound, except the distant foot-fall of a sentinel, who came to relieve guard. She now thought she might venture towards the turret, and, having gently opened the chamber door to examine the corridor, and to listen if any person was stirring in the castle, found all around in perfect stillness. Yet no sooner had she left the room, than she perceived a light flash on the walls of the corridor, and, without waiting to see by whom it was carried, she shrunk back, and closed her door. No one approaching, she conjectured, that it was Montoni going to pay his midnight visit to her unknown neighbour, and she determined to wait, till he should have retired to his own apartment.

When the chimes had tolled another half hour, she once more opened the door, and, perceiving that no person was in the corridor, hastily crossed into a passage, that led along the south side of the castle towards the stair-case, whence she believed she could easily find her way to the turret. Often pausing on her way, listening apprehensively to the murmurs of the wind, and looking fearfully onward into the gloom of the long passages, she, at length, reached the stair-case; but there her perplexity began. Two passages appeared, of which she knew not how to prefer one, and was compelled, at last, to decide by chance, rather than by circumstances. That she entered, opened first into a wide gallery, along which she passed lightly and swiftly; for the lonely aspect of the place awed her, and she started at the echo of her own steps.

On a sudden, she thought she heard a voice, and, not distinguishing from whence it came, feared equally to proceed, or to return. For some moments, she stood in an attitude of listening expectation, shrinking almost from herself and scarcely daring to look round her. The voice came again, but, though it was now near her, terror did not allow her to judge exactly whence it proceeded. She thought, however, that it was the voice of complaint, and her belief was soon confirmed by a low moaning sound, that seemed to proceed from one of the chambers, opening into the gallery. It instantly occurred to her, that Madame Montoni might be there confined, and she advanced to the door to speak, but was checked by considering, that she was, perhaps, going to commit herself to a stranger, who might discover her to Montoni; for, though this person, whoever it was, seemed to be in affliction, it did not follow, that he was a prisoner.

While these thoughts passed over her mind, and left her still in hesitation, the voice spoke again, and, calling "Ludovico," she then perceived it to be that of Annette; on which, no longer hesitating, she went in joy to answer her.

"Ludovico!" cried Annette, sobbing—"Ludovico!"

"It is I," said Emily, trying to open the door. "How came you here? Who shut you up?"

"Ludovico!" repeated Annette—"O Ludovico!"

"It is not Ludovico, it is I—Mademoiselle Emily."

Annette ceased sobbing, and was silent.

"If you can open the door, let me in," said Emily, "here is no person to hurt you."

"Ludovico!—O, Ludovico!" cried Annette.

Emily now lost her patience, and, her fear of being overheard increasing, she was even nearly about to leave the door, when she considered, that Annette might, possibly, know something of the situation of Madame Montoni, or direct her to the turret. At length, she obtained a reply, though little satisfactory, to her questions, for Annette knew nothing of Madame Montoni, and only conjured Emily to tell her what was become of Ludovico. Of him she had no information to give, and she again asked who had shut Annette up.

"Ludovico," said the poor girl, "Ludovico shut me up. When I ran away from the dressing-room door to-day, I went I scarcely knew where, for safety; and, in this gallery, here, I met Ludovico, who hurried me into this chamber, and locked me up to keep me out of harm, as he said. But he was in such a hurry himself, he hardly spoke ten words, but he told me he would come, and let me out, when all was quiet, and he took away the key with him. Now all these hours are passed, and I have neither seen, or heard a word of him; they have murdered him—I know they have!"

Emily suddenly remembered the wounded person, whom she had seen borne into the servants' hall, and she scarcely doubted, that he was Ludovico, but she concealed the circumstance from Annette, and endeavoured to comfort her. Then, impatient to learn something of her aunt, she again enquired the way to the turret.

"O! you are not going, ma'amselle," said Annette, "for Heaven's sake, do not go, and leave me here by myself."

"Nay, Annette, you do not think I can wait in the gallery all night," replied Emily. "Direct me to the turret; in the morning I will endeavour to release you."

"O holy Mary!" exclaimed Annette, "am I to stay here by myself all night! I shall be frightened out of my senses, and I shall die of hunger; I have had nothing to eat since dinner!"

Emily could scarcely forbear smiling at the heterogeneous distresses of Annette, though she sincerely pitied them, and said what she could to soothe her. At length, she obtained something like a direction to the east turret, and quitted the door, from whence, after many intricacies and perplexities, she reached the steep and winding stairs of the turret, at the foot of which she stopped to rest, and to re-animate her courage with a sense of her duty. As she surveyed this dismal place, she perceived a door on the opposite side of the staircase, and, anxious to know whether it would lead her to Madame Montoni, she tried to undraw the bolts, which fastened it. A fresher air came to her face, as she unclosed the door, which opened upon the east rampart, and the sudden current had nearly extinguished her light, which she now removed to a distance; and again, looking out upon the obscure terrace, she perceived only the faint outline of the walls and of some towers, while, above, heavy clouds, borne along the wind, seemed to mingle with the stars, and wrap the night in thicker darkness. As she gazed, now willing to defer the moment of certainty, from which she expected only confirmation of evil, a distant footstep reminded her, that she might be observed by the men on watch, and, hastily closing the door, she took her lamp, and passed up the stair-case. Trembling came upon her, as she ascended through the gloom. To her melancholy fancy this seemed to be a place of death, and the chilling silence, that reigned, confirmed its character. Her spirits faltered. "Perhaps," said she, "I am come hither only to learn a dreadful truth, or to witness some horrible spectacle; I feel that my senses would not survive such an addition of horror."

The image of her aunt murdered—murdered, perhaps, by the hand of Montoni, rose to her mind; she trembled, gasped for breath—repented that she had dared to venture hither, and checked her steps. But, after she had paused a few minutes, the consciousness of her duty returned, and she went on. Still all was silent. At length a track of blood, upon a stair, caught her eyes; and instantly she perceived, that the wall and several other steps were stained. She paused, again struggled to support herself, and the lamp almost fell from her trembling hand. Still no sound was heard, no living being seemed to inhabit the turret; a thousand times she wished herself again in her chamber; dreaded to enquire farther—dreaded to encounter some horrible spectacle, and yet could not resolve, now that she was so near the termination of her efforts, to desist from them. Having again recollected courage to proceed, after ascending about half way up the turret, she came to another door, but here again she stopped in hesitation; listened for sounds within, and then, summoning all her resolution, unclosed it, and entered a chamber, which, as her lamp shot its feeble rays through the darkness, seemed to exhibit only dew-stained and deserted walls. As she stood examining it, in fearful expectation of discovering the remains of her unfortunate aunt, she perceived something lying in an obscure corner of the room, and, struck with an horrible conviction, she became, for an instant, motionless and nearly insensible. Then, with a kind of desperate resolution, she hurried towards the object that excited her terror, when, perceiving the clothes of some person, on the floor, she caught hold of them, and found in her grasp the old uniform of a soldier, beneath which appeared a heap of pikes and other arms. Scarcely daring to trust her sight, she continued, for some moments, to gaze on the object of her late alarm, and then left the chamber, so much comforted and occupied by the conviction, that her aunt was not there, that she was going to descend the turret, without enquiring farther; when, on turning to do so, she observed upon some steps on the second flight an appearance of blood, and remembering, that there was yet another chamber to be explored, she again followed the windings of the ascent. Still, as she ascended, the track of blood glared upon the stairs.

It led her to the door of a landing-place, that terminated them, but she was unable to follow it farther. Now that she was so near the sought-for certainty, she dreaded to know it, even more than before, and had not fortitude sufficient to speak, or to attempt opening the door.

Having listened, in vain, for some sound, that might confirm, or destroy her fears, she, at length, laid her hand on the lock, and, finding it fastened, called on Madame Montoni; but only a chilling silence ensued.

"She is dead!" she cried,—"murdered!—her blood is on the stairs!"

Emily grew very faint; could support herself no longer,

and had scarcely presence of mind to set down the lamp, and place herself on a step.

When her recollection returned, she spoke again at the door, and again attempted to open it, and, having lingered for some time, without receiving any answer, or hearing a sound, she descended the turret, and, with all the swiftness her feebleness would permit, sought her own apartment.

As she turned into the corridor, the door of a chamber opened, from whence Montoni came forth; but Emily, more terrified than ever to behold him, shrunk back into the passage soon enough to escape being noticed, and heard him close the door, which she had perceived was the same she formerly observed. Having here listened to his departing steps, till their faint sound was lost in distance, she ventured to her apartment, and, securing it once again, retired to her bed, leaving the lamp burning on the hearth. But sleep was fled from her harassed mind, to which images of horror alone occurred. She endeavoured to think it possible, that Madame Montoni had not been taken to the turret; but, when she recollected the former menaces of her husband and the terrible spirit of vengeance, which he had displayed on a late occasion; when she remembered his general character, the looks of the men, who had forced Madame Montoni from her apartment, and the written traces on the stairs of the turret—she could not doubt, that her aunt had been carried thither, and could scarcely hope, that she had not been carried to be murdered.

The grey of morning had long dawned through her casements, before Emily closed her eyes in sleep; when wearied nature, at length, yielded her a respite from suffering. . . .

Volume Three

[from] CHAPTER III

Montoni at length impatiently enquired what she had to say? "I have no time for trifling," he added, "my moments are important."

Emily then told him, that she wished to return to France, and came to beg, that he would permit her to do so.—But when he looked surprised, and enquired for the motive of the request, she hesitated, became paler than before, trembled, and had nearly sunk at his feet. He observed her emotion, with apparent indifference, and interrupted the silence by telling her, he must be gone. Emily, however, recalled her spirits sufficiently to enable her to repeat her request. And, when Montoni absolutely refused it, her slumbering mind was roused.

"I can no longer remain here with propriety, sir," said she, "and I may be allowed to ask, by what right you detain me."

"It is my will that you remain here," said Montoni, laying his hand on the door to go; "let that suffice you."

Emily, considering that she had no appeal from this will, forbore to dispute his right, and made a feeble effort to persuade him to be just. "While my aunt lived, sir," said she, in a tremulous voice, "my residence here was not improper; but now, that she is no more, I may surely be permitted to depart. My stay cannot benefit you, sir, and will only distress me."

"Who told you, that Madame Montoni was dead?" said Montoni, with an inquisitive eye. Emily hesitated, for nobody had told her so, and she did not dare to avow the having seen that spectacle in the portal-chamber, which had compelled her to the belief.

"Who told you so?" he repeated, more sternly.

"Alas! I know it too well," replied Emily: "spare me on this terrible subject!"

She sat down on a bench to support herself.

"If you wish to see her," said Montoni, "you may; she lies in the east turret."

He now left the room, without awaiting her reply, and returned to the cedar chamber, where such of the chevaliers as had not before seen Emily, began to rally him, on the discovery they had made; but Montoni did not appear disposed to bear this mirth, and they changed the subject.

Having talked with the subtle Orsino, on the plan of an excursion, which he meditated for a future day, his friend advised, that they should lie in wait for the enemy, which Verezzi impetuously opposed, reproached Orsino with want of spirit, and swore, that, if Montoni would let him lead on fifty men, he would conquer all that should oppose him.

Orsino smiled contemptuously; Montoni smiled too, but he also listened. Verezzi then proceeded with vehement declamation and assertion, till he was stopped by an argument of Orsino, which he knew not how to answer better than by invective. His fierce spirit detested the cunning caution of Orsino, whom he constantly opposed, and whose inveterate, though silent, hatred he had long ago incurred. And Montoni was a calm observer of both, whose different qualifications he knew, and how to bend their opposite character to the perfection of his own designs. But Verezzi, in the heat of opposition, now did not scruple to accuse Orsino of cowardice, at which the countenance of the latter, while he made no reply, was over-spread with a livid paleness; and Montoni, who watched his lurking eye, saw him put his hand hastily into his bosom. But Verezzi, whose face, glowing with crimson, formed a striking contrast to the complexion of Orsino, remarked not the action, and continued boldly declaiming against cowards to Cavigni, who was slily laughing at his vehemence, and at the silent mortification of Orsino, when the latter, retiring a few steps behind, drew forth a stilletto to stab his adversary in the back. Montoni arrested his half-extended arm, and, with a significant look, made him return the poinard into his bosom, unseen by all except himself; for most of the party were disputing at a distant window, on the situation of a dell where they meant to form an ambuscade.

When Verezzi had turned round, the deadly hatred, expressed on the features of his opponent, raising, for the first time, a suspicion of his intention, he laid his hand on his sword, and then, seeming to recollect himself, strode up to Montoni.

"Signor," said he, with a significant look at Orsino, "we are not a band of assassins; if you have business for brave men employ me on this expedition: you shall have the last drop of my blood; if you have only work for cowards—keep him," pointing to Orsino, "and let me quit Udolpho."

Orsino, still more incensed, again drew forth his stilletto, and rushed towards Verezzi, who, at the same instant, advanced with his sword, when Montoni and the rest of the party interfered and separated them.

"This is the conduct of a boy," said Montoni to Verezzi, "not of a man: be more moderate in your speech."

"Moderation is the virtue of cowards," retorted Verezzi; "they are moderate in every thing—but in fear."

"I accept your words," said Montoni, turning upon him with a fierce and haughty look, and drawing his sword out of the scabbard.

"With all my heart," cried Verezzi, "though I did not mean them for you."

He directed a pass at Montoni; and, while they fought,

the villain Orsino made another attempt to stab Verezzi, and was again prevented.

The combatants were, at length, separated; and, after a very long and violent dispute, reconciled. Montoni then left the room with Orsino, whom he detained in private consultation for a considerable time.

Emily, meanwhile, stunned by the last words of Montoni, forgot, for the moment, his declaration, that she should continue in the castle, while she thought of her unfortunate aunt, who, he had said, was laid in the east turret. In suffering the remains of his wife to lie thus long unburied, there appeared a degree of brutality more shocking than she had suspected even Montoni could practise.

After a long struggle, she determined to accept his permission to visit the turret, and to take a last look of her ill-fated aunt: with which design she returned to her chamber, and, while she waited for Annette to accompany her, endeavoured to acquire fortitude sufficient to support her through the approaching scene; for, though she trembled to encounter it, she knew that to remember the performance of this last act of duty would hereafter afford her consoling satisfaction.

Annette came, and Emily mentioned her purpose, from which the former endeavoured to dissuade her, though without effect, and Annette was, with much difficulty, prevailed upon to accompany her to the turret; but no consideration could make her promise to enter the chamber of death.

They now left the corridor, and, having reached the foot of the stair-case, which Emily had formerly ascended, Annette declared she would go no further, and Emily proceeded alone. When she saw the track of blood, which she had before observed, her spirits fainted, and, being compelled to rest on the stairs, she almost determined to proceed no further. The pause of a few moments restored her resolution, and she went on.

As she drew near the landing-place, upon which the upper chamber opened, she remembered, that the door was formerly fastened, and apprehended, that it might still be so. In this expectation, however, she was mistaken; for the door opened at once, into a dusky and silent chamber, round which she fearfully looked, and then slowly advanced, when a hollow voice spoke. Emily, who was unable to speak, or to move from the spot, uttered no sound of terror. The voice spoke again; and, then, thinking that it resembled that of Madame Montoni, Emily's spirits were instantly roused; she rushed towards a bed, that stood in a remote part of the room, and drew aside the curtains. Within, appeared a pale and emaciated face. She started back, then again advanced, shuddered as she took up the skeleton hand, that lay stretched upon the quilt; then let it drop, and then viewed the face with a long, unsettled gaze. It was that of Madame Montoni, though so changed by illness, that the resemblance of what it had been, could scarcely be traced in what it now appeared. She was still alive, and, raising her heavy eyes, she turned them on her niece.

"Where have you been so long?" said she, in the same hollow tone, "I thought you had forsaken me."

"Do you indeed live," said Emily, at length, "or is this but a terrible apparition?" She received no answer, and again she snatched up the hand. "This is substance," she exclaimed, "but it is cold—cold as marble!" She let it fall. "O, if you really live, speak!" said Emily, in a voice of desperation, "that I may not lose my senses—say you know me!"

"I do live," replied Madame Montoni, "but—I feel that I am about to die."

Emily clasped the hand she held, more eagerly, and groaned. They were both silent for some moments. Then Emily endeavoured to soothe her, and enquired what had reduced her to this present deplorable state.

Montoni, when he removed her to the turret under the improbable suspicion of having attempted his life, had ordered the men employed on the occasion, to observe a strict secrecy concerning her. To this he was influenced by a double motive. He meant to debar her from the comfort of Emily's visits, and to secure an opportunity of privately dispatching her, should any new circumstances occur to confirm the present suggestions of his suspecting mind. His consciousness of the hatred he deserved, it was natural enough should at first lead him to attribute to her the attempt that had been made upon his life; and, though there was no other reason to believe that she was concerned in that atrocious design, his suspicions remained; he continued to confine her in the turret, under a strict guard; and, without pity or remorse, had suffered her to lie, forlorn and neglected, under a raging fever, till it had reduced to the present state.

The track of blood, which Emily had seen on the stairs, had flowed from the unbound wound of one of the men employed to carry Madame Montoni, and which he had received in the late affray. At night these men, having contented themselves with securing the door of their prisoner's room, had retired from guard; and then it was, that Emily, at the time of her first enquiry, had found the turret so silent and deserted.

When she had attempted to open the door of the chamber, her aunt was sleeping, and this occasioned the silence, which had contributed to delude her into a belief, that she was no more; yet had her terror permitted her to persevere longer in the call, she would probably have awakened Madame Montoni, and have been spared much suffering. The spectacle in the portal-chamber, which afterwards confirmed Emily's horrible suspicion, was the corpse of a man, who had fallen in the affray, and the same which had been borne into the servants' hall, where she took refuge from the tumult. This man had lingered under his wounds for some days; and, soon after his death, his body had been removed on the couch, on which he died, for interment in the vault beneath the chapel, through which Emily and Barnardine had passed to the chamber.

Emily, after asking Madame Montoni a thousand questions concerning herself, left her, and sought Montoni; for the more solemn interest she felt for her aunt, made her now regardless of the resentment her remonstrances might draw upon herself, and of the improbability of his granting what she meant to entreat.

"Madame Montoni is now dying, sir," said Emily, as soon as she saw him—"Your resentment, surely, will not pursue her to the last moment! Suffer her to be removed from that forlorn room to her own apartment, and to have necessary comforts administered."

"Of what service will that be, if she is dying?" said Montoni, with apparent indifference.

"The service, at least, of saving you, sir, from a few of those pangs of conscience you must suffer, when you shall be in the same situation," said Emily, with imprudent indignation, of which Montoni soon made her sensible, by commanding her to quit his presence. Then, forgetting her resentment, and impressed only by compassion for the piteous state of her aunt, dying without succour, she submitted to humble herself to Montoni, and to adopt every persuasive means, that might reduce him to relent towards his wife.

For a considerable time he was proof against all she said, and all she looked; but at length the divinity of pity, beaming in Emily's eyes, seemed to touch his heart. He turned away, ashamed of his better feelings, half sullen and half relenting; but finally consented, that his wife should be removed to her own apartment, and that Emily should attend her. Dreading equally, that this relief might arrive too late, and that Montoni might retract his concession, Emily scarcely staid to thank him for it, but, assisted by Annette, she quickly prepared Madame Montoni's bed, and they carried her a cordial, that might enable her feeble frame to sustain the fatigue of a removal.

Madame was scarcely arrived in her own apartment, when an order was given by her husband, that she should remain in the turret; but Emily, thankful that she had made such dispatch, hastened to inform him of it, as well as that a second removal would instantly prove fatal, and he suffered his wife to continue where she was.

During this day, Emily never left Madame Montoni, except to prepare such little nourishing things as she judged necessary to sustain her, and which Madame Montoni received with quiet acquiescence, though she seemed sensible that they could not save her from approaching dissolution, and scarcely appeared to wish for life. Emily meanwhile watched over her with the most tender solicitude, no longer seeing her imperious aunt in the poor object before her, but the sister of her late beloved father, in a situation that called for all her compassion and kindness. When night came, she determined to sit up with her aunt, but this the latter positively forbade, commanding her to retire to rest, and Annette alone to remain in her chamber. Rest was, indeed, necessary to Emily, whose spirits and frame were equally wearied by the occurrences and exertions of the day; but she would not leave Madame Montoni, till after the turn of midnight, a period then thought so critical by the physicians.

Soon after twelve, having enjoined Annette to be wakeful, and to call her, should any change appear for the worse, Emily sorrowfully bade Madame Montoni good night, and withdrew to her chamber. Her spirits were more than usually depressed by the piteous condition of her aunt, whose recovery she scarcely dared to expect. To her own misfortunes she saw no period, inclosed as she was, in a remote castle, beyond the reach of any friends, had she possessed such, and beyond the pity even of strangers; while she knew herself to be in the power of a man capable of any action, which his interest, or his ambition, might suggest.

Occupied by melancholy reflections and by anticipations as sad, she did not retire immediately to rest, but leaned thoughtfully on her open casement. The scene before her of woods and mountains, reposing in the moon-light, formed a regretted contrast with the state of her mind; but the lonely murmur of these woods, and the view of this sleeping landscape, gradually soothed her emotions and softened her to tears.

She continued to weep, for some time, lost to every thing, but to a gentle sense of her misfortunes. When she, at length, took the handkerchief from her eyes, she perceived, before her, on the terrace below, the figure she had formerly observed, which stood fixed and silent, immediately oppo-site to her casement. On perceiving it, she started back, and terror for some time overcame curiosity;—at length, she re-turned to the casement, and still the figure was before it, which she now compelled herself to observe, but was utterly unable to speak, as she had formerly intended. The moon shone with a clear light, and it was, perhaps, the agitation of her mind, that prevented her distinguishing, with any degree of accuracy, the form before her. It was still station-ary, and she began to doubt, whether it was really animated.

Her scattered thoughts were now so far returned as to remind her, that her light exposed her to dangerous obser-vation, and she was stepping back to remove it, when she perceived the figure move, and then wave what seemed to be its arm, as if to beckon her; and, while she gazed, fixed in fear, it repeated the action. She now attempted to speak, but the words died on her lips, and she went from the casement to remove her light; as she was doing which, she heard, from without, a faint groan. Listening, but not daring to return, she presently heard it repeated.

"Good God!—what can this mean!" said she.

Again she listened, but the sound came no more; and, after a long interval of silence, she recovered courage enough to go to the casement, when she again saw the same appearance! It beckoned again, and again uttered a low sound.

"That groan was surely human!" said she. "I *will* speak." "Who is it," cried Emily in a faint voice, "that wanders at this late hour?"

The figure raised its head but suddenly started away, and glided down the terrace. She watched it, for a long while, passing swiftly in the moon-light, but heard no footstep, till a sentinel from the other extremity of the rampart walked slowly along. The man stopped under her window, and, looking up, called her by name. She was retiring precipitately, but, a second summons inducing her to reply, the soldier then respectfully asked if she had seen any thing pass. On her answering, that she had; he said no more, but walked away down the terrace, Emily following him with her eyes, till he was lost in the distance. But, as he was on guard, she knew he could not go beyond the rampart, and, therefore, resolved to await his return.

Soon after, his voice was heard, at a distance, calling loudly; and then a voice still more distant answered, and, in the next moment, the watch-word was given, and passed along the terrace. As the soldiers moved hastily under the casement, she called to enquire what had happened, but they passed without regarding her.

Emily's thoughts returning to the figure she had seen, "It cannot be a person, who has designs upon the castle," said she; "such an one would conduct himself very differently. He would not venture where sentinels were on watch, nor fix himself opposite to a window, where he perceived he must be observed; much less would he beckon, or utter a sound of complaint. Yet it cannot be a prisoner, for how could he obtain the opportunity to wander thus?"

If she had been subject to vanity, she might have supposed this figure to be some inhabitant of the castle, who wandered under her casement in the hope of seeing her, and of being allowed to declare his admiration; but this opinion never occurred to Emily, and, if it had, she would have dismissed it as improbable, on considering, that, when the opportunity of speaking had occurred, it had been suffered to pass in silence; and that, even at the moment in which she had spoken, the form had abruptly quitted the place.

While she mused, two sentinels walked up the rampart in earnest conversation, of which she caught a few words, and learned from these, that one of their comrades had fallen down senseless. Soon after, three other soldiers appeared slowly advancing from the bottom of the terrace, but she heard only a low voice, that came at intervals. As they drew near, she perceived this to be the voice of him, who walked in the middle, apparently supported by his comrades; and she again called to them, enquiring what had happened. At the sound of her voice, they stopped, and looked up, while she repeated her question, and was told, that Roberto, their fellow of the watch, had been seized with a fit, and that his cry, as he fell, had caused a false alarm.

"Is he subject to fits?" said Emily.

"Yes, Signora," replied Roberto; "but if I had not, what I saw was enough to have frightened the Pope himself."

"What was it?" enquired Emily, trembling.

"I cannot tell what it was, lady, or what I saw, or how it vanished," replied the soldier, who seemed to shudder at the recollection.

"Was it the person, whom you followed down the rampart, that has occasioned you this alarm?" said Emily, endeavouring to conceal her own.

"Person!" exclaimed the man,—"it was the devil, and this is not the first time I have seen him!"

"Nor will it be the last," observed one of his comrades, laughing.

"No, no, I warrant not," said another.

"Well," rejoined Roberto, "you may be as merry now, as you please; you was none so jocose the other night, Sebastian, when you was on watch with Launcelot."

"Launcelot need not talk of that," replied Sebastian, "let him remember how he stood trembling, and unable to give the *word*, till the man was gone. If the man had not come so silently upon us, I would have seized him, and soon made him tell who he was."

"What man?" enquired Emily.

"It was no man, lady," said Launcelot, who stood by, "but the devil himself, as my comrade says. What man, who does not live in the castle, could get within the walls at midnight? Why, I might just as well pretend to march to Venice, and get among all the Senators, when they are counselling; and I warrant I should have more chance of getting out again alive, than any fellow, that we should catch within the gates after dark. So I think I have proved plainly enough, that this can be nobody that lives out of the castle; and now I will prove, that it can be nobody that lives in the castle—for, if he did—why should he be afraid to be seen? So after this, I hope nobody will pretend to tell me it was anybody. No, I say again, by holy Pope! it was the devil, and Sebastian, there, knows this is not the first time we have seen him."

"When did you see the figure, then, before?" said Emily half smiling, who, though she thought the conversation somewhat too much, felt an interest, which would not permit her to conclude it.

"About a week ago, lady," said Sebastian, taking up the story.

"And where?"

"On the rampart, lady, higher up."

"Did you pursue it, that it fled?"

"No, Signora. Launcelot and I were on watch together, and every thing was so still, you might have heard a mouse stir, when, suddenly, Launcelot says—Sebastian! do you see nothing? I turned my head a little to the left, as it might be —thus. No, says I. Hush! said Launcelot,—look yonder—just by the last cannon on the rampart! I looked, and then thought I did see something move; but there being no light, but what the stars gave, I could not be certain. We stood quite silent, to watch it, and presently saw something pass along the castle wall just opposite to us!"

"Why did you not seize it, then?" cried a soldier, who had scarcely spoken till now.

"Aye, why did you not seize it?" said Roberto.

"You should have been there to have done that," replied Sebastian. "You would have been bold enough to have taken it by the throat, though it had been the devil himself; we could not take such a liberty, perhaps because we are not so well acquainted with him, as you are. But, as I was saying, it stole by us so quickly, that we had not time to get rid of our surprise, before it was gone. Then, we knew it was in vain to follow. We kept constant watch all that night, but we saw it no more. Next morning, we told some of our comrades, who were on duty on other parts of the ramparts, what we had seen; but they had seen nothing, and laughed at us, and it was not till to-night, that the same figure walked again."

"Where did you lose it, friend?" said Emily to Roberto.

"When I left you, lady," replied the man, "you might see me go down the rampart, but it was not till I reached the east terrace, that I saw any thing. Then, the moon shining bright, I saw something like a shadow flitting before me, as it were, at some distance. I stopped, when I turned the corner of the east tower, where I had seen this figure not a moment before,—but it was gone! As I stood, looking through the old arch, which leads to the east rampart, and where I am sure it had passed, I heard, all of a sudden, such a sound!—It was not like a groan, or a cry, or a shout, or any thing I ever heard in my life. I heard it only once, and that was enough for me; for I know nothing that happened after, till I found my comrades, here, about me."

"Come," said Sebastian, "let us go to our posts—the moon is setting. Good night, lady!"

"Aye, let us go," rejoined Roberto. "Good night, lady."

"Good night; the holy mother guard you!" said Emily, as she closed her casement and retired to reflect upon the strange circumstance that had just occurred, connecting which with what had happened on former nights, she endeavoured to derive from the whole something more positive, than conjecture. But her imagination was inflamed, while her judgment was not enlightened, and the terrors of superstition again pervaded her mind. . . .

[from] CHAPTER VIII

The night was stormy; the battlements of the castle appeared to rock in the wind, and, at intervals, long groans seemed to pass on the air, such as those, which often deceive the melancholy mind, in tempests, and amidst scenes of desolation. Emily heard, as formerly, the sentinels pass along the terrace to their posts, and, looking out from her casement, observed, that the watch was doubled; a precaution, which appeared necessary enough, when she threw her eyes on the walls, and saw their shattered condition. The well-known sounds of the soldiers' march, and of their distant voices, which passed her in the wind, and were lost again, recalled to her memory the melancholy sensations she had suffered, when she formerly heard the same sounds; and occasioned almost involuntary comparisons between her present, and her late situation. But this was no subject for congratulation, and she wisely checked the course of her thoughts, while, as the hour was not yet come, in which she had been accustomed to hear the music, she closed the casement, and endeavoured to await it in patience. The door of the stair-case she tried to secure, as usual, with some of the furniture of the room; but this expedient her fears now represented to her to be very inadequate to the power and perseverance of Verezzi; and she often looked at a large and heavy chest, that stood in the chamber, with wishes that she and Annette had strength enough to move it. While she blamed the long stay of this girl, who was still with Ludovico and some other of the servants, she trimmed her wood fire, to make the room appear less desolate, and sat down beside it with a book, which her eyes perused, while her thoughts wandered to Valancourt, and her own misfortunes. As she sat thus, she thought, in a pause of the wind, she distinguished music, and went to the casement to listen, but the loud swell of the gust overcame every other sound. When the wind sunk again, she heard distinctly, in the deep pause that succeeded, the sweet strings of a lute; but again the rising tempest bore away the notes, and again was succeeded by a solemn pause. Emily, trembling with hope and fear, opened her casement to listen, and to try whether her own voice could be heard by the musician; for to endure any longer this state of torturing suspense concerning Valancourt, seemed to be utterly impossible. There was a kind of breathless stillness in the chambers, that permitted her to distinguish from below the tender notes of the very lute she had formerly heard, and with it, a plaintive voice, made sweeter by the low rustling sound, that now began to creep along the wood-tops, till it was lost in the rising wind. Their tall heads then began to wave, while, through a forest of pine, on the left, the wind, groaning heavily, rolled onward over the woods below, bending them almost to their roots; and, as the long-resounding gale swept away, other woods, on the right, seemed to answer the "loud lament;" then, others, further still, softened it into a murmur, that died into silence. Emily listened, with mingled awe and expectation, hope and fear; and again the melting sweetness of the lute was heard, and the same solemn-breathing voice. Convinced that these came from an apartment underneath, she leaned far out of her window, that she might discover whether any light was there; but the casements below, as well as those above, were sunk so deep in the thick walls of the castle, that she could not see them, or even the faint ray, that probably glimmered through their bars. She then ventured to call; but the wind bore her voice to the other end of the terrace, and then the music was heard as before, in the pause of the gust. Suddenly, she thought she heard a

noise in her chamber, and she drew herself within the casement; but, in a moment after, distinguishing Annette's
voice at the door, she concluded it was her she had heard
before, and she let her in. "Move softly, Annette, to the
casement," said she, "and listen with me; the music is returned." They were silent till, the measure changing, Annette exclaimed, "Holy Virgin! I know that song well; it is
a French song, one of the favourite songs of my dear country." This was the ballad Emily had heard on a former
night, though not the one she had first listened to from the
fishing-house in Gascony. "O! it is a Frenchman, that sings,"
said Annette: "it must be Monsieur Valancourt." "Hark!
Annette, do not speak so loud," said Emily, "we may be
overheard." "What! by the Chevalier?" said Annette. "No,"
replied Emily mournfully, "but by somebody, who may report us to the Signor. What reason have you to think it is
Monsieur Valancourt, who sings? But hark! now the voice
swells louder! Do you recollect those tones? I fear to trust
my own judgment." "I never happened to hear the Chevalier sing, Mademoiselle," replied Annette, who, as Emily
was disappointed to perceive, had no stronger reason for
concluding this to be Valancourt, than that the musician
must be a Frenchman. Soon after, she heard the song of
the fishing-house, and distinguished her own name, which
was repeated so distinctly, that Annette had heard it also.
She trembled, sunk into a chair by the window, and Annette
called aloud, "Monsieur Valancourt! Monsieur Valancourt!"
while Emily endeavoured to check her, but she repeated the
call more loudly than before, and the lute and the voice suddenly stopped. Emily listened, for some time, in a state of
intolerable suspense; but, no answer being returned, "It
does not signify, Mademoiselle," said Annette; "it is the
Chevalier, and I will speak to him." "No, Annette," said
Emily, "I think I will speak myself; if it is he, he will know

my voice, and speak again." "Who is it," said she, "that sings at this late hour?"

A long silence ensued, and, having repeated the question, she perceived some faint accents, mingling in the blast, that swept by; but the sounds were so distant, and passed so suddenly, that she could scarcely hear them, much less distinguish the words they uttered, or recognise the voice. After another pause, Emily called again; and again they heard a voice, but as faintly as before; and they perceived, that there were other circumstances, besides the strength, and direction of the wind, to contend with; for the great depth, at which the casements were fixed in the castle walls, contributed, still more than the distance, to prevent articulated sounds from being understood, though general ones were easily heard. Emily, however, ventured to believe, from the circumstance of her voice alone having been answered, that the stranger was Valancourt, as well as that he knew her, and she gave herself up to speechless joy. Annette, however, was not speechless.—She renewed her calls, but received no answer; and Emily, fearing, that a further attempt, which certainly was, at present, highly dangerous, might expose them to the guards of the castle, while it could not perhaps terminate her suspense, insisted on Annette's dropping the enquiry for this night; though she determined herself to question Ludovico, on the subject, in the morning, more urgently than she had yet done. She was now enabled to say, that the stranger, whom she had formerly heard, was still in the castle, and to direct Ludovico to that part of it, in which he was confined.

Emily, attended by Annette, continued at the casement, for some time, but all remained still; they heard neither lute or voice again, and Emily was now as much oppressed by anxious joy, as she lately was by a sense of her misfortunes. With hasty steps she paced the room, now half calling on Valancourt's name, then suddenly stopping, and now going to the casement and listening, where, however, she heard nothing but the solemn waving of the woods. Sometimes her impatience to speak to Ludovico prompted her to send Annette to call him; but a sense of the impropriety of this at midnight restrained her. Annette, meanwhile, as impatient as her mistress, went as often to the casement to listen, and returned almost as much disappointed. She, at length, mentioned Signor Verezzi, and her fear, lest he should enter the chamber by the stair-case door. "But the night is now almost past, Mademoiselle," said she, recollecting herself: "there is the morning light, beginning to peep over those mountains yonder in the east."

Emily had forgotten, till this moment, that such a person existed as Verezzi, and all the danger that had appeared to threaten her; but the mention of his name renewed her alarm, and she remembered the old chest, that she had wished to place against the door, which she now, with Annette, attempted to move, but it was so heavy, that they could not lift it from the floor. "What is in this great old chest, Mademoiselle," said Annette, "that makes it so weighty?" Emily having replied, "that she found it in the chamber, when she first came to the castle, and had never examined it,"—"Then I will, Ma'amselle," said Annette, and she tried to lift the lid; but this was held by a lock, for which she had no key, and which, indeed, appeared, from its peculiar construction, to open with a spring. The morning now glimmered through the casements, and the wind had sunk into a calm. Emily looked out upon the dusky woods, and on the twilight mountains, just stealing on the eye, and saw the whole scene, after the storm, lying in profound stillness, the woods motionless, and the clouds above, through which the dawn trembled, scarcely appearing to move along the heavens. One soldier was pacing the terrace beneath, with measured steps; and two, more distant, were sunk asleep on the walls, wearied with the night's watch.

Having inhaled, for a while, the pure spirit of the air, and of vegetation, which the late rains had called forth; and having listened, once more, for a note of music, she now closed the casement, and retired to rest. . . .

Volume Four

CHAPTER XVII

——"But in these cases,
We still have judgment here; that we but teach
Bloody instructions, which, being taught, return
To plague the inventor: thus even-handed justice
Commends the ingredients of our poison'd chalice
To our own lips."

MACBETH

Some circumstances of an extraordinary nature now withdrew Emily from her own sorrows, and excited emotions, which partook of both surprise and horror.

A few days following that, on which Signora Laurentini died, her will was opened at the monastery, in the presence of the superiors and Mons. Bonnac, when it was found, that one third of her personal property was bequeathed to the nearest surviving relative of the late Marchioness de Villeroi, and that Emily was the person.

With the secret of Emily's family the abbess had long been acquainted, and it was in observance of the earnest request of St. Aubert, who was known to the friar, that attended him on his death-bed, that his daughter had remained in ignorance of her relationship to the Marchioness. But some hints, which had fallen from Signora Laurentini, during her last interview with Emily, and a confession of a very extraordinary nature, given in her dying hours, had made the abbess think it necessary to converse with her young friend, on the topic she had not before ventured to introduce; and it was for this purpose, that she had requested to see her on the morning that followed her interview with the nun. Emily's indisposition had then prevented the intended conversation; but now, after the will had been examined, she received a summons, which she immediately obeyed, and became informed of circumstances, that powerfully affected her. As the narrative of the abbess was, however, deficient in many particulars, of which the reader may wish to be informed, and the history of the nun is materially connected with the fate of the Marchioness de Villeroi, we shall omit the conversation, that passed in the parlour of the convent, and mingle with our relation a brief history of

LAURENTINI DI UDOLPHO,

Who was the only child of her parents, and heiress of the ancient house of Udolpho, in the territory of Venice. It was the first misfortune of her life, and that which led to all her succeeding misery, that the friends, who ought to have restrained her strong passions, and mildly instructed her in the art of governing them, nurtured them by early indulgence. But they cherished their own failings in her; for their conduct was not the result of rational kindness, and, when they either indulged, or opposed the passions of their child, they gratified their own. Thus they indulged her with weakness, and reprehended her with violence; her spirit was exasperated by their vehemence, instead of being corrected by their wisdom; and their oppositions became contests for victory, in which the due tenderness of the parents, and the affectionate duties of the child, were equally forgotten; but, as returning fondness disarmed the parents' resentment soonest, Laurentini was suffered to believe that she had conquered, and her passions became stronger by every effort, that had been employed to subdue them.

The death of her father and mother in the same year left

her to her own discretion, under the dangerous circumstances attendant on youth and beauty. She was fond of company, delighted with admiration, yet disdainful of the opinion of the world, when it happened to contradict her inclinations; had a gay and brilliant wit, and was mistress of all the arts of fascination. Her conduct was such as might have been expected, from the weakness of her principles and the strength of her passions.

Among her numerous admirers was the late Marquis de Villeroi, who, on his tour through Italy, saw Laurentini at Venice, where she usually resided, and became her passionate adorer. Equally captivated by the figure and accomplishments of the Marquis, who was at that period one of the most distinguished noblemen of the French court, she had the art so effectually to conceal from him the dangerous traits of her character and the blemishes of her late conduct, that he solicited her hand in marriage.

Before the nuptials were concluded, she retired to the castle of Udolpho, whither the Marquis followed, and, where her conduct, relaxing from the propriety, which she had lately assumed, discovered to him the precipice, on which he stood. A minuter enquiry than he had before thought it necessary to make, convinced him, that he had been deceived in her character, and she, whom he had designed for his wife, afterwards became his mistress.

Having passed some weeks at Udolpho, he was called abruptly to France, whither he returned with extreme reluctance, for his heart was still fascinated by the arts of Laurentini, with whom, however, he had on various pretences delayed his marriage; but, to reconcile her to this separation, he now gave repeated promises of returning to conclude the nuptials, as soon as the affair, which thus suddenly called him to France, should permit.

Soothed, in some degree, by these assurances, she suffered him to depart; and, soon after, her relative, Montoni, arriving at Udolpho, renewed the addresses, which she had before refused, and which she now again rejected. Meanwhile, her thoughts were constantly with the Marquis de Villeroi, for whom she suffered all the delirium of Italian love, cherished by the solitude, to which she confined herself; for she had now lost all taste for the pleasures of society and the gaiety of amusement. Her only indulgences were to sigh and weep over a miniature of the Marquis; to visit the scenes, that had witnessed their happiness, to pour forth her heart to him in writing, and to count the weeks, the days, which must intervene before the period that he had mentioned as probable for his return. But this period passed without bringing him; and week after week followed in heavy and almost intolerable expectation. During this interval, Laurentini's fancy, occupied incessantly by one idea, became disordered; and, her whole heart being devoted to one object, life became hateful to her, when she believed that object lost.

Several months passed, during which she heard nothing from the Marquis de Villeroi, and her days were marked, at intervals, with the phrensy of passion and the sullenness of despair. She secluded herself from all visitors, and, sometimes, remained in her apartment, for weeks together, refusing to speak to every person, except her favourite female attendant, writing scraps of letters, reading, again and again, those she had received from the Marquis, weeping over his picture, and speaking to it, for many hours, upbraiding, reproaching and caressing it alternately.

At length, a report reached her, that the Marquis had married in France, and, after suffering all the extremes of love, jealousy and indignation, she formed the desperate resolution of going secretly to that country, and, if the report proved true, of attempting a deep revenge. To her favourite woman only she confided the plan of her journey, and she engaged her to partake of it. Having collected her jewels, which, descending to her from many branches of her family, were of immense value, and all her cash, to a very large amount, they were packed in a trunk, which was privately conveyed to a neighbouring town, whither Laurentini, with this only servant, followed, and thence proceeded secretly to Leghorn, where they embarked for France.

When, on her arrival in Languedoc, she found, that the Marquis de Villeroi had been married, for some months, her despair almost deprived her of reason, and she alternately projected and abandoned the horrible design of murdering the Marquis, his wife and herself. At length she contrived to throw herself in his way, with an intention of reproaching him, for his conduct, and of stabbing herself in his presence; but, when she again saw him, who so long had been the constant object of her thoughts and affections, resentment yielded to love; her resolution failed; she trembled with the conflict of emotions, that assailed her heart, and fainted away.

The Marquis was not proof against her beauty and sensibility; all the energy, with which he had first loved, returned, for his passion had been resisted by prudence, rather than overcome by indifference; and, since the honour of his family would not permit him to marry her, he had endeavoured to subdue his love, and had so far succeeded, as to select the then Marchioness for his wife, whom he loved at first with a tempered and rational affection. But the mild virtues of that amiable lady did not recompense him for her indifference, which appeared, notwithstanding her efforts to conceal it; and he had, for some time, suspected that her affections were engaged by another person, when Laurentini arrived in Languedoc. This artful Italian soon perceived, that she had regained her influence over him, and, soothed by the discovery, she determined to live, and to employ all her enchantments to win his consent to the diabolical deed, which she believed was necessary to the security of her happiness. She conducted her scheme with deep dissimulation and patient perseverance, and, having completely estranged the affections of the Marquis from his wife, whose gentle goodness and unimpassioned manners had ceased to please, when contrasted with the captivations of the Italian, she proceeded to awaken in his mind the jealousy of pride, for it was no longer that of love, and even pointed out to him the person, to whom she affirmed the Marchioness had sacrificed her honour; but Laurentini had first extorted from him a solemn promise to forbear avenging himself upon his rival. This was an important part of her plan, for she knew, that, if his desire of vengeance was restrained towards one party, it would burn more fiercely towards the other, and he might then, perhaps, be prevailed on to assist in the horrible act, which would release him from the only barrier, that withheld him from making her his wife.

The innocent Marchioness, meanwhile, observed, with extreme grief, the alteration in her husband's manners. He became reserved and thoughtful in her presence; his conduct was austere, and sometimes even rude; and he left her, for many hours together, to weep for his unkindness, and to form plans for the recovery of his affection. His conduct afflicted her the more, because, in obedience to the command of her father, she had accepted his hand, though her affections were engaged to another, whose amiable disposition, she had reason to believe, would have endured her happiness. This circumstance Laurentini had discovered, soon after her arrival in France, and had made ample use of it in assisting her designs upon the Marquis, to whom she adduced such seeming proof of his wife's infidelity, that, in the frantic rage of wounded honour, he consented to destroy his wife. A slow poison was administered, and she fell a victim to the jealousy and subtlety of Laurentini and to the guilty weakness of her husband.

But the moment of Laurentini's triumph, the moment, to which she had looked forward for the completion of all her wishes, proved only the commencement of a suffering, that never left her to her dying hour.

The passion of revenge, which had in part stimulated her to the commission of this atrocious deed, died, even at the moment when it was gratified, and left her to the horrors of unavailing pity and remorse, which would probably have empoisoned all the years she had promised herself with the Marquis de Villeroi, had her expectations of an alliance with him been realized. But he, too, had found the moment of his revenge to be that of remorse, as to himself, and detestation, as to the partner of his crime; the feeling, which he had mistaken for conviction, was no more; and he stood astonished, and aghast, that no proof remained of his wife's infidelity, now that she had suffered the punishment of guilt. Even when he was informed, that she was dying, he had felt suddenly and unaccountably reassured of her innocence, nor was the solemn assurance she made him in her last hour, capable of affording him a stronger conviction of her blameless conduct.

In the first horrors of remorse and despair, he felt inclined to deliver up himself and the woman, who had plunged him into this abyss of guilt, into the hands of justice; but, when the paroxysm of his suffering was over, his intention changed. Laurentini, however, he saw only once afterwards, and that was, to curse her as the instigator of his crime, and to say, that he spared her life only on condition, that she passed the rest of her days in prayer and penance. Overwhelmed with disappointment, on receiving contempt and abhorrence from the man, for whose sake she had not scrupled to stain her conscience with human blood, and, touched with horror of the unavailing crime she had committed, she renounced the world, and retired to the monastery of St. Claire, a dreadful victim to unresisted passion.

The Marquis, immediately after the death of his wife, quitted Chateau-le-Blanc, to which he never returned, and endeavoured to lose the sense of his crime amidst the tumult of war, or the dissipations of a capital; but his efforts were vain; a deep dejection hung over him ever after, for which his most intimate friends could not account, and he, at length, died, with a degree of horror nearly equal to that, which Laurentini had suffered. The physician, who had observed the singular appearance of the unfortunate Marchioness, after death, had been bribed to silence; and, as the surmises of a few of the servants had proceeded no further than a whisper, the affair had never been investigated. Whether this whisper ever reached the father of the Marchioness, and, if it did, whether the difficulty of obtaining proof deterred him from prosecuting the Marquis de Villeroi, is uncertain; but her death was deeply lamented by some part of her family, and particularly by her brother, M. St. Aubert; for that was the degree of relationship, which had existed between Emily's father and the Marchioness; and there is no doubt, that he suspected the manner of her death. Many letters passed between the Marquis and him, soon after the decease of this beloved sister, the subject of which was not known, but there is reason to believe, that they related to the cause of her death; and these were the papers, together with some letters of the Marchioness, who had confided to her brother the occasion of her unhappiness, which St. Aubert had so solemnly enjoined his daughter to destroy: and anxiety for her peace had probably made him forbid her to enquire into the melancholy story, to which they alluded. Such, indeed, had been his affliction, on the premature death of this his favourite sister, whose unhappy marriage had from the first excited his tenderest pity, that he never could hear her named, or mention her himself after her death, except to Madame St. Aubert. From Emily, whose sensibility he feared to awaken, he had so carefully concealed her history and name, that she was ignorant, till now, that she ever had such a relative as the Marchioness de Villeroi; and from this motive he had enjoined silence to his only surviving sister, Madame Cheron, who had scrupulously observed his request.

It was over some of the last pathetic letters of the Marchioness, that St. Aubert was weeping, when he was observed by Emily, on the eve of her departure from La Vallée, and it was her picture, which he had so tenderly caressed. Her disastrous death may account for the emotion he had betrayed, on hearing her named by La Voisin, and for his request to be interred near the monument of the Villerois, where her remains were deposited, but not those of her husband, who was buried, where he died, in the north of France.

The confessor, who attended St. Aubert in his last moments, recollected him to be the brother of the late Marchioness, when St. Aubert, from tenderness to Emily, had conjured him to conceal the circumstance, and to request that the abbess, to whose care he particularly recommended her, would do the same; a request, which had been exactly observed.

Laurentini, on her arrival in France, had carefully concealed her name and family, and, the better to disguise her real history, had, on entering the convent, caused the story to be circulated, which had imposed on sister Frances, and it is probable, that the abbess, who did not preside in the convent, at the time of her noviciation, was also entirely ignorant of the truth. The deep remorse, that seized on the mind of Laurentini, together with the sufferings of disappointed passion, for she still loved the Marquis, again unsettled her intellects, and, after the first paroxysms of despair were passed, a heavy and silent melancholy had settled upon her spirits, which suffered few interruptions from fits of phrensy, till the time of her death. During many years, it had been her only amusement to walk in the woods near the monastery, in the solitary hours of night, and to play upon a favourite instrument, to which she sometimes joined the delightful melody of her voice, in the most solemn and melancholy airs of her native country, modulated by all the energetic feeling, that dwelt in her heart. The physician, who had attended her, recommended it to the superior to indulge her in this whim, as the only means of soothing her distempered fancy; and she was suffered to walk in the lonely hours of night, attended by the servant, who had accompanied her from Italy; but, as the indulgence transgressed against the rules of the convent, it was kept as secret as possible; and thus the mysterious music of Laurentini had combined with other circumstances, to produce a report, that not only the chateau, but its neighbourhood, was haunted.

Soon after her entrance into this holy community, and before she had shewn any symptoms of insanity there, she made a will, in which, after bequeathing a considerable legacy to the convent, she divided the remainder of her personal property, which her jewels made very valuable, between the wife of Mons. Bonnac, who was an Italian lady and her relation, and the nearest surviving relative of the late Marchioness de Villeroi. As Emily St. Aubert was not only the nearest, but the sole relative, this legacy descended to her, and thus explained to her the whole mystery of her father's conduct.

The resemblance between Emily and her unfortunate aunt had frequently been observed by Laurentini, and had occasioned the singular behaviour, which had formerly alarmed her; but it was in the nun's dying hour, when her conscience gave her perpetually the idea of the Marchioness, that she became more sensible, than ever, of this likeness, and, in her phrensy, deemed it no resemblance of the person

she had injured, but the original herself. The bold assertion, that had followed, on the recovery of her senses, that
Emily was the daughter of the Marchioness de Villeroi,
arose from a suspicion that she was so; for, knowing that
her rival, when she married the Marquis, was attached to
another lover, she had scarcely scrupled to believe, that her
honour had been sacrificed, like her own, to an unresisted
passion.

Of a crime, however, to which Emily had suspected, from
her phrensied confession of murder, that she had been in-
strumental in the castle of Udolpho, Laurentini was innocent; and she had herself been deceived, concerning the
spectacle, that formerly occasioned her so much terror, and
had since compelled her, for a while, to attribute the horrors of the nun to a consciousness of a murder, committed
in that castle.

It may be remembered, that, in a chamber of Udolpho,
hung a black veil, whose singular situation had excited
Emily's curiosity, and which afterwards disclosed an object, that had overwhelmed her with horror; for, on lifting it,
there appeared, instead of the picture she had expected,
within a recess of the wall, a human figure of ghastly paleness, stretched at its length, and dressed in the habiliments
of the grave. What added to the horror of the spectacle, was,
that the face appeared partly decayed and disfigured by
worms, which were visible on the features and hands. On
such an object, it will be readily believed, that no person
could endure to look twice. Emily, it may be recollected,
had, after the first glance, let the veil drop, and her terror
had prevented her from ever after provoking a renewal of
such suffering, as she had then experienced. Had she dared
to look again, her delusion and her fears would have vanished together, and she would have perceived, that the
figure before her was not human, but formed of wax. The

history of it is somewhat extraordinary, though not without example in the records of that fierce severity, which monkish superstition has sometimes inflicted on mankind. A member of the house of Udolpho, having committed some offence against the prerogative of the church, had been condemned to the penance of contemplating, during certain hours of the day, a waxen image, made to resemble a human body in the state, to which it is reduced after death. This penance, serving as a memento of the condition at which he must himself arrive, had been designed to reprove the pride of the Marquis of Udolpho, which had formerly so much exasperated that of the Romish church; and he had not only superstitiously observed this penance himself, which, he had believed, was to obtain a pardon for all his sins, but had made it a condition in his will, that his descendants should preserve the image, on pain of forfeiting to the church a certain part of his domain, that they also might profit by the humiliating moral it conveyed. The figure, therefore, had been suffered to retain its station in the wall of the chamber, but his descendants excused themselves from observing the penance, to which he had been enjoined.

This image was so horribly natural, that it is not surprising Emily should have mistaken it for the object it resembled, nor, since she had heard such an extraordinary account, concerning the disappearing of the late lady of the castle, and had such experience of the character of Montoni, that she should have believed this to be the murdered body of the lady Laurentini, and that he had been the contriver of her death.

The situation, in which she had discovered it, occasioned her, at first, much surprise and perplexity; but the vigilance, with which the doors of the chamber, where it was deposited, were afterwards secured, had compelled her to believe, that Montoni, not daring to confide the secret of her death to any person, had suffered her remains to decay in this obscure chamber. The ceremony of the veil, however, and the circumstance of the doors having been left open, even for a moment, had occasioned her much wonder and some doubts; but these were not sufficient to overcome her suspicion of Montoni; and it was the dread of his terrible vengeance, that had sealed her lips in silence, concerning what she had seen in the west chamber.

Emily, in discovering the Marchioness de Villeroi to have been the sister of Mons. St. Aubert, was variously affected; but, amidst the sorrow, which she suffered for her untimely death, she was released from an anxious and painful conjecture, occasioned by the rash assertion of Signora Laurentini, concerning her birth and the honour of her parents. Her faith in St. Aubert's principles would scarcely allow her to suspect that he had acted dishonourably; and she felt such reluctance to believe herself the daughter of any other, than her, whom she had always considered and loved as a mother, that she would hardly admit such a circumstance to be possible; yet the likeness, which it had frequently been affirmed she bore to the late Marchioness, the former behaviour of Dorothée the old housekeeper, the assertion of Laurentini, and the mysterious attachment, which St. Aubert had discovered, awakened doubts, as to his connection with the Marchioness, which her reason could neither vanquish, or confirm. From these, however, she was now relieved, and all the circumstances of her father's conduct were fully explained; but her heart was oppressed by the melancholy catastrophe of her amiable relative, and by the awful lesson, which the history of the nun exhibited, the indulgence of whose passions had been the means of leading her gradually to the commission of a crime, from the prophecy of which in her early years she would have recoiled in horror, and exclaimed—that it could not be!—a crime, which whole years of repentance and of the severest penance had not been able to obliterate from her conscience.*

---

* Space does not permit recounting the series of adventures and misadventures that occur before Emily and Valancourt are reunited— "restored to each other—to the beloved landscapes of their native country,—to the securest felicity of this life, that of aspiring to moral and labouring for intellectual improvement—to the pleasures of enlightened society, and to the exercise of the benevolence, which had always animated their hearts; while the bowers of La Vallée became once more the reatreat of goodness, wisdom, and domestic blessedness!"—ED.

Northanger Abbey

BY

JANE AUSTEN

NORTHANGER ABBEY:

AND

PERSUASION.

BY THE AUTHOR OF " PRIDE AND PREJUDICE,"
" MANSFIELD-PARK," &c.

WITH A BIOGRAPHICAL NOTICE OF THE
AUTHOR.

IN FOUR VOLUMES.

VOL. I.

LONDON:

JOHN MURRAY, ALBEMARLE-STREET,

1818.

Volume One

CHAPTER I

No one who had ever seen Catherine Morland in her infancy, would have supposed her born to be an heroine. Her situation in life, the character of her father and mother, her own person and disposition, were all equally against her. Her father was a clergyman, without being neglected, or poor, and a very respectable man, though his name was Richard—and he had never been handsome. He had a considerable independence, besides two good livings—and he was not in the least addicted to locking up his daughters. Her mother was a woman of useful plain sense, with a good temper, and, what is more remarkable, with a good constitution. She had three sons before Catherine was born; and instead of dying in bringing the latter into the world, as any body might expect, she still lived on—lived to have six children more—to see them growing up around her, and to enjoy excellent health herself. A family of ten children will be always called a fine family, where there are heads and arms and legs enough for the number; but the Morlands had little other right to the word, for they were in general very plain, and Catherine, for many years of her life, as plain as any. She had a thin awkward figure, a sallow skin without colour, dark lank hair, and strong features;—so much for her person;—and not less unpropitious for heroism seemed her mind. She was fond of all boys' plays, and greatly preferred cricket not merely to dolls, but to the more heroic enjoyments of infancy, nursing a dormouse, feeding a canary-bird, or watering a rose-bush. Indeed she had no taste for a garden; and if she gathered flowers at all, it was chiefly for the pleasure of mischief—at least so it was conjectured from her always preferring those which she was forbidden to take.—Such were her propensities—her abilities were quite as extraordinary. She never could learn or understand any thing before she was taught; and sometimes not even then, for she was often inattentive, and occasionally stupid. Her mother was three months in teaching her only to repeat the "Beggar's Petition;" and after all, her next sister, Sally, could say it better than she did. Not that Catherine was always stupid,—by no means; she learnt the fable of "The Hare and many Friends," as quickly as any girl in England. Her mother wished her to learn music; and Catherine was sure she should like it, for she was very fond of tinkling the keys of the old forlorn spinnet; so, at eight years old she began. She learnt a year, and could not bear it;—and Mrs. Morland, who did not insist on her daughters being accomplished in spite of incapacity or distaste, allowed her to leave off. The day which dismissed the music-master was one of the happiest of Catherine's life. Her taste for drawing was not superior; though whenever she could obtain the outside of a letter from her mother, or seize upon any other odd piece of paper, she did what she could in that way, by drawing houses and trees, hens and chickens, all very much like one another.—Writing and accounts she was taught by her father; French by her mother: her proficiency in either was not remarkable, and she shirked her lessons in both whenever she could. What a strange, unaccountable character!—for with all these symptoms of profligacy at ten years old, she had neither a bad heart nor a bad temper; was seldom stubborn, scarcely ever quarrelsome, and very kind to the little ones, with few interruptions of tyranny; she was moreover noisy and wild, hated confinement and cleanliness, and loved nothing so well in the world as rolling down the green slope at the back of the house.

Such was Catherine Morland at ten. At fifteen, appearances were mending; she began to curl her hair and long for balls; her complexion improved, her features were softened by plumpness and colour, her eyes gained more animation, and her figure more consequence. Her love of dirt gave way to an inclination for finery, and she grew clean as she grew smart; she had now the pleasure of sometimes hearing her father and mother remark on her personal improvement. "Catherine grows quite a good-looking girl,—she is almost pretty to day," were words which caught her ears now and then; and how welcome were the sounds! To look *almost* pretty, is an acquisition of higher delight to a girl who has been looking plain the first fifteen years of her life, than a beauty from her cradle can ever receive.

Mrs. Morland was a very good woman, and wished to see her children every thing they ought to be; but her time was so much occupied in lying-in and teaching the little ones, that her elder daughters were inevitably left to shift for themselves; and it was not very wonderful that Catherine, who had by nature nothing heroic about her, should prefer cricket, base ball, riding on horseback, and running about the country at the age of fourteen, to books—or at least books of information—for, provided that nothing like useful knowledge could be gained from them, provided they were all story and no reflection, she had never any objection to books at all. But from fifteen to seventeen she was in training for a heroine; she read all such works as heroines must read to supply their memories with those quotations which are so serviceable and so soothing in the vicissitudes of their eventful lives.

From Pope, she learnt to censure those who

> "bear about the mockery of woe."

From Gray, that

> "Many a flower is born to blush unseen,
> "And waste its fragrance on the desert air."

From Thompson, that

>   ———"It is a delightful task
> "To teach the young idea how to shoot."

And from Shakespeare she gained a great store of information—amongst the rest, that

>   ———"Trifles light as air,
> "Are, to the jealous, confirmation strong,
> "As proofs of Holy Writ."

That

> "The poor beetle, which we tread upon,
> "In corporal sufferance feels a pang as great
> "As when a giant dies."

And that a young woman in love always looks

>   ———"like Patience on a monument
> "Smiling at Grief."

So far her improvement was sufficient—and in many other points she came on exceedingly well; for though she could not write sonnets, she brought herself to read them; and though there seemed no chance of her throwing a whole party into raptures by a prelude on the pianoforte, of her own composition, she could listen to other people's performance with very little fatigue. Her greatest deficiency was in the pencil—she had no notion of drawing—not enough even to attempt a sketch of her lover's profile, that she might be detected in the design. There she fell miserably short of the true heroic height. At present she did not know her own poverty, for she had no lover to pourtray. She had reached the age of seventeen, without having seen one amiable youth who could call forth her sensibility; without having inspired one real passion, and without having excited even any admiration but what was very moderate and very transient. This was strange indeed! But strange things may be generally accounted for if their cause be fairly searched out. There was not one lord in the neighbourhood; no—not even a baronet. There was not one family among their acquaintance who had reared and supported a boy accidentally found at their door—not one young man whose origin was unknown. Her father had no ward, and the squire of the parish no children.

But when a young lady is to be a heroine, the perverseness of forty surrounding families cannot prevent her. Something must and will happen to throw a hero in her way.

Mr. Allen, who owned the chief of the property about Fullerton, the village in Wiltshire where the Morlands lived, was ordered to Bath for the benefit of a gouty constitution;—and his lady, a good-humoured woman, fond of Miss Morland, and probably aware that if adventures will not befal a young lady in her own village, she must seek them abroad, invited her to go with them. Mr. and Mrs. Morland were all compliance, and Catherine all happiness.

CHAPTER II

In addition to what has already been said of Catherine Morland's personal and mental endowments, when about to be launched into all the difficulties and dangers of a six weeks' residence in Bath, it may be stated, for the reader's more certain information, lest the following pages should otherwise fail of giving any idea of what her character is meant to be; that her heart was affectionate, her disposition cheerful and open, without conceit or affectation of any kind—her manners just removed from the awkwardness and shyness of a girl; her person pleasing, and, when in good looks, pretty—and her mind about as ignorant and uninformed as the female mind at seventeen usually is.

When the hour of departure drew near, the maternal anxiety of Mrs. Morland will be naturally supposed to be most severe. A thousand alarming presentiments of evil to her beloved Catherine from this terrific separation must oppress her heart with sadness, and drown her in tears for the last day or two of their being together; and advice of the most important and applicable nature must of course flow from her wise lips in their parting conference in her closet. Cautions against the violence of such noblemen and baronets as delight in forcing young ladies away to some remote farm-house, must, at such a moment, relieve the fulness of her heart. Who would not think so? But Mrs. Morland knew so little of lords and baronets, that she entertained no notion of their general mischievousness, and was wholly unsuspicious of danger to her daughter from their machinations. Her cautions were confined to the following points. "I beg, Catherine, you will always wrap yourself up very warm about the throat, when you come from the Rooms at night; and I wish you would try to keep some account of the money you spend;—I will give you this little book on purpose."

Sally, or rather Sarah, (for what young lady of common gentility will reach the age of sixteen without altering her name as far as she can?) must from situation be at this time the intimate friend and confidante of her sister. It is remarkable, however, that she neither insisted on Catherine's writing by every post, nor exacted her promise of transmitting the character of every new acquaintance, nor a detail of every interesting conversation that Bath might produce. Every thing indeed relative to this important journey was done, on the part of the Morlands, with a degree of moderation and composure, which seemed rather consistent with the common feelings of common life, than with the refined susceptibilities, the tender emotions which the first separation of a heroine from her family ought always to excite. Her father, instead of giving her an unlimited order on his banker, or even putting an hundred pounds bank-bill into her hands, gave her only ten guineas, and promised her more when she wanted it.

Under these unpromising auspices, the parting took place, and the journey began. It was performed with suitable quietness and uneventful safety. Neither robbers nor tempests befriended them, nor one lucky overturn to introduce them to the hero. Nothing more alarming occurred than a fear on Mrs. Allen's side, of having once left her clogs behind her at an inn, and that fortunately proved to be groundless.

They arrived at Bath. Catherine was all eager delight;— her eyes were here, there, every where, as they approached its fine and striking environs, and afterwards drove through those streets which conducted them to the hotel. She was come to be happy, and she felt happy already.

They were soon settled in comfortable lodgings in Pulteney-street.

It is now expedient to give some description of Mrs. Allen, that the reader may be able to judge, in what manner her actions will hereafter tend to promote the general distress of the work, and how she will, probably, contribute to reduce poor Catherine to all the desperate wretchedness of which a last volume is capable—whether by her imprudence, vulgarity, or jealousy—whether by intercepting her letters, ruining her character, or turning her out of doors.

Mrs. Allen was one of that numerous class of females, whose society can raise no other emotion than surprise at there being any men in the world who could like them well enough to marry them. She had neither beauty, genius, accomplishment, nor manner. The air of a gentle-woman, a great deal of quiet, inactive good temper, and a trifling turn of mind, were all that could account for her being the choice of a sensible, intelligent man, like Mr. Allen. In one respect she was admirably fitted to introduce a young lady into public, being as fond of going every where and seeing every thing herself as any young lady could be. Dress was her passion. She had a most harmless delight in being fine; and our heroine's entrée into life could not take place till after three or four days had been spent in learning what was mostly worn, and her chaperon was provided with a dress of the newest fashion. Catherine too made some purchases herself, and when all these matters were arranged, the important evening came which was to usher her into the Upper Rooms. Her hair was cut and dressed by the best hand, her clothes put on with care, and both Mrs. Allen and her maid declared she looked quite as she should do. With such encouragement, Catherine hoped at least to pass uncensured through the crowd. As for admiration, it was always very welcome when it came, but she did not depend on it.

Mrs. Allen was so long in dressing, that they did not

enter the ball-room till late. The season was full, the room crowded, and the two ladies squeezed in as well as they could. As for Mr. Allen, he repaired directly to the card-room, and left them to enjoy a mob by themselves. With more care for the safety of her new gown than for the comfort of her protegée, Mrs. Allen made her way through the throng of men by the door, as swiftly as the necessary caution would allow; Catherine, however, kept close at her side, and linked her arm too firmly within her friend's to be torn asunder by any common effort of a struggling assembly. But to her utter amazement she found that to proceed along the room was by no means the way to disengage themselves from the crowd; it seemed rather to increase as they went on, whereas she had imagined that when once fairly within the door, they should easily find seats and be able to watch the dances with perfect convenience. But this was far from being the case, and though by unwearied diligence they gained even the top of the room, their situation was just the same; they saw nothing of the dancers but the high feathers of some of the ladies. Still they moved on—something better was yet in view; and by a continued exertion of strength and ingenuity they found themselves at last in the passage behind the highest bench. Here there was something less of crowd than below; and hence Miss Morland had a comprehensive view of all the company beneath her, and of all the dangers of her late passage through them. It was a splendid sight, and she began, for the first time that evening, to feel herself at a ball: she longed to dance, but she had not an acquaintance in the room. Mrs. Allen did all that she could do in such a case by saying very placidly, every now and then, "I wish you could dance, my dear,—I wish you could get a partner." For some time her young friend felt obliged to her for these wishes; but they were repeated so often, and proved so totally ineffectual, that Catherine grew tired at last, and would thank her no more.

They were not long able, however, to enjoy the repose of the eminence they had so laboriously gained.—Every body was shortly in motion for tea, and they must squeeze out like the rest. Catherine began to feel something of disappointment—she was tired of being continually pressed against by people, the generality of whose faces possessed nothing to interest, and with all of whom she was so wholly unacquainted, that she could not relieve the irksomeness of imprisonment by the exchange of a syllable with any of her fellow captives; and when at last arrived in the tea-room, she felt yet more the awkwardness of having no party to join, no acquaintance to claim, no gentleman to assist them.— They saw nothing of Mr. Allen; and after looking about them in vain for a more eligible situation, were obliged to sit down at the end of a table, at which a large party were already placed, without having any thing to do there, or any body to speak to, except each other.

Mrs. Allen congratulated herself, as soon as they were seated, on having preserved her gown from injury. "It would have been very shocking to have it torn," said she, "would not it?—It is such a delicate muslin.—For my part I have not seen any thing I like so well in the whole room, I assure you."

"How uncomfortable it is," whispered Catherine, "not to have a single acquaintance here!"

"Yes, my dear," replied Mrs. Allen, with perfect serenity, "it is very uncomfortable indeed."

"What shall we do?—The gentlemen and ladies at this table look as if they wondered why we came here—we seem forcing ourselves into their party."

"Aye, so we do.—That is very disagreeable. I wish we had a large acquaintance here."

"I wish we had *any*;—it would be somebody to go to."

"Very true, my dear; and if we knew anybody we would

join them directly. The Skinners were here last year—I wish they were here now."

"Had not we better go away as it is?—Here are no tea things for us, you see."

"No more there are, indeed.—How very provoking! But I think we had better sit still, for one gets so tumbled in such a crowd! How is my head, my dear?—Somebody gave me a push that has hurt it I am afraid."

"No, indeed, it looks very nice.—But, dear Mrs. Allen, are you sure there is nobody you know in all this multitude of people? I think you *must* know somebody."

"I don't upon my word—I wish I did. I wish I had a large acquaintance here with all my heart, and then I should get you a partner.—I should be so glad to have you dance. There goes a strange-looking woman! What an odd gown she has got on!—How old fashioned it is! Look at the back."

After some time they received an offer of tea from one of their neighbours; it was thankfully accepted, and this introduced a light conversation with the gentleman who offered it, which was the only time that any body spoke to them during the evening, till they were discovered and joined by Mr. Allen when the dance was over.

"Well, Miss Morland," said he, directly, "I hope you have had an agreeable ball."

"Very agreeable indeed," she replied, vainly endeavouring to hide a great yawn.

"I wish she had been able to dance," said his wife, "I wish we could have got a partner for her.—I have been saying how glad I should be if the Skinners were here this winter instead of last; or if the Parrys had come, as they talked of once, she might have danced with George Parry. I am so sorry she has not had a partner!"

"We shall do better another evening I hope," was Mr. Allen's consolation.

The company began to disperse when the dancing was

over—enough to leave space for the remainder to walk about in some comfort; and now was the time for a heroine, who had not yet played a very distinguished part in the events of the evening, to be noticed and admired. Every five minutes, by removing some of the crowd, gave greater openings for her charms. She was now seen by many young men who had not been near her before. Not one, however, started with rapturous wonder on beholding her, no whisper of eager inquiry ran round the room, nor was she once called a divinity by any body. Yet Catherine was in very good looks, and had the company only seen her three years before, they would *now* have thought her exceedingly handsome.

She *was* looked at however, and with some admiration; for, in her own hearing, two gentlemen pronounced her to be a pretty girl. Such words had their due effect; she immediately thought the evening pleasanter than she had found it before—her humble vanity was contented—she felt more obliged to the two young men for this simple praise than a true quality heroine would have been for fifteen sonnets in celebration of her charms, and went to her chair in good humour with every body, and perfectly satisfied with her share of public attention.

CHAPTER III

Every morning now brought its regular duties;—shops were to be visited; some new part of the town to be looked at; and the Pump-room to be attended, where they paraded up and down for an hour, looking at every body and speaking to no one. The wish of a numerous acquaintance in Bath was still uppermost with Mrs. Allen, and she repeated it after every fresh proof, which every morning brought, of her knowing nobody at all.

They made their appearance in the Lower Rooms; and here fortune was more favourable to our heroine. The master of the ceremonies introduced to her a very gentleman-like young man as a partner;—his name was Tilney. He seemed to be about four or five and twenty, was rather tall, had a pleasing countenance, a very intelligent and lively eye, and, if not quite handsome, was very near it. His address was good, and Catherine felt herself in high luck. There was little leisure for speaking while they danced; but when they were seated at tea, she found him as agreeable as she had already given him credit for being. He talked with fluency and spirit—and there was an archness and pleasantry in his manner which interested, though it was hardly understood by her. After chatting some time on such matters as naturally arose from the objects around them, he suddenly addressed her with—"I have hitherto been very remiss, madam, in the proper attentions of a partner here; I have not yet asked you how long you have been in Bath; whether you were ever here before; whether you have been at the Upper Rooms, the theatre, and the concert; and how you like the place altogether. I have been very negligent—but are you now at leisure to satisfy me in these particulars? If you are I will begin directly."

"You need not give yourself that trouble, sir."

"No trouble I assure you, madam." Then forming his features into a set smile, and affectedly softening his voice, he added, with a simpering air, "Have you been long in Bath, madam?"

"About a week, sir," replied Catherine, trying not to laugh.

"Really!" with affected astonishment.

"Why should you be surprized, sir?"

"Why, indeed!" said he, in his natural tone—"but some emotion must appear to be raised by your reply, and surprize is more easily assumed, and not less reasonable than any other.—Now let us go on. Were you never here before, madam?"

"Never, sir."

"Indeed! Have you yet honoured the Upper Rooms?"

"Yes, sir, I was there last Monday."

"Have you been to the theatre?"

"Yes, sir, I was at the play on Tuesday."

"To the concert?"

"Yes, sir, on Wednesday."

"And are you altogether pleased with Bath?"

"Yes—I like it very well."

"Now I must give one smirk, and then we may be rational again."

Catherine turned away her head, not knowing whether she might venture to laugh.

"I see what you think of me," said he gravely—"I shall make but a poor figure in your journal to-morrow."

"My journal!"

"Yes, I know exactly what you will say: Friday, went to the Lower Rooms; wore my sprigged muslin robe with blue trimmings—plain black shoes—appeared to much advantage; but was strangely harassed by a queer, half-witted man, who would make me dance with him, and distressed me by his nonsense."

"Indeed I shall say no such thing."

"Shall I tell you what you ought to say?"

"If you please."

"I danced with a very agreeable young man, introduced by Mr. King; had a great deal of conversation with him—seems a most extraordinary genius—hope I may know more of him. *That*, madam, is what I *wish* you to say."

"But, perhaps, I keep no journal."

"Perhaps you are not sitting in this room, and I am not sitting by you. These are points in which a doubt is equally possible. Not keep a journal! How are your absent cousins to understand the tenour of your life in Bath without one? How are the civilities and compliments of every day to be related as they ought to be, unless noted down every evening in a journal? How are your various dresses to be remembered, and the particular state of your complexion, and curl of your hair to be described in all their diversities, without having constant recourse to a journal?—My dear madam, I am not so ignorant of young ladies' ways as you wish to believe me; it is this delightful habit of journalizing which largely contributes to form the easy style of writing for which ladies are so generally celebrated. Every body allows that the talent of writing agreeable letters is peculiarly female. Nature may have done something, but I am sure it must be essentially assisted by the practice of keeping a journal."

"I have sometimes thought," said Catherine, doubtingly, "whether ladies do write so much better letters than gentlemen! That is—I should not think the superiority was always on our side."

"As far as I have had opportunity of judging, it appears

to me that the usual style of letter-writing among women is faultless, except in three particulars."

"And what are they?"

"A general deficiency of subject, a total inattention to stops, and a very frequent ignorance of grammar."

"Upon my word! I need not have been afraid of disclaiming the compliment. You do not think too highly of us in that way."

"I should no more lay it down as a general rule that women write better letters than men, than that they sing better duets, or draw better landscapes. In every power, of which taste is the foundation, excellence is pretty fairly divided between the sexes."

They were interrupted by Mrs. Allen:—"My dear Catherine," said she, "do take this pin out of my sleeve; I am afraid it has torn a hole already; I shall be quite sorry if it has, for this is a favourite gown, though it cost but nine shillings a yard."

"That is exactly what I should have guessed it, madam," said Mr. Tilney, looking at the muslin.

"Do you understand muslins, sir?"

"Particularly well; I always buy my own cravats, and am allowed to be an excellent judge; and my sister has often trusted me in the choice of a gown. I bought one for her the other day, and it was pronounced to be a prodigious bargain by every lady who saw it. I gave but five shillings a yard for it, and a true Indian muslin."

Mrs. Allen was quite struck by his genius. "Men commonly take so little notice of those things," said she: "I can never get Mr. Allen to know one of my gowns from another. You must be a great comfort to your sister, sir."

"I hope I am, madam."

"And pray, sir, what do you think of Miss Morland's gown?"

"It is very pretty, madam," said he, gravely examining

it; "but I do not think it will wash well; I am afraid it will fray."

"How can you," said Catherine, laughing, "be so ——" she had almost said, strange.

"I am quite of your opinion, sir," replied Mrs. Allen: "and so I told Miss Morland when she bought it."

"But then you know, madam, muslin always turns to some account or other; Miss Morland will get enough out of it for a handkerchief, or a cap, or a cloak.—Muslin can never be said to be wasted. I have heard my sister say so forty times, when she has been extravagant in buying more than she wanted, or careless in cutting it to pieces."

"Bath is a charming place, sir; there are so many good shops here.—We are sadly off in the country; not but what we have very good shops in Salisbury, but it is so far to go; —eight miles is a long way; Mr. Allen says it is nine, measured nine; but I am sure it cannot be more than eight; and it is such a fag—I come back tired to death. Now here one can step out of doors and get a thing in five minutes."

Mr. Tilney was polite enough to seem interested in what she said; and she kept him on the subject of muslins till the dancing recommenced. Catherine feared, as she listened to their discourse, that he indulged himself a little too much with the foibles of others.—"What are you thinking of so earnestly?" said he, as they walked back to the ball-room;— "not of your partner, I hope, for, by that shake of the head, your meditations are not satisfactory."

Catherine coloured, and said, "I was not thinking of any thing."

"That is artful and deep, to be sure; but I had rather be told at once that you will not tell me."

"Well then, I will not."

"Thank you; for now we shall soon be acquainted, as I am authorized to tease you on this subject whenever we meet, and nothing in the world advances intimacy so much."

They danced again; and, when the assembly closed, parted, on the lady's side at least, with a strong inclination for continuing the acquaintance. Whether she thought of him so much, while she drank her warm wine and water, and prepared herself for bed, as to dream of him when there, cannot be ascertained; but I hope it was no more than in a slight slumber, or a morning doze at most; for if it be true, as a celebrated writer has maintained, that no young lady can be justified in falling in love before the gentleman's love is declared,* it must be very improper that a young lady should dream of a gentleman before the gentleman is first known to have dreamt of her. How proper Mr. Tilney might be as a dreamer or a lover, had not yet perhaps entered Mr. Allen's head, but that he was not objectionable as a common acquaintance for his young charge he was on inquiry satisfied; for he had early in the evening taken pains to know who her partner was, and had been assured of Mr. Tilney's being a clergyman, and of a very respectable family in Gloucestershire.

* Vide a letter from Mr. Richardson, No. 97, vol. ii. Rambler.

CHAPTER IV

With more than usual eagerness did Catherine hasten to the Pump-room the next day, secure within herself of seeing Mr. Tilney there before the morning were over, and ready to meet him with a smile:—but no smile was demanded—Mr. Tilney did not appear. Every creature in Bath, except himself, was to be seen in the room at different periods of the fashionable hours; crowds of people were every moment passing in and out, up the steps and down; people whom nobody cared about, and nobody wanted to see; and he only was absent. "What a delightful place Bath is," said Mrs. Allen, as they sat down near the great clock, after parading the room till they were tired; "and how pleasant it would be if we had any acquaintance here."

This sentiment had been uttered so often in vain, that Mrs. Allen had no particular reason to hope it would be followed with more advantage now; but we are told to "despair of nothing we would attain," as "unwearied diligence our point would gain;" and the unwearied diligence with which she had every day wished for the same thing was at length to have its just reward, for hardly had she been seated ten minutes before a lady of about her own age, who was sitting by her, and had been looking at her attentively for several minutes, addressed her with great complaisance in these words:—"I think, madam, I cannot be mistaken; it is a long time since I had the pleasure of seeing you, but is not your name Allen?" This question answered, as it readily was, the stranger pronounced her's to be Thorpe; and Mrs. Allen immediately recognized the features of a former school-fellow and intimate, whom she had seen only once since their respective marriages, and that many years ago. Their joy on this meeting was very great, as well it might, since they had been contented to know nothing of each other for the last fifteen years. Compliments on good looks now passed; and, after observing how time had slipped away since they were last together, how little they had thought of meeting in Bath, and what a pleasure it was to see an old friend, they proceeded to make inquiries and give intelligence as to their families, sisters, and cousins, talking both together, far more ready to give than to receive information, and each hearing very little of what the other said. Mrs. Thorpe, however, had one great advantage as a talker, over Mrs. Allen, in a family of children; and when she expatiated on the talents of her sons, and the beauty of her daughters, —when she related their different situations and views,— that John was at Oxford, Edward at Merchant-Taylors', and William at sea,—and all of them more beloved and respected in their different station than any other three beings ever were, Mrs. Allen had no similar information to give, no similar triumphs to press on the unwilling and unbelieving ear of her friend, and was forced to sit and appear to listen to all these maternal effusions, consoling herself, however, with the discovery, which her keen eye soon made, that the lace on Mrs. Thorpe's pelisse was not half so handsome as that on her own.

"Here come my dear girls," cried Mrs. Thorpe, pointing at three smart looking females, who, arm in arm, were then moving towards her. "My dear Mrs. Allen, I long to introduce them; they will be so delighted to see you: the tallest is Isabella, my eldest; is not she a fine young woman? The others are very much admired too, but I believe Isabella is the handsomest."

The Miss Thorpes were introduced; and Miss Morland, who had been for a short time forgotten, was introduced likewise. The name seemed to strike them all; and, after speaking to her with great civility, the eldest young lady observed aloud to the rest, "How excessively like her brother Miss Morland is!"

"The very picture of him indeed!" cried the mother— and "I should have known her any where for his sister!" was repeated by them all, two or three times over. For a moment Catherine was surprized; but Mrs. Thorpe and her daughters had scarcely begun the history of their acquaintance with Mr. James Morland, before she remembered that her eldest brother had lately formed an intimacy with a young man of his own college, of the name of Thorpe; and that he had spent the last week of the Christmas vacation with his family, near London.

The whole being explained, many obliging things were said by the Miss Thorpes of their wish of being better acquainted with her; of being considered as already friends, through the friendship of their brothers, &c. which Catherine heard with pleasure, and answered with all the pretty expressions she could command; and, as the first proof of amity, she was soon invited to accept an arm of the eldest Miss Thorpe, and take a turn with her about the room. Catherine was delighted with this extension of her Bath acquaintance, and almost forgot Mr. Tilney while she talked to Miss Thorpe. Friendship is certainly the finest balm for the pangs of disappointed love.

Their conversation turned upon those subjects, of which the free discussion has generally much to do in perfecting a sudden intimacy between two young ladies; such as dress, balls, flirtations, and quizzes. Miss Thorpe, however, being four years older than Miss Morland, and at least four years better informed, had a very decided advantage in discussing such points; she could compare the balls of Bath with those of Tunbridge; its fashions with the fashions of London; could rectify the opinions of her new friend in many articles of tasteful attire; could discover a flirtation between any gentleman and lady who only smiled on each other; and point out a quiz through the thickness of a crowd. These powers received due admiration from Catherine, to whom they were entirely new; and the respect which they naturally inspired might have been too great for familiarity, had not the easy gaiety of Miss Thorpe's manners, and her frequent expressions of delight on this acquaintance with her, softened down every feeling of awe, and left nothing but tender affection. Their increasing attachment was not to be satisfied with half a dozen turns in the Pump-room, but required, when they all quitted it together, that Miss Thorpe should accompany Miss Morland to the very door of Mr. Allen's house; and that they should there part with a most affectionate and lengthened shake of hands, after learning, to their mutual relief, that they should see each other across the theatre at night, and say their prayers in the same chapel the next morning. Catherine then ran directly up stairs, and watched Miss Thorpe's progress down the street from the drawing-room window; admired the graceful spirit of her walk, the fashionable air of her figure and dress, and felt grateful, as well she might, for the chance which had procured her such a friend.

Mrs. Thorpe was a widow, and not a very rich one; she was a good-humoured, well-meaning woman, and a very indulgent mother. Her eldest daughter had great personal beauty, and the younger ones, by pretending to be as handsome as their sister, imitating her air, and dressing in the same style, did very well.

This brief account of the family is intended to supersede the necessity of a long and minute detail from Mrs. Thorpe herself, of her past adventures and sufferings, which might otherwise be expected to occupy the three or four following chapters; in which the worthlessness of lords and attornies might be set forth, and conversations, which had passed twenty years before, be minutely repeated.

CHAPTER V

Catherine was not so much engaged at the theatre that evening, in returning the nods and smiles of Miss Thorpe, though they certainly claimed much of her leisure, as to forget to look with an inquiring eye for Mr. Tilney in every box which her eye could reach; but she looked in vain. Mr. Tilney was no fonder of the play than the Pump-room. She hoped to be more fortunate the next day; and when her wishes for fine weather were answered by seeing a beautiful morning, she hardly felt a doubt of it; for a fine Sunday in Bath empties every house of its inhabitants, and all the world appears on such an occasion to walk about and tell their acquaintance what a charming day it is.

As soon as divine service was over, the Thorpes and Allens eagerly joined each other; and after staying long enough in the Pump-room to discover that the crowd was insupportable, and that there was not a genteel face to be seen, which every body discovers every Sunday throughout the season, they hastened away to the Crescent, to breathe the fresh air of better company. Here Catherine and Isabella, arm in arm, again tasted the sweets of friendship in an unreserved conversation;—they talked much, and with much enjoyment; but again was Catherine disappointed in her hope of re-seeing her partner. He was no where to be met with; every search for him was equally unsuccessful, in morning lounges or evening assemblies; neither at the upper nor lower rooms, at dressed or undressed balls, was he perceivable; nor among the walkers, the horsemen, or the curricle-drivers of the morning. His name was not in the Pump-room book, and curiosity could do no more. He must be gone from Bath. Yet he had not mentioned that his stay would be so short! This sort of mysteriousness, which is always so becoming in a hero, threw a fresh grace in Catherine's imagination around his person and manners, and increased her anxiety to know more of him. From the Thorpes she could learn nothing, for they had been only two days in Bath before they met with Mrs. Allen. It was a subject, however, in which she often indulged with her fair friend, from whom she received every possible encouragement to continue to think of him; and his impression on her fancy was not suffered therefore to weaken. Isabella was very sure that he must be a charming young man; and was equally sure that he must have been delighted with her dear Catherine, and would therefore shortly return. She liked him the better for being a clergyman, "for she must confess herself very partial to the profession;" and something like a sigh escaped her as she said it. Perhaps Catherine was wrong in not demanding the cause of that gentle emotion—but she was not experienced enough in the finesse of love, or the duties of friendship, to know when delicate raillery was properly called for, or when a confidence should be forced.

Mrs. Allen was now quite happy—quite satisfied with Bath. She had found some acquaintance, had been so lucky too as to find in them the family of a most worthy old friend; and, as the completion of good fortune, had found these friends by no means so expensively dressed as herself. Her daily expressions were no longer, "I wish we had some acquaintance in Bath!" They were changed into—"How glad I am we have met with Mrs. Thorpe!"—and she was as eager in promoting the intercourse of the two families, as her young charge and Isabella themselves could be; never satisfied with the day unless she spent the chief of it by the side of Mrs. Thorpe, in what they called conversation, but in which there was scarcely ever any exchange of opinion, and not often any resemblance of subject, for Mrs. Thorpe talked chiefly of her children, and Mrs. Allen of her gowns.

The progress of the friendship between Catherine and Isabella was quick as its beginning had been warm, and they passed so rapidly through every gradation of increasing tenderness, that there was shortly no fresh proof of it to be given to their friends or themselves. They called each other by their Christian name, were always arm in arm when they walked, pinned up each other's train for the dance, and were not to be divided in the set; and if a rainy morning deprived them of other enjoyments, they were still resolute in meeting in defiance of wet and dirt, and shut themselves up, to read novels together. Yes, novels;—for I will not adopt that ungenerous and impolitic custom so common with novel writers, of degrading by their contemptuous censure the very performances, to the number of which they are themselves adding—joining with their greatest enemies in bestowing the harshest epithets on such works, and scarcely ever permitting them to be read by their own heroine, who, if she accidentally take up a novel, is sure to turn over its insipid pages with disgust. Alas! if the heroine of one novel be not patronized by the heroine of another, from whom can she expect protection and regard? I cannot approve of it. Let us leave it to the Reviewers to abuse such effusions of fancy at their leisure, and over every new novel to talk in threadbare strains of the trash with which the press now groans. Let us not desert one another; we are an injured body. Although our productions have afforded more extensive and unaffected pleasure than those of any other literary corporation in the world, no species of composition has been so much decried. From pride, ignorance, or fashion, our foes are almost as many as our readers. And while the abilities of the nine-hundredth abridger of the History of England, or of the man who collects and publishes in a volume some dozen lines of Milton, Pope, and Prior, with a paper from the Spectator, and a chapter from Sterne, are eulogized by a thousand pens,—there seems almost a general wish of decrying the capacity and undervaluing the labour of the novelist, and of slighting the performances which have only genius, wit, and taste to recommend them. "I am no novel reader—I seldom look into novels—Do not imagine that *I* often read novels—It is really very well for a novel."— Such is the common cant.—"And what are you reading, Miss ——?" "Oh! it is only a novel!" replies the young lady; while she lays down her book with affected indifference, or momentary shame.—"It is only Cecilia, or Camilla, or Belinda;" or, in short, only some work in which the greatest powers of the mind are displayed, in which the most thorough knowledge of human nature, the happiest delineation of its varieties, the liveliest effusions of wit and humour are conveyed to the world in the best chosen language. Now, had the same young lady been engaged with a volume of the Spectator, instead of such a work, how proudly would she have produced the book, and told its name; though the chances must be against her being occupied by any part of that voluminous publication, of which either the matter or manner would not disgust a young person of taste: the substance of its papers so often consisting in the statement of improbable circumstances, unnatural characters, and topics of conversation, which no longer concern any one living; and their language, too, frequently so coarse as to give no very favourable idea of the age that could endure it.

CHAPTER VI

The following conversation, which took place between the two friends in the Pump-room one morning, after an acquaintance of eight or nine days, is given as a specimen of their very warm attachment, and of the delicacy, discretion, originality of thought, and literary taste which marked the reasonableness of that attachment.

They met by appointment; and as Isabella had arrived nearly five minutes before her friend, her first address naturally was—"My dearest creature, what can have made you so late? I have been waiting for you at least this age!"

"Have you, indeed!—I am very sorry for it; but really I thought I was in very good time. It is but just one. I hope you have not been here long?"

"Oh! these ten ages at least. I am sure I have been here this half hour. But now, let us go and sit down at the other end of the room, and enjoy ourselves. I have an hundred things to say to you. In the first place, I was so afraid it would rain this morning, just as I wanted to set off; it looked very showery, and that would have thrown me into agonies! Do you know, I saw the pretiest hat you can imagine, in a shop window in Milsom-street just now—very like yours, only with coquelicot ribbons instead of green; I quite longed for it. But, my dearest Catherine, what have you been doing with yourself all this morning?—Have you gone on with Udolpho?"

"Yes, I have been reading it ever since I woke; and I am got to the black veil."

"Are you, indeed? How delightful! Oh! I would not tell

you what is behind the black veil for the world! Are not you wild to know?"

"Oh! yes, quite; what can it be?—But do not tell me—I would not be told upon any account. I know it must be a skeleton, I am sure it is Laurentina's skeleton. Oh! I am delighted with the book! I should like to spend my whole life in reading it. I assure you, if it had not been to meet you, I would not have come away from it for all the world."

"Dear creature! how much I am obliged to you; and when you have finished Udolpho, we will read the Italian together; and I have made out a list of ten or twelve more of the same kind for you."

"Have you, indeed! How glad I am!—What are they all?"

"I will read you their names directly; here they are, in my pocket-book. Castle of Wolfenbach, Clermont, Mysterious Warnings, Necromancer of the Black Forest, Midnight Bell, Orphan of the Rhine, and Horrid Mysteries. Those will last us some time."

"Yes, pretty well; but are they all horrid, are you sure they are all horrid?"

"Yes, quite sure; for a particular friend of mine, a Miss Andrews, a sweet girl, one of the sweetest creatures in the world, has read every one of them. I wish you knew Miss Andrews, you would be delighted with her. She is netting herself the sweetest cloak you can conceive. I think her as beautiful as an angel, and I am so vexed with the men for not admiring her!—I scold them all amazingly about it."

"Scold them! Do you scold them for not admiring her?"

"Yes, that I do. There is nothing I would not do for those who are really my friends. I have no notion of loving people by halves, it is not my nature. My attachments are always excessively strong. I told Capt. Hunt at one of our assemblies this winter, that if he was to tease me all night, I would not dance with him, unless he would allow Miss Andrews to be as beautiful as an angel. The men think us incapable of real friendship you know, and I am determined to shew them the difference. Now, if I were to hear any body speak slightingly of you, I should fire up in a moment: —but that is not at all likely, for *you* are just the kind of girl to be a great favourite with the men."

"Oh! dear," cried Catherine, colouring, "how can you say so?"

"I know you very well; you have so much animation, which is exactly what Miss Andrews wants, for I must confess there is something amazingly insipid about her. Oh! I must tell you, that just after we parted yesterday, I saw a young man looking at you so earnestly—I am sure he is in love with you." Catherine coloured, and disclaimed again. Isabella laughed. "It is very true, upon my honour, but I see how it is; you are indifferent to every body's admiration, except that of one gentleman, who shall be nameless. Nay, I cannot blame you—(speaking more seriously)—your feelings are easily understood. Where the heart is really attached, I know very well how little one can be pleased with the attention of any body else. Every thing is so insipid, so uninteresting, that does not relate to the beloved object! I can perfectly comprehend your feelings."

"But you should not persuade me that I think so very much about Mr. Tilney, for perhaps I may never see him again."

"Not see him again! My dearest creature, do not talk of it. I am sure you would be miserable if you thought so."

"No, indeed, I should not. I do not pretend to say that I was not very much pleased with him; but while I have Udolpho to read, I feel as if nobody could make me miserable. Oh! the dreadful black veil! My dear Isabella, I am sure there must be Laurentina's skeleton behind it."

"It is so odd to me, that you should never have read Udolpho before; but I suppose Mrs. Morland objects to novels."

"No, she does not. She very often reads Sir Charles Grandison herself; but new books do not fall in our way."

"Sir Charles Grandison! That is an amazing horrid book, is it not?—I remember Miss Andrews could not get through the first volume."

"It is not like Udolpho at all; but yet I think it is very entertaining."

"Do you indeed!—you surprize me; I thought it had not been readable. But, my dearest Catherine, have you settled what to wear on your head to-night? I am determined at all events to be dressed exactly like you. The men take notice of *that* sometimes you know."

"But it does not signify if they do;" said Catherine, very innocently.

"Signify! Oh, heavens! I make it a rule never to mind what they say. They are very often amazingly impertinent if you do not treat them with spirit, and make them keep their distance."

"Are they?—Well, I never observed *that*. They always behave very well to me."

"Oh! they give themselves such airs. They are the most conceited creatures in the world, and think themselves of so much importance!—By the bye, though I have thought of it a hundred times, I have always forgot to ask you what is your favourite complexion in a man. Do you like them best dark or fair?"

"I hardly know. I never much thought about it. Something between both, I think. Brown—not fair, and not very dark."

"Very well, Catherine. That is exactly he. I have not forgot your description of Mr. Tilney;—'a brown skin, with dark eyes, and rather dark hair.'—Well, my taste is different. I prefer light eyes, and as to complexion—do you know—I like a sallow better than any other. You must not betray me, if you should ever meet with one of your acquaintance answering that description."

"Betray you!—What do you mean?"

"Nay, do not distress me. I believe I have said too much. Let us drop the subject."

Catherine, in some amazement, complied; and after remaining a few moments silent, was on the point of reverting to what interested her at that time rather more than any thing else in the world, Laurentina's skeleton; when her friend prevented her, by saying,—"For Heaven's sake! let us move away from this end of the room. Do you know, there are two odious young men who have been staring at me this half hour. They really put me quite out of countenance. Let us go and look at the arrivals. They will hardly follow us there."

Away they walked to the book; and while Isabella examined the names, it was Catherine's employment to watch the proceedings of these alarming young men.

"They are not coming this way, are they? I hope they are not so impertinent as to follow us. Pray let me know if they are coming. I am determined I will not look up."

In a few moments Catherine, with unaffected pleasure, assured her that she need not be longer uneasy, as the gentlemen had just left the Pump-room.

"And which way are they gone?" said Isabella, turning hastily round. "One was a very good-looking young man."

"They went towards the churchyard."

"Well, I am amazingly glad I have got rid of them! And now, what say you to going to Edgar's Buildings with me, and looking at my new hat? You said you should like to see it."

Catherine readily agreed. "Only," she added, "perhaps we may overtake the two young men."

"Oh! never mind that. If we make haste, we shall pass by them presently, and I am dying to shew you my hat."

"But if we only wait a few minutes, there will be no danger of our seeing them at all."

"I shall not pay them any such compliment, I assure you. I have no notion of treating men with such respect. *That* is the way to spoil them."

Catherine had nothing to oppose against such reasoning; and therefore, to shew the independence of Miss Thorpe, and her resolution of humbling the sex, they set off immediately as fast as they could walk, in pursuit of the two young men.

CHAPTER VII

Half a minute conducted them through the Pump-yard to the archway, opposite Union-passage; but here they were stopped. Every body acquainted with Bath may remember the difficulties of crossing Cheap-street at this point; it is indeed a street of so impertinent a nature, so unfortunately connected with the great London and Oxford roads, and the principal inn of the city, that a day never passes in which parties of ladies, however important their business, whether in quest of pastry, millinery, or even (as in the present case) of young men, are not detained on one side or other by carriages, horsemen, or carts. This evil had been felt and lamented, at least three times a day, by Isabella since her residence in Bath; and she was now fated to feel and lament it once more, for at the very moment of coming opposite to Union-passage, and within view of the two gentlemen who were proceeding through the crowds, and threading the gutters of that interesting alley, they were prevented crossing by the approach of a gig, driven along on bad pavement by a most knowing-looking coachman with all the vehemence that could most fitly endanger the lives of himself, his companion, and his horse.

"Oh, these odious gigs!" said Isabella, looking up, "how I detest them." But this detestation, though so just, was of short duration, for she looked again and exclaimed, "Delightful! Mr. Morland and my brother!"

"Good heaven! 'tis James!" was uttered at the same moment by Catherine; and, on catching the young men's eyes, the horse was immediately checked with a violence which almost threw him on his haunches, and the servant having now scampered up, the gentlemen jumped out, and the equipage was delivered to his care.

Catherine, by whom this meeting was wholly unexpected, received her brother with the liveliest pleasure; and he, being of a very amiable disposition, and sincerely attached to her, gave every proof on his side of equal satisfaction, which he could have leisure to do, while the bright eyes of Miss Thorpe were incessantly challenging his notice; and to her his devoirs were speedily paid, with a mixture of joy and embarrassment which might have informed Catherine, had she been more expert in the development of other people's feelings, and less simply engrossed by her own, that her brother thought her friend quite as pretty as she could do herself.

John Thorpe, who in the mean time had been giving orders about the horses, soon joined them, and from him she directly received the amends which were her due; for while he slightly and carelessly touched the hand of Isabella, on her he bestowed a whole scrape and half a short bow. He was a stout young man of middling height, who, with a plain face and ungraceful form, seemed fearful of being too handsome unless he wore the dress of a groom, and too much like a gentleman unless he were easy where he ought to be civil, and impudent where he might be allowed to be easy. He took out his watch: "How long do you think we have been running it from Tetbury, Miss Morland?"

"I do not know the distance." Her brother told her that it was twenty-three miles.

"*Three*-and-twenty!" cried Thorpe; "five-and-twenty if it is an inch." Morland remonstrated, pleaded the authority of road-books, innkeepers, and milestones; but his friend disregarded them all; he had a surer test of distance. "I know it must be five-and-twenty," said he, "by the time we have been doing it. It is now half after one; we drove out of the inn-yard at Tetbury as the town-clock struck eleven; and I defy any man in England to make my horse go less than ten miles an hour in harness; that makes it exactly twenty-five."

"You have lost an hour," said Morland; "it was only ten o'clock when we came from Tetbury."

"Ten o'clock! it was eleven, upon my soul! I counted every stroke. This brother of yours would persuade me out of my senses, Miss Morland; do but look at my horse; did you ever see an animal so made for speed in your life?" (The servant had just mounted the carriage and was driving off.) "Such true blood! Three hours and a half indeed coming only three-and-twenty miles! look at that creature, and suppose it possible if you can."

"He *does* look very hot to be sure."

"Hot! he had not turned a hair till we came to Walcot Church: but look at his forehand; look at his loins; only see how he moves; that horse *cannot* go less than ten miles an hour: tie his legs and he will get on. What do you think of my gig, Miss Morland? a neat one, is not it? Well hung; town built; I have not had it a month. It was built for a Christchurch man, a friend of mine, a very good sort of fellow; he ran it a few weeks, till, I believe, it was convenient to have done with it. I happened just then to be looking out for some light thing of the kind, though I had pretty well determined on a curricle too; but I chanced to meet him on Magdalen Bridge, as he was driving into Oxford, last term: 'Ah! Thorpe,' said he, 'do you happen to want such a little thing as this? it is a capital one of the kind, but I am cursed tired of it.' 'Oh! d——,' said I, 'I am your man; what do you ask?' And how much do you think he did, Miss Morland?"

"I am sure I cannot guess at all."

"Curricle-hung you see; seat, trunk, sword-case, splashing-board, lamps, silver moulding, all you see complete; the iron-work as good as new, or better. He asked fifty guineas;

I closed with him directly, threw down the money, and the carriage was mine."

"And I am sure," said Catherine, "I know so little of such things that I cannot judge whether it was cheap or dear."

"Neither one nor t'other; I might have got it for less I dare say; but I hate haggling, and poor Freeman wanted cash."

"That was very good-natured of you," said Catherine, quite pleased.

"Oh! d—— it, when one has the means of doing a kind thing by a friend, I hate to be pitiful."

An inquiry now took place into the intended movements of the young ladies; and, on finding whither they were going, it was decided that the gentlemen should accompany them to Edgar's Buildings, and pay their respects to Mrs. Thorpe. James and Isabella led the way; and so well satisfied was the latter with her lot, so contentedly was she endeavouring to ensure a pleasant walk to him who brought the double recommendation of being her brother's friend, and her friend's brother, so pure and uncoquettish were her feelings, that, though they overtook and passed the two offending young men in Milsom-street, she was so far from seeking to attract their notice, that she looked back at them only three times.

John Thorpe kept of course with Catherine, and, after a few minutes' silence, renewed the conversation about his gig—"You will find, however, Miss Morland, it would be reckoned a cheap thing by some people, for I might have sold it for ten guineas more the next day; Jackson, of Oriel, bid me sixty at once; Morland was with me at the time."

"Yes," said Morland, who overheard this; "but you forget that your horse was included."

"My horse! oh, d—— it! I would not sell my horse for a hundred. Are you fond of an open carriage, Miss Morland?"

"Yes, very; I have hardly ever an opportunity of being in one; but I am particularly fond of it."

"I am glad of it; I will drive you out in mine every day."

"Thank you," said Catherine, in some distress, from a doubt of the propriety of accepting such an offer.

"I will drive you up Lansdown Hill to-morrow."

"Thank you; but will not your horse want rest?"

"Rest! he has only come three-and-twenty miles to-day; all nonsense; nothing ruins horses so much as rest; nothing knocks them up so soon. No, no; I shall exercise mine at the average of four hours every day while I am here."

"Shall you indeed!" said Catherine very seriously, "that will be forty miles a day."

"Forty! aye fifty, for what I care. Well, I will drive you up Lansdown to-morrow; mind, I am engaged."

"How delightful that will be!" cried Isabella, turning round; "my dearest Catherine, I quite envy you; but I am afraid, brother, you will not have room for a third."

"A third indeed! no, no; I did not come to Bath to drive my sisters about; that would be a good joke, faith! Morland must take care of you."

This brought on a dialogue of civilities between the other two; but Catherine heard neither the particulars nor the result. Her companion's discourse now sunk from its hitherto animated pitch, to nothing more than a short decisive sentence of praise or condemnation on the face of every woman they met; and Catherine, after listening and agreeing as long as she could, with all the civility and deference of the youthful female mind, fearful of hazarding an opinion of its own in opposition to that of a self-assured man, especially where the beauty of her own sex is concerned, ventured at length to vary the subject by a question which had been long uppermost in her thoughts; it was, "Have you ever read Udolpho, Mr. Thorpe?"

"Udolpho! Oh, Lord! not I; I never read novels; I have something else to do."

Catherine, humbled and ashamed, was going to apologize for her question, but he prevented her by saying, "Novels are all so full of nonsense and stuff; there has not been a tolerably decent one come out since Tom Jones, except the Monk; I read that t'other day; but as for all the others, they are the stupidest things in creation."

"I think you must like Udolpho, if you were to read it; it is so very interesting."

"Not I, faith! No, if I read any, it shall be Mrs. Radcliff's; her novels are amusing enough; they are worth reading; some fun and nature in *them*."

"Udolpho was written by Mrs. Radcliff," said Catherine, with some hesitation, from the fear of mortifying him.

"No sure; was it? Aye, I remember, so it was; I was thinking of that other stupid book, written by that woman they make such a fuss about, she who married the French emigrant."

"I suppose you mean Camilla?"

"Yes, that's the book; such unnatural stuff!—An old man playing at see-saw! I took up the first volume once, and looked it over, but I soon found it would not do; indeed I guessed what sort of stuff it must be before I saw it: as soon as I heard she had married an emigrant, I was sure I should never be able to get through it."

"I have never read it."

"You had no loss I assure you; it is the horridest nonsense you can imagine; there is nothing in the world in it but an old man's playing at see-saw and learning Latin; upon my soul there is not."

This critique, the justness of which was unfortunately lost on poor Catherine, brought them to the door of Mrs. Thorpe's lodgings, and the feelings of the discerning and unprejudiced reader of Camilla gave way to the feelings of the dutiful and affectionate son, as they met Mrs. Thorpe, who had descried them from above, in the passage. "Ah, mother! how do you do?" said he, giving her a hearty shake of the hand: "where did you get that quiz of a hat, it makes you look like an old witch? Here is Morland and I come to stay a few days with you, so you must look out for a couple of good beds some where near." And this address seemed to satisfy all the fondest wishes of the mother's heart, for she received him with the most delighted and exulting affection. On his two younger sisters he then bestowed an equal portion of his fraternal tenderness, for he asked each of them how they did, and observed that they both looked very ugly.

These manners did not please Catherine; but he was James's friend and Isabella's brother; and her judgment was further bought off by Isabella's assuring her, when they withdrew to see the new hat, that John thought her the most charming girl in the world, and by John's engaging her before they parted to dance with him that evening. Had she been older or vainer, such attacks might have done little; but, where youth and diffidence are united, it requires uncommon steadiness of reason to resist the attraction of being called the most charming girl in the world, and of being so very early engaged as a partner; and the consequence was, that, when the two Morlands, after sitting an hour with the Thorpes, set off to walk together to Mr. Allen's, and James, as the door was closed on them, said, "Well, Catherine, how do you like my friend Thorpe?" instead of answering, as she probably would have done, had there been no friendship and no flattery in the case, "I do not like him at all;" she directly replied, "I like him very much; he seems very agreeable."

"He is as good-natured a fellow as ever lived; a little of a rattle; but that will recommend him to your sex I believe: and how do you like the rest of the family?"

"Very, very much indeed: Isabella particularly."

"I am very glad to hear you say so; she is just the kind of young woman I could wish to see you attached to; she has so much good sense, and is so thoroughly unaffected and amiable; I always wanted you to know her; and she seems very fond of you. She said the highest things in your praise that could possibly be; and the praise of such a girl as Miss Thorpe even you, Catherine," taking her hand with affection, "may be proud of."

"Indeed I am," she replied; "I love her exceedingly, and am delighted to find that you like her too. You hardly mentioned any thing of her, when you wrote to me after your visit there."

"Because I thought I should soon see you myself. I hope you will be a great deal together while you are in Bath. She is a most amiable girl; such a superior understanding! How fond all the family are of her; she is evidently the general favourite; and how much she must be admired in such a place as this—is not she?"

"Yes, very much indeed, I fancy; Mr. Allen thinks her the prettiest girl in Bath."

"I dare say he does; and I do not know any man who is a better judge of beauty than Mr. Allen. I need not ask you whether you are happy here, my dear Catherine; with such a companion and friend as Isabella Thorpe, it would be impossible for you to be otherwise; and the Allens I am sure are very kind to you?"

"Yes, very kind; I never was so happy before; and now you are come it will be more delightful than ever; how good it is of you to come so far on purpose to see *me*."

James accepted this tribute of gratitude, and qualified his conscience for accepting it too, by saying with perfect sincerity, "Indeed, Catherine, I love you dearly."

Inquiries and communications concerning brothers and sisters, the situation of some, the growth of the rest, and other family matters, now passed between them, and continued, with only one small digression on James's part, in praise of Miss Thorpe, till they reached Pulteney-street, where he was welcomed with great kindness by Mr. and Mrs. Allen, invited by the former to dine with them, and summoned by the latter to guess the price and weigh the merits of a new muff and tippet. A pre-engagement in Edgar's Buildings prevented his accepting the invitation of one friend, and obliged him to hurry away as soon as he had satisfied the demands of the other. The time of the two parties uniting in the Octagon Room being correctly adjusted, Catherine was then left to the luxury of a raised, restless, and frightened imagination over the pages of Udolpho, lost from all worldly concerns of dressing and dinner, incapable of soothing Mrs. Allen's fears on the delay of an expected dress-maker, and having only one minute in sixty to bestow even on the reflection of her own felicity, in being already engaged for the evening.

CHAPTER VIII

In spite of Udolpho and the dress-maker, however, the party from Pulteney-street reached the Upper-rooms in very good time. The Thorpes and James Morland were there only two minutes before them; and Isabella having gone through the usual ceremonial of meeting her friend with the most smiling and affectionate haste, of admiring the set of her gown, and envying the curl of her hair, they followed their chaperons, arm in arm, into the ball-room, whispering to each other whenever a thought occurred, and supplying the place of many ideas by a squeeze of the hand or a smile of affection.

The dancing began within a few minutes after they were seated; and James, who had been engaged quite as long as his sister, was very importunate with Isabella to stand up; but John was gone into the card-room to speak to a friend, and nothing, she declared, should induce her to join the set before her dear Catherine could join it too: "I assure you," said she, "I would not stand up without your dear sister for all the world; for if I did we should certainly be separated the whole evening." Catherine accepted this kindness with gratitude, and they continued as they were for three minutes longer, when Isabella, who had been talking to James on the other side of her, turned again to his sister and whispered, "My dear creature, I am afraid I must leave you, your brother is so amazingly impatient to begin; I know you will not mind my going away, and I dare say John will be back in a moment, and then you may easily find me out." Catherine, though a little disappointed, had too much good-nature to make any opposition, and the others rising up, Isabella had only time to press her friend's hand and say, "Good bye, my dear love," before they hurried off. The younger Miss Thorpes being also dancing, Catherine was left to the mercy of Mrs. Thorpe and Mrs. Allen, between whom she now remained. She could not help being vexed at the non-appearance of Mr. Thorpe, for she not only longed to be dancing, but was likewise aware that, as the real dignity of her situation could not be known, she was sharing with the scores of other young ladies still sitting down all the discredit of wanting a partner. To be disgraced in the eye of the world, to wear the appearance of infamy while her heart is all purity, her actions all innocence, and the misconduct of another the true source of her debasement, is one of those circumstances which peculiarly belong to the heroine's life, and her fortitude under it what particularly dignifies her character. Catherine had fortitude too; she suffered, but no murmur passed her lips.

From this state of humiliation, she was roused, at the end of ten minutes, to a pleasanter feeling, by seeing, not Mr. Thorpe, but Mr. Tilney, within three yards of the place where they sat; he seemed to be moving that way, but he did not see her, and therefore the smile and the blush, which his sudden reappearance raised in Catherine, passed away without sullying her heroic importance. He looked as handsome and as lively as ever, and was talking with interest to a fashionable and pleasing-looking young woman, who leant on his arm, and whom Catherine immediately guessed to be his sister; thus unthinkingly throwing away a fair opportunity of considering him lost to her for ever, by being married already. But guided only by what was simple and probable, it had never entered her head that Mr. Tilney could be married; he had not behaved, he had not talked, like the married men to whom she had been used; he had never mentioned a wife, and he had acknowledged a sister. From these circumstances sprang the instant conclusion of his sister's now being by his side; and therefore, instead of turning of a deathlike paleness, and falling in a fit on Mrs. Allen's bosom, Catherine sat erect, in the perfect use of her senses, and with cheeks only a little redder than usual.

Mr. Tilney and his companion, who continued, though slowly, to approach, were immediately preceded by a lady, an acquaintance of Mrs. Thorpe; and this lady stopping to speak to her, they, as belonging to her, stopped likewise, and Catherine, catching Mr. Tilney's eye, instantly received from him the smiling tribute of recognition. She returned it with pleasure, and then advancing still nearer, he spoke both to her and Mrs. Allen, by whom he was very civilly acknowledged. "I am very happy to see you again, sir, indeed; I was afraid you had left Bath." He thanked her for her fears, and said that he had quitted it for a week, on the very morning after his having had the pleasure of seeing her.

"Well, sir, and I dare say you are not sorry to be back again, for it is just the place for young people—and indeed for every body else too. I tell Mr. Allen, when he talks of being sick of it, that I am sure he should not complain, for it is so very agreeable a place, that it is much better to be here than at home at this dull time of year. I tell him he is quite in luck to be sent here for his health."

"And I hope, madam, that Mr. Allen will be obliged to like the place, from finding it of service to him."

"Thank you, sir. I have no doubt that he will.—A neighbour of ours, Dr. Skinner, was here for his health last winter, and came away quite stout."

"That circumstance must give great encouragement."

"Yes, sir—and Dr. Skinner and his family were here three months; so I tell Mr. Allen he must not be in a hurry to get away."

Here they were interrupted by a request from Mrs. Thorpe to Mrs. Allen, that she would move a little to accommodate Mrs. Hughes and Miss Tilney with seats, as they had agreed to join their party. This was accordingly done, Mr. Tilney still continuing standing before them and after a few minutes consideration, he asked Catherine to dance with him. This compliment, delightful as it was, produced severe mortification to the lady; and in giving her denial, she expressed her sorrow on the occasion so very much as if she really felt it, that had Thorpe, who joined her just afterwards, been half a minute earlier, he might have thought her sufferings rather too acute. The very easy manner in which he then told her that he had kept her waiting, did not by any means reconcile her more to her lot; nor did the particulars which he entered into while they were standing up, of the horses and dogs of the friend whom he had just left, and of a proposed exchange of terriers between them, interest her so much as to prevent her looking very often towards that part of the room where she had left Mr. Tilney. Of her dear Isabella, to whom she particularly longed to point out that gentleman, she could see nothing. They were in different sets. She was separated from all her party, and away from all her acquaintance;—one mortification succeeded another, and from the whole she deduced this useful lesson, that to go previously engaged to a ball, does not necessarily increase either the dignity or enjoyment of a young lady. From such a moralizing strain as this, she was suddenly roused by a touch on the shoulder, and turning round, perceived Mrs. Hughes directly behind her, attended by Miss Tilney and a gentleman. "I beg your pardon, Miss Morland," said she, "for this liberty,—but I cannot any how get to Miss Thorpe, and Mrs. Thorpe said she was sure you would not have the least objection to letting in this young lady by you." Mrs. Hughes could not have applied to any creature in the room more happy to oblige her than Catherine. The young ladies were introduced to each other, Miss Tilney expressing a proper sense of such goodness,

Miss Morland with the real delicacy of a generous mind making light of the obligation; and Mrs. Hughes, satisfied with having so respectably settled her young charge, returned to her party.

Miss Tilney had a good figure, a pretty face, and a very agreeable countenance; and her air, though it had not all the decided pretension, the resolute stilishness of Miss Thorpe's, had more real elegance. Her manners shewed good sense and good breeding; they were neither shy, nor affectedly open; and she seemed capable of being young, attractive, and at a ball, without wanting to fix the attention of every man near her, and without exaggerated feelings of extatic delight or inconceivable vexation on every little trifling occurrence. Catherine, interested at once by her appearance and her relationship to Mr. Tilney, was desirous of being acquainted with her, and readily talked therefore whenever she could think of any thing to say, and had courage and leisure for saying it. But the hindrance thrown in the way of a very speedy intimacy, by the frequent want of one or more of these requisites, prevented their doing more than going through the first rudiments of an acquaintance, by informing themselves how well the other liked Bath, how much she admired its buildings and surrounding country, whether she drew, or played or sang, and whether she was fond of riding on horseback.

The two dances were scarcely concluded before Catherine found her arm gently seized by her faithful Isabella, who in great spirits exclaimed—"At last I have got you. My dearest creature, I have been looking for you this hour. What could induce you to come into this set, when you knew I was in the other? I have been quite wretched without you."

"My dear Isabella, how was it possible for me to get at you? I could not even see where you were."

"So I told your brother all the time—but he would not believe me. Do go and see for her, Mr. Morland, said I—but

she had not looked round long before she saw him leading a young lady to the dance.

"Ah! he has got a partner, I wish he had asked *you*," said Mrs. Allen; and after a short silence, she added, "he is a very agreeable young man."

"Indeed he is, Mrs. Allen," said Mrs. Thorpe, smiling complacently; "I must say it, though I *am* his mother, that there is not a more agreeable young man in the world."

This inapplicable answer might have been too much for the comprehension of many; but it did not puzzle Mrs. Allen, for after only a moment's consideration, she said, in a whisper to Catherine, "I dare say she thought I was speaking of her son."

Catherine was disappointed and vexed. She seemed to have missed by so little the very object she had had in view; and this persuasion did not incline her to a very gracious reply, when John Thorpe came up to her soon afterwards, and said, "Well, Miss Morland, I suppose you and I are to stand up and jig it together again."

"Oh, no; I am much obliged to you, our two dances are over; and, besides, I am tired, and do not mean to dance any more."

"Do not you?—then let us walk about and quiz people. Come along with me, and I will shew you the four greatest quizzers in the room; my two younger sisters and their partners. I have been laughing at them this half hour."

Again Catherine excused herself; and at last he walked off to quiz his sisters by himself. The rest of the evening she found very dull; Mr. Tilney was drawn away from their party at tea, to attend that of his partner; Miss Tilney, though belonging to it, did not sit near her, and James and Isabella were so much engaged in conversing together, that the latter had no leisure to bestow more on her friend than one smile, one squeeze, and one "dearest Catherine."

CHAPTER IX

The progress of Catherine's unhappiness from the events of the evening, was as follows. It appeared first in a general dissatisfaction with every body about her, while she remained in the rooms, which speedily brought on considerable weariness and a violent desire to go home. This, on arriving in Pulteney-street, took the direction of extraordinary hunger, and when that was appeased, changed into an earnest longing to be in bed; such was the extreme point of her distress; for when there she immediately fell into a sound sleep which lasted nine hours, and from which she awoke perfectly revived, in excellent spirits, with fresh hopes and fresh schemes. The first wish of her heart was to improve her acquaintance with Miss Tilney, and almost her first resolution, to seek her for that purpose, in the Pump-room at noon. In the Pump-room, one so newly arrived in Bath must be met with, and that building she had already found so favourable for the discovery of female excellence, and the completion of female intimacy, so admirably adapted for secret discourses and unlimited confidence, that she was most reasonably encouraged to expect another friend from within its walls. Her plan for the morning thus settled, she sat quietly down to her book after breakfast, resolving to remain in the same place and the same employment till the clock struck one; and from habitude very little incommoded by the remarks and ejaculations of Mrs. Allen, whose vacancy of mind and incapacity for thinking were such, that as she never talked a great deal, so she could never be entirely silent; and, therefore, while she sat at her work, if she lost her needle or broke her thread, if she heard a carriage in the street, or saw a speck upon her gown, she must observe it aloud, whether there were any one at leisure to answer her or not. At about half past twelve, a remarkably loud rap drew her in haste to the window, and scarcely had she time to inform Catherine of there being two open carriages at the door, in the first only a servant, her brother driving Miss Thorpe in the second, before John Thorpe came running up stairs, calling out, "Well, Miss Morland, here I am. Have you been waiting long? We could not come before; the old devil of a coachmaker was such an eternity finding out a thing fit to be got into, and now it is ten thousand to one, but they break down before we are out of the street. How do you do, Mrs. Allen? a famous ball last night, was not it? Come, Miss Morland, be quick, for the others are in a confounded hurry to be off. They want to get their tumble over."

"What do you mean?" said Catherine, "where are you all going to?"

"Going to? why, you have not forgot our engagement! Did not we agree together to take a drive this morning? What a head you have! We are going up Claverton Down."

"Something was said about it, I remember," said Catherine, looking at Mrs. Allen for her opinion; "but really I did not expect you."

"Not expect me! that's a good one! And what a dust you would have made, if I had not come."

Catherine's silent appeal to her friend, meanwhile, was entirely thrown away, for Mrs. Allen, not being at all in the habit of conveying any expression herself by a look, was not aware of its being ever intended by any body else; and Catherine, whose desire of seeing Miss Tilney again could at that moment bear a short delay in favour of a drive, and who thought there could be no impropriety in her going with Mr. Thorpe, as Isabella was going at the same time with James, was therefore obliged to speak plainer. "Well, ma'am, what do you say to it? Can you spare me for an hour or two? shall I go?"

"Do just as you please, my dear," replied Mrs. Allen, with the most placid indifference. Catherine took the advice, and ran off to get ready. In a very few minutes she re-appeared, having scarcely allowed the two others time enough to get through a few short sentences in her praise, after Thorpe had procured Mrs. Allen's admiration of his gig; and then receiving her friend's parting good wishes, they both hurried down stairs. "My dearest creature," cried Isabella, to whom the duty of friendship immediately called her before she could get into the carriage, "you have been at least three hours getting ready. I was afraid you were ill. What a delightful ball we had last night. I have a thousand things to say to you; but make haste and get in, for I long to be off."

Catherine followed her orders and turned away, but not too soon to hear her friend exclaim aloud to James, "What a sweet girl she is! I quite doat on her."

"You will not be frightened, Miss Morland," said Thorpe, as he handed her in, "if my horse should dance about a little at first setting off. He will, most likely, give a plunge or two, and perhaps take the rest for a minute; but he will soon know his master. He is full of spirits, playful as can be, but there is no vice in him."

Catherine did not think the portrait a very inviting one, but it was too late to retreat, and she was too young to own herself frightened; so, resigning herself to her fate, and trusting to the animal's boasted knowledge of its owner, she sat peaceably down, and saw Thorpe sit down by her. Every thing being then arranged, the servant who stood at the horse's head was bid in an important voice "to let him go," and off they went in the quietest manner imaginable, without a plunge or a caper, or any thing like one. Catherine, delighted at so happy an escape, spoke her pleasure aloud with grateful surprise; and her companion immediately made the matter perfectly simple by asssuring her that it was entirely owing to the peculiarly judicious manner in which he had then held the reins, and the singular discernment and dexterity with which he had directed his whip. Catherine, though she could not help wondering that with such perfect command of his horse, he should think it necessary to alarm her with a relation of its tricks, congratulated herself sincerely on being under the care of so excellent a coachman; and perceiving that the animal continued to go on in the same quiet manner, without shewing the smallest propensity towards any unpleasant vivacity, and (considering its inevitable pace was ten miles an hour) by no means alarmingly fast, gave herself up to all the enjoyment of air and exercise of the most invigorating kind, in a fine mild day of February, with the consciousness of safety. A silence of several minutes succeeded their first short dialogue;—it was broken by Thorpe's saying very abruptly, "Old Allen is as rich as a Jew—is not he?" Catherine did not understand him—and he repeated his question, adding in explanation, "Old Allen, the man you are with."

"Oh! Mr. Allen, you mean. Yes, I believe, he is very rich."

"And no children at all?"

"No—not any."

"A famous thing for his next heirs. He is *your* godfather, is not he?"

"My godfather!—no."

"But you are always very much with them."

"Yes, very much."

"Aye, that is what I meant. He seems a good kind of old fellow enough, and has lived very well in his time, I dare say; he is not gouty for nothing. Does he drink his bottle a-day now?"

"His bottle a-day!—no. Why should you think of such a thing? He is a very temperate man, and you could not fancy him in liquor last night?"

"Lord help you!—You women are always thinking of men's being in liquor. Why you do not suppose a man is overset by a bottle? I am sure of *this*—that if every body was to drink their bottle a-day, there would not be half the disorders in the world there are now. It would be a famous good thing for us all."

"I cannot believe it."

"Oh! lord, it would be the saving of thousands. There is not the hundredth part of the wine consumed in this kingdom, that there ought to be. Our foggy climate wants help."

"And yet I have heard that there is a great deal of wine drank in Oxford."

"Oxford! There is no drinking at Oxford now, I assure you. Nobody drinks there. You would hardly meet with a man who goes beyond his four pints at the utmost. Now, for instance, it was reckoned a remarkable thing at the last party in my rooms, that upon an average we cleared about five pints a head. It was looked upon as something out of the common way. *Mine* is famous good stuff to be sure. You would not often meet with any thing like it in Oxford— and that may account for it. But this will just give you a notion of the general rate of drinking there."

"Yes, it does give a notion," said Catherine, warmly, "and that is, that you all drink a great deal more wine than I thought you did. However, I am sure James does not drink so much."

This declaration brought on a loud and overpowering reply, of which no part was very distinct, except the frequent exclamations, amounting almost to oaths, which adorned it, and Catherine was left, when it ended, with rather a strengthened belief of there being a great deal of wine drank in Oxford, and the same happy conviction of her brother's comparative sobriety.

Thorpe's ideas then all reverted to the merits of his own equipage, and she was called on to admire the spirit and freedom with which his horse moved along, and the ease which his paces, as well as the excellence of the springs, gave the motion of the carriage. She followed him in all his admiration as well as she could. To go before, or beyond him was impossible. His knowledge and her ignorance of the subject, his rapidity of expression, and her diffidence of herself put that out of her power; she could strike out nothing new in commendation, but she readily echoed whatever he chose to assert, and it was finally settled between them without any difficulty, that his equipage was altogether the most complete of its kind in England, his carriage the neatest, his horse the best goer, and himself the best coachman.— "You do not really think, Mr. Thorpe," said Catherine, venturing after some time to consider the matter as entirely decided, and to offer some little variation on the subject, "that James's gig will break down?"

"Break down! Oh! lord! Did you ever see such a little tittuppy thing in your life? There is not a sound piece of iron about it. The wheels have been fairly worn out these ten years at least—and as for the body! Upon my soul, you might shake it to pieces yourself with a touch. It is the most devilish little ricketty business I ever beheld!—Thank God! we have got a better. I would not be bound to go two miles in it for fifty thousand pounds."

"Good heavens!" cried Catherine, quite frightened, "then pray let us turn back; they will certainly meet with an accident if we go on. Do let us turn back, Mr. Thorpe; stop and speak to my brother, and tell him how very unsafe it is."

"Unsafe! Oh, lord! what is there in that? they will only get a roll if it does break down; and there is plenty of dirt, it will be excellent falling. Oh, curse it! the carriage is safe enough, if a man knows how to drive it; a thing of that sort in good hands will last above twenty years after it is fairly worn out. Lord bless you! I would undertake for five pounds to drive it to York and back again, without losing a nail."

Catherine listened with astonishment; she knew not how to reconcile two such very different accounts of the same thing; for she had not been brought up to understand the propensities of a rattle, nor to know to how many idle assertions and impudent falsehoods the excess of vanity will lead. Her own family were plain matter-of-fact people, who seldom aimed at wit of any kind; her father, at the utmost, being contented with a pun, and her mother with a proverb; they were not in the habit therefore of telling lies to increase their importance, or of asserting at one moment what they would contradict the next. She reflected on the affair for some time in much perplexity, and was more than once on the point of requesting from Mr. Thorpe a clearer insight into his real opinion on the subject; but she checked herself, because it appeared to her that he did not excel in giving those clearer insights, in making those things plain which he had before made ambiguous; and, joining to this, the consideration, that he would not really suffer his sister and his friend to be exposed to a danger from which he might easily preserve them, she concluded at last, that he must know the carriage to be in fact perfectly safe, and therefore would alarm herself no longer. By him the whole matter seemed entirely forgotten; and all the rest of his conversation, or rather talk, began and ended with himself and his own concerns. He told her of horses which he had bought for a trifle and sold for incredible sums; of racing matches, in which his judgment had infallibly foretold the winner; of shooting parties, in which he had killed more birds (though without having one good shot) than all his companions together; and described to her some famous day's sport, with the fox-hounds, in which his foresight and skill in directing the dogs had repaired the mistakes of the most experienced huntsman, and in which the boldness of his riding, though it had never endangered his own life for a moment, had been constantly leading others into difficulties, which he calmly concluded had broken the necks of many.

Little as Catherine was in the habit of judging for herself, and unfixed as were her general notions of what men ought to be, she could not entirely repress a doubt, while she bore with the effusions of his endless conceit, of his being alto-gether completely agreeable. It was a bold surmise, for he was Isabella's brother; and she had been assured by James, that his manners would recommend him to all her sex; but in spite of this, the extreme weariness of his company, which crept over her before they had been out an hour, and which continued unceasingly to increase till they stopped in Pulteney-street again, induced her, in some small degree, to resist such high authority, and to distrust his powers of giving universal pleasure.

When they arrived at Mrs. Allen's door, the astonish-ment of Isabella was hardly to be expressed, on finding that it was too late in the day for them to attend her friend into the house:—"Past three o'clock!" it was inconceivable, in-credible, impossible! and she would neither believe her own watch, nor her brother's, nor the servant's; she would be-lieve no assurance of it founded on reason or reality, till Morland produced his watch, and ascertained the fact; to have doubted a moment longer *then*, would have been equally inconceivable, incredible, and impossible; and she could only protest, over and over again, that no two hours and a half had ever gone off so swiftly before, as Catherine was called on to confirm; Catherine could not tell a false-hood even to please Isabella; but the latter was spared the misery of her friend's dissenting voice, by not waiting for her answer. Her own feelings entirely engrossed her; her wretchedness was most acute on finding herself obliged to go directly home.—It was ages since she had had a moment's conversation with her dearest Catherine; and, though she had such thousands of things to say to her, it appeared as if they were never to be together again; so, with smiles of most exquisite misery, and the laughing eye of utter despondency, she bade her friend adieu and went on.

Catherine found Mrs. Allen just returned from all the busy idleness of the morning, and was immediately greeted with, "Well, my dear, here you are;" a truth which she had no greater inclination than power to dispute; "and I hope you have had a pleasant airing?"

"Yes, ma'am, I thank you; we could not have had a nicer day."

"So Mrs. Thorpe said; she was vastly pleased at your all going."

"You have seen Mrs. Thorpe then?"

"Yes, I went to the Pump-room as soon as you were gone, and there I met her, and we had a great deal of talk together. She says there was hardly any veal to be got at market this morning, it is so uncommonly scarce."

"Did you see any body else of our acquaintance?"

"Yes; we agreed to take a turn in the Crescent, and there we met Mrs. Hughes, and Mr. and Miss Tilney walking with her."

"Did you indeed? and did they speak to you?"

"Yes, we walked along the Crescent together for half an hour. They seem very agreeable people. Miss Tilney was in a very pretty spotted muslin, and I fancy, by what I can learn, that she always dresses very handsomely. Mrs. Hughes talked to me a great deal about the family."

"And what did she tell you of them?"

"Oh! a vast deal indeed; she hardly talked of any thing else."

"Did she tell you what part of Gloucestershire they come from?"

"Yes, she did; but I cannot recollect now. But they are very good kind of people, and very rich. Mrs. Tilney was a Miss Drummond, and she and Mrs. Hughes were schoolfellows; and Miss Drummond had a very large fortune; and, when she married, her father gave her twenty thousand pounds, and five hundred to buy wedding-clothes. Mrs. Hughes saw all the clothes after they came from the ware-house."

"And are Mr. and Mrs. Tilney in Bath?"

"Yes, I fancy they are, but I am not quite certain. Upon recollection, however, I have a notion they are both dead; at least the mother is; yes, I am sure Mrs. Tilney is dead, because Mrs. Hughes told me there was a very beautiful set of pearls that Mr. Drummond gave his daughter on her wedding-day and that Miss Tilney has got now, for they were put by for her when her mother died."

"And is Mr. Tilney, my partner, the only son?"

"I cannot be quite positive about that, my dear; I have some idea he is; but, however, he is a very fine young man Mrs. Hughes says, and likely to do very well."

Catherine inquired no further; she had heard enough to feel that Mrs. Allen had no real intelligence to give, and that she was most particularly unfortunate herself in having missed such a meeting with both brother and sister. Could she have foreseen such a circumstance, nothing should have persuaded her to go out with the others; and, as it was, she could only lament her ill-luck, and think over what she had lost, till it was clear to her, that the drive had by no means been very pleasant and that John Thorpe himself was quite disagreeable.

CHAPTER X

The Allens, Thorpes, and Morlands, all met in the evening at the theatre; and, as Catherine and Isabella sat together, there was then an opportunity for the latter to utter some few of the many thousand things which had been collecting within her for communication, in the immeasurable length of time which had divided them.—"Oh, heavens! my beloved Catherine, have I got you at last?" was her address on Catherine's entering the box and sitting by her. "Now, Mr. Morland," for he was close to her on the other side, "I shall not speak another word to you all the rest of the evening; so I charge you not to expect it. My sweetest Catherine, how have you been this long age? but I need not ask you, for you look delightfully. You really have done your hair in a more heavenly style than ever: you mischievous creature, do you want to attract every body? I assure you, my brother is quite in love with you already; and as for Mr. Tilney—but *that* is a settled thing—even *your* modesty cannot doubt his attachment now; his coming back to Bath makes it too plain. Oh! what would not I give to see him! I really am quite wild with impatience. My mother says he is the most delightful young man in the world; she saw him this morning you know: you must introduce him to me. Is he in the house now?—Look about for heaven's sake! I assure you, I can hardly exist till I see him."

"No," said Catherine, "he is not here; I cannot see him any where."

"Oh, horrid! am I never to be acquainted with him? How do you like my gown? I think it does not look amiss; the sleeves were entirely my own thought. Do you know I get so immoderately sick of Bath; your brother and I were agreeing this morning that, though it is vastly well to be here for a few weeks, we would not live here for millions. We soon found out that our tastes were exactly alike in preferring the country to every other place; really, our opinions were so exactly the same, it was quite ridiculous! There was not a single point in which we differed; I would not have had you by for the world; you are such a sly thing, I am sure you would have made some droll remark or other about it."

"No, indeed I should not."

"Oh, yes you would indeed; I know you better than you know yourself. You would have told us that we seemed born for each other, or some nonsense of that kind, which would have distressed me beyond conception; my cheeks would have been as red as your roses; I would not have had you by for the world."

"Indeed you do me injustice; I would not have made so improper a remark upon any account; and besides, I am sure it would never have entered my head."

Isabella smiled incredulously, and talked the rest of the evening to James.

Catherine's resolution of endeavouring to meet Miss Tilney again continued in full force the next morning; and till the usual moment of going to the Pump-room, she felt some alarm from the dread of a second prevention. But nothing of that kind occurred, no visitors appeared to delay them, and they all three set off in good time for the Pump-room, where the ordinary course of events and conversation took place; Mr. Allen, after drinking his glass of water, joined some gentlemen to talk over the politics of the day and compare the accounts of their newspapers; and the ladies walked about together, noticing every new face, and almost every new bonnet in the room. The female part of the Thorpe family, attended by James Morland, appeared among the crowd in less than a quarter of an hour, and Catherine immediately took her usual place by the side of her friend. James, who was now in constant attendance, maintained a similar position, and separating themselves from the rest of their party, they walked in that manner for some time, till Catherine began to doubt the happiness of a situation which confining her entirely to her friend and brother, gave her very little share in the notice of either. They were always engaged in some sentimental discussion or lively dispute, but their sentiment was conveyed in such whispering voices, and their vivacity attended with so much laughter, that though Catherine's supporting opinion was not unfrequently called for by one or the other, she was never able to give any, from not having heard a word of the subject. At length however she was empowered to disengage herself from her friend, by the avowed necessity of speaking to Miss Tilney, whom she most joyfully saw just entering the room with Mrs. Hughes, and whom she instantly joined, with a firmer determination to be acquainted, than she might have had courage to command, had she not been urged by the disappointment of the day before. Miss Tilney met her with great civility, returned her advances with equal good will, and they continued talking together as long as both parties remained in the room; and though in all probability not an observation was made, nor an expression used by either which had not been made and used some thousands of times before, under that roof, in every Bath season, yet the merit of their being spoken with simplicity and truth, and without personal conceit, might be something uncommon.—

"How well your brother dances!" was an artless exclamation of Catherine's towards the close of their conversation, which at once surprized and amused her companion.

"Henry!" she replied with a smile. "Yes, he does dance very well."

"He must have thought it very odd to hear me say I was engaged the other evening, when he saw me sitting down.

But I really had been engaged the whole day to Mr. Thorpe." Miss Tilney could only bow. "You cannot think," added Catherine after a moment's silence, "how surprized I was to see him again. I felt so sure of his being quite gone away."

"When Henry had the pleasure of seeing you before, he was in Bath but for a couple of days. He came only to engage lodgings for us."

"*That* never occurred to me; and of course, not seeing him any where, I thought he must be gone. Was not the young lady he danced with on Monday a Miss Smith?"

"Yes, an acquaintance of Mrs. Hughes."

"I dare say she was very glad to dance. Do you think her pretty?"

"Not very."

"He never comes to the Pump-room, I suppose?"

"Yes, sometimes; but he has rid out this morning with my father."

Mrs. Hughes now joined them, and asked Miss Tilney if she was ready to go. "I hope I shall have the pleasure of seeing you again soon," said Catherine. "Shall you be at the cotillion ball to-morrow?"

"Perhaps we——yes, I think we certainly shall."

"I am glad of it, for we shall all be there."—This civility was duly returned; and they parted—on Miss Tilney's side with some knowledge of her new acquaintance's feelings, and on Catherine's, without the smallest consciousness of having explained them.

She went home very happy. The morning had answered all her hopes, and the evening of the following day was now the object of expectation, the future good. What gown and what head-dress she should wear on the occasion became her chief concern. She cannot be justified in it. Dress is at all times a frivolous distinction, and excessive solicitude about it often destroys its own aim. Catherine knew all this

very well; her great aunt had read her a lecture on the subject only the Christmas before; and yet she lay awake ten
minutes on Wednesday night debating between her spotted
and her tamboured muslin, and nothing but the shortness
of the time prevented her buying a new one for the evening.
This would have been an error in judgment, great though
not uncommon, from which one of the other sex rather
than her own, a brother rather than a great aunt might have
warned her, for man only can be aware of the insensibility of
man towards a new gown. It would be mortifying to the feelings of many ladies, could they be made to understand how
little the heart of man is affected by what is costly or new in
their attire; how little it is biassed by the texture of their
muslin, and how unsusceptible of peculiar tenderness towards the spotted, the sprigged, the mull or the jackonet.
Woman is fine for her own satisfaction alone. No man will
admire her the more, no woman will like her the better for
it. Neatness and fashion are enough for the former, and a
something of shabbiness or impropriety will be most endearing to the latter.—But not one of these grave reflections
troubled the tranquillity of Catherine.

She entered the rooms on Thursday evening with feelings
very different from what had attended her thither the
Monday before. She had then been exulting in her engagement to Thorpe, and was now chiefly anxious to avoid his
sight, lest he should engage her again; for though she could
not, dared not expect that Mr. Tilney should ask her a
third time to dance, her wishes, hopes and plans all cen-
tered in nothing less. Every young lady may feel for my
heroine in this critical moment, for every young lady has at
some time or other known the same agitation. All have been,
or at least all have believed themselves to be, in danger from
the pursuit of some one whom they wished to avoid; and
all have been anxious for the attentions of some one whom
they wished to please. As soon as they were joined by the

Thorpes, Catherine's agony began; she fidgetted about if John Thorpe came towards her, hid herself as much as possible from his view, and when he spoke to her pretended not to hear him. The cotillions were over, the country-dancing beginning, and she saw nothing of the Tilneys. "Do not be frightened, my dear Catherine," whispered Isabella, "but I am really going to dance with your brother again. I declare positively it is quite shocking. I tell him he ought to be ashamed of himself, but you and John must keep us in countenance. Make haste, my dear creature, and come to us. John is just walked off, but he will be back in a moment."

Catherine had neither time nor inclination to answer. The others walked away, John Thorpe was still in view, and she gave herself up for lost. That she might not appear, however, to observe or expect him, she kept her eyes intently fixed on her fan; and a self-condemnation for her folly, in supposing that among such a crowd they should even meet with the Tilneys in any reasonable time, had just passed through her mind, when she suddenly found herself addressed and again solicited to dance, by Mr. Tilney himself. With what sparkling eyes and ready motion she granted his request, and with how pleasing a flutter of heart she went with him to the set, may be easily imagined. To escape, and, as she believed, so narrowly escape John Thorpe, and to be asked, so immediately on his joining her, asked by Mr. Tilney, as if he had sought her on purpose!—it did not appear to her that life could supply any greater felicity.

Scarcely had they worked themselves into the quiet possession of a place, however, when her attention was claimed by John Thorpe, who stood behind her. "Hey-day, Miss Morland!" said he, "what is the meaning of this?—I thought you and I were to dance together."

"I wonder you should think so, for you never asked me."

"That is a good one, by Jove!—I asked you as soon as I came into the room, and I was just going to ask you again, but when I turned round, you were gone!—this is a cursed shabby trick! I only came for the sake of dancing with *you*, and I firmly believe you were engaged to me ever since Monday. Yes; I remember, I asked you while you were waiting in the lobby for your cloak. And here have I been telling all my acquaintance that I was going to dance with the prettiest girl in the room; and when they see you standing up with somebody else, they will quiz me famously."

"Oh, no; they will never think of *me*, after such a description as that."

"By heavens, if they do not, I will kick them out of the room for blockheads. What chap have you there?" Catherine satisfied his curiosity. "Tilney," he repeated, "Hum—I do not know him. A good figure of a man; well put together.—Does he want a horse?—Here is a friend of mine, Sam Fletcher, has got one to sell that would suit any body. A famous clever animal for the road—only forty guineas. I had fifty minds to buy it myself, for it is one of my maxims always to buy a good horse when I meet with one; but it would not answer my purpose, it would not do for the field. I would give any money for a real good hunter. I have three now, the best that ever were back'd. I would not take eight hundred guineas for them. Fletcher and I mean to get a house in Leicestershire, against the next season. It is so d—— uncomfortable, living at an inn."

This was the last sentence by which he could weary Catherine's attention, for he was just then born off by the resistless pressure of a long string of passing ladies. Her partner now drew near, and said, "That gentleman would have put me out of patience, had he staid with you half a minute longer. He has no business to withdraw the attention of my partner from me. We have entered into a contract of mutual agreeableness for the space of an evening, and all our agreeableness belongs solely to each other for that time. Nobody can fasten themselves on the notice of one, without injuring the rights of the other. I consider a country-dance as an emblem of marriage. Fidelity and complaisance are the principal duties of both; and those men who do not chuse to dance or marry themselves, have no business with the partners or wives of their neighbours."

"But they are such very different things!—"

"—That you think they cannot be compared together."

"To be sure not. People that marry can never part, but must go and keep house together. People that dance, only stand opposite each other in a long room for half an hour."

"And such is your definition of matrimony and dancing. Taken in that light certainly, their resemblance is not striking; but I think I could place them in such a view.—You will allow, that in both, man has the advantage of choice, woman only the power of refusal; that in both, it is an engagement between man and woman, formed for the advantage of each; and that when once entered into, they belong exclusively to each other till the moment of its dissolution; that it is their duty, each to endeavour to give the other no cause for wishing that he or she had bestowed themselves elsewhere, and their best interest to keep their own imaginations from wandering towards the perfections of their neighbours, or fancying that they should have been better off with any one else. You will allow all this?"

"Yes, to be sure, as you state it, all this sounds very well; but still they are so very different.—I cannot look upon them at all in the same light, nor think the same duties belong to them."

"In one respect, there certainly is a difference. In marriage, the man is supposed to provide for the support of the woman; the woman to make the home agreeable to the man; he is to purvey, and she is to smile. But in dancing, their duties are exactly changed; the agreeableness, the compliance are expected from him, while she furnishes the fan and the lavender water. *That,* I suppose, was the difference of duties which struck you, as rendering the conditions incapable of comparison."

"No, indeed, I never thought of that."

"Then I am quite at a loss. One thing, however, I must observe. This disposition on your side is rather alarming. You totally disallow any similarity in the obligations; and may I not thence infer, that your notions of the duties of the dancing state are not so strict as your partner might wish? Have I not reason to fear, that if the gentleman who spoke to you just now were to return, or if any other gentleman were to address you, there would be nothing to restrain you from conversing with him as long as you chose?"

"Mr. Thorpe is such a very particular friend of my brother's, that if he talks to me, I must talk to him again; but there are hardly three young men in the room besides him, that I have any acquaintance with."

"And is that to be my only security? alas, alas!"

"Nay, I am sure you cannot have a better; for if I do not know any body, it is impossible for me to talk to them; and, besides, I do not *want* to talk to any body."

"Now you have given me a security worth having; and I shall proceed with courage. Do you find Bath as agreeable as when I had the honour of making the inquiry before?"

"Yes, quite—more so, indeed."

"More so!—Take care, or you will forget to be tired of it at the proper time.—You ought to be tired at the end of six weeks."

"I do not think I should be tired, if I were to stay here six months."

"Bath, compared with London, has little variety, and so every body finds out every year. 'For six weeks, I allow Bath is pleasant enough; but beyond *that,* it is the most tiresome place in the world.' You would be told so by people of all descriptions, who come regularly every winter, lengthen their six weeks into ten or twelve, and go away at last because they can afford to stay no longer."

"Well, other people must judge for themselves, and those who go to London may think nothing of Bath. But I, who live in a small retired village in the country, can never find greater sameness in such a place as this, than in my own home; for here are a variety of amusements, a variety of things to be seen and done all day long, which I can know nothing of there."

"You are not fond of the country."

"Yes, I am. I have always lived there, and always been very happy. But certainly there is much more sameness in a country life than in a Bath life. One day in the country is exactly like another."

"But then you spend your time so much more rationally in the country."

"Do I?"

"Do you not?"

"I do not believe there is much difference."

"Here you are in pursuit only of amusement all day long."

"And so I am at home—only I do not find so much of it. I walk about here, and so I do there;—but here I see a variety of people in every street, and there I can only go and call on Mrs. Allen."

Mr. Tilney was very much amused. "Only go and call on Mrs. Allen!" he repeated. "What a picture of intellectual poverty! However, when you sink into this abyss again, you will have more to say. You will be able to talk of Bath, and of all that you did here."

"Oh! yes. I shall never be in want of something to talk of again to Mrs. Allen, or any body else. I really believe I shall always be talking of Bath, when I am at home again—I *do* like it so very much. If I could but have papa and mamma, and the rest of them here, I suppose I should be too happy! James's coming (my eldest brother) is quite delightful—and especially as it turns out, that the very family we are just got so intimate with, are his intimate friends already. Oh! who can ever be tired of Bath?"

"Not those who bring such fresh feelings of every sort to it, as you do. But papas and mammas, and brothers and intimate friends are a good deal gone by, to most of the frequenters of Bath—and the honest relish of balls and plays, and every-day sights, is past with them."

Here their conversation closed; the demands of the dance becoming now too importunate for a divided attention.

Soon after their reaching the bottom of the set, Catherine perceived herself to be earnestly regarded by a gentleman who stood among the lookers-on, immediately behind her partner. He was a very handsome man, of a commanding aspect, past the bloom, but not past the vigour of life; and with his eye still directed towards her, she saw him presently address Mr. Tilney in a familiar whisper. Confused by his notice, and blushing from the fear of its being excited by something wrong in her appearance, she turned away her head. But while she did so, the gentleman retreated, and her partner coming nearer, said, "I see that you guess what I have just been asked. That gentleman knows your name, and you have a right to know his. It is General Tilney, my father."

Catherine's answer was only "Oh!"—but it was an "Oh!" expressing every thing needful; attention to his words, and perfect reliance on their truth. With real interest and strong admiration did her eye now follow the General, as he moved through the crowd, and "How handsome a family they are!" was her secret remark.

In chatting with Miss Tilney before the evening concluded, a new source of felicity arose to her. She had never taken a country walk since her arrival in Bath. Miss Tilney, to whom all the commonly-frequented environs were familiar, spoke of them in terms which made her all eagerness to know them too; and on her openly fearing that she might find nobody to go with her, it was proposed by the brother and sister that they should join in a walk, some morning or other. "I shall like it," she cried, "beyond any thing in the world; and do not let us put it off—let us go to-morrow." This was readily agreed to, with only a proviso of Miss Tilney's, that it did not rain, which Catherine was sure it would not. At twelve o'clock, they were to call for her in Pulteney-street—and "remember—twelve o'clock," was her parting speech to her new friend. Of her other, her older, her more established friend, Isabella, of whose fidelity and worth she had enjoyed a fortnight's experience, she scarcely saw any thing during the evening. Yet, though longing to make her acquainted with her happiness, she cheerfully submitted to the wish of Mr. Allen, which took them rather early away, and her spirits danced within her, as she danced in her chair all the way home.

CHAPTER XI

The morrow brought a very sober looking morning; the sun making only a few efforts to appear; and Catherine augured from it, every thing most favourable to her wishes. A bright morning so early in the year, she allowed would generally turn to rain, but a cloudy one foretold improvement as the day advanced. She applied to Mr. Allen for confirmation of her hopes, but Mr. Allen not having his own skies and barometer about him, declined giving any absolute promise of sunshine. She applied to Mrs. Allen, and Mrs. Allen's opinion was more posittive. "She had no doubt in the world of its being a very fine day, if the clouds would only go off, and the sun keep out."

At about eleven o'clock however, a few specks of small rain upon the windows caught Catherine's watchful eye, and "Oh! dear, I do believe it will be wet," broke from her in a most desponding tone.

"I thought how it would be," said Mrs. Allen.

"No walk for me to-day," sighed Catherine;—"but perhaps it may come to nothing, or it may hold up before twelve."

"Perhaps it may, but then, my dear, it will be so dirty."

"Oh! that will not signify; I never mind dirt."

"No," replied her friend very placidly, "I know you never mind dirt."

After a short pause, "It comes on faster and faster!" said Catherine, as she stood watching at a window.

"So it does indeed. If it keeps raining, the streets will be very wet."

"There are four umbrellas up already. How I hate the sight of an umbrella!"

"They are disagreeable things to carry. I would much rather take a chair at any time."

"It was such a nice looking morning! I felt so convinced it would be dry!"

"Any body would have thought so indeed. There will be very few people in the Pump-room, if it rains all the morning. I hope Mr. Allen will put on his great coat when he goes, but I dare say he will not, for he had rather do any thing in the world than walk out in a great coat; I wonder he should dislike it, it must be so comfortable."

The rain continued—fast, though not heavy. Catherine went every five minutes to the clock, threatening on each return that, if it still kept on raining another five minutes, she would give up the matter as hopeless. The clock struck twelve, and it still rained.—"You will not be able to go, my dear."

"I do not quite despair yet. I shall not give it up till a quarter after twelve. This is just the time of day for it to clear up, and I do think it looks a little lighter. There, it is twenty minutes after twelve, and now I *shall* give it up entirely. Oh! that we had such weather here as they had at Udolpho, or at least in Tuscany and the South of France!—the night that poor St. Aubin died!—such beautiful weather!"

At half past twelve, when Catherine's anxious attention to the weather was over, and she could no longer claim any merit from its amendment, the sky began voluntarily to clear. A gleam of sunshine took her quite by surprise; she looked round; the clouds were parting, and she instantly returned to the window to watch over and encourage the happy appearance. Ten minutes more made it certain that a bright afternoon would succeed, and justified the opinion of Mrs. Allen, who had "always thought it would clear up."

But whether Catherine might still expect her friends, whether there had not been too much rain for Miss Tilney to venture, must yet be a question.

It was too dirty for Mrs. Allen to accompany her husband to the Pump-room; he accordingly set off by himself, and Catherine had barely watched him down the street, when her notice was claimed by the approach of the same two open carriages, containing the same three people that had surprized her so much a few mornings back.

"Isabella, my brother, and Mr. Thorpe, I declare! They are coming for me perhaps—but I shall not go—I cannot go indeed, for you know Miss Tilney may still call." Mrs. Allen agreed to it. John Thorpe was soon with them, and his voice was with them yet sooner, for on the stairs he was calling out to Miss Morland to be quick. "Make haste! make haste!" as he threw open the door—"put on your hat this moment—there is no time to be lost—we are going to Bristol. —How d'ye do, Mrs. Allen?"

"To Bristol! Is not that a great way off?—But, however, I cannot go with you to-day, because I am engaged; I expect some friends every moment." This was of course vehemently talked down as no reason at all; Mrs. Allen was called on to second him, and the two others walked in, to give their assistance. "My sweetest Catherine, is not this delightful? We shall have a most heavenly drive. You are to thank your brother and me for the scheme; it darted into our heads at breakfast-time, I verily believe at the same instant; and we should have been off two hours ago if it had not been for this detestable rain. But it does not signify, the nights are moonlight, and we shall do delightfully. Oh! I am in such extasies at the thoughts of a little country air and quiet!—so much better than going to the Lower Rooms. We shall drive directly to Clifton and dine there; and, as soon as dinner is over, if there is time for it, go on to Kingsweston."

"I doubt our being able to do so much," said Morland.

"You croaking fellow!" cried Thorpe, "we shall be able to do ten times more. Kingsweston! aye, and Blaize Castle too, and any thing else we can hear of; but here is your sister says she will not go."

"Blaize Castle!" cried Catherine; "what is that?"

"The finest place in England—worth going fifty miles at any time to see."

"What, is it really a castle, an old castle?"

"The oldest in the kingdom."

"But is it like what one reads of?"

"Exactly—the very same."

"But now really—are there towers and long galleries?"

"By dozens."

"Then I should like to see it; but I cannot——I cannot go."

"Not go!—my beloved creature, what do you mean?"

"I cannot go, because"——(looking down as she spoke, fearful of Isabella's smile) "I expect Miss Tilney and her brother to call on me to take a country walk. They promised to come at twelve, only it rained; but now, as it is so fine, I dare say they will be here soon."

"Not they indeed," cried Thorpe; "for, as we turned into Broad-street, I saw them—does he not drive a phaeton with bright chesnuts?"

"I do not know indeed."

"Yes, I know he does; I saw him. You are talking of the man you danced with last night, are not you?"

"Yes."

"Well, I saw him at that moment turn up the Lansdown Road,—driving a smart-looking girl."

"Did you indeed?"

"Did upon my soul; knew him again directly, and he seemed to have got some very pretty cattle too."

"It is very odd! but I suppose they thought it would be too dirty for a walk."

"And well they might, for I never saw so much dirt in my life. Walk! you could no more walk than you could fly! it has not been so dirty the whole winter; it is ancle-deep every where."

Isabella corroborated it:—"My dearest Catherine, you cannot form an idea of the dirt; come, you must go; you cannot refuse going now."

"I should like to see the castle; but may we go all over it? may we go up every staircase, and into every suite of rooms?"

"Yes, yes, every hole and corner."

"But then,—if they should only be gone out for an hour till it is drier, and call by and bye?"

"Make yourself easy, there is no danger of that, for I heard Tilney hallooing to a man who was just passing by on horseback, that they were going as far as Wick Rocks."

"Then I will. Shall I go, Mrs. Allen?"

"Just as you please, my dear."

"Mrs. Allen, you must persuade her to go," was the general cry. Mrs. Allen was not inattentive to it:—"Well, my dear," said she, "suppose you go."—And in two minutes they were off.

Catherine's feelings, as she got into the carriage, were in a very unsettled state; divided between regret for the loss of one great pleasure, and the hope of soon enjoying another, almost its equal in degree, however unlike in kind. She could not think the Tilneys had acted quite well by her, in so readily giving up their engagement, without sending her any message of excuse. It was now but an hour later than the time fixed on for the beginning of their walk; and, in spite of what she had heard of the prodigious accumulation of dirt in the course of that hour, she could not from her own observation help thinking, that they might have gone with very little inconvenience. To feel herself slighted by them was very painful. On the other hand, the delight

of exploring an edifice like Udolpho, as her fancy represented Blaize Castle to be, was such a counterpoise of good,
as might console her for almost any thing.

They passed briskly down Pulteney-street, and through
Laura-place, without the exchange of many words. Thorpe
talked to his horse, and she meditated, by turns, on broken
promises and broken arches, phaetons and false hangings,
Tilneys and trap-doors. As they entered Argyle-buildings,
however, she was roused by this address from her companion, "Who is that girl who looked at you so hard as she went
by?"

"Who?—where?"

"On the right-hand pavement—she must be almost out of
sight now." Catherine looked round and saw Miss Tilney
leaning on her brother's arm, walking slowly down the
street. She saw them both looking back at her. "Stop, stop,
Mr. Thorpe," she impatiently cried, "it is Miss Tilney; it is
indeed.—How could you tell me they were gone?—Stop, stop,
I will get out this moment and go to them." But to what
purpose did she speak?—Thorpe only lashed his horse into
a brisker trot; the Tilneys, who had soon ceased to look after
her, were in a moment out of sight round the corner of
Laura-place, and in another moment she was herself whisked
into the Market-place. Still, however, and during the length
of another street, she intreated him to stop. "Pray, pray stop,
Mr. Thorpe.—I cannot go on.—I will not go on.—I must go
back to Miss Tilney." But Mr. Thorpe only laughed,
smacked his whip, encouraged his horse, made odd noises,
and drove on; and Catherine, angry and vexed as she was,
having no power of getting away, was obliged to give up the
point and submit. Her reproaches, however, were not
spared. "How could you deceive me so, Mr. Thorpe?—How
could you say, that you saw them driving up the Lansdown-
road?—I would not have had it happen so for the world.—
They must think it so strange; so rude of me! to go by them,

too, without saying a word! You do not know how vexed I am.—I shall have no pleasure at Clifton, nor in any thing else. I had rather, ten thousand times rather get out now, and walk back to them. How could you say, you saw them driving out in a phaeton?" Thorpe defended himself very stoutly, declared he had never seen two men so much alike in his life, and would hardly give up the point of its having been Tilney himself.

Their drive, even when this subject was over, was not likely to be very agreeable. Catherine's complaisance was no longer what it had been in their former airing. She listened reluctantly, and her replies were short. Blaize Castle remained her only comfort; towards *that,* she still looked at intervals with pleasure; though rather than be disappointed of the promised walk, and especially rather than be thought ill of by the Tilneys, she would willingly have given up all the happiness which its walls could supply—the happiness of a progress through a long suite of lofty rooms, exhibiting the remains of magnificent furniture, though now for many years deserted—the happiness of being stopped in their way along narrow, winding vaults, by a low, grated door; or even of having their lamp, their only lamp, extinguished by a sudden gust of wind, and of being left in total darkness. In the meanwhile, they proceeded on their journey without any mischance; and were within view of the town of Keynsham, when a halloo from Morland, who was behind them, made his friend pull up, to know what was the matter. The others then came close enough for conversation, and Morland said, "We had better go back, Thorpe; it is too late to go on to-day; your sister thinks so as well as I. We have been exactly an hour coming from Pulteney-street, very little more than seven miles; and, I suppose, we have at least eight more to go. It will never do. We set out a great deal too late. We had much better put it off till another day, and turn round."

"It is all one to me," replied Thorpe rather angrily; and instantly turning his horse, they were on their way back to Bath.

"If your brother had not got such a d—— beast to drive," said he soon afterwards, "we might have done it very well. My horse would have trotted to Clifton within the hour, if left to himself, and I have almost broke my arm with pulling him in to that cursed broken-winded jade's pace. Morland is a fool for not keeping a horse and gig of his own."

"No, he is not," said Catherine warmly, "for I am sure he could not afford it."

"And why cannot he afford it?"

"Because he has not money enough."

"And whose fault is that?"

"Nobody's, that I know of." Thorpe then said something in the loud, incoherent way to which he had often recourse, about its being a d—— thing to be miserly; and that if people who rolled in money could not afford things, he did not know who could; which Catherine did not even endeavour to understand. Disappointed of what was to have been the consolation for her first disappointment, she was less and less disposed either to be agreeable herself, or to find her companion so; and they returned to Pulteney-street without her speaking twenty words.

As she entered the house, the footman told her, that a gentleman and lady had called and inquired for her a few minutes after her setting off; that, when he told them she was gone out with Mr. Thorpe, the lady had asked whether any message had been left for her; and on his saying no, had felt for a card, but said she had none about her, and went away. Pondering over these heart-rending tidings, Catherine walked slowly up stairs. At the head of them she was met by Mr. Allen, who, on hearing the reason of their speedy return, said, "I am glad your brother had so much sense; I am glad you are come back. It was a strange, wild scheme."

They all spent the evening together at Thorpe's. Catherine was disturbed and out of spirits; but Isabella seemed to find a pool of commerce, in the fate of which she shared, by private partnership with Morland, a very good equivalent for the quiet and country air of an inn at Clifton. Her satisfaction, too, in not being at the Lower Rooms, was spoken more than once. "How I pity the poor creatures that are going there! How glad I am that I am not amongst them! I wonder whether it will be a full ball or not! They have not begun dancing yet. I would not be there for all the world. It is so delightful to have an evening now and then to oneself. I dare say it will not be a very good ball. I know the Mitchells will not be there. I am sure I pity every body that is. But I dare say, Mr. Morland, you long to be at it, do not you? I am sure you do. Well, pray do not let any body here be a restraint on you. I dare say we could do very well without you; but you men think yourselves of such consequence."

Catherine could almost have accused Isabella of being wanting in tenderness towards herself and her sorrows; so very little did they appear to dwell on her mind, and so very inadequate was the comfort she offered. "Do not be so dull, my dearest creature," she whispered. "You will quite break my heart. It was amazingly shocking to be sure; but the Tilneys were entirely to blame. Why were not they more punctual? It was dirty, indeed, but what did that signify? I am sure John and I should not have minded it. I never mind going through any thing, where a friend is concerned; that is my disposition, and John is just the same; he has amazing strong feelings. Good heavens! what a delightful hand you have got! Kings, I vow! I never was so happy in my life! I would fifty times rather you should have them than myself."

And now I may dismiss my heroine to the sleepless

couch, which is the true heroine's portion; to a pillow strewed with thorns and wet with tears. And lucky may she think herself, if she get another good night's rest in the course of the next three months.

CHAPTER XII

"Mrs. Allen," said Catherine the next morning, "will there be any harm in my calling on Miss Tilney to-day? I shall not be easy till I have explained every thing."

"Go by all means, my dear; only put on a white gown; Miss Tilney always wears white."

Catherine cheerfully complied; and being properly equipped, was more impatient than ever to be at the Pump-room, that she might inform herself of General Tilney's lodgings, for though she believed they were in Milsom-street, she was not certain of the house, and Mrs. Allen's wavering convictions only made it more doubtful. To Milsom-street she was directed; and having made herself perfect in the number, hastened away with eager steps and a beating heart to pay her visit, explain her conduct, and be forgiven; tripping lightly through the church-yard, and resolutely turning away her eyes, that she might not be obliged to see her beloved Isabella and her dear family, who, she had reason to believe, were in a shop hard by. She reached the house without any impediment, looked at the number, knocked at the door, and inquired for Miss Tilney. The man believed Miss Tilney to be at home, but was not quite certain. Would she be pleased to send up her name? She gave her card. In a few minutes the servant returned, and with a look which did not quite confirm his words, said he had been mistaken, for that Miss Tilney was walked out. Catherine, with a blush of mortification, left the house. She felt almost persuaded that Miss Tilney *was* at home, and too much offended to admit her; and as she retired down the street, could not withhold one glance at the drawing-room windows, in expectation of seeing her there, but no one appeared at them. At the bottom of the street, however, she looked back again, and then, not at a window, but issuing from the door, she saw Miss Tilney herself. She was followed by a gentleman, whom Catherine believed to be her father, and they turned up towards Edgar's-buildings. Catherine, in deep mortification, proceeded on her way. She could almost be angry herself at such angry incivility; but she checked the resentful sensation; she remembered her own ignorance. She knew not how such an offence as her's might be classed by the laws of worldly politeness, to what a degree of unforgivingness it might with propriety lead, nor to what rigours of rudeness in return it might justly make her amenable.

Dejected and humbled, she had even some thoughts of not going with the others to the theatre that night; but it must be confessed that they were not of long continuance: for she soon recollected, in the first place, that she was without any excuse for staying at home; and, in the second, that it was a play she wanted very much to see. To the theatre accordingly they all went; no Tilneys appeared to plague or please her; she feared that, amongst the many perfections of the family, a fondness for plays was not to be ranked; but perhaps it was because they were habituated to the finer performances of the London stage, which she knew, on Isabella's authority, rendered every thing else of the kind "quite horrid." She was not deceived in her own expectation of pleasure; the comedy so well suspended her care, that no one, observing her during the first four acts, would have supposed she had any wretchedness about her. On the beginning of the fifth, however, the sudden view of Mr. Henry Tilney and his father, joining a party in the opposite box, recalled her to anxiety and distress. The stage could no longer excite genuine merriment—no longer keep her whole attention. Every other look upon an average was directed towards the opposite box; and, for the space of two entire scenes, did she thus watch Henry Tilney, without being once able to catch his eye. No longer could he be suspected of indifference for a play; his notice was never withdrawn from the stage during two whole scenes. At length, however, he did look towards her, and he bowed—but such a bow! no smile, no continued observance attended it; his eyes were immediately returned to their former direction. Catherine was restlessly miserable; she could almost have run around to the box in which he sat, and forced him to hear her explanation. Feelings rather natural than heroic possessed her; instead of considering her own dignity injured by this ready condemnation—instead of proudly resolving, in conscious innocence, to shew her resentment towards him who could harbour a doubt of it, to leave to him all the trouble of seeking an explanation, and to enlighten him on the past only by avoiding his sight, or flirting with somebody else, she took to herself all the shame of misconduct, or at least of its appearance, and was only eager for an opportunity of explaining its cause.

The play concluded—the curtain fell—Henry Tilney was no longer to be seen where he had hitherto sat, but his father remained, and perhaps he might be now coming round to their box. She was right; in a few minutes he appeared, and, making his way through the then thinning rows, spoke with like calm politeness to Mrs. Allen and her friend.—Not with such calmness was he answered by the latter: "Oh! Mr. Tilney, I have been quite wild to speak to you, and make my apologies. You must have thought me so rude; but indeed it was not my own fault,—was it, Mrs. Allen? Did not they tell me that Mr. Tilney and his sister were gone out in a phaeton together? and then what could I do? But I had ten thousand times rather have been with you; now had not I, Mrs. Allen?"

"My dear, you tumble my gown," was Mrs. Allen's reply.

Her assurance, however, standing sole as it did, was not thrown away; it brought a more cordial, more natural smile into his countenance, and he replied in a tone which retained only a little affected reserve:—"We were much obliged to you at any rate for wishing us a pleasant walk after our passing you in Argyle-street: you were so kind as to look back on purpose."

"But indeed I did not wish you a pleasant walk; I never thought of such a thing; but I begged Mr. Thorpe so earnestly to stop; I called out to him as soon as ever I saw you; now, Mrs. Allen, did not——Oh! you were not there; but indeed I did; and, if Mr. Thorpe would only have stopped, I would have jumped out and run after you."

Is there a Henry in the world who could be insensible to such a declaration? Henry Tilney at least was not. With a yet sweeter smile, he said every thing that need be said of his sister's concern, regret, and dependence on Catherine's honour.—"Oh! do not say Miss Tilney was not angry," cried Catherine, "because I know she was; for she would not see me this morning when I called; I saw her walk out of the house the next minute after my leaving it; I was hurt, but I was not affronted. Perhaps you did not know I had been there."

"I was not within at the time; but I heard of it from Eleanor, and she has been wishing ever since to see you, to explain the reason of such incivility; but perhaps I can do it as well. It was nothing more than that my father——they were just preparing to walk out, and he being hurried for time, and not caring to have it put off, made a point of her being denied. That was all, I do assure you. She was very much vexed, and meant to make her apology as soon as possible."

Catherine's mind was greatly eased by this information, yet a something of solicitude remained, from which sprang the following question, thoroughly artless in itself, though rather distressing to the gentleman:—"But, Mr. Tilney, why were *you* less generous than your sister? If she felt such confidence in my good intentions, and could suppose it to be only a mistake, why should *you* be so ready to take offence?"

"Me!—I take offence!"

"Nay, I am sure by your look, when you came into the box, you were angry."

"I angry! I could have no right."

"Well, nobody would have thought you had no right who saw your face." He replied by asking her to make room for him, and talking of the play.

He remained with them some time, and was only too agreeable for Catherine to be contented when he went away. Before they parted, however, it was agreed that the projected walk should be taken as soon as possible; and, setting aside the misery of his quitting their box, she was, upon the whole, left one of the happiest creatures in the world.

While talking to each other, she had observed with some surprize, that John Thorpe, who was never in the same part of the house for ten minutes together, was engaged in conversation with General Tilney; and she felt something more than surprize, when she thought she could perceive herself the object of their attention and discourse. What could they have to say of her? She feared General Tilney did not like her appearance: she found it was implied in his preventing her admittance to his daughter, rather than postpone his own walk a few minutes. "How came Mr. Thorpe to know your father?" was her anxious inquiry, as she pointed them out to her companion. He knew nothing about it; but his father, like every military man, had a very large acquaintance.

When the entertainment was over, Thorpe came to assist them in getting out. Catherine was the immediate object of his gallantry; and, while they waited in the lobby for a chair, he prevented the inquiry which had travelled from her heart almost to the tip of her tongue, by asking, in a consequential manner, whether she had seen him talking with General Tilney:—"He is a fine old fellow, upon my soul!—stout, active,—looks as young as his son. I have a great regard for him, I assure you: a gentleman-like, good sort of fellow as ever lived."

"But how came you to know him?"

"Know him!—There are few people much about town that I do not know. I have met him for ever at the Bedford; and I knew his face again to-day the moment he came into the billiard-room. One of the best players we have, by the bye; and we had a little touch together, though I was almost afraid of him at first: the odds were five to four against me; and, if I had not made one of the cleanest strokes that perhaps ever was made in this world——I took his ball exactly——but I could not make you understand it without a table;—however I *did* beat him. A very fine fellow; as rich as a Jew. I should like to dine with him; I dare say he gives famous dinners. But what do you think we have been talking of?—You. Yes, by heavens!—and the General thinks you the finest girl in Bath."

"Oh! nonsense! how can you say so?"

"And what do you think I said?" (lowering his voice) "Well done, General, said I, I am quite of your mind."

Here, Catherine, who was much less gratified by his admiration than by General Tilney's, was not sorry to be called away by Mr. Allen. Thorpe, however, would see her to her chair, and, till she entered it, continued the same kind of delicate flattery, in spite of her entreating him to have done.

That General Tilney, instead of disliking, should admire her, was very delightful; and she joyfully thought, that there was not one of the family whom she need now fear to meet. —The evening had done more, much more, for her, than could have been expected.

CHAPTER XIII

Monday, Tuesday, Wednesday, Thursday, Friday and Saturday have now passed in review before the reader; the events of each day, its hopes and fears, mortifications and pleasures have been separately stated, and the pangs of Sunday only now remain to be described, and close the week. The Clifton scheme had been deferred, not relinquished, and on the afternoon's Crescent of this day, it was brought forward again. In a private consultation between Isabella and James, the former of whom had particularly set her heart upon going, and the latter no less anxiously placed his upon pleasing her, it was agreed that, provided the weather were fair, the party should take place on the following morning; and they were to set off very early, in order to be at home in good time. The affair thus determined, and Thorpe's approbation secured, Catherine only remained to be apprized of it. She had left them for a few minutes to speak to Miss Tilney. In that interval the plan was completed, and as soon as she came again, her agreement was demanded; but instead of the gay acquiescence expected by Isabella, Catherine looked grave, was very sorry, but could not go. The engagement which ought to have kept her from joining in the former attempt, would make it impossible for her to accompany them now. She had that moment settled with Miss Tilney to take their promised walk to-morrow; it was quite determined, and she would not, upon any account, retract. But that she *must* and *should* retract, was instantly the eager cry of both the Thorpes; they must go to Clifton to-morrow, they would not go without her, it would be nothing to put off a mere walk for one day longer, and they would not hear of a refusal. Catherine was distressed, but not subdued. "Do not urge me, Isabella. I am engaged to Miss Tilney. I cannot go." This availed nothing. The same arguments assailed her again; she must go, she should go, and they would not hear of a refusal. "It would be so easy to tell Miss Tilney that you had just been reminded of a prior engagement, and must only beg to put off the walk till Tuesday."

"No, it would not be easy. I could not do it. There has been no prior engagement." But Isabella became only more and more urgent; calling on her in the most affectionate manner; addressing her by the most endearing names. She was sure her dearest, sweetest Catherine would not seriously refuse such a trifling request to a friend who loved her so dearly. She knew her beloved Catherine to have so feeling a heart, so sweet a temper, to be so easily persuaded by those she loved. But all in vain; Catherine felt herself to be in the right, and though pained by such tender, such flattering supplication, could not allow it to influence her. Isabella then tried another method. She reproached her with having more affection for Miss Tilney, though she had known her so little a while, than for her best and oldest friends; with being grown cold and indifferent, in short, towards herself. "I cannot help being jealous, Catherine, when I see myself slighted for strangers, I, who love you so excessively! When once my affections are placed, it is not in the power of any thing to change them. But I believe my feelings are stronger than any body's; I am sure they are too strong for my own peace; and to see myself supplanted in your friendship by strangers, does cut me to the quick, I own. These Tilneys seem to swallow up every thing else."

Catherine thought this reproach equally strange and unkind. Was it the part of a friend thus to expose her feelings to the notice of others? Isabella appeared to her ungenerous and selfish, regardless of every thing but her own gratification. These painful ideas crossed her mind, though she said nothing. Isabella, in the meanwhile, had applied her handkerchief to her eyes; and Morland, miserable at such a sight, could not help saying, "Nay, Catherine. I think you cannot stand out any longer now. The sacrifice is not much; and to oblige such a friend—I shall think you quite unkind, if you still refuse."

This was the first time of her brother's openly siding against her, and anxious to avoid his displeasure, she proposed a compromise. If they would only put off their scheme till Tuesday, which they might easily do, as it depended only on themselves, she could go with them, and every body might then be satisfied. But "No, no, no!" was the immediate answer; "that could not be, for Thorpe did not know that he might not go to town on Tuesday." Catherine was sorry, but could do no more; and a short silence ensued, which was broken by Isabella; who in a voice of cold resentment said, "Very well, then there is an end of the party. If Catherine does not go, I cannot. I cannot be the only woman. I would not, upon any account in the world, do so improper a thing."

"Catherine, you must go," said James.

"But why cannot Mr. Thorpe drive one of his other sisters? I dare say either of them would like to go."

"Thank ye," cried Thorpe, "but I did not come to Bath to drive my sisters about, and look like a fool. No, if you do not go, d—— me if I do. I only go for the sake of driving you."

"That is a compliment which gives me no pleasure." But her words were lost on Thorpe, who had turned abruptly away.

The three others still continued together, walking in a most uncomfortable manner to poor Catherine; sometimes not a word was said, sometimes she was again attacked with supplications or reproaches, and her arm was still linked within Isabella's, though their hearts were at war. At one moment she was softened, at another irritated; always distressed, but always steady.

"I did not think you had been so obstinate, Catherine," said James; "you were not used to be so hard to persuade; you once were the kindest, best-tempered of my sisters."

"I hope I am not less so now," she replied, very feelingly; "but indeed I cannot go. If I am wrong, I am doing what I believe to be right."

"I suspect," said Isabella, in a low voice, "there is no great struggle."

Catherine's heart swelled; she drew away her arm, and Isabella made no opposition. Thus passed a long ten minutes, till they were again joined by Thorpe, who coming to them with a gayer look, said, "Well, I have settled the matter, and now we may all go to-morrow with a safe conscience. I have been to Miss Tilney, and made your excuses."

"You have not!" cried Catherine.

"I have, upon my soul. Left her this moment. Told her you had sent me to say, that having just recollected a prior engagement of going to Clifton with us to-morrow, you could not have the pleasure of walking with her till Tuesday. She said very well, Tuesday was just as convenient to her; so there is an end of all our difficulties.—A pretty good thought of mine—hey?"

Isabella's countenance was once more all smiles and good-humour, and James too looked happy again.

"A most heavenly thought indeed! Now, my sweet Catherine, all our distresses are over; you are honourably acquitted, and we shall have a most delightful party."

"This will not do," said Catherine; "I cannot submit to this. I must run after Miss Tilney directly and set her right."

Isabella, however, caught hold of one hand; Thorpe of the other; and remonstrances poured in from all three. Even

James was quite angry. When every thing was settled, when Miss Tilney herself said that Tuesday would suit her as well, it was quite ridiculous, quite absurd to make any further objection.

"I do not care. Mr. Thorpe had no business to invent any such message. If I had thought it right to put it off, I could have spoken to Miss Tilney myself. This is only doing it in a ruder way; and how do I know that Mr. Thorpe has—— he may be mistaken again perhaps; he led me into one act of rudeness by his mistake on Friday. Let me go, Mr. Thorpe; Isabella, do not hold me."

Thorpe told her it would be in vain to go after the Tilneys; they were turning the corner into Brock-street, when he had overtaken them, and were at home by this time.

"Then I will go after them," said Catherine; "wherever they are I will go after them. It does not signify talking. If I could not be persuaded into doing what I thought wrong, I never will be tricked into it." And with these words she broke away and hurried off. Thorpe would have darted after her, but Morland withheld him. "Let her go, let her go, if she will go."

"She is as obstinate as——"

Thorpe never finished the simile, for it could hardly have been a proper one.

Away walked Catherine in great agitation, as fast as the crowd would permit her, fearful of being pursued, yet determined to persevere. As she walked, she reflected on what had passed. It was painful to her to disappoint and displease them, particularly to displease her brother; but she could not repent her resistance. Setting her own inclination apart, to have failed a second time in her engagement to Miss Tilney, to have retracted a promise voluntarily made only five minutes before, and on a false pretence too, must have been wrong. She had not been withstanding them on selfish principles alone, she had not consulted merely her own gratification; *that* might have been ensured in some degree by the excursion itself, by seeing Blaize Castle; no, she had attended to what was due to others, and to her own character in their opinion. Her conviction of being right however was not enough to restore her composure, till she had spoken to Miss Tilney she could not be at ease; and quickening her pace when she got clear of the Crescent, she almost ran over the remaining ground till she gained the top of Milsom-street. So rapid had been her movements, that in spite of the Tilneys' advantage in the outset, they were but just turning into their lodgings as she came within view of them; and the servant still remaining at the open door, she used only the ceremony of saying that she must speak with Miss Tilney that moment, and hurrying by him proceeded up stairs. Then, opening the first door before her, which happened to be the right, she immediately found herself in the drawing-room with General Tilney, his son and daughter. Her explanation, defective only in being—from her irritation of nerves and shortness of breath—no explanation at all, was instantly given. "I am come in a great hurry—It was all a mistake—I never promised to go—I told them from the first I could not go.—I ran away in a great hurry to explain it.—I did not care what you thought of me.—I would not stay for the servant."

The business however, though not perfectly elucidated by this speech, soon ceased to be a puzzle. Catherine found that John Thorpe *had* given the message; and Miss Tilney had no scruple in owning herself greatly surprized by it. But whether her brother had still exceeded her in resentment, Catherine, though she instinctively addressed herself as much to one as to the other in her vindication, had no means of knowing. Whatever might have been felt before her arrival, her eager declarations immediately made every look and sentence as friendly as she could desire.

The affair thus happily settled, she was introduced by

Miss Tilney to her father, and received by him with such ready, such solicitous politeness as recalled Thorpe's information to her mind, and made her think with pleasure that he might be sometimes depended on. To such anxious attention was the general's civility carried, that not aware of her extraordinary swiftness in entering the house, he was quite angry with the servant whose neglect had reduced her to open the door of the apartment herself. "What did William mean by it? He should make a point of inquiring into the matter." And if Catherine had not most warmly asserted his innocence, it seemed likely that William would lose the favour of his master for ever, if not his place, by her rapidity.

After sitting with them a quarter of an hour, she rose to take leave, and was then most agreeably surprized by General Tilney's asking her if she would do his daughter the honour of dining and spending the rest of the day with her. Miss Tilney added her own wishes. Catherine was greatly obliged; but it was quite out of her power. Mr. and Mrs. Allen would expect her back every moment. The general declared he could say no more; the claims of Mr. and Mrs. Allen were not to be superseded; but on some other day he trusted, when longer notice could be given, they would not refuse to spare her to her friend. "Oh, no; Catherine was sure they would not have the least objection, and she should have great pleasure in coming." The general attended her himself to the street-door, saying every thing gallant as they went down stairs, admiring the elasticity of her walk, which corresponded exactly with the spirit of her dancing, and making her one of the most graceful bows she had ever beheld, when they parted.

Catherine, delighted by all that had passed, proceeded gaily to Pulteney-street; walking, as she concluded, with great elasticity, though she had never thought of it before. She reached home without seeing any thing more of the offended party; and now that she had been triumphant throughout, had carried her point and was secure of her walk, she began (as the flutter of her spirits subsided) to doubt whether she had been perfectly right. A sacrifice was always noble; and if she had given way to their entreaties, she should have been spared the distressing idea of a friend displeased, a brother angry, and a scheme of great happiness to both destroyed, perhaps through her means. To ease her mind, and ascertain by the opinion of an unprejudiced person what her own conduct had really been, she took occasion to mention before Mr. Allen the half-settled scheme of her brother and the Thorpes for the following day. Mr. Allen caught at it directly. "Well," said he, "and do you think of going too?"

"No; I had just engaged myself to walk with Miss Tilney before they told me of it; and therefore you know I could not go with them, could I?"

"No, certainly not; and I am glad you do not think of it. These schemes are not at all the thing. Young men and women driving about the country in open carriages! Now and then it is very well; but going to inns and public places together! It is not right; and I wonder Mrs. Thorpe should allow it. I am glad you do not think of going; I am sure Mrs. Morland would not be pleased. Mrs. Allen, are not you of my way of thinking? Do not you think these kind of projects objectionable?"

"Yes, very much so indeed. Open carriages are nasty things. A clean gown is not five minutes wear in them. You are splashed getting in and getting out; and the wind takes your hair and your bonnet in every direction. I hate an open carriage myself."

"I know you do; but that is not the question. Do not you think it has an odd appearance, if young ladies are frequently driven about in them by young men, to whom they are not even related?"

"Yes, my dear, a very odd appearance indeed. I cannot bear to see it."

"Dear madam," cried Catherine, "then why did not you tell me so before? I am sure if I had known it to be improper, I would not have gone with Mr. Thorpe at all; but I always hoped you would tell me, if you thought I was doing wrong."

"And so I should, my dear, you may depend on it; for as I told Mrs. Morland at parting, I would always do the best for you in my power. But one must not be over particular. Young people *will* be young people, as your good mother says herself. You know I wanted you, when we first came, not to buy that sprigged muslin, but you would. Young people do not like to be always thwarted."

"But this was something of real consequence; and I do not think you would have found me hard to persuade."

"As far as it has gone hitherto, there is no harm done," said Mr. Allen; "and I would only advise you, my dear, not to go out with Mr. Thorpe any more."

"That is just what I was going to say," added his wife.

Catherine, relieved for herself, felt uneasy for Isabella; and after a moment's thought, asked Mr. Allen whether it would not be both proper and kind in her to write to Miss Thorpe, and explain the indecorum of which she must be as insensible as herself; for she considered that Isabella might otherwise perhaps be going to Clifton the next day, in spite of what had passed. Mr. Allen however discouraged her from doing any such thing. "You had better leave her alone, my dear, she is old enough to know what she is about; and if not, has a mother to advise her. Mrs. Thorpe is too indulgent beyond a doubt; but however you had better not interfere. She and your brother chuse to go, and you will be only getting ill-will."

Catherine submitted; and though sorry to think that Isabella should be doing wrong, felt greatly relieved by Mr.

Allen's approbation of her own conduct, and truly rejoiced to be preserved by his advice from the danger of falling into such an error herself. Her escape from being one of the party to Clifton was now an escape indeed; for what would the Tilneys have thought of her, if she had broken her promise to them in order to do what was wrong in itself? if she had been guilty of one breach of propriety, only to enable her to be guilty of another?

CHAPTER XIV

The next morning was fair, and Catherine almost expected another attack from the assembled party. With Mr. Allen to support her, she felt no dread of the event: but she would gladly be spared a contest, where victory itself was painful; and was heartily rejoiced therefore at neither seeing nor hearing any thing of them. The Tilneys called for her at the appointed time; and no new difficulty arising, no sudden recollection, no unexpected summons, no impertinent intrusion to disconcert their measures, my heroine was most unnaturally able to fulfil her engagement, though it was made with the hero himself. They determined on walking round Beechen Cliff, that noble hill, whose beautiful verdure and hanging coppice render it so striking an object from almost every opening in Bath.

"I never look at it," said Catherine, as they walked along the side of the river, "without thinking of the south of France."

"You have been abroad then?" said Henry, a little surprized.

"Oh! no, I only mean what I have read about. It always puts me in mind of the country that Emily and her father travelled through, in the 'Mysteries of Udolpho.' But you never read novels, I dare say?"

"Why not?"

"Because they are not clever enough for you—gentlemen read better books."

"The person, be it gentleman or lady, who has not pleasure in a good novel, must be intolerably stupid. I have read all Mrs. Radcliffe's works, and most of them with great

394

pleasure. The Mysteries of Udolpho, when I had once be-gun it, I could not lay down again;—I remember finishing it in two days—my hair standing on end the whole time."

"Yes," added Miss Tilney, "and I remember that you undertook to read it aloud to me, and that when I was called away for only five minutes to answer a note, instead of waiting for me, you took the volume into the Hermitage-walk, and I was obliged to stay till you had finished it."

"Thank you, Eleanor;—a most honourable testimony. You see, Miss Morland, the injustice of your suspicions. Here was I, in my eagerness to get on, refusing to wait only five minutes for my sister; breaking the promise I had made of reading it aloud, and keeping her in suspense at a most interesting part, by running away with the volume, which, you are to observe, was her own, particularly her own. I am proud when I reflect on it, and I think it must establish me in your good opinion."

"I am very glad to hear it indeed, and now I shall never be ashamed of liking Udolpho myself. But I really thought before, young men despised novels amazingly."

"It is *amazingly;* it may well suggest *amazement* if they do —for they read nearly as many as women. I myself have read hundreds and hundreds. Do not imagine that you can cope with me in a knowledge of Julias and Louisas. If we proceed to particulars, and engage in the never-ceasing inquiry of 'Have you read this?' and 'Have you read that?' I shall soon leave you as far behind me as—what shall I say?—I want an appropriate simile;—as far as your friend Emily herself left poor Valancourt when she went with her aunt into Italy. Consider how many years I have had the start of you. I had entered on my studies at Oxford, while you were a good little girl working your sampler at home!"

"Not very good I am afraid. But now really, do not you think Udolpho the nicest book in the world?"

"The nicest;—by which I suppose you mean the neatest. That must depend upon the binding."

"Henry," said Miss Tilney, "you are very impertinent. Miss Morland, he is treating you exactly as he does his sister. He is for ever finding fault with me, for some incorrectness of language, and now he is taking the same liberty with you. The word 'nicest,' as you used it, did not suit him; and you had better change it as soon as you can, or we shall be overpowered with Johnson and Blair all the rest of the way."

"I am sure," cried Catherine, "I did not mean to say any thing wrong; but it *is* a nice book, and why should not I call it so?"

"Very true," said Henry, "and this is a very nice day, and we are taking a very nice walk, and you are two very nice young ladies. Oh! it is a very nice word indeed!—it does for every thing. Originally perhaps it was applied only to express neatness, propriety, delicacy, or refinement;—people were nice in their dress, in their sentiments, or their choice. But now every commendation on every subject is comprised in that one word."

"While, in fact," cried his sister, "it ought only to be applied to you, without any commendation at all. You are more nice than wise. Come, Miss Morland, let us leave him to meditate over our faults in the utmost propriety of diction, while we praise Udolpho in whatever terms we like best. It is a most interesting work. You are fond of that kind of reading?"

"To say the truth, I do not much like any other."

"Indeed!"

"That is, I can read poetry and plays, and things of that sort, and do not dislike travels. But history, real solemn history, I cannot be interested in. Can you?"

"Yes, I am fond of history."

"I wish I were too. I read it a little as a duty, but it tells me nothing that does not either vex or weary me. The quarrels of popes and kings, with wars or pestilences, in every page; the men all so good for nothing, and hardly any women at all—it is very tiresome: and yet I often think it odd that it should be so dull, for a great deal of it must be invention. The speeches that are put into the heroes' mouths, their thoughts and designs—the chief of all this must be invention, and invention is what delights me in other books."

"Historians, you think," said Miss Tilney, "are not happy in their flights of fancy. They display imagination without raising interest. I am fond of history—and am very well contented to take the false with the true. In the principal facts they have sources of intelligence in former histories and records, which may be as much depended on, I conclude, as any thing that does not actually pass under one's own observation; and as for the little embellishments you speak of, they are embellishments, and I like them as such. If a speech be well drawn up, I read it with pleasure, by whomsoever it may be made—and probably with much greater, if the production of Mr. Hume or Mr. Robertson, than if the genuine words of Caractacus, Agricola, or Alfred the Great."

"You are fond of history!—and so are Mr. Allen and my father; and I have two brothers who do not dislike it. So many instances within my small circle of friends is remarkable! At this rate, I shall not pity the writers of history any longer. If people like to read their books, it is all very well, but to be at so much trouble in filling great volumes, which, as I used to think, nobody would willingly ever look into, to be labouring only for the torment of little boys and girls, always struck me as a hard fate; and though I know it is all very right and necessary, I have often wondered at the person's courage that could sit down on purpose to do it."

"That little boys and girls should be tormented," said Henry, "is what no one at all acquainted with human nature in a civilized state can deny; but in behalf of our most distinguished historians, I must observe, that they might well be offended at being supposed to have no higher aim; and that by their method and style, they are perfectly well qualified to torment readers of the most advanced reason and mature time of life. I use the verb 'to torment,' as I observed to be your own method, instead of 'to instruct,' supposing them to be now admitted as synonimous."

"You think me foolish to call instruction a torment, but if you had been as much used as myself to hear poor little children first learning their letters and then learning to spell, if you had ever seen how stupid they can be for a whole morning together, and how tired my poor mother is at the end of it, as I am in the habit of seeing almost every day of my life at home, you would allow that to *torment* and to *instruct* might sometimes be used as synonimous words."

"Very probably. But historians are not accountable for the difficulty of learning to read; and even you yourself, who do not altogether seem particularly friendly to very severe, very intense aplication, may perhaps be brought to acknowledge that it is very well worth while to be tormented for two or three years of one's life, for the sake of being able to read all the rest of it. Consider—if reading had not been taught, Mrs. Radcliffe would have written in vain—or perhaps might not have written at all."

Catherine assented—and a very warm panegyric from her on that lady's merits, closed the subject.—The Tilneys were soon engaged in another on which she had nothing to say. They were viewing the country with the eyes of persons accustomed to drawing, and decided on its capability of being formed into pictures, with all the eagerness of real taste. Here Catherine was quite lost. She knew nothing of drawing—nothing of taste:—and she listened to them with an attention which brought her little profit, for they talked in phrases which conveyed scarcely any idea to her. The little which she could understand however appeared to contradict the very few notions she had entertained on the matter before. It seemed as if a good view were no longer to be taken from the top of an high hill, and that a clear blue sky was no longer a proof of a fine day. She was heartily ashamed of her ignorance. A misplaced shame. Where people wish to attach, they should always be ignorant. To come with a well-informed mind, is to come with an inability of administering to the vanity of others, which a sensible person would always wish to avoid. A woman especially, if she have the misfortune of knowing any thing, should conceal it as well as she can.

The advantages of natural folly in a beautiful girl have been already set forth by the capital pen of a sister author; —and to her treatment of the subject I will only add in justice to men, that though to the larger and more trifling part of the sex, imbecility in females is a great enhancement of their personal charms, there is a portion of them too reasonable and too well informed themselves to desire any thing more in woman than ignorance. But Catherine did not know her own advantages—did not know that a good-looking girl, with an affectionate heart and a very ignorant mind, cannot fail of attracting a clever young man, unless circumstances are particularly untoward. In the present instance, she confessed and lamented her want of knowledge; declared that she would give any thing in the world to be able to draw; and a lecture on the picturesque immediately followed, in which his instructions were so clear that she soon began to see beauty in every thing admired by him, and her attention was so earnest, that he became perfectly satisfied of her having a great deal of natural taste. He talked of fore-grounds, distances, and second distances—side-screens and perspectives—lights and shades;—and Catherine was so hopeful a scholar, that when they gained the top of Beechen Cliff, she voluntarily rejected the whole city of Bath, as unworthy to make part of a landscape. Delighted with her progress, and fearful of wearying her with too much wisdom at once, Henry suffered the subject to decline, and by an easy transition from a piece of rocky fragment and the withered oak which he had placed near its summit, to oaks in general, to forests, the inclosure of them, waste lands, crown lands and government, he shortly found himself arrived at politics; and from politics, it was an easy step to silence. The general pause which succeeded his short disquisition on the state of the nation, was put an end to by Catherine, who, in rather a solemn tone of voice, uttered these words, "I have heard that something very shocking indeed, will soon come out in London."

Miss Tilney, to whom this was chiefly addressed, was startled, and hastily replied, "Indeed!—and of what nature?"

"That I do not know, nor who is the author. I have only heard that it is to be more horrible than any thing we have met with yet."

"Good heaven!—Where could you hear of such a thing?"

"A particular friend of mine had an account of it in a letter from London yesterday. It is to be uncommonly dreadful. I shall expect murder and every thing of the kind."

"You speak with astonishing composure! But I hope your friend's accounts have been exaggerated;—and if such a design is known beforehand, proper measures will undoubtedly be taken by government to prevent its coming to effect."

"Government," said Henry, endeavouring not to smile, "neither desires nor dares to interfere in such matters. There must be murder; and government cares not how much."

The ladies stared. He laughed, and added, "Come, shall I make you understand each other, or leave you to puzzle out an explanation as you can? No—I will be noble. I will prove myself a man, no less by the generosity of my soul than the clearness of my head. I have no patience with such of my sex as disdain to let themselves sometimes down to the comprehension of yours. Perhaps the abilities of women are neither sound nor acute—neither vigorous nor keen. Perhaps they may want observation, discernment, judgment, fire, genius, and wit."

"Miss Morland, do not mind what he says;—but have the goodness to satisfy me as to this dreadful riot."

"Riot!—what riot?"

"My dear Eleanor, the riot is only in your own brain. The confusion there is scandalous. Miss Morland has been talking of nothing more dreadful than a new publication which is shortly to come out, in three duodecimo volumes, two hundred and seventy-six pages in each, with a frontispiece to the first, of two tombstones and a lantern—do you understand?—And you, Miss Morland—my stupid sister has mistaken all your clearest expressions. You talked of expected horrors in London—and instead of instantly conceiving, as any rational creature would have done, that such words could relate only to a circulating library, she immediately pictured to herself a mob of three thousand men assembling in St. George's Fields; the Bank attacked, the Tower threatened, the streets of London flowing with blood, a detachment of the 12th Light Dragoons, (the hopes of the nation,) called up from Northampton to quell the insurgents, and gallant Capt. Frederick Tilney, in the moment of charging at the head of his troop, knocked off his horse by a brickbat from an upper window. Forgive her stupidity. The fears of the sister have added to the weakness of the woman; but she is by no means a simpleton in general."

Catherine looked grave. "And now, Henry," said Miss Tilney, "that you have made us understand each other, you may as well make Miss Morland understand yourself—unless you mean to have her think you intolerably rude to your sister, and a great brute in your opinion of women in general. Miss Morland is not used to your odd ways."

"I shall be most happy to make her better acquainted with them."

"No doubt;—but that is no explanation of the present."

"What am I to do?"

"You know what you ought to do. Clear your character handsomely before her. Tell her that you think very highly of the understanding of women."

"Miss Morland, I think very highly of the understanding of all the women in the world—especially of those—whoever they may be—with whom I happen to be in company."

"That is not enough. Be more serious."

"Miss Morland, no one can think more highly of the understanding of women than I do. In my opinion, nature has given them so much, that they never find it necessary to use more than half."

"We shall get nothing more serious from him now, Miss Morland. He is not in a sober mood. But I do assure you that he must be entirely misunderstood, if he can ever appear to say an unjust thing of any woman at all, or an unkind one of me."

It was no effort to Catherine to believe that Henry Tilney could never be wrong. His manner might sometimes surprize, but his meaning must always be just:—and what she did not understand, she was almost as ready to admire, as what she did. The whole walk was delightful, and though it ended too soon, its conclusion was delightful too;—her friends attended her into the house, and Miss Tilney, before they parted, addressing herself with respectful form, as much to Mrs. Allen as to Catherine, petitioned for the pleasure of her company to dinner on the day after the next. No difficulty was made on Mrs. Allen's side—and the only difficulty on Catherine's was in concealing the excess of her pleasure.

The morning had passed away so charmingly as to banish all her friendship and natural affection; for no thought of

Isabella or James had crossed her during their walk. When the Tilneys were gone, she became amiable again, but she was amiable for some time to little effect; Mrs. Allen had no intelligence to give that could relieve her anxiety, she had heard nothing of any of them. Towards the end of the morning however, Catherine having occasion for some indispensable yard of ribbon which must be bought without a moment's delay, walked out into the town, and in Bond-street overtook the second Miss Thorpe, as she was loitering towards Edgar's Buildings between two of the sweetest girls in the world, who had been her dear friends all the morning. From her, she soon learned that the party to Clifton had taken place. "They set off at eight this morning," said Miss Anne, "and I am sure I do not envy them their drive. I think you and I are very well off to be out of the scrape.— It must be the dullest thing in the world, for there is not a soul at Clifton at this time of year. Belle went with your brother, and John drove Maria."

Catherine spoke the pleasure she really felt on hearing this part of the arrangement.

"Oh! yes," rejoined the other, "Maria is gone. She was quite wild to go. She thought it would be something very fine. I cannot say I admire her taste; and for my part I was determined from the first not to go, if they pressed me ever so much."

Catherine, a little doubtful of this, could not help answering, "I wish you could have gone too. It is a pity you could not all go."

"Thank you; but it is quite a matter of indifference to me. Indeed, I would not have gone on any account. I was saying so to Emily and Sophia when you over took us."

Catherine was still unconvinced; but glad that Anne should have the friendship of an Emily and a Sophia to console her, she bade her adieu without much uneasiness, and returned home, pleased that the party had not been prevented by her refusing to join it, and very heartily wishing that it might be too pleasant to allow either James or Isabella to resent her resistance any longer.

CHAPTER XV

Early the next day, a note from Isabella, speaking peace and tenderness in every line, and entreating the immediate presence of her friend on a matter of the utmost importance, hastened Catherine, in the happiest state of confidence and curiosity, to Edgar's Buildings.—The two youngest Miss Thorpes were by themselves in the parlour; and, on Anne's quitting it to call her sister, Catherine took the opportunity of asking the other for some particulars of their yesterday's party. Maria desired no greater pleasure than to speak of it; and Catherine immediately learnt that it had been altogether the most delightful scheme in the world; that nobody could imagine how charming it had been, and that it had been more delightful than any body could conceive. Such was the information of the first five minutes; the second unfolded thus much in detail,—that they had driven directly to the York Hotel, ate some soup, and bespoke an early dinner, walked down to the Pump-room, tasted the water, and laid out some shillings in purses and spars; thence adjourned to eat ice at a pastry-cook's, and hurrying back to the Hotel, swallowed their dinner in haste, to prevent being in the dark; and then had a delightful drive back, only the moon was not up, and it rained a little, and Mr. Morland's horse was so tired he could hardly get it along.

Catherine listened with heartfelt satisfaction. It appeared that Blaize Castle had never been thought of; and, as for all the rest, there was nothing to regret for half an instant. —Maria's intelligence concluded with a tender effusion of pity for her sister Anne, whom she represented as insupportably cross, from being excluded the party.

"She will never forgive me, I am sure; but, you know, how could I help it? John would have me go, for he vowed he would not drive her, because she had such thick ancles. I dare say she will not be in good humour again this month; but I am determined I will not be cross; it is not a little matter that puts me out of temper."

Isabella now entered the room with so eager a step, and a look of such happy importance, as engaged all her friend's notice. Maria was without ceremony sent away, and Isabella, embracing Catherine, thus began:—"Yes, my dear Catherine, it is so indeed; your penetration has not deceived you.—Oh! that arch eye of yours!—It sees through every thing."

Catherine replied only by a look of wondering ignorance.

"Nay, my beloved, sweetest friend," continued the other, "compose yourself.—I am amazingly agitated, as you perceive. Let us sit down and talk in comfort. Well, and so you guessed it the moment you had my note?—Sly creature!—Oh! my dear Catherine, you alone who know my heart can judge of my present happiness. Your brother is the most charming of men. I only wish I were more worthy of him.—But what will your excellent father and mother say?—Oh! heavens! when I think of them I am so agitated!"

Catherine's understanding began to awake: an idea of the truth suddenly darted into her mind; and, with the natural blush of so new an emotion, she cried out, "Good heaven!—my dear Isabella, what do you mean? Can you—can you really be in love with James?"

This bold surmise, however, she soon learnt comprehended but half the fact. The anxious affection, which she was accused of having continually watched in Isabella's every look and action, had, in the course of their yesterday's party, received the delightful confession of an equal love. Her heart and faith were alike engaged to James.—Never had Catherine listened to any thing so full of interest, wonder, and joy. Her brother and her friend engaged!—New to such circumstances, the importance of it appeared unspeakably great, and she contemplated it as one of those grand events, of which the ordinary course of life can hardly afford a return. The strength of her feelings she could not express; the nature of them, however, contented her friend. The happiness of having such a sister was their first effusion, and the fair ladies mingled in embraces and tears of joy.

Delighting, however, as Catherine sincerely did in the prospect of the connexion, it must be acknowledged that Isabella far surpassed her in tender anticipations.—"You will be so infinitely dearer to me, my Catherine, than either Anne or Maria: I feel that I shall be so much more attached to my dear Morland's family than to my own."

This was a pitch of friendship beyond Catherine.

"You are so like your dear brother," continued Isabella, "that I quite doated on you the first moment I saw you. But so it always is with me; the first moment settles every thing. The very first day that Morland came to us last Christmas —the very first moment I beheld him—my heart was irrecoverably gone. I remember I wore my yellow gown, with my hair done up in braids; and when I came into the drawing-room, and John introduced him, I thought I never saw any body so handsome before."

Here Catherine secretly acknowledged the power of love; for, though exceedingly fond of her brother, and partial to all his endowments, she had never in her life thought him handsome.

"I remember too, Miss Andrews drank tea with us that evening, and wore her puce-coloured sarsenet; and she looked so heavenly, that I thought your brother must certainly fall in love with her; I could not sleep a wink all night for thinking of it. Oh! Catherine, the many sleepless nights I have had on your brother's account!—I would not have you suffer half what I have done! I am grown wretchedly thin I know; but I will not pain you by describing my

anxiety; you have seen enough of it. I feel that I have betrayed myself perpetually;—so unguarded in speaking of my
partiality for the church!—But my secret I was always sure
would be safe with *you*."

Catherine felt that nothing could have been safer; but
ashamed of an ignorance little expected, she dared no longer
contest the point, nor refuse to have been as full of arch
penetration and affectionate sympathy as Isabella chose to
consider her. Her brother she found was preparing to set
off with all speed to Fullerton, to make known his situation
and ask consent; and here was a source of some real agitation to the mind of Isabella. Catherine endeavoured to persuade her, as she was herself persuaded, that her father and
mother would never oppose their son's wishes.—"It is impossible," said she, "for parents to be more kind, or more
desirous of their children's happiness; I have no doubt of
their consenting immediately."

"Morland says exactly the same," replied Isabella; "and
yet I dare not expect it; my fortune will be so small; they
never can consent to it. Your brother, who might marry
any body!"

Here Catherine again discerned the force of love.

"Indeed, Isabella, you are too humble.—The difference of
fortune can be nothing to signify."

"Oh! my sweet Catherine, in *your* generous heart I know
it would signify nothing; but we must not expect such dis-
interestedness in many. As for myself, I am sure I only wish
our situations were reversed. Had I the command of millions, were I mistress of the whole world, your brother
would be my only choice."

This charming sentiment, recommended as much by sense
as novelty, gave Catherine a most pleasing remembrance of
all the heroines of her acquaintance; and she thought her
friend never looked more lovely than in uttering the grand
idea.—"I am sure they will consent," was her frequent dec-

laration; "I am sure they will be delighted with you."

"For my own part," said Isabella, "my wishes are so moderate, that the smallest income in nature would be enough for me. Where people are really attached, poverty itself is wealth: grandeur I detest: I would not settle in London for the universe. A cottage in some retired village would be extasy. There are some charming little villas about Richmond."

"Richmond!" cried Catherine.—"You must settle near Fullerton. You must be near us."

"I am sure I shall be miserable if we do not. If I can but be near *you,* I shall be satisfied. But this is idle talking! I will not allow myself to think of such things, till we have your father's answer. Morland says that by sending it to-night to Salisbury, we may have it to-morrow.—To-morrow? —I know I shall never have courage to open the letter. I know it will be the death of me."

A reverie succeeded this conviction—and when Isabella spoke again, it was to resolve on the quality of her wedding-gown.

Their conference was put an end to by the anxious young lover himself, who came to breathe his parting sigh before he set off for Wiltshire. Catherine wished to congratulate him, but knew not what to say, and her eloquence was only in her eyes. From them however the eight parts of speech shone out most expressively, and James could combine them with ease. Impatient for the realization of all that he hoped at home, his adieus were not long; and they would have been yet shorter, had he not been frequently detained by the urgent entreaties of his fair one that he would go. Twice was he called almost from the door by her eagerness to have him gone. "Indeed, Morland, I must drive you away. Consider how far you have to ride. I cannot bear to see you linger so. For Heaven's sake, waste no more time. There, go, go—I insist on it."

The two friends, with hearts now more united than ever, were inseparable for the day; and in schemes of sisterly happiness the hours flew along. Mrs. Thorpe and her son, who were acquainted with every thing, and who seemed only to want Mr. Morland's consent, to consider Isabella's engagement as the most fortunate circumstance imaginable for their family, were allowed to join their counsels, and add their quota of significant looks and mysterious expressions to fill up the measure of curiosity to be raised in the unprivileged younger sisters. To Catherine's simple feelings, this odd sort of reserve seemed neither kindly meant, nor consistently supported; and its unkindness she would hardly have forborn pointing out, had its inconsistency been less their friend;—but Anne and Maria soon set her heart at ease by the sagacity of their "I know what;" and the evening was spent in a sort of war of wit, a display of family ingenuity; on one side in the mystery of an affected secret, on the other of undefined discovery, all equally acute.

Catherine was with her friend again the next day, endeavouring to support her spirits, and while away the many tedious hours before the delivery of the letters; a needful exertion, for as the time of reasonable expectation drew near, Isabella became more and more desponding, and before the letter arrived, had worked herself into a state of real distress. But when it did come, where could distress be found? "I have had no difficulty in gaining the consent of my kind parents, and am promised that every thing in their power shall be done to forward my happiness," were the first three lines, and in one moment all was joyful security. The brightest glow was instantly spread over Isabella's features, all care and anxiety seemed removed, her spirits became almost too high for controul, and she called herself without scruple the happiest of mortals.

Mrs. Thorpe, with tears of joy, embraced her daughter, her son, her visitor, and could have embraced half the

inhabitants of Bath with satisfaction. Her heart was overflowing with tenderness. It was "dear John," and "dear Catherine" at every word;—"dear Anne and dear Maria" must
immediately be made sharers in their felicity; and two
"dears" at once before the name of Isabella were not more
than that beloved child had now well earned. John himself
was no skulker in joy. He not only bestowed on Mr. Morland the high commendation of being one of the finest
fellows in the world, but swore off many sentences in his
praise.

The letter, whence sprang all this felicity, was short, containing little more than this assurance of success; and every
particular was deferred till James could write again. But
for particulars Isabella could well afford to wait. The needful was comprised in Mr. Morland's promise; his honour
was pledged to make every thing easy; and by what means
their income was to be formed, whether landed property
were to be resigned, or funded money made over, was a matter in which her disinterested spirit took no concern. She
knew enough to feel secure of an honourable and speedy
establishment, and her imagination took a rapid flight over
its attendant felicities. She saw herself at the end of a few
weeks, the gaze and admiration of every new acquaintance
at Fullerton, the envy of every valued old friend in Putney,
with a carriage at her command, a new name on her tickets,
and a brilliant exhibition of hoop rings on her finger.

When the contents of the letter were ascertained, John
Thorpe, who had only waited its arrival to begin his journey
to London, prepared to set off. "Well, Miss Morland," said
he, on finding her alone in the parlour, "I am come to bid
you good bye." Catherine wished him a good journey. Without appearing to hear her, he walked to the window,
fidgetted about, hummed a tune, and seemed wholly self-
occupied.

"Shall not you be late at Devizes?" said Catherine. He

made no answer; but after a minute's silence burst out with, "A famous good thing this marrying scheme, upon my soul! A clever fancy of Morland's and Belle's. What do you think of it, Miss Morland? *I* say it is no bad notion."

"I am sure I think it a very good one."

"Do you?—that's honest, by heavens! I am glad you are no enemy to matrimony however. Did you ever hear the old song, 'Going to one wedding brings on another?' I say, you will come to Belle's wedding, I hope."

"Yes; I have promised your sister to be with her, if possible."

"And then you know"—twisting himself about and forcing a foolish laugh—"I say, then you know, we may try the truth of this same old song."

"May we?—but I never sing. Well, I wish you a good journey. I dine with Miss Tilney to-day, and must now be going home."

"Nay, but there is no such confounded hurry.—Who knows when we may be together again?—Not but that I shall be down again by the end of a fortnight, and a devilish long fortnight it will appear to me."

"Then why do you stay away so long?" replied Catherine —finding that he waited for an answer.

"That is kind of you, however—kind and good-natured.— I shall not forget it in a hurry.—But you have more good-nature and all that, than any body living I believe. A monstrous deal of good-nature, and it is not only good-nature, but you have so much, so much of every thing; and then you have such—upon my soul I do not know any body like you."

"Oh! dear, there are a great many people like me, I dare say, only a great deal better. Good morning to you."

"But I say, Miss Morland, I shall come and pay my respects at Fullerton before it is long, if not disagreeable."

"Pray do.—My father and mother will be very glad to see you."

"And I hope—I hope, Miss Morland, *you* will not be sorry to see me."

"Oh! dear, not at all. There are very few people I am sorry to see. Company is always cheerful."

"That is just my way of thinking. Give me but a little cheerful company, let me only have the company of the people I love, let me only be where I like and with whom I like, and the devil take the rest, say I.—And I am heartily glad to hear you say the same. But I have a notion, Miss Morland, you and I think pretty much alike upon most matters."

"Perhaps we may; but it is more than I ever thought of. And as to *most matters,* to say the truth, there are not many that I know my own mind about."

"By Jove, no more do I. It is not my way to bother my brains with what does not concern me. My notion of things is simple enough. Let me only have the girl I like, say I, with a comfortable house over my head, and what care I for all the rest? Fortune is nothing. I am sure of a good income of my own; and if she had not a penny, why so much the better."

"Very true. I think like you there. If there is a good fortune on one side, there can be no occasion for any on the other. No matter which has it, so that there is enough. I hate the idea of one great fortune looking out for another. And to marry for money I think the wickedest thing in existence.—Good day.—We shall be very glad to see you at Fullerton, whenever it is convenient." And away she went. It was not in the power of all his gallantry to detain her longer. With such news to communicate, and such a visit to prepare for, her departure was not to be delayed by any thing in his nature to urge; and she hurried away, leaving him to the undivided consciousness of his own happy address, and her explicit encouragement.

The agitation which she had herself experienced on first learning her brother's engagement, made her expect to raise no inconsiderable emotion in Mr. and Mrs. Allen, by the communication of the wonderful event. How great was her disappointment! The important affair, which many words of preparation ushered in, had been foreseen by them both ever since her brother's arrival; and all that they felt on the occasion was comprehended in a wish for the young people's happiness, with a remark, on the gentleman's side, in favour of Isabella's beauty, and on the lady's, of her great good luck. It was to Catherine the most surprizing insensibility. The disclosure however of the great secret of James's going to Fullerton the day before, did raise some emotion in Mrs. Allen. She could not listen to that with perfect calmness; but repeatedly regretted the necessity of its concealment, wished she could have known his intention, wished she could have seen him before he went, as she should certainly have troubled him with her best regards to his father and mother, and her kind compliments to all the Skinners.

Volume Two

CHAPTER I

Catherine's expectations of pleasure from her visit in Milsom-street were so very high, that disappointment was inevitable; and accordingly, though she was most politely received by General Tilney, and kindly welcomed by his daughter, though Henry was at home, and no one else of the party, she found, on her return, without spending many hours in the examination of her feelings, that she had gone to her appointment preparing for happiness which it had not afforded. Instead of finding herself improved in acquaintance with Miss Tilney, from the intercourse of the day, she seemed hardly so intimate with her as before; instead of seeing Henry Tilney to greater advantage than ever, in the ease of a family party, he had never said so little, nor been so little agreeable; and, in spite of their father's great civilities to her—in spite of his thanks, invitations, and compliments—it had been a release to get away from him. It puzzled her to account for all this. It could not be General Tilney's fault. That he was perfectly agreeable and good-natured, and altogether a very charming man, did not admit of a doubt, for he was tall and handsome, and Henry's father. *He* could not be accountable for his children's want of spirits, or for her want of enjoyment in his company. The former she hoped at last might have been accidental, and the latter she could only attribute to her own stupidity. Isabella, on hearing the particulars of the visit, gave a different explanation: "It was all pride, pride, insufferable haughtiness and pride! She had long suspected the family to be very high, and this made it certain. Such insolence of behaviour as Miss Tilney's she had never heard of in her life! Not to do the honours of her house with common good-breeding!—To behave to her guest with such superciliousness!—Hardly even to speak to her!"

"But it was not so bad as that, Isabella; there was no superciliousness; she was very civil."

"Oh! don't defend her! And then the brother, he, who had appeared so attached to you! Good heavens! well, some people's feelings are incomprehensible. And so he hardly looked once at you the whole day?"

"I do not say so; but he did not seem in good spirits."

"How contemptible! Of all things in the world inconstancy is my aversion. Let me entreat you never to think of him again, my dear Catherine; indeed he is unworthy of you."

"Unworthy! I do not suppose he ever thinks of me."

"That is exactly what I say; he never thinks of you.—Such fickleness! Oh! how different to your brother and to mine! I really believe John has the most constant heart."

"But as for General Tilney, I assure you it would be impossible for any body to behave to me with greater civility and attention; it seemed to be his only care to entertain and make me happy."

"Oh! I know no harm of him; I do not suspect him of pride. I believe he is a very gentleman-like man. John thinks very well of him, and John's judgment——"

"Well, I shall see how they behave to me this evening; we shall meet them at the rooms."

"And must I go?"

"Do not you intend it? I thought it was all settled."

"Nay, since you make such a point of it, I can refuse you nothing. But do not insist upon my being very agreeable, for my heart, you know, will be some forty miles off. And as for dancing, do not mention it I beg; *that* is quite out of the question. Charles Hodges will plague me to death I dare say; but I shall cut him very short. Ten to one but he guesses the reason, and that is exactly what I want to avoid, so I shall insist on his keeping his conjecture to himself."

Isabella's opinion of the Tilneys did not influence her friend; she was sure there had been no insolence in the manners either of brother or sister; and she did not credit there being any pride in their hearts. The evening rewarded her confidence; she was met by one with the same kindness, and by the other with the same attention as heretofore: Miss Tilney took pains to be near her, and Henry asked her to dance.

Having heard the day before in Milsom-street, that their elder brother, Captain Tilney, was expected almost every hour, she was at no loss for the name of a very fashionable-looking, handsome young man, whom she had never seen before, and who now evidently belonged to their party. She looked at him with great admiration, and even supposed it possible, that some people might think him handsomer than his brother, though, in her eyes, his air was more assuming, and his countenance less prepossessing. His taste and manners were beyond a doubt decidedly inferior; for, within her hearing, he not only protested against every thought of dancing himself, but even laughed openly at Henry for finding it possible. From the latter circumstance it may be presumed, that, whatever might be our heroine's opinion of him, his admiration of her was not of a very dangerous kind; not likely to produce animosities between the brothers, nor persecutions to the lady. *He* cannot be the instigator of the three villains in horsemen's great coats, by whom she will hereafter be forced into a travelling-chaise and four, which will drive off with incredible speed. Catherine, meanwhile, undisturbed by presentiments of such an evil, or of any evil at all, except that of having but a short set to dance down, enjoyed her usual happiness with Henry Tilney, listening with sparkling eyes to every thing he said; and, in finding him irresistible, becoming so herself.

At the end of the first dance, Captain Tilney came towards them again, and, much to Catherine's dissatisfaction, pulled his brother away. They retired whispering together; and, though her delicate sensibility did not take immediate alarm, and lay it down as fact, that Captain Tilney must have heard some malevolent misrepresentation of her, which he now hastened to communicate to his brother, in the hope of separating them for ever, she could not have her partner conveyed from her sight without very uneasy sensations. Her suspense was of full five minutes' duration; and she was beginning to think it a very long quarter of an hour, when they both returned, and an explanation was given, by Henry's requesting to know, if she thought her friend, Miss Thorpe, would have any objection to dancing, as his brother would be most happy to be introduced to her. Catherine, without hesitation, replied, that she was very sure Miss Thorpe did not mean to dance at all. The cruel reply was passed on to the other, and he immediately walked away.

"Your brother will not mind it I know," said she, "because I heard him say before, that he hated dancing; but it was very good-natured in him to think of it. I suppose he saw Isabella sitting down, and fancied she might wish for a partner; but he is quite mistaken, for she would not dance upon any account in the world."

Henry smiled, and said, "How very little trouble it can give you to understand the motive of other people's actions."

"Why?—What do you mean?"

"With you, it is not, How is such a one likely to be influenced? What is the inducement most likely to act upon such a person's feelings, age, situation, and probable habits of life considered?—but, how should *I* be influenced, what would be *my* inducement in acting so and so?"

"I do not understand you."

"Then we are on very unequal terms, for I understand you perfectly well."

"Me?—yes; I cannot speak well enough to be unintelligible."

"Bravo!—an excellent satire on modern language."

"But pray tell me what you mean."

"Shall I indeed?—Do you really desire it?—But you are not aware of the consequences; it will involve you in a very cruel embarrassment, and certainly bring on a disagreement between us."

"No, no; it shall not do either; I am not afraid."

"Well then, I only meant that your attributing my brother's wish of dancing with Miss Thorpe to good-nature alone, convinced me of your being superior in good-nature yourself to all the rest of the world."

Catherine blushed and disclaimed, and the gentleman's predictions were verified. There was a something, however, in his words which repaid her for the pain of confusion; and that something occupied her mind so much, that she drew back for some time, forgetting to speak or to listen, and almost forgetting where she was; till, roused by the voice of Isabella, she looked up and saw her with Captain Tilney preparing to give them hands across.

Isabella shrugged her shoulders and smiled, the only explanation of this extraordinary change which could at that time be given; but as it was not quite enough for Catherine's comprehension, she spoke her astonishment in very plains terms to her partner.

"I cannot think how it could happen! Isabella was so determined not to dance."

"And did Isabella never change her mind before?"

"Oh! but, because——and your brother!—After what you told him from me, how could he think of going to ask her?"

"I cannot take surprize to myself on that head. You bid

me be surprized on your friend's account, and therefore I am; but as for my brother, his conduct in the business, I must own, has been no more than I believed him perfectly equal to. The fairness of your friend was an open attraction; her firmness, you know, could only be understood by yourself."

"You are laughing; but, I assure you, Isabella is very firm in general."

"It is as much as should be said of any one. To be always firm must be to be often obstinate. When properly to relax is the trial of judgment; and, without reference to my brother, I really think Miss Thorpe has by no means chosen ill in fixing on the present hour."

The friends were not able to get together for any confidential discourse till all the dancing was over; but then, as they walked about the room arm in arm, Isabella thus explained herself:—"I do not wonder at your surprize; and I am really fatigued to death. He is such a rattle!—Amusing enough, if my mind had been disengaged; but I would have given the world to sit still."

"Then why did not you?"

"Oh! my dear! it would have looked so particular; and you know how I abhor doing that. I refused him as long as I possibly could, but he would take no denial. You have no idea how he pressed me. I begged him to excuse me, and get some other partner—but no, not he; after aspiring to my hand, there was nobody else in the room he could bear to think of; and it was not that he wanted merely to dance, he wanted to be with *me*. Oh! such nonsense!—I told him he had taken a very unlikely way to prevail upon me; for, of all things in the world, I hated fine speeches and compliments; —and so——and so then I found there would be no peace if I did not stand up. Besides, I thought Mrs. Hughes, who introduced him, might take it ill if I did not: and your dear brother, I am sure he would have been miserable if I had sat down the whole evening. I am so glad it is over! My spirits are quite jaded with listening to his nonsense: and then,— being such a smart young fellow, I saw every eye was upon us."

"He is very handsome indeed."

"Handsome!—Yes, I suppose he may. I dare say people would admire him in general; but he is not at all in my style of beauty. I hate a florid complexion and dark eyes in a man. However, he is very well. Amazingly conceited, I am sure. I took him down several times you know in my way."

When the young ladies next met, they had a far more interesting subject to discuss. James Morland's second letter was then received, and the kind intentions of his father fully explained. A living, of which Mr. Morland was himself patron and incumbent, of about four hundred pounds yearly value, was to be resigned to his son as soon as he should be old enough to take it; no trifling deduction from the family income, no niggardly assignment to one of ten children. An estate of at least equal value, moreover, was assured as his future inheritance.

James expressed himself on the occasion with becoming gratitude; and the necessity of waiting between two and three years before they could marry, being, however unwelcome, no more than he had expected, was born by him without discontent. Catherine, whose expectations had been as unfixed as her ideas of her father's income, and whose judgment was now entirely led by her brother, felt equally well satisfied, and heartily congratulated Isabella on having every thing so pleasantly settled.

"It is very charming indeed," said Isabella, with a grave face. "Mr. Morland has behaved vastly handsome indeed," said the gentle Mrs. Thorpe, looking anxiously at her daughter. "I only wish I could do as much. One could not expect more from him you know. If he finds he *can* do more by and bye, I dare say he will, for I am sure he must be an excellent good hearted man. Four hundred is but a small income to begin on indeed, but your wishes, my dear Isabella, are so moderate, you do not consider how little you ever want, my dear."

"It is not on my own account I wish for more; but I cannot bear to be the means of injuring my dear Morland, making him sit down upon an income hardly enough to find one in the common necessaries of life. For myself, it is nothing; I never think of myself."

"I know you never do, my dear; and you will always find your reward in the affection it makes every body feel for you. There never was a young woman so beloved as you are by every body that knows you; and I dare say when Mr. Morland sees you, my dear child—but do not let us distress our dear Catherine by talking of such things. Mr. Morland has behaved so very handsome you know. I always heard he was a most excellent man; and you know, my dear, we are not to suppose but what, if you had had a suitable fortune, he would have come down with something more, for I am sure he must be a most liberal-minded man."

"Nobody can think better of Mr. Morland than I do, I am sure. But every body has their failing you know, and every body has a right to do what they like with their own money." Catherine was hurt by these insinuations. "I am very sure," said she, "that my father has promised to do as much as he can afford."

Isabella recollected herself. "As to that, my sweet Catherine, there cannot be a doubt, and you know me well enough to be sure that a much smaller income would satisfy me. It is not the want of more money that makes me just at present a little out of spirits; I hate money; and if our union could take place now upon only fifty pounds a year, I should not have a wish unsatisfied. Ah! my Catherine, you have found me out. There's the sting. The long, long, endless two years and half that are to pass before your brother can hold the living."

"Yes, yes, my darling Isabella," said Mrs. Thorpe, "we perfectly see into your heart. You have no disguise. We perfectly understand the present vexation; and every body must love you the better for such a noble honest affection."

Catherine's uncomfortable feelings began to lessen. She endeavoured to believe that the delay of the marriage was the only source of Isabella's regret; and when she saw her at their next interview as cheerful and amiable as ever, endeavoured to forget that she had for a minute thought otherwise. James soon followed his letter, and was received with the most gratifying kindnesss.

CHAPTER II

The Allens had now entered on the sixth week of their stay in Bath; and whether it should be the last, was for some time a question, to which Catherine listened with a beating heart. To have her acquaintance with the Tilneys end so soon, was an evil which nothing could counterbalance. Her whole happiness seemed at stake, while the affair was in suspense, and every thing secured when it was determined that the lodgings should be taken for another fortnight. What this additional fortnight was to produce to her beyond the pleasure of sometimes seeing Henry Tilney, made but a small part of Catherine's speculation. Once or twice indeed, since James's engagement had taught her what *could* be done, she had got so far as to indulge in a secret "perhaps," but in general the felicity of being with him for the present bounded her views: the present was now comprised in another three weeks, and her happiness being certain for that period, the rest of her life was at such a distance as to excite but little interest. In the course of the morning which saw this business arranged, she visited Miss Tilney, and poured forth her joyful feelings. It was doomed to be a day of trial. No sooner had she expressed her delight in Mr. Allen's lengthened stay, than Miss Tilney told her of her father's having just determined upon quitting Bath by the end of another week. Here was a blow! The past suspense of the morning had been ease and quiet to the present disappointment. Catherine's countenance fell, and in a voice of most sincere concern she echoed Miss Tilney's concluding words, "By the end of another week!"

"Yes, my father can seldom be prevailed on to give the

waters what I think a fair trial. He has been disappointed of some friends' arrival whom he expected to meet here, and as he is now pretty well, is in a hurry to get home."

"I am very sorry for it," said Catherine dejectedly, "if I had known this before—"

"Perhaps," said Miss Tilney in an embarrassed manner, "you would be so good—it would make me very happy if—"

The entrance of her father put a stop to the civility, which Catherine was beginning to hope might introduce a desire of their corresponding. After addressing her with his usual politeness, he turned to his daughter and said, "Well, Eleanor, may I congratulate you on being successful in your application to your fair friend?"

"I was just beginning to make the request, sir, as you came in."

"Well, proceed by all means. I know how much your heart is in it. My daughter, Miss Morland," he continued, without leaving his daughter time to speak, "has been forming a very bold wish. We leave Bath, as she has perhaps told you, on Saturday se'nnight. A letter from my steward tells me that my presence is wanted at home; and being disappointed in my hope of seeing the Marquis of Longtown and General Courteney here, some of my very old friends, there is nothing to detain me longer in Bath. And could we carry our selfish point with you, we should leave it without a single regret. Can you, in short, be prevailed on to quit this scene of public triumph and oblige your friend Eleanor with your company in Gloucestershire? I am almost ashamed to make the request, though its presumption would certainly appear greater to every creature in Bath than yourself. Modesty such as your's—but not for the world would I pain it by open praise. If you can be induced to honour us with a visit, you will make us happy beyond expression. 'Tis true, we can offer you nothing like the gaieties of this lively place; we can tempt you neither by amusement nor splendour, for our mode of living, as you see, is plain and unpretending; yet no endeavours shall be wanting on our side to make Northanger Abbey not wholly disagreeable."

Northanger Abbey!—These were thrilling words, and wound up Catherine's feelings to the highest point of extasy. Her grateful and gratified heart could hardly restrain its expressions within the language of tolerable calmness. To receive so flattering an invitation! To have her company so warmly solicited! Every thing honourable and soothing, every present enjoyment, and every future hope was contained in it; and her acceptance, with only the saving clause of papa and mamma's approbation, was eagerly given.—"I will write home directly," said she, "and if they do not object, as I dare say they will not"—

General Tilney was not less sanguine, having already waited on her excellent friends in Pulteney-street, and obtained their sanction of his wishes. "Since they can consent to part with you," said he, "we may expect philosophy from all the world."

Miss Tilney was earnest, though gentle, in her secondary civilities, and the affair became in a few minutes as nearly settled, as this necessary reference to Fullerton would allow.

The circumstances of the morning had led Catherine's feelings through the varieties of suspense, security, and disappointment; but they were now safely lodged in perfect bliss; and with spirits elated to rapture, with Henry at her heart, and Northanger Abbey on her lips, she hurried home to write her letter. Mr. and Mrs. Morland, relying on the discretion of the friends to whom they had already entrusted their daughter, felt no doubt of the propriety of an acquaintance which had been formed under their eye, and sent therefore by return of post their ready consent to her visit in Gloucestershire. This indulgence, though not more than Catherine had hoped for, completed her conviction of being favoured beyond every other human creature, in friends and fortune, circumstance and chance. Every thing seemed to co-operate for her advantage. By the kindness of her first friends the Allens, she had been introduced into scenes, where pleasures of every kind had met her. Her feelings, her preferences had each known the happiness of a return. Wherever she felt attachment, she had been able to create it. The affection of Isabella was to be secured to her in a sister. The Tilneys, they, by whom above all, she desired to be favourably thought of, outstripped even her wishes in the flattering measures by which their intimacy was to be continued. She was to be their chosen visitor, she was to be for weeks under the same roof with the person whose society she mostly prized—and, in addition to all the rest, this roof was to be the roof of an abbey!—Her passion for ancient edifices was next in degree to her passion for Henry Tilney—and castles and abbies made usually the charm of those reveries which his image did not fill. To see and explore either the ramparts and keep of the one, or the cloisters of the other, had been for many weeks a darling wish, though to be more than the visitor of an hour, had seemed too nearly impossible for desire. And yet, this was to happen. With all the chances against her of house, hall, place, park, court, and cottage, Northanger turned up an abbey, and she was to be its inhabitant. Its long, damp passages, its narrow cells and ruined chapel, were to be within her daily reach, and she could not entirely subdue the hope of some traditional legends, some awful memorials of an injured and ill-fated nun.

It was wonderful that her friends should seem so little elated by the possession of such a home; that the consciousness of it should be so meekly born. The power of early habit only could account for it. A distinction to which they had been born gave no pride. Their superiority of abode was no more to them than their superiority of person.

Many were the inquiries she was eager to make of Miss

Tilney; but so active were her thoughts, that when these inquiries were answered, she was hardly more assured than before, of Northanger Abbey having been a richly-endowed convent at the time of the Reformation, of its having fallen into the hands of an ancestor of the Tilneys on its dissolution, of a large portion of the ancient building still making a part of the present dwelling although the rest was decayed, or of its standing low in a valley, sheltered from the north and east by rising woods of oak.

CHAPTER III

With a mind thus full of happiness, Catherine was hardly aware that two or three days had passed away, without her seeing Isabella for more than a few minutes together. She began first to be sensible of this, and to sigh for her conversation, as she walked along the Pump-room one morning, by Mrs. Allen's side, without any thing to say or to hear; and scarcely had she felt a five minutes' longing of friendship, before the object of it appeared, and inviting her to a secret conference, led the way to a seat. "This is my favourite place," said she, as they sat down on a bench between the doors, which commanded a tolerable view of every body entering at either, "it is so out of the way."

Catherine, observing that Isabella's eyes were continually bent towards one door or the other, as in eager expectation, and remembering how often she had been falsely accused of being arch, thought the present a fine opportunity for being really so; and therefore gaily said, "Do not be uneasy, Isabella. James will soon be here."

"Psha! my dear creature," she replied, "do not think me such a simpleton as to be always wanting to confine him to my elbow. It would be hideous to be always together; we should be the jest of the place. And so you are going to Northanger!—I am amazingly glad of it. It is one of the finest old places in England, I understand. I shall depend upon a most particular description of it."

"You shall certainly have the best in my power to give. But who are you looking for? Are your sisters coming?"

"I am not looking for any body. One's eyes must be somewhere, and you know what a foolish trick I have of fixing mine, when my thoughts are an hundred miles off. I am amazingly absent; I believe I am the most absent creature in the world. Tilney says it is always the case with minds of a certain stamp."

"But I thought, Isabella, you had something in particular to tell me?"

"Oh! yes, and so I have. But here is a proof of what I was saying. My poor head! I had quite forgot it. Well, the thing is this, I have just had a letter from John;—you can guess the contents."

"No, indeed, I cannot."

"My sweet love, do not be so abominably affected. What can he write about, but yourself? You know he is over head and ears in love with you."

"With *me*, dear Isabella!"

"Nay, my sweetest Catherine, this is being quite absurd! Modesty, and all that, is very well in its way, but really a little common honesty is sometimes quite as becoming. I have no idea of being so overstrained! It is fishing for compliments. His attentions were such as a child must have noticed. And it was but half an hour before he left Bath, that you gave him the most positive encouragement. He says so in this letter, says that he as good as made you an offer, and that you received his advances in the kindest way; and now he wants me to urge his suit, and say all manner of pretty things to you. So it is in vain to affect ignorance."

Catherine, with all the earnestness of truth, expressed her astonishment at such a charge, protesting her innocence of every thought of Mr. Thorpe's being in love with her, and the consequent impossibility of her having ever intended to encourage him. "As to any attentions on his side, I do declare, upon my honour, I never was sensible of them for a moment—except just his asking me to dance the first day of his coming. And as to making me an offer, or any thing like it, there must be some unaccountable mistake. I could not have misunderstood a thing of that kind, you know!—and, as I ever wish to be believed, I solemnly protest that no syllable of such a nature ever passed between us. The last half hour before he went away!—It must be all and completely a mistake—for I did not see him once that whole morning."

"But *that* you certainly did, for you spent the whole morning in Edgar's Buildings—it was the day your father's consent came—and I am pretty sure that you and John were alone in the parlour, some time before you left the house."

"Are you?—Well, if you say it, it was so, I dare say—but for the life of me, I cannot recollect it.—I *do* remember now being with you, and seeing him as well as the rest—but that we were ever alone for five minutes—However, it is not worth arguing about, for whatever might pass on his side, you must be convinced, by my having no recollection of it, that I never thought, nor expected, nor wished for any thing of the kind from him. I am excessively concerned that he should have any regard for me—but indeed it has been quite unintentional on my side, I never had the smallest idea of it. Pray undeceive him as soon as you can, and tell him I beg his pardon—that is—I do not know what I ought to say—but make him understand what I mean, in the properest way. I would not speak disrespectfully of a brother of your's, Isabella, I am sure; but you know very well that if I could think of one man more than another—*he* is not the person." Isabella was silent. "My dear friend, you must not be angry with me. I cannot suppose your brother cares so very much about me. And, you know, we shall still be sisters."

"Yes, yes," (with a blush) "there are more ways than one of our being sisters.—But where am I wandering to?—Well, my dear Catherine, the case seems to be, that you are determined against poor John—is not it so?"

"I certainly cannot return his affection, and as certainly never meant to encourage it."

"Since that is the case, I am sure I shall not tease you any further. John desired me to speak to you on the subject, and therefore I have. But I confess, as soon as I read his letter, I thought it a very foolish, imprudent business, and not likely to promote the good of either; for what were you to live upon, supposing you came together? You have both of you something to be sure, but it is not a trifle that will support a family now-a-days; and after all that romancers may say, there is no doing without money. I only wonder John could think of it; he could not have received my last."

"You *do* acquit me then of any thing wrong?—You are convinced that I never meant to deceive your brother, never suspected him of liking me till this moment?"

"Oh! as to that," answered Isabella laughingly, "I do not pretend to determine what your thoughts and designs in time past may have been. All that is best known to yourself. A little harmless flirtation or so will occur, and one is often drawn on to give more encouragement than one wishes to stand by. But you may be assured that I am the last person in the world to judge you severely. All those things should be allowed for in youth and high spirits. What one means one day, you know, one may not mean the next. Circumstances change, opinions alter."

"But my opinion of your brother never did alter; it was always the same. You are describing what never happened."

"My dearest Catherine," continued the other without at all listening to her, "I would not for all the world be the means of hurrying you into an engagement before you knew what you were about. I do not think any thing would justify me in wishing you to sacrifice all your happiness merely to oblige my brother, because he is my brother, and who perhaps after all, you know, might be just as happy without you, for people seldom know what they would be at, young men especially, they are so amazingly changeable and inconstant. What I say is, why should a brother's happiness be dearer to me than a friend's? You know I carry my notions of friendship pretty high. But, above all things, my dear Catherine, do not be in a hurry. Take my word for it, that if you are in too great a hurry, you will certainly live to repent it. Tilney says, there is nothing people are so often deceived in, as the state of their own affections, and I believe he is very right. Ah! here he comes; never mind, he will not see us, I am sure."

Catherine, looking up, perceived Captain Tilney; and Isabella, earnestly fixing her eye on him as she spoke, soon caught his notice. He approached immediately, and took the seat to which her movements invited him. His first address made Catherine start. Though spoken low, she could distinguish, "What! always to be watched, in person or by proxy!"

"Psha, nonsense!" was Isabella's answer in the same half whisper. "Why do you put such things into my head? If I could believe it—my spirit, you know, is pretty independent."

"I wish your heart were independent. That would be enough for me."

"My heart, indeed! What can you have to do with hearts? You men have none of you any hearts."

"If we have not hearts, we have eyes; and they give us torment enough."

"Do they? I am sorry for it; I am sorry they find any thing so disagreeable in me. I will look another way. I hope this pleases you, (turning her back on him,) I hope your eyes are not tormented now."

"Never more so; for the edge of a blooming cheek is still in view—at once too much and too little."

Catherine heard all this, and quite out of countenance could listen no longer. Amazed that Isabella could endure it, and jealous for her brother, she rose up, and saying she should join Mrs. Allen, proposed their walking. But for this Isabella shewed no inclination. She was so amazingly tired, and it was so odious to parade about the Pump-room; and if she moved from her seat she should miss her sisters, she was expecting her sisters every moment; so that her dearest Catherine must excuse her, and must sit quietly down again. But Catherine could be stubborn too; and Mrs. Allen just then coming up to propose their returning home, she joined her and walked out of the Pump-room, leaving Isabella still sitting with Captain Tilney. With much uneasiness did she thus leave them. It seemed to her that Captain Tilney was falling in love with Isabella, and Isabella unconsciously encouraging him; unconsciously it must be, for Isabella's attachment to James was as certain and well acknowledged as her engagement. To doubt her truth or good intentions was impossible; and yet, during the whole of their conversation her manner had been odd. She wished Isabella had talked more like her usual self, and not so much about money; and had not looked so well pleased at the sight of Captain Tilney. How strange that she should not perceive his admiration! Catherine longed to give her a hint of it, to put her on her guard, and prevent all the pain which her too lively behaviour might otherwise create both for him and her brother.

The compliment of John Thorpe's affection did not make amends for this thoughtlessness in his sister. She was almost as far from believing as from wishing it to be sincere; for she had not forgotten that he could mistake, and his assertion of the offer and of her encouragement convinced her that his mistakes could sometimes be very egregious. In vanity therefore she gained but little, her chief profit was in wonder. That he should think it worth his while to fancy himself in love with her, was a matter of lively astonishment. Isabella talked of his attentions; *she* had never been sensible of any; but Isabella had said many things which she hoped had been spoken in haste, and would never be said again; and upon this she was glad to rest altogether for present ease and comfort.

CHAPTER IV

A few days passed away, and Catherine, though not allowing herself to suspect her friend, could not help watching her closely. The result of her observations was not agreeable. Isabella seemed an altered creature. When she saw her indeed surrounded only by their immediate friends in Edgar's Buildings or Pulteney-street, her change of manners was so trifling that, had it gone no farther, it might have passed unnoticed. A something of languid indifference, or of that boasted absence of mind which Catherine had never heard of before, would occasionally come across her; but had nothing worse appeared, *that* might only have spread a new grace and inspired a warmer interest. But when Catherine saw her in public, admitting Captain Tilney's attentions as readily as they were offered, and allowing him almost an equal share with James in her notice and smiles, the alteration became too positive to be past over. What could be meant by such unsteady conduct, what her friend could be at, was beyond her comprehension. Isabella could not be aware of the pain she was inflicting; but it was a degree of wilful thoughtlessness which Catherine could not but resent. James was the sufferer. She saw him grave and uneasy; and however careless of his present comfort the woman might be who had given him her heart, to *her* it was always an object. For poor Captain Tilney too she was greatly concerned. Though his looks did not please her, his name was a passport to her good will, and she thought with sincere compassion of his approaching disappointment; for, in spite of what she had believed herself to overhear in the Pump-room, his behaviour was so incompatible with a knowledge of Isabella's engagement, that she could not, upon reflection, imagine him aware of it. He might be jealous of her brother as a rival, but if more had seemed implied, the fault must have been in her misapprehension. She wished, by a gentle remonstrance, to remind Isabella of her situation, and make her aware of this double unkindness; but for remonstrance, either opportunity or comprehension was always against her. If able to suggest a hint, Isabella could never understand it. In this distress, the intended departure of the Tilney family became her chief consolation; their journey into Gloucestershire was to take place within a few days, and Captain Tilney's removal would at least restore peace to every heart but his own. But Captain Tilney had at present no intention of removing; he was not to be of the party to Northanger, he was to continue at Bath. When Catherine knew this, her resolution was directly made. She spoke to Henry Tilney on the subject, regretting his brother's evident partiality for Miss Thorpe, and entreating him to make known her prior engagement.

"My brother does know it," was Henry's answer.

"Does he?—then why does he stay here?"

He made no reply, and was beginning to talk of something else; but she eagerly continued, "Why do not you persuade him to go away? The longer he stays, the worse it will be for him at last. Pray advise him for his own sake, and for every body's sake, to leave Bath directly. Absence will in time make him comfortable again; but he can have no hope here, and it is only staying to be miserable." Henry smiled and said, "I am sure my brother would not wish to do that."

"Then you will persuade him to go away?"

"Persuasion is not at command; but pardon me, if I cannot even endeavour to persuade him. I have myself told him that Miss Thorpe is engaged. He knows what he is about, and must be his own master."

"No, he does not know what he is about," cried Catherine; "he does not know the pain he is giving my brother. Not that James has ever told me so, but I am sure he is very uncomfortable."

"And are you sure it is my brother's doing?"

"Yes, very sure."

"Is it my brother's attentions to Miss Thorpe, or Miss Thorpe's admission of them, that gives the pain?"

"Is not it the same thing?"

"I think Mr. Morland would acknowledge a difference. No man is offended by another man's admiration of the woman he loves; it is the woman only who can make it a torment."

Catherine blushed for her friend, and said, "Isabella is wrong. But I am sure she cannot mean to torment, for she is very much attached to my brother. She has been in love with him ever since they first met, and while my father's consent was uncertain, she fretted herself almost into a fever. You know she must be attached to him."

"I understand: she is in love with James, and flirts with Frederick."

"Oh! no, not flirts. A woman in love with one man cannot flirt with another."

"It is probable that she will neither love so well, nor flirt so well, as she might do either singly. The gentlemen must each give up a little."

After a short pause, Catherine resumed with "Then you do not believe Isabella so very much attached to my brother?"

"I can have no opinion on that subject."

"But what can your brother mean? If he knows her engagement, what can he mean by his behaviour?"

"You are a very close questioner."

"Am I?—I only ask what I want to be told."

"But do you only ask what I can be expected to tell?"

"Yes, I think so; for you must know your brother's heart."

"My brother's heart, as you term it, on the present occasion, I assure you I can only guess at."

"Well?"

"Well!—Nay, if it is to be guess-work, let us all guess for ourselves. To be guided by second-hand conjecture is pitiful. The premises are before you. My brother is a lively, and perhaps sometimes a thoughtless young man; he has had about a week's acquaintance with your friend, and he has known her engagement almost as long as he has known her."

"Well," said Catherine, after some moments' consideration, "*you* may be able to guess at your brother's intentions from all this; but I am sure I cannot. But is not your father uncomfortable about it?—Does not he want Captain Tilney to go away?—Sure, if your father were to speak to him, he would go."

"My dear Miss Morland," said Henry, "in this amiable solicitude for your brother's comfort, may you not be a little mistaken? Are you not carried a little too far? Would he thank you, either on his own account or Miss Thorpe's, for supposing that her affection, or at least her good-behaviour, is only to be secured by her seeing nothing of Captain Tilney? Is he safe only in solitude?—or, is her heart constant to him only when unsolicited by any one else?—He cannot think this—and you may be sure that he would not have you think it. I will not say, 'Do not be uneasy,' because I know that you are so, at this moment; but be as little uneasy as you can. You have no doubt of the mutual attachment of your brother and your friend; depend upon it therefore, that real jealousy never can exist between them; depend upon it that no disagreement between them can be of any duration. Their hearts are open to each other, as neither heart can be to you; they know exactly what is required and what can be borne; and you may be certain, that one will never tease the other beyond what is known to be pleasant."

Perceiving her still to look doubtful and grave, he added, "Though Frederick does not leave Bath with us, he will probably remain but a very short time, perhaps only a few days behind us. His leave of absence will soon expire, and he must return to his regiment.—And what will then be their acquaintance?—The mess-room will drink Isabella Thorpe for a fortnight, and she will laugh with your brother over poor Tilney's passion for a month."

Catherine would contend no longer against comfort. She had resisted its approaches during the whole length of a speech, but it now carried her captive. Henry Tilney must know best. She blamed herself for the extent of her fears, and resolved never to think so seriously on the subject again.

Her resolution was supported by Isabella's behaviour in their parting interview. The Thorpes spent the last evening of Catherine's stay in Pulteney-street, and nothing passed between the lovers to excite her uneasiness, or make her quit them in apprehension. James was in excellent spirits, and Isabella most engagingly placid. Her tenderness for her friend seemed rather the first feeling of her heart; but that at such a moment was allowable; and once she gave her lover a flat contradiction, and once she drew back her hand; but Catherine remembered Henry's instructions, and placed it all to judicious affection. The embraces, tears, and promises of the parting fair ones may be fancied.

CHAPTER V

Mr. and Mrs. Allen were sorry to lose their young friend, whose good-humour and cheerfulness had made her a valuable companion, and in the promotion of whose enjoyment their own had been gently increased. Her happiness in going with Miss Tilney, however, prevented their wishing it otherwise; and, as they were to remain only one more week in Bath themselves, her quitting them now would not long be felt. Mr. Allen attended her to Milsom-street, where she was to breakfast, and saw her seated with the kindest welcome among her new friends; but so great was her agitation in finding herself as one of the family, and so fearful was she of not doing exactly what was right, and of not being able to preserve their good opinion, that, in the embarrassment of the first five minutes, she could almost have wished to return with him to Pulteney-street.

Miss Tilney's manners and Henry's smile soon did away some of her unpleasant feelings; but still she was far from being at ease; nor could the incessant attentions of the General himself entirely reassure her. Nay, perverse as it seemed, she doubted whether she might not have felt less, had she been less attended to. His anxiety for her comfort— his continual solicitations that she would eat, and his often-expressed fears of her seeing nothing to her taste—though never in her life before had she beheld half such variety on a breakfast-table—made it impossible for her to forget for a moment that she was a visitor. She felt utterly unworthy of such respect, and knew not how to reply to it. Her tranquillity was not improved by the General's impatience for the appearance of his eldest son, nor by the displeasure he

expressed at his laziness when Captain Tilney at last came
down. She was quite pained by the severity of his father's
reproof, which seemed disproportionate to the offence; and
much was her concern increased, when she found herself the
principal cause of the lecture; and that his tardiness was
chiefly resented from being disrespectful to her. This was
placing her in a very uncomfortable situation, and she felt
great compassion for Captain Tilney, without being able to
hope for his good-will.

He listened to his father in silence, and attempted not
any defence, which confirmed her in fearing, that the inquietude of his mind, on Isabella's account, might, by
keeping him long sleepless, have been the real cause of his
rising late.—It was the first time of her being decidedly in
his company, and she had hoped to be now able to form
her opinion of him; but she scarcely heard his voice while
his father remained in the room; and even afterwards, so
much were his spirits affected, she could distinguish nothing
but these words, in a whisper to Eleanor, "How glad I shall
be when you are all off."

The bustle of going was not pleasant.—The clock struck
ten while the trunks were carrying down, and the General
had fixed to be out of Milsom-street by that hour. His great
coat, instead of being brought for him to put on directly,
was spread out in the curricle in which he was to accompany
his son. The middle seat of the chaise was not drawn out,
though there were three people to go in it, and his daughter's maid had so crowded it with parcels, that Miss Morland would not have room to sit; and, so much was he
influenced by this apprehension when he handed her in,
that she had some difficulty in saving her own new writing-
desk from being thrown out into the street.—At last, however, the door was closed upon the three females, and they
set off at the sober pace in which the handsome, highly-fed
four horses of a gentleman usually perform a journey of

thirty miles: such was the distance of Northanger from Bath, to be now divided into two equal stages. Catherine's spirits revived as they drove from the door; for with Miss Tilney she felt no restraint; and, with the interest of a road entirely new to her, of an abbey before, and a curricle behind, she caught the last view of Bath without any regret, and met with every mile-stone before she expected it. The tediousness of a two hours' bait at Petty-France, in which there was nothing to be done but to eat without being hungry, and loiter about without any thing to see, next followed —and her admiration of the style in which they travelled, of the fashionable chaise-and-four—postilions handsomely liveried, rising so regularly in their stirrups, and numerous out-riders properly mounted, sunk a little under this conquent inconvenience. Had their party been perfectly agreeable, the delay would have been nothing; but General Tilney, though so charming a man, seemed always a check upon his children's spirits, and scarcely any thing was said but by himself; the observation of which, with his discontent at whatever the inn afforded, and his angry impatience at the waiters, made Catherine grow every moment more in awe of him, and appeared to lengthen the two hours into four.—At last, however, the order of release was given; and much was Catherine then surprized by the General's proposal of her taking his place in his son's curricle for the rest of the journey:—"the day was fine, and he was anxious for her seeing as much of the country as possible."

The remembrance of Mr. Allen's opinion, respecting young men's open carriages, made her blush at the mention of such a plan, and her first thought was to decline it; but her second was of greater deference for General Tilney's judgment; he could not propose any thing improper for her; and, in the course of a few minutes, she found herself with Henry in the curricle, as happy a being as ever existed. A very short trial convinced her that a curricle was the prettiest equipage in the world; the chaise-and-four wheeled off with some grandeur, to be sure, but it was a heavy and troublesome business, and she could not easily forget its having stopped two hours at Petty-France. Half the time would have been enough for the curricle, and so nimbly were the light horses disposed to move, that, had not the General chosen to have his own carriage lead the way, they could have passed it with ease in half a minute. But the merit of the curricle did not all belong to the horses;— Henry drove so well,—so quietly—without making any disturbance, without parading to her, or swearing at them; so different from the only gentleman-coachman whom it was in her power to compare him with!—And then his hat sat so well, and the innumerable capes of his great coat looked so becomingly important!—To be driven by him, next to being dancing with him, was certainly the greatest happiness in the world. In addition to every other delight, she had now that of listening to her own praise; of being thanked at least, on his sister's account, for her kindness in thus becoming her visitor; of hearing it ranked as real friendship, and described as creating real gratitude. His sister, he said, was uncomfortably circumstanced—she had no female companion—and, in the frequent absence of her father, was sometimes without any companion at all.

"But how can that be?" said Catherine, "are not you with her?"

"Northanger is not more than half my home; I have an establishment at my own house in Woodston, which is nearly twenty miles from my father's, and some of my time is necessarily spent there."

"How sorry you must be for that!"

"I am always sorry to leave Eleanor."

"Yes; but besides your affection for her, you must be so fond of the abbey!—After being used to such a home as the abbey, an ordinary parsonage-house must be very disagreeable."

He smiled, and said, "You have formed a very favourable idea of the abbey."

"To be sure I have. Is not it a fine old place, just like what one reads about?"

"And are you prepared to encounter all the horrors that a building such as 'what one reads about' may produce?—Have you a stout heart?—Nerves fit for sliding pannels and tapestry?"

"Oh! yes—I do not think I should be easily frightened, because there would be so many people in the house—and besides, it has never been uninhabited and left deserted for years, and then the family come back to it unawares, without giving any notice, as generally happens."

"No, certainly.—We shall not have to explore our way into a hall dimly lighted by the expiring embers of a wood fire—nor be obliged to spread our beds on the floor of a room without windows, doors, or furniture. But you must be aware that when a young lady is (by whatever means) introduced into a dwelling of this kind, she is always lodged apart from the rest of the family. While they snugly repair to their own end of the house, she is formally conducted by Dorothy the ancient housekeeper up a different staircase, and along many gloomy passages, into an apartment never used since some cousin or kin died in it about twenty years before. Can you stand such a ceremony as this? Will not your mind misgive you, when you find yourself in this gloomy chamber—too lofty and extensive for you, with only the feeble rays of a single lamp to take in its size—its walls hung with tapestry exhibiting figures as large as life, and the bed, of dark green stuff or purple velvet, presenting even a funereal appearance. Will not your heart sink within you?"

"Oh! but this will not happen to me, I am sure."

"How fearfully will you examine the furniture of your apartment!—And what will you discern?—Not tables, toilettes, wardrobes, or drawers, but on one side perhaps the remains of a broken lute, on the other a ponderous chest which no efforts can open, and over the fire-place the portrait of some handsome warrior, whose features will so incomprehensibly strike you, that you will not be able to withdraw your eyes from it. Dorothy meanwhile, no less struck by your appearance, gazes on you in great agitation, and drops a few unintelligible hints. To raise your spirits, moreover, she gives you reason to suppose that the part of the abbey you inhabit is undoubtedly haunted, and informs you that you will not have a single domestic within call. With this parting cordial she curtseys off—you listen to the sound of her receding footsteps as long as the last echo can reach you—and when, with fainting spirits, you attempt to fasten your door, you discover, with increased alarm, that it has no lock."

"Oh! Mr. Tilney, how frightful!—This is just like a book!—But it cannot really happen to me. I am sure your housekeeper is not really Dorothy.—Well, what then?"

"Nothing further to alarm perhaps may occur the first night. After surmounting your *unconquerable* horror of the bed, you will retire to rest, and get a few hours' unquiet slumber. But on the second, or at farthest the *third* night after your arrival, you will probably have a violent storm. Peals of thunder so loud as to seem to shake the edifice to its foundation will roll round the neighbouring mountains —and during the frightful gusts of wind which accompany it, you will probably think you discern (for your lamp is not extinguished) one part of the hanging more violently agitated than the rest. Unable of course to repress your curiosity in so favourable a moment for indulging it, you will instantly arise, and throwing your dressing-gown around you, proceed to examine this mystery. After a very short search, you will discover a division in the tapestry so artfully constructed as to defy the minutest inspection, and on opening it, a door will immediately appear—which door being only secured by massy bars and a padlock, you will, after a few efforts, succeed in opening,—and, with your lamp in your hand, will pass through it into a small vaulted room."

"No, indeed; I should be too much frightened to do any such thing."

"What! not when Dorothy has given you to understand that there is a secret subterraneous communication between your apartment and the chapel of St. Anthony, scarcely two miles off—Could you shrink from so simple an adventure? No, no, you will proceed into this small vaulted room, and through this into several others, without perceiving any thing very remarkable in either. In one perhaps there may be a dagger, in another a few drops of blood, and in a third the remains of some instrument of torture; but there being nothing in all this out of the common way, and your lamp being nearly exhausted, you will return towards your own apartment. In repassing through the small vaulted room, however, your eyes will be attracted towards a large, old-fashioned cabinet of ebony and gold, which, though narrowly examining the furniture before, you had passed unnoticed. Impelled by an irresistible presentiment, you will eagerly advance to it, unlock its folding doors, and search into every drawer;—but for some time without discovering any thing of importance—perhaps nothing but a considerable hoard of diamonds. At last, however, by touching a secret spring, an inner compartment will open—a roll of paper appears:—you seize it—it contains many sheets of manuscript—you hasten with the precious treasure into your own chamber, but scarcely have you been able to decipher 'Oh! thou—whomsoever thou mayst be, into whose hands these memoirs of the wretched Matilda may fall'—when your lamp suddenly expires in the socket, and leaves you in total darkness."

"Oh! no, no—do not say so. Well, go on."

But Henry was too much amused by the interest he had raised, to be able to carry it farther; he could no longer command solemnity either of subject or voice, and was obliged to entreat her to use her own fancy in the perusal of Matilda's woes. Catherine, recollecting herself, grew ashamed of her eagerness, and began earnestly to assure him that her attention had been fixed without the smallest apprehension of really meeting with what he related. "Miss Tilney, she was sure, would never put her into such a chamber as he had described!—She was not at all afraid."

As they drew near the end of their journey—her impatience for a sight of the abbey—for some time suspended by his conversation on subjects very different—returned in full force, and every bend in the road was expected with solemn awe to afford a glimpse of its massy walls of grey stone, rising amidst a grove of ancient oaks, with the last beams of the sun playing in beautiful splendour on its high Gothic windows. But so low did the building stand, that she found herself passing through the great gates of the lodge into the very grounds of Northanger, without having discerned even an antique chimney.

She knew not that she had any right to be surprized, but there was a something in this mode of approach which she certainly had not expected. To pass between lodges of a modern appearance, to find herself with such ease in the very precincts of the abbey, and driven so rapidly along a smooth, level road of fine gravel, without obstacle, alarm or solemnity of any kind, struck her as odd and inconsistent. She was not long at leisure however for such considerations. A sudden scud of rain driving full in her face, made it impossible for her to observe any thing further, and fixed all her thoughts on the welfare of her new straw bonnet:—

and she was actually under the Abbey walls, was springing, with Henry's assistance, from the carriage, was beneath the shelter of the old porch, and had even passed on to the hall, where her friend and the General were waiting to welcome her, without feeling one aweful foreboding of future misery to herself, or one moment's suspicion of any past scenes of horror being acted within the solemn edifice. The breeze had not seemed to waft the sighs of the murdered to her; it had wafted nothing worse than a thick mizzling rain; and having given a good shake to her habit, she was ready to be shewn into the common drawing-room, and capable of considering where she was.

An abbey!—yes, it was delightful to be really in an abbey! —but she doubted, as she looked round the room, whether any thing within her observation, would have given her the consciousness. The furniture was in all the profusion and elegance of modern taste. The fire-place, where she had expected the ample width and ponderous carving of former times, was contracted to a Rumford, with slabs of plain though handsome marble, and ornaments over it of the prettiest English china. The windows, to which she looked with peculiar dependence, from having heard the General talk of his preserving them in their Gothic form with reverential care, were yet less what her fancy had portrayed. To be sure, the pointed arch was preserved—the form of them was Gothic—they might be even casements—but every pane was so large, so clear, so light! To an imagination which had hoped for the smallest divisions, and the heaviest stone-work, for painted glass, dirt and cobwebs, the difference was very distressing.

The General, perceiving how her eye was employed, began to talk of the smallness of the room and simplicity of the furniture, where every thing being for daily use, pretended only to comfort, &c.; flattering himself however that there were some apartments in the Abbey not unworthy her notice—and was proceeding to mention the costly gilding of one in particular, when taking out his watch, he stopped short to pronounce it with surprize within twenty minutes of five! This seemed the word of separation, and Catherine found herself hurried away by Miss Tilney in such a manner as convinced her that the strictest punctuality to the family hours would be expected at Northanger.

Returning through the large and lofty hall, they ascended a broad staircase of shining oak, which, after many flights and many landing-places, brought them upon a long wide gallery. On one side it had a range of doors, and it was lighted on the other by windows which Catherine had only time to discover looked into a quadrangle, before Miss Tilney led the way into a chamber, and scarcely staying to hope she would find it comfortable, left her with an anxious entreaty that she would make as little alteration as possible in her dress.

CHAPTER VI

A moment's glance was enough to satisfy Catherine that her apartment was very unlike the one which Henry had endeavoured to alarm her by the description of.—It was by no means unreasonably large, and contained neither tapestry nor velvet.—The walls were papered, the floor was carpeted; the windows were neither less perfect, nor more dim than those of the drawing-room below; the furniture, though not of the latest fashion, was handsome and comfortable, and the air of the room altogether far from uncheerful. Her heart instantaneously at ease on this point, she resolved to lose no time in particular examination of any thing, as she greatly dreaded disobliging the General by any delay. Her habit therefore was thrown off with all possible haste, and she was preparing to unpin the linen package, which the chaise-seat had conveyed for her immediate accommodation, when her eye suddenly fell on a large high chest, standing back in a deep recess on one side of the fire-place. The sight of it made her start; and, forgetting every thing else, she stood gazing on it in motionless wonder, while these thoughts crossed her:—

"This is strange indeed! I did not expect such a sight as this!—An immense heavy chest!—What can it hold?—Why should it be placed here?—Pushed back too, as if meant to be out of sight!—I will look into it—cost me what it may, I will look into it—and directly too—by day-light.—If I stay till evening my candle may go out." She advanced and examined it closely: it was of cedar, curiously inlaid with some darker wood, and raised, about a foot from the ground, on a carved stand of the same. The lock was silver, though tarnished from age; at each end were the imperfect remains of handles also of silver, broken perhaps prematurely by some strange violence; and, on the centre of the lid, was a mysterious cypher, in the same metal. Catherine bent over it intently, but without being able to distinguish any thing with certainty. She could not, in whatever direction she took it, believe the last letter to be a *T;* and yet that it should be any thing else in that house was a circumstance to raise no common degree of astonishment. If not originally their's, by what strange events could it have fallen into the Tilney family?

Her fearful curiosity was every moment growing greater; and seizing, with trembling hands, the hasp of the lock, she resolved at all hazards to satisfy herself at least as to its contents. With difficulty, for something seemed to resist her efforts, she raised the lid a few inches; but at that moment a sudden knocking at the door of the room made her, starting, quit her hold, and the lid closed with alarming violence. This ill-timed intruder was Miss Tilney's maid, sent by her mistress to be of use to Miss Morland; and though Catherine immediately dismissed her, it recalled her to the sense of what she ought to be doing, and forced her, in spite of her anxious desire to penetrate this mystery, to proceed in her dressing without further delay. Her progress was not quick, for her thoughts and her eyes were still bent on the object so well calculated to interest and alarm; and though she dared not waste a moment upon a second attempt, she could not remain many paces from the chest. At length, however, having slipped one arm into her gown, her toilette seemed so nearly finished, that the impatience of her curiosity might safely be indulged. One moment surely might be spared; and, so desperate should be the exertion of her strength, that, unless secured by supernatural means, the lid in one moment should be thrown back. With this spirit she sprang forward, and her confidence did not deceive her. Her resolute effort threw back the lid, and gave to her astonished eyes the view of a white cotton counterpane, properly folded, reposing at one end of the chest in undisputed possession!

She was gazing on it with the first blush of surprise, when Miss Tilney, anxious for her friend's being ready, entered the room, and to the rising shame of having harboured for some minutes an absurd expectation, was then added the shame of being caught in so idle a search. "That is a curious old chest, is not it?" said Miss Tilney, as Catherine hastily closed it and turned away to the glass. "It is impossible to say how many generations it has been here. How it came to be first put in this room I know not, but I have not had it moved, because I thought it might sometimes be of use in holding hats and bonnets. The worst of it is that its weight makes it difficult to open. In that corner, however, it is at least out of the way."

Catherine had no leisure for speech, being at once blushing, tying her gown, and forming wise resolutions with the most violent dispatch. Miss Tilney gently hinted her fear of being late; and in half a minute they ran down stairs together, in an alarm not wholly unfounded, for General Tilney was pacing the drawing-room, his watch in his hand, and having, on the very instant of their entering, pulled the bell with violence, ordered "Dinner to be on table *directly!*"

Catherine trembled at the emphasis with which he spoke, and sat pale and breathless, in a most humble mood, concerned for his children, and detesting old chests; and the General recovering his politeness as he looked at her, spent the rest of his time in scolding his daughter, for so foolishly hurrying her fair friend, who was absolutely out of breath from haste, when there was not the least occasion for hurry in the world: but Catherine could not at all get over the double distress of having involved her friend in a lecture and been a great simpleton herself, till they were happily seated at the dinner-table, when the General's complacent smiles, and a good appetite of her own, restored her to peace. The dining-parlour was a noble room, suitable in its dimensions to a much larger drawing-room than the one in common use, and fitted up in a style of luxury and expense which was almost lost on the unpractised eye of Catherine, who saw little more than its spaciousness and the number of their attendants. Of the former, she spoke aloud her admiration; and the General, with a very gracious countenance, acknowledged that it was by no means an ill-sized room; and further confessed, that, though as careless on such subjects as most people, he did look upon a tolerably large eating-room as one of the necessaries of life; he supposed, however, "that she must have been used to much better sized apartments at Mr. Allen's?"

"No, indeed," was Catherine's honest assurance; "Mr. Allen's dining-parlour was not more than half as large:" and she had never seen so large a room as this in her life. The General's good-humour increased.—Why, as he *had* such rooms, he thought it would be simple not to make use of them; but, upon his honour, he believed there might be more comfort in rooms of only half their size. Mr. Allen's house, he was sure, must be exactly of the true size for rational happiness.

The evening passed without any further disturbance, and, in the occasional absence of General Tilney, with much positive cheerfulness. It was only in his presence that Catherine felt the smallest fatigue from her journey; and even then, even in moments of languor or restraint, a sense of general happiness preponderated, and she could think of her friends in Bath without one wish of being with them.

The night was stormy; the wind had been rising at intervals the whole afternoon; and by the time the party broke up, it blew and rained violently. Catherine, as she crossed the hall, listened to the tempest with sensations of awe; and,

when she heard it rage round a corner of the ancient building and close with sudden fury a distant door, felt for the
first time that she was really in an Abbey.—Yes, these were
characteristic sounds;—they brought to her recollection a
countless variety of dreadful situations and horrid scenes,
which such buildings had witnessed, and such storms
ushered in; and most heartily did she rejoice in the happier
circumstances attending her entrance within walls so
solemn!—*She* had nothing to dread from midnight assassins
or drunken gallants. Henry had certainly been only in jest
in what he had told her that morning. In a house so furnished, and so guarded, she could have nothing to explore
or to suffer; and might go to her bedroom as securely as if
it had been her own chamber at Fullerton. Thus wisely
fortifying her mind, as she proceeded up stairs, she was
enabled, especially on perceiving that Miss Tilney slept only
two doors from her, to enter her room with a tolerably stout
heart; and her spirits were immediately assisted by the
cheerful blaze of a wood fire. "How much better is this,"
said she, as she walked to the fender—"how much better to
find a fire ready lit, than to have to wait shivering in the
cold till all the family are in bed, as so many poor girls have
been obliged to do, and then to have a faithful old servant
frightening one by coming in with a faggot! How glad I am
that Northanger is what it is! If it had been like some other
places, I do not know that, in such a night as this, I could
have answered for my courage:—but now, to be sure, there
is nothing to alarm one."

She looked round the room. The window curtains seemed
in motion. It could be nothing but the violence of the wind
penetrating through the divisions of the shutters; and she
stept boldly forward, carelessly humming a tune, to assure
herself of its being so, peeped courageously behind each
curtain, saw nothing on either low window seat to scare
her, and on placing a hand against the shutter, felt the

strongest conviction of the wind's force. A glance at the old chest, as she turned away from this examination, was not without its use; she scorned the causeless fears of an idle fancy, and began with a most happy indifference to prepare herself for bed. "She should take her time; she should not hurry herself; she did not care if she were the last person up in the house. But she would not make up her fire; *that* would seem cowardly, as if she wished for the protection of light after she were in bed." The fire therefore died away, and Catherine, having spent the best part of an hour in her arrangements, was beginning to think of stepping into bed, when, on giving a parting glance round the room, she was struck by the appearance of a high, old-fashioned black cabinet, which, though in a situation conspicuous enough, had never caught her notice before. Henry's words, his description of the ebony cabinet which was to escape her observation at first, immediately rushed across her; and though there could be nothing really in it, there was something whimsical, it was certainly a very remarkable coincidence! She took her candle and looked closely at the cabinet. It was not absolutely ebony and gold; but it was Japan, black and yellow Japan of the handsomest kind; and as she held her candle, the yellow had very much the effect of gold. The key was in the door, and she had a strange fancy to look into it; not however with the smallest expectation of finding any thing, but it was so very odd, after what Henry had said. In short, she could not sleep till she had examined it. So, placing the candle with great caution on a chair, she seized the key with a very tremulous hand and tried to turn it; but it resisted her utmost strength. Alarmed, but not discouraged, she tried it another way; a bolt flew, and she believed herself successful; but how strangely mysterious!—the door was still immoveable. She paused a moment in breathless wonder. The wind roared down the chimney, the rain beat in torrents against the windows, and every thing seemed to

speak the awfulness of her situation. To retire to bed, however, unsatisfied on such a point, would be vain, since sleep
must be impossible with the consciousness of a cabinet so
mysteriously closed in her immediate vicinity. Again therefore she applied herself to the key, and after moving it in
every possible way for some instants with the determined
celerity of hope's last effort, the door suddenly yielded to her
hand: her heart leaped with exultation at such a victory,
and having thrown open each folding door, the second being secured only by bolts of less wonderful construction
than the lock, though in that her eye could not discern any
thing unusual, a double range of small drawers appeared in
view, with some larger drawers above and below them; and
in the centre, a small door, closed also with a lock and key,
secured in all probability a cavity of importance.

Catherine's heart beat quick, but her courage did not fail
her. With a cheek flushed by hope, and an eye straining with
curiosity, her fingers grasped the handle of a drawer and
drew it forth. It was entirely empty. With less alarm and
greater eagerness she seized a second, a third, a fourth; each
was equally empty. Not one was left unsearched, and in not
one was any thing found. Well read in the art of concealing a treasure, the possibility of false linings to the drawers
did not escape her, and she felt round each with anxious
acuteness in vain. The place in the middle alone remained
now unexplored; and though she had "never from the first
had the smallest idea of finding any thing in any part of
the cabinet, and was not in the least disappointed at her ill
success thus far, it would be foolish not to examine it thoroughly while she was about it." It was some time however
before she could unfasten the door, the same difficulty occurring in the management of this inner lock as of the
outer; but at length it did open; and not vain, as hitherto,
was her search; her quick eyes directly fell on a roll of paper
pushed back into the further part of the cavity, apparently

for concealment, and her feelings at that moment were indescribable. Her heart fluttered, her knees trembled, and her cheeks grew pale. She seized, with an unsteady hand, the precious manuscript, for half a glance sufficed to ascertain written characters; and while she acknowledged with awful sensations this striking exemplification of what Henry had foretold, resolved instantly to peruse every line before she attempted to rest.

The dimness of the light her candle emitted made her turn to it with alarm; but there was no danger of its sudden extinction, it had yet some hours to burn; and that she might not have any greater difficulty in distinguishing the writing than what its ancient date might occasion, she hastily snuffed it. Alas! it was snuffed and extinguished in one. A lamp could not have expired with more awful effect. Catherine, for a few moments, was motionless with horror. It was done completely; not a remnant of light in the wick could give hope to the rekindling breath. Darkness impenetrable and immovable filled the room. A violent gust of wind, rising with sudden fury, added fresh horror to the moment. Catherine trembled from head to foot. In the pause which succeeded, a sound like receding footsteps and the closing of a distant door struck on her affrighted ear. Human nature could support no more. A cold sweat stood on her forehead, the manuscript fell from her hand, and groping her way to the bed, she jumped hastily in, and sought some suspension of agony by creeping far underneath the clothes. To close her eyes in sleep that night, she felt must be entirely out of the question. With a curiosity so justly awakened, and feelings in every way so agitated, repose must be absolutely impossible. The storm too abroad so dreadful!—She had not been used to feel alarm from wind, but now every blast seemed fraught with awful intelligence. The manuscript so wonderfully found, so wonderfully accomplishing the morning's prediction, how was it to be accounted for?—What could it contain?—to whom could it relate?—by what means could it have been so long concealed?—and how singularly strange that it should fall to her lot to discover it! Till she had made herself mistress of its contents, however, she could have neither repose nor comfort; and with the sun's first rays she was determined to peruse it. But many were the tedious hours which must yet intervene. She shuddered, tossed about in her bed, and envied every quiet sleeper. The storm still raged, and various were the noises, more terrific even than the wind, which struck at intervals on her startled ear. The very curtains of her bed seemed at one moment in motion, and at another the lock of her door was agitated, as if by the attempt of somebody to enter. Hollow murmurs seemed to creep along the gallery, and more than once her blood was chilled by the sound of distant moans. Hour after hour passed away, and the wearied Catherine had heard three proclaimed by all the clocks in the house, before the tempest subsided, or she unknowingly fell fast asleep.

CHAPTER VII

The housemaid's folding back her window-shutters at eight o'clock the next day, was the sound which first roused Catherine; and she opened her eyes, wondering that they could ever have been closed, on objects of cheerfulness; her fire was already burning, and a bright morning had succeeded the tempest of the night. Instantaneously with the consciousness of existence, returned her recollection of the manuscript; and springing from the bed in the very moment of the maid's going away, she eagerly collected every scattered sheet which had burst from the roll on its falling to the ground, and flew back to enjoy the luxury of their perusal on her pillow. She now plainly saw that she must not expect a manuscript of equal length with the generality of what she had shuddered over in books, for the roll, seeming to consist entirely of small disjointed sheets, was altogether but of trifling size, and much less than she had supposed it to be at first.

Her greedy eye glanced rapidly over a page. She started at its import. Could it be possible, or did not her senses play her false?—An inventory of linen, in coarse and modern characters, seemed all that was before her! If the evidence of sight might be trusted, she held a washing-bill in her hand. She seized another sheet, and saw the same articles with little variation; a third, a fourth, and a fifth presented nothing new. Shirts, stockings, cravats and waistcoats faced her in each. Two others, penned by the same hand, marked an expenditure scarcely more interesting, in letters, hair-powder, shoe-string and breeches-ball. And the larger sheet, which had inclosed the rest, seemed by its first cramp line,

"To poultice chesnut mare,"—a farrier's bill! Such was the collection of papers, (left perhaps, as she could then suppose, by the negligence of a servant in the place whence she had taken them,) which had filled her with expectation and alarm, and robbed her of half her night's rest! She felt humbled to the dust. Could not the adventure of the chest have taught her wisdom? A corner of it catching her eye as she lay, seemed to rise up in judgment against her. Nothing could now be clearer than the absurdity of her recent fancies. To suppose that a manuscript of many generations back could have remained undiscovered in a room such as that, so modern, so habitable!—or that she should be the first to possess the skill of unlocking a cabinet, the key of which was open to all!

How could she have so imposed on herself?—Heaven forbid that Henry Tilney should ever know her folly! And it was in a great measure his own doing, for had not the cabinet appeared so exactly to agree with his description of her adventures, she should never have felt the smallest curiosity about it. This was the only comfort that occurred. Impatient to get rid of those hateful evidences of her folly, those detestable papers then scattered over the bed, she rose directly, and folding them up as nearly as possible in the same shape as before, returned them to the same spot within the cabinet, with a very hearty wish that no untoward accident might ever bring them forward again, to disgrace her even with herself.

Why the locks should have been so difficult to open however, was still something remarkable, for she could now manage them with perfect ease. In this there was surely something mysterious, and she indulged in the flattering suggestion for half a minute, till the possibility of the door's having been at first unlocked, and of being herself its fastener, darted into her head, and cost her another blush.

She got away as soon as she could from a room in which

her conduct produced such unpleasant reflections, and found her way with all speed to the breakfast-parlour, as it had been pointed out to her by Miss Tilney the evening before. Henry was alone in it; and his immediate hope of her having been undisturbed by the tempest, with an arch reference to the character of the building they inhabited, was rather distressing. For the world would she not have her weakness suspected; and yet, unequal to an absolute falsehood, was constrained to acknowledge that the wind had kept her awake a little. "But we have a charming morning after it," she added, desiring to get rid of the subject; "and storms and sleeplessness are nothing when they are over. What beautiful hyacinths!—I have just learnt to love a hyacinth."

"And how might you learn?—By accident or argument?"

"Your sister taught me; I cannot tell how. Mrs. Allen used to take pains, year after year, to make me like them; but I never could, till I saw them the other day in Milsom-street; I am naturally indifferent about flowers."

"But now you love a hyacinth. So much the better. You have gained a new source of enjoyment, and it is well to have as many holds upon happiness as possible. Besides, a taste for flowers is always desirable in your sex, as a means of getting you out of doors, and tempting you to more frequent exercise than you would otherwise take. And though the love of a hyacinth may be rather domestic, who can tell, the sentiment once raised, but you may in time come to love a rose?"

"But I do not want any such pursuit to get me out of doors. The pleasure of walking and breathing fresh air is enough for me, and in fine weather I am out more than half my time.—Mamma says, I am never within."

"At any rate, however, I am pleased that you have learnt to love a hyacinth. The mere habit of learning to love is the thing; and a teachableness of disposition in a young lady is a great blessing.—Has my sister a pleasant mode of instruction?"

Catherine was saved the embarrassment of attempting an answer, by the entrance of the General, whose smiling compliments announced a happy state of mind, but whose gentle hint of sympathetic early rising did not advance her composure.

The elegance of the breakfast set forced itself on Catherine's notice when they were seated at table; and, luckily, it had been the General's choice. He was enchanted by her approbation of his taste, confessed it to be neat and simple, thought it right to encourage the manufacture of his country; and for his part, to his uncritical palate, the tea was as well flavoured from the clay of Staffordshire, as from that of Dresden or Sêve. But this was quite an old set, purchased two years ago. The manufacture was much improved since that time; he had seen some beautiful specimens when last in town, and had he not been perfectly without vanity of that kind, might have been tempted to order a new set. He trusted, however, that an opportunity might ere long occur of selecting one—though not for himself. Catherine was probably the only one of the party who did not understand him.

Shortly after breakfast Henry left them for Woodston, where business required and would keep him two or three days. They all attended in the hall to see him mount his horse, and immediately on re-entering the breakfast room, Catherine walked to a window in the hope of catching another glimpse of his figure. "This is a somewhat heavy call upon your brother's fortitude," observed the General to Eleanor. "Woodston will make but a sombre appearance to-day."

"Is it a pretty place?" asked Catherine.

"What say you, Eleanor?—speak your opinion, for ladies can best tell the taste of ladies in regard to places as well as men. I think it would be acknowledged by the most impartial eye to have many recommendations. The house stands among fine meadows facing the south-east, with an excellent kitchen-garden in the same aspect; the walls surrounding which I built and stocked myself about ten years ago, for the benefit of my son. It is a family living, Miss Morland; and the property in the place being chiefly my own, you may believe I take care that it shall not be a bad one. Did Henry's income depend solely on this living, he would not be ill provided for. Perhaps it may seem odd, that with only two younger children, I should think any profession necessary for him; and certainly there are moments when we could all wish him disengaged from every tie of business. But though I may not exactly make converts of you young ladies, I am sure your father, Miss Morland, would agree with me in thinking it expedient to give every young man some employment. The money is nothing, it is not an object, but employment is the thing. Even Frederick, my eldest son, you see, who will perhaps inherit as considerable a landed property as any private man in the county, has his profession."

The imposing effect of this last argument was equal to his wishes. The silence of the lady proved it to be unanswerable.

Something had been said the evening before of her being shewn over the house, and he now offered himself as her conductor; and though Catherine had hoped to explore it accompanied only by his daughter, it was a proposal of too much happiness in itself, under any circumstances, not to be gladly accepted; for she had been already eighteen hours in the Abbey, and had seen only a few of its rooms. The netting-box, just leisurely drawn forth, was closed with joyful haste, and she was ready to attend him in a moment. "And when they had gone over the house, he promised himself moreover the pleasure of accompanying her into the shrubberies and garden." She curtsied her acquiescence.

"But perhaps it might be more agreeable to her to make those her first object. The weather was at present favourable, and at this time of year the uncertainty was very great of its continuing so.—Which would she prefer? He was equally at her service.—Which did his daughter think would most accord with her fair friend's wishes?—But he thought he could discern.—Yes, he certainly read in Miss Morland's eyes a judicious desire of making use of the present smiling weather.—But when did she judge amiss?—The Abbey would be always safe and dry.—He yielded implicitly, and would fetch his hat and attend them in a moment." He left the room, and Catherine, with a disappointed, anxious face, began to speak of her unwillingness that he should be taking them out of doors against his own inclination, under a mistaken idea of pleasing her; but she was stopt by Miss Tilney's saying, with a little confusion, "I believe it will be wisest to take the morning while it is so fine; and do not be uneasy on my father's account, he always walks out at this time of day."

Catherine did not exactly know how this was to be understood. Why was Miss Tilney embarrassed? Could there be any unwillingness on the General's side to shew her over the Abbey? The proposal was his own. And was not it odd that he should *always* take his walk so early? Neither her father nor Mr. Allen did so. It was certainly very provoking. She was all impatience to see the house, and had scarcely any curiosity about the grounds. If Henry had been with them indeed!—but now she should not know what was picturesque when she saw it. Such were her thoughts, but she kept them to herself, and put on her bonnet in patient discontent.

She was struck however, beyond her expectation, by the grandeur of the Abbey, as she saw it for the first time from the lawn. The whole building enclosed a large court; and two sides of the quadrangle, rich in Gothic ornaments, stood forward for admiration. The remainder was shut off by knolls of old trees, or luxuriant plantations, and the steep woody hills rising behind to give it shelter, were beautiful even in the leafless month of March. Catherine had seen nothing to compare with it; and her feelings of delight were so strong, that without waiting for any better authority, she boldly burst forth in wonder and praise. The General listened with assenting gratitude; and it seemed as if his own estimation of Northanger had waited unfixed till that hour.

The kitchen-garden was to be next admired, and he led the way to it across a small portion of the park.

The number of acres contained in this garden was such as Catherine could not listen to without dismay, being more than double the extent of Mr. Allen's, as well as her father's, including church-yard and orchard. The walls seemed countless in number, endless in length; a village of hot-houses seemed to arise among them, and a whole parish to be at work within the inclosure. The General was flattered by her looks of surprize, which told him almost as plainly, as he soon forced her to tell him in words, that she had never seen any gardens at all equal to them before;—and he then modestly owned that, "without any ambition of that sort himself—without any solicitude about it,—he did believe them to be unrivalled in the kingdom. If he had a hobby-horse, it was *that*. He loved a garden. Though careless enough in most matters of eating, he loved good fruit—or if he did not, his friends and children did. There were great vexations however attending such a garden as his. The utmost care could not always secure the most valuable fruits. The pinery had yielded only one hundred in the last year. Mr. Allen, he supposed, must feel these inconveniences as well as himself."

"No, not at all. Mr. Allen did not care about the garden, and never went into it."

With a triumphant smile of self-satisfaction, the General

wished he could do the same, for he never entered his, without being vexed in some way or other, by its falling short of his plan.

"How were Mr. Allen's succession-houses worked?" describing the nature of his own as they entered them.

"Mr. Allen had only one small hot-house, which Mrs. Allen had the use of for her plants in winter, and there was a fire in it now and then."

"He is a happy man!" said the General, with a look of very happy contempt.

Having taken her into every division, and led her under every wall, till she was heartily weary of seeing and wondering, he suffered the girls at last to seize the advantage of an outer door, and then expressing his wish to examine the effect of some recent alterations about the tea-house, proposed it as no unpleasant extension of their walk, if Miss Morland were not tired. "But where are you going, Eleanor? —Why do you chuse that cold, damp path to it? Miss Morland will get wet. Our best way is across the park."

"This is so favourite a walk of mine," said Miss Tilney, "that I always think it the best and nearest way. But perhaps it may be damp."

It was a narrow winding path through a thick grove of old Scotch firs; and Catherine, struck by its gloomy aspect, and eager to enter it, could not, even by the General's disapprobation, be kept from stepping forward. He perceived her inclination, and having again urged the plea of health in vain, was too polite to make further opposition. He excused himself however from attending them:—"The rays of the sun were not too cheerful for him, and he would meet them by another course." He turned away; and Catherine was shocked to find how much her spirits were relieved by the separation. The shock however being less real than the relief, offered it no injury; and she began to talk with easy gaiety of the delightful melancholy which such a grove inspired.

"I am particularly fond of this spot," said her companion, with a sigh. "It was my mother's favourite walk."

Catherine had never heard Mrs. Tilney mentioned in the family before, and the interest excited by this tender remembrance, shewed itself directly in her altered countenance, and in the attentive pause with which she waited for something more.

"I used to walk here so often with her!" added Eleanor; "though I never loved it then, as I have loved it since. At that time indeed I used to wonder at her choice. But her memory endears it now."

"And ought it not," reflected Catherine, "to endear it to her husband? Yet the General would not enter it." Miss Tilney continuing silent, she ventured to say, "Her death must have been a great affliction!"

"A great and increasing one," replied the other, in a low voice. "I was only thirteen when it happened; and though I felt my loss perhaps as strongly as one so young could feel it, I did not, I could not then know what a loss it was." She stopped for a moment, and then added, with great firmness, "I have no sister, you know—and though Henry—though my brothers are very affectionate, and Henry is a great deal here, which I am most thankful for, it is impossible for me not to be often solitary."

"To be sure you must miss him very much."

"A mother would have been always present. A mother would have been a constant friend; her influence would have been beyond all other."

"Was she a very charming woman? Was she handsome? Was there any picture of her in the Abbey? And why had she been so partial to that grove? Was it from dejection of spirits?"—were questions now eagerly poured forth;—the first three received a ready affirmative, the two others were passed by; and Catherine's interest in the deceased Mrs. Tilney augmented with every question, whether answered or not. Of her unhappiness in marriage, she felt persuaded. The General certainly had been an unkind husband. He did not love her walk:—could he therefore have loved her? And besides, handsome as he was, there was a something in the turn of his features which spoke his not having behaved well to her.

"Her picture, I suppose," blushing at the consummate art of her own question, "hangs in your father's room?"

"No;—it was intended for the drawing-room; but my father was dissatisfied with the painting, and for some time it had no place. Soon after her death I obtained it for my own, and hung it in my bed-chamber—where I shall be happy to shew it you;—it is very like."—Here was another proof. A portrait—very like—of a departed wife, not valued by the husband!—He must have been dreadfully cruel to her!

Catherine attempted no longer to hide from herself the nature of the feelings which, in spite of all his attentions, he had previously excited; and what had been terror and dislike before, was now absolute aversion. Yes, aversion! His cruelty to such a charming woman made him odious to her. She had often read of such characters; characters, which Mr. Allen had been used to call unnatural and overdrawn; but here was proof positive of the contrary.

She had just settled this point, when the end of the path brought them directly upon the General; and in spite of all her virtuous indignation, she found herself again obliged to walk with him, listen to him, and even to smile when he smiled. Being no longer able however to receive pleasure from the surrounding objects, she soon began to walk with lassitude; the General perceived it, and with a concern for her health, which seemed to reproach her for her opinion of him, was most urgent for returning with his daughter to the house. He would follow them in a quarter of an hour.

Again they parted—but Eleanor was called back in half a minute to receive a strict charge against taking her friend round the Abbey till his return. This second instance of his anxiety to delay what she so much wished for, struck Catherine as very remarkable.

CHAPTER VIII

An hour passed away before the General came in, spent, on the part of his young guest, in no very favourable consideration of his character.—"This lengthened absence, these solitary rambles, did not speak a mind at ease, or a conscience void of reproach."—At length he appeared; and, whatever might have been the gloom of his meditations, he could still smile with *them*. Miss Tilney, understanding in part her friend's curiosity to see the house, soon revived the subject; and her father being, contrary to Catherine's expectations, unprovided with any pretence for further delay, beyond that of stopping five minutes to order refreshments to be in the room by their return, was at last ready to escort them.

They set forward; and, with a grandeur of air, a dignified step, which caught the eye, but could not shake the doubts of the well-read Catherine, he led the way across the hall, through the common drawing-room and one useless anti-chamber, into a room magnificent both in size and furniture—the real drawing-room, used only with company of consequence.—It was very noble—very grand—very charming!—was all that Catherine had to say, for her indiscriminating eye scarcely discerned the colour of the satin; and all minuteness of praise, all praise that had much meaning, was supplied by the General: the costliness or elegance of any room's fitting-up could be nothing to her; she cared for no furniture of a more modern date than the fifteenth century. When the General had satisfied his own curiosity, in a close examination of every well-known ornament, they proceeded into the library, an apartment, in its way, of equal magnificence, exhibiting a collection of books, on which an humble man might have looked with pride.—Catherine heard, admired, and wondered with more genuine feeling than before—gathered all that she could from this store-house of knowledge, by running over the titles of half a shelf, and was ready to proceed. But suites of apartments did not spring up with her wishes.—Large as was the building, she had already visited the greatest part; though, on being told that, with the addition of the kitchen, the six or seven rooms she had now seen surrounded three sides of the court, she could scarcely believe it, or overcome the suspicion of there being many chambers secreted. It was some relief, however, that they were to return to the rooms in common use, by passing through a few of less importance, looking into the court, which, with occasional passages, not wholly unintricate, connected the different sides;—and she was further soothed in her progress, by being told, that she was treading what had once been a cloister, having traces of cells pointed out, and observing several doors, that were neither opened nor explained to her;—by finding herself successively in a billiard-room, and in the General's private apartment, without comprehending their connexion, or being able to turn aright when she left them; and lastly, by passing through a dark little room, owning Henry's authority, and strewed with his litter of books, guns, and great coats.

From the dining-room of which, though already seen, and always to be seen at five o'clock, the General could not forego the pleasure of pacing out the length, for the more certain information of Miss Morland, as to what she neither doubted nor cared for, they proceeded by quick communication to the kitchen—the ancient kitchen of the convent, rich in the massy walls and smoke of former days, and in the stoves and hot closets of the present. The General's improving hand had not loitered here: every modern invention to facilitate the labour of the cooks, had been adopted within this, their spacious theatre; and, when the genius of others had failed, his own had often produced the perfection wanted. His endowments of this spot alone might at any time have placed him high among the benefactors of the convent.

With the walls of the kitchen ended all the antiquity of the Abbey; the fourth side of the quadrangle having, on account of its decaying state, been removed by the General's father, and the present erected in its place. All that was venerable ceased here. The new building was not only new, but declared itself to be so; intended only for offices, and enclosed behind by stable-yards, no uniformity of architecture had been thought necessary. Catherine could have raved at the hand which had swept away what must have been beyond the value of all the rest, for the purposes of mere domestic economy; and would willingly have been spared the mortification of a walk through scenes so fallen, had the General allowed it; but if he had a vanity, it was in the arrangement of his offices; and as he was convinced, that, to a mind like Miss Morland's, a view of the accommodations and comforts, by which the labours of her inferiors were softened, must always be gratifying, he should make no apology for leading her on. They took a slight survey of all; and Catherine was impressed, beyond her expectation, by their multiplicity and their convenience. The purposes for which a few shapeless pantries and a comfortless scullery were deemed sufficient at Fullerton, were here carried on in appropriate divisions, commodious and roomy. The number of servants continually appearing, did not strike her less than the number of their offices. Wherever they went, some pattened girl stopped to curtsey, or some footman in dishabille sneaked off. Yet this was an Abbey!—How inexpressibly different in these domestic arrangements from such as she had read about—from abbeys and castles, in which, though certainly larger than Northanger, all the dirty work of the house was to be done by two pair of female hands at the utmost. How they could get through it all, had often amazed Mrs. Allen; and, when Catherine saw what was necessary here, she began to be amazed herself.

They returned to the hall, that the chief stair-case might be ascended, and the beauty of its wood, and ornaments of rich carving might be pointed out: having gained the top, they turned in an opposite direction from the gallery in which her room lay, and shortly entered one on the same plan, but superior in length and breadth. She was here shewn successively into three large bed-chambers, with their dressing-rooms, most completely and handsomely fitted up; every thing that money and taste could do, to give comfort and elegance to apartments, had been bestowed on these; and, being furnished within the last five years, they were perfect in all that would be generally pleasing, and wanting in all that could give pleasure to Catherine. As they were surveying the last, the General, after slightly naming a few of the distinguished characters, by whom they had at times been honoured, turned with a smiling countenance to Catherine, and ventured to hope, that henceforward some of their earliest tenants might be "our friends from Fullerton." She felt the unexpected compliment, and deeply regretted the impossibility of thinking well of a man so kindly disposed towards herself, and so full of civility to all her family.

The gallery was terminated by folding doors, which Miss Tilney, advancing, had thrown open, and passed through, and seemed on the point of doing the same by the first door to the left, in another long reach of gallery, when the General, coming forwards, called her hastily, and, as Catherine thought, rather angrily back, demanding whither she were going?—And what was there more to be seen?—Had not Miss Morland already seen all that could be worth her notice?—And did she not suppose her friend might be glad of some refreshment after so much exercise? Miss Tilney drew back directly, and the heavy doors were closed upon the mortified Catherine, who, having seen, in a momentary glance beyond them, a narrower passage, more numerous openings, and symptoms of a winding stair-case, believed herself at last within the reach of something worth her notice; and felt, as she unwillingly paced back the gallery, that she would rather be allowed to examine that end of the house, than see all the finery of all the rest.—The General's evident desire of preventing such an examination was an additional stimulant. Something was certainly to be concealed; her fancy, though it had trespassed lately once or twice, could not mislead her here; and what that something was, a short sentence of Miss Tilney's, as they followed the General at some distance down stairs, seemed to point out:—"I was going to take you into what was my mother's room—the room in which she died——" were all her words; but few as they were, they conveyed pages of intelligence to Catherine. It was no wonder that the General should shrink from the sight of such objects as that room must contain; a room in all probability never entered by him since the dreadful scene had passed, which released his suffering wife, and left him to the stings of conscience.

She ventured, when next alone with Eleanor, to express her wish of being permitted to see it, as well as all the rest of that side of the house; and Eleanor promised to attend her there, whenever they should have a convenient hour. Catherine understood her:—the General must be watched from home, before that room could be entered. "It remains as it was, I suppose?" said she, in a tone of feeling.

"Yes, entirely."

"And how long ago may it be that your mother died?"

"She has been dead these nine years." And nine years, Catherine knew was a trifle of time, compared with what generally elapsed after the death of an injured wife, before her room was put to rights.

"You were with her, I suppose, to the last?"

"No," said Miss Tilney, sighing; "I was unfortunately from home.—Her illness was sudden and short; and, before I arrived it was all over."

Catherine's blood ran cold with the horrid suggestions which naturally sprang from these words. Could it be possible?—Could Henry's father?——And yet how many were the examples to justify even the blackest suspicions!—And, when she saw him in the evening, while she worked with her friend, slowly pacing the drawing-room for an hour together in silent thoughtfulness, with downcast eyes and contracted brow, she felt secure from all possibility of wronging him. It was the air and attitude of a Montoni!—What could more plainly speak the gloomy workings of a mind not wholly dead to every sense of humanity, in its fearful review of past scenes of guilt? Unhappy man!—And the anxiousness of her spirits directed her eyes towards his figure so repeatedly, as to catch Miss Tilney's notice. "My father," she whispered, "often walks about the room in this way; it is nothing unusual."

"So much the worse!" thought Catherine; such ill-timed exercise was of a piece with the strange unseasonableness of his morning walks, and boded nothing good.

After an evening, the little variety and seeming length of which made her peculiarly sensible of Henry's importance among them, she was heartily glad to be dismissed; though it was a look from the General not designed for her observation which sent his daughter to the bell. When the butler would have lit his master's candle, however, he was forbidden. The latter was not going to retire. "I have many pamphlets to finish," said he to Catherine, "before I can close my eyes; and perhaps may be poring over the affairs of the nation for hours after you are asleep. Can either of us be more meetly employed? *My* eyes will be blinding for the good of others; and *yours* preparing by rest for future mischief."

But neither the business alleged, nor the magnificent compliment, could win Catherine from thinking, that some very different object must occasion so serious a delay of proper repose. To be kept up for hours, after the family were in bed, by stupid pamphlets, was not very likely. There must be some deeper cause: something was to be done which could be done only while the household slept; and the probability that Mrs. Tilney yet lived, shut up for causes unknown, and receiving from the pitiless hands of her husband a nightly supply of coarse food, was the conclusion which necessarily followed. Shocking as was the idea, it was at least better than a death unfairly hastened, as, in the natural course of things, she must ere long be released. The suddenness of her reputed illness; the absence of her daughter, and probably of her other children, at the time— all favoured the supposition of her imprisonment.—Its origin—jealousy perhaps, or wanton cruelty—was yet to be unravelled.

In revolving these matters, while she undressed, it suddenly struck her as not unlikely, that she might that morning have passed near the very spot of this unfortunate woman's confinement—might have been within a few paces of the cell in which she languished out her days; for what part of the Abbey could be more fitted for the purpose than that which yet bore the traces of monastic division? In the high-arched passage, paved with stone, which already she had trodden with peculiar awe, she well remembered the doors of which the General had given no account. To what might not those doors lead? In support of the plausibility of this conjecture, it further occurred to her, that the forbidden gallery, in which lay the apartments of the unfortunate Mrs. Tilney, must be, as certainly as her memory could guide her, exactly over this suspected range of cells, and the stair-case by the side of those apartments of which she had caught a transient glimpse, communicating by some secret means with those cells, might well have favoured the barbarous proceedings of her husband. Down that stair-case she had perhaps been conveyed in a state of well-prepared insensi-bility!

Catherine sometimes started at the boldness of her own surmises, and sometimes hoped or feared that she had gone too far; but they were supported by such appearances as made their dismissal impossible.

The side of the quadrangle, in which she supposed the guilty scene to be acting, being, according to her belief, just opposite her own, it struck her that, if judiciously watched, some rays of light from the General's lamp might glimmer through the lower windows, as he passed to the prison of his wife; and, twice before she stepped into bed, she stole gently from her room to the corresponding window in the gallery, to see if it appeared; but all abroad was dark, and it must yet be too early. The various ascending noises con-vinced her that the servants must still be up. Till midnight, she supposed it would be in vain to watch; but then, when the clock had struck twelve, and all was quiet, she would, if not quite appalled by darkness, steal out and look once more. The clock struck twelve—and Catherine had been half an hour asleep.

CHAPTER IX

The next day afforded no opportunity for the proposed examination of the mysterious apartments. It was Sunday, and the whole time between morning and afternoon service was required by the General in exercise abroad or eating cold meat at home; and great as was Catherine's curiosity, her courage was not equal to a wish of exploring them after dinner, either by the fading light of the sky between six and seven o'clock, or by the yet more partial though stronger illumination of a treacherous lamp. The day was unmarked therefore by any thing to interest her imagination beyond the sight of a very elegant monument to the memory of Mrs. Tilney, which immediately fronted the family pew. By that her eye was instantly caught and long retained; and the perusal of the highly-strained epitaph, in which every virtue was ascribed to her by the inconsolable husband, who must have been in some way or other her destroyer, affected her even to tears.

That the General, having erected such a monument, should be able to face it, was not perhaps very strange, and yet that he could sit so boldly collected within its view, maintain so elevated an air, look so fearlessly around, nay, that he should even enter the church, seemed wonderful to Catherine. Not however that many instances of beings equally hardened in guilt might not be produced. She could remember dozens who had persevered in every possible vice, going on from crime to crime, murdering whomsoever they chose, without any feeling of humanity or remorse; till a violent death or a religious retirement closed their black career. The erection of the monument itself could not in the smallest degree affect her doubts of Mrs. Tilney's actual decease. Were she even to descend into the family vault where her ashes were supposed to slumber, were she to behold the coffin in which they were said to be enclosed—what could it avail in such a case? Catherine had read too much not to be perfectly aware of the ease with which a waxen figure might be introduced, and a supposititious funeral carried on.

The succeeding morning promised something better. The General's early walk, ill-timed as it was in every other view, was favourable here; and when she knew him to be out of the house, she directly proposed to Miss Tilney the accomplishment of her promise. Eleanor was ready to oblige her; and Catherine reminding her as they went of another promise, their first visit in consequence was to the portrait in her bed-chamber. It represented a very lovely woman, with a mild and pensive countenance, justifying, so far, the expectations of its new observer; but they were not in every respect answered, for Catherine had depended upon meeting with features, air, complexion that should be the very counterpart, the very image, if not of Henry's, of Eleanor's; —the only portraits of which she had been in the habit of thinking, bearing always an equal resemblance of mother and child. A face once taken was taken for generations. But here she was obliged to look and consider and study for a likeness. She contemplated it, however, in spite of this drawback, with much emotion; and, but for a yet stronger interest, would have left it unwillingly.

Her agitation as they entered the great gallery was too much for any endeavour at discourse; she could only look at her companion. Eleanor's countenance was dejected, yet sedate; and its composure spoke her enured to all the gloomy objects to which they were advancing. Again she passed through the folding-doors, again her hand was upon the important lock, and Catherine, hardly able to breathe, was turning to close the former with fearful caution, when the figure, the dreaded figure of the General himself at the further end of the gallery, stood before her! The name of "Eleanor" at the same moment, in his loudest tone, resounded through the building, giving to his daughter the first intimation of his presence, and to Catherine terror upon terror. An attempt at concealment had been her first instinctive movement on perceiving him, yet she could scarcely hope to have escaped his eye; and when her friend, who with an apologizing look darted hastily by her, had joined and disappeared with him, she ran for safety to her own room, and, locking herself in, believed that she should never have courage to go down again. She remained there at least an hour, in the greatest agitation, deeply commiserating the state of her poor friend, and expecting a summons herself from the angry General to attend him in his own apartment. No summons however arrived; and at last, on seeing a carriage drive up to the Abbey, she was emboldened to descend and meet him under the protection of visitors. The breakfast-room was gay with company; and she was named to them by the General, as the friend of his daughter, in a complimentary style, which so well concealed his resentful ire, as to make her feel secure at least of life for the present. And Eleanor, with a command of countenance which did honour to her concern for his character, taking an early occasion of saying to her, "My father only wanted me to answer a note," she began to hope that she had either been unseen by the General, or that from some consideration of policy she should be allowed to suppose herself so. Upon this trust she dared still to remain in his presence, after the company left them, and nothing occurred to disturb it.

In the course of this morning's reflections, she came to a resolution of making her next attempt on the forbidden door alone. It would be much better in every respect that

Eleanor should know nothing of the matter. To involve her in the danger of a second detection, to court her into an apartment which must wring her heart, could not be the office of a friend. The General's utmost anger could not be to herself what it might be to a daughter; and, besides, she thought the examination itself would be more satisfactory if made without any companion. It would be impossible to explain to Eleanor the suspicions, from which the other had, in all likelihood, been hitherto happily exempt; nor could she therefore, in *her* presence, search for those proofs of the General's cruelty, which however they might yet have escaped discovery, she felt confident of somewhere drawing forth, in the shape of some fragmented journal, continued to the last gasp. Of the way to the apartment she was now perfectly mistress; and as she wished to get it over before Henry's return, who was expected on the morrow, there was no time to be lost. The day was bright, her courage high; at four o'clock, the sun was now two hours above the horizon, and it would be only her retiring to dress half an hour earlier than usual.

It was done; and Catherine found herself alone in the gallery before the clocks had ceased to strike. It was no time for thought; she hurried on, slipped with the least possible noise through the folding doors, and without stopping to look or breathe, rushed forward to the one in question. The lock yielded to her hand, and, luckily, with no sullen sound that could alarm a human being. On tip-toe she entered; the room was before her; but it was some minutes before she could advance another step. She beheld what fixed her to the spot and agitated every feature.—She saw a large, well-proportioned apartment, an handsome dimity bed, arranged as unoccupied with an housemaid's care, a bright Bath stove, mahogany wardrobes and neatly-painted chairs, on which the warm beams of a western sun gaily poured through two sash windows! Catherine had expected to have her feelings worked, and worked they were. Astonishment and doubt first seized them; and a shortly succeeding ray of common sense added some bitter emotions of shame. She could not be mistaken as to the room; but how grossly mistaken in every thing else!—in Miss Tilney's meaning, in her own calculation! This apartment, to which she had given a date so ancient, a position so awful, proved to be one end of what the General's father had built. There were two other doors in the chamber, leading probably into dressing-closets; but she had no inclination to open either. Would the veil in which Mrs. Tilney had last walked, or the volume in which she had last read, remain to tell what nothing else was allowed to whisper? No: whatever might have been the General's crimes, he had certainly too much wit to let them sue for detection. She was sick of exploring, and desired but to be safe in her own room, with her own heart only privy to its folly; and she was on the point of retreating as softly as she had entered, when the sound of footsteps, she could hardly tell where, made her pause and tremble. To be found there, even by a servant, would be unpleasant; but by the General, (and he seemed always at hand when least wanted,) much worse!—She listened—the sound had ceased; and resolving not to lose a moment, she passed through and closed the door. At that instant a door underneath was hastily opened; some one seemed with swift steps to ascend the stairs, by the head of which she had yet to pass before she could gain the gallery. She had no power to move. With a feeling of terror not very definable, she fixed her eyes on the staircase, and in a few moments it gave Henry to her view. "Mr. Tilney!" she exclaimed in a voice of more than common astonishment. He looked astonished too. "Good God!" she continued, not attending to his address, "how came you here?—how came you up that staircase?"

"How came I up that staircase!" he replied, greatly surprized. "Because it is my nearest way from the stable-yard to my own chamber; and why should I not come up it?"

Catherine recollected herself, blushed deeply, and could say no more. He seemed to be looking in her countenance for that explanation which her lips did not afford. She moved on towards the gallery. "And may I not, in my turn," said he, as he pushed back the folding doors, "ask how *you* came here?—This passage is at least as extraordinary a road from the breakfast-parlour to your apartment, as that staircase can be from the stables to mine."

"I have been," said Catherine, looking down, "to see your mother's room."

"My mother's room!—Is there any thing extraordinary to be seen there?"

"No, nothing at all.—I thought you did not mean to come back till to-morrow."

"I did not expect to be able to return sooner, when I went away; but three hours ago I had the pleasure of finding nothing to detain me.—You look pale.—I am afraid I alarmed you by running so fast up those stairs. Perhaps you did not know—you were not aware of their leading from the offices in common use?"

"No, I was not.—You have had a very fine day for your ride."

"Very;—and does Eleanor leave you to find your way into all the rooms in the house by yourself?"

"Oh! no; she shewed me over the greatest part on Saturday—and we were coming here to these rooms—but only—(dropping her voice)—your father was with us."

"And that prevented you;" said Henry, earnestly regarding her.—"Have you looked into all the rooms in that passage?"

"No, I only wanted to see—Is not it very late? I must go and dress."

"It is only a quarter past four, (shewing his watch) and

you are not now in Bath. No theatre, no rooms to prepare for. Half an hour at Northanger must be enough."

She could not contradict it, and therefore suffered herself to be detained, though her dread of further questions made her, for the first time in their acquaintance, wish to leave him. They walked slowly up the gallery. "Have you had any letter from Bath since I saw you?"

"No, and I am very much surprized. Isabella promised so faithfully to write directly."

"Promised so faithfully!—A faithful promise!—That puzzles me.—I have heard of a faithful performance. But a faithful promise—the fidelity of promising! It is a power little worth knowing however, since it can deceive and pain you. My mother's room is very commodious, is it not? Large and cheerful-looking, and the dressing closets so well disposed! It always strikes me as the most comfortable apartment in the house, and I rather wonder that Eleanor should not take it for her own. She sent you to look at it, I suppose?"

"No."

"It has been your own doing entirely?"—Catherine said nothing—After a short silence, during which he had closely observed her, he added, "As there is nothing in the room in itself to raise curiosity, this must have proceeded from a sentiment of respect for my mother's character, as described by Eleanor, which does honour to her memory. The world, I believe, never saw a better woman. But it is not often that virtue can boast an interest such as this. The domestic, unpretending merits of a person never known, do not often create that kind of fervent, venerating tenderness which would prompt a visit like yours. Eleanor, I suppose, has talked of her a great deal?"

"Yes, a great deal. That is—no, not much, but what she did say, was very interesting. Her dying so suddenly," (slowly, and with hesitation it was spoken,) "and you—none of you being at home—and your father, I thought—perhaps had not been very fond of her."

"And from these circumstances," he replied, (his quick eye fixed on her's,) "you infer perhaps the probability of some negligence—some—(involuntarily she shook her head)—or it may be—of something still less pardonable." She raised her eyes towards him more fully than she had ever done before. "My mother's illness," he continued, "the seizure which ended in her death *was* sudden. The malady itself, one from which she had often suffered, a bilious fever—its cause therefore constitutional. On the third day, in short as soon as she could be prevailed on, a physician attended her, a very respectable man, and one in whom she had always placed great confidence. Upon his opinion of her danger, two others were called in the next day, and remained in almost constant attendance for four-and-twenty hours. On the fifth day she died. During the progress of her disorder, Frederick and I (*we* were both at home) saw her repeatedly; and from our own observation can bear witness to her having received every possible attention which could spring from the affection of those about her, or which her situation in life could command. Poor Eleanor *was* absent, and at such a distance as to return only to see her mother in her coffin."

"But your father," said Catherine, "was *he* afflicted?"

"For a time, greatly so. You have erred in supposing him not attached to her. He loved her, I am persuaded, as well as it was possible for him to—We have not all, you know, the same tenderness of disposition—and I will not pretend to say that while she lived, she might not often have had much to bear, but though his temper injured her, his judgment never did. His value of her was sincere; and, if not permanently, he was truly afflicted by her death."

"I am very glad of it," said Catherine, "it would have been very shocking!"—

"If I understand you rightly, you had formed a surmise

of such horror as I have hardly words to—Dear Miss Morland, consider the dreadful nature of the suspicions you have entertained. What have you been judging from? Remember the country and the age in which we live. Remember that we are English, that we are Christians. Consult your own understanding, your own sense of the probable, your own observation of what is passing around you—Does our education prepare us for such atrocities? Do our laws connive at them? Could they be perpetrated without being known, in a country like this, where social and literary intercourse is on such a footing; where every man is surrounded by a neighbourhood of voluntary spies, and where roads and newspapers lay every thing open? Dearest Miss Morland, what ideas have you been admitting?"

They had reached the end of the gallery; and with tears of shame she ran off to her own room.

CHAPTER X

The visions of romance were over. Catherine was completely awakened. Henry's address, short as it had been, had more thoroughly opened her eyes to the extravagance of her late fancies than all their several disappointments had done. Most grievously was she humbled. Most bitterly did she cry. It was not only with herself that she was sunk—but with Henry. Her folly, which now seemed even criminal, was all exposed to him, and he must despise her for ever. The liberty which her imagination had dared to take with the character of his father, could he ever forgive it? The absurdity of her curiosity and her fears, could they ever be forgotten? She hated herself more than she could express. He had—she thought he had, once or twice before this fatal morning, shewn something like affection for her.—But now —in short, she made herself as miserable as possible for about half an hour, went down when the clock struck five, with a broken heart, and could scarcely give an intelligible answer to Eleanor's inquiry, if she was well. The formidable Henry soon followed her into the room, and the only difference in his behaviour to her, was that he paid her rather more attention than usual. Catherine had never wanted comfort more, and he looked as if he was aware of it.

The evening wore away with no abatement of this soothing politeness; and her spirits were gradually raised to a modest tranquillity. She did not learn either to forget or defend the past; but she learned to hope that it would never transpire farther, and that it might not cost her Henry's entire regard. Her thoughts being still chiefly fixed on what she had with such causeless terror felt and done, nothing could shortly be clearer, than that it had been all a voluntary, self-created delusion, each trifling circumstance receiving importance from an imagination resolved on alarm, and every thing forced to bend to one purpose by a mind which, before she entered the Abbey, had been craving to be frightened. She remembered with what feelings she had prepared for a knowledge of Northanger. She saw that the infatuation had been created, the mischief settled long before her quitting Bath, and it seemed as if the whole might be traced to the influence of that sort of reading which she had there indulged.

Charming as were all Mrs. Radcliffe's works, and charming even as were the works of all her imitators, it was not in them perhaps that human nature, at least in the midland counties of England, was to be looked for. Of the Alps and Pyrenees, with their pine forests and their vices, they might give a faithful delineation; and Italy, Switzerland, and the South of France, might be as fruitful in horrors as they were there represented. Catherine dared not doubt beyond her own country, and even of that, if hard pressed, would have yielded the northern and western extremities. But in the central part of England there was surely some security for the existence even of a wife not beloved, in the laws of the land, and the manners of the age. Murder was not tolerated, servants were not slaves, and neither poison nor sleeping potions to be procured, like rhubarb, from every druggist. Among the Alps and Pyrenees, perhaps, there were no mixed characters. There, such as were not as spotless as an angel, might have the dispositions of a fiend. But in England it was not so; among the English, she believed, in their hearts and habits, there was a general though unequal mixture of good and bad. Upon this conviction, she would not be surprized if even in Henry and Eleanor Tilney, some slight imperfection might hereafter appear; and upon this conviction she need not fear to acknowledge some actual specks in the character of their father, who, though cleared from the grossly injurious suspicions which she must ever blush to have entertained, she did believe, upon serious consideration, to be not perfectly amiable.

Her mind made up on these several points, and her resolution formed, of always judging and acting in future with the greatest good sense, she had nothing to do but to forgive herself and be happier than ever; and the lenient hand of time did much for her by insensible gradations in the course of another day. Henry's astonishing generosity and nobleness of conduct, in never alluding in the slightest way to what had passed, was of the greatest assistance to her; and sooner than she could have supposed it possible in the beginning of her distress, her spirits became absolutely comfortable, and capable, as heretofore, of continual improvement by any thing he said. There were still some subjects indeed, under which she believed they must always tremble;—the mention of a chest or a cabinet, for instance—and she did not love the sight of japan in any shape: but even *she* could allow, that an occasional memento of past folly, however painful, might not be without use.

The anxieties of common life began soon to succeed to the alarms of romance. Her desire of hearing from Isabella grew every day greater. She was quite impatient to know how the Bath world went on, and how the Rooms were attended; and especially was she anxious to be assured of Isabella's having matched some fine netting-cotton, on which she had left her intent; and of her continuing on the best terms with James. Her only dependence for information of any kind was on Isabella. James had protested against writing to her till his return to Oxford; and Mrs. Allen had given her no hopes of a letter till she had got back to Fullerton.—But Isabella had promised and promised again; and when she promised a thing, she was so scrupulous in performing it! this made it so particularly strange!

For nine successive mornings, Catherine wondered over the repetition of a disappointment, which each morning became more severe: but, on the tenth, when she entered the breakfast-room, her first object was a letter, held out by Henry's willing hand. She thanked him as heartily as if he had written it himself. " 'Tis only from James, however," as she looked at the direction. She opened it; it was from Oxford; and to this purpose:—

"Dear Catherine,

"Though, God knows, with little inclination for writing, I think it my duty to tell you, that every thing is at an end between Miss Thorpe and me.—I left her and Bath yesterday, never to see either again. I shall not enter into particulars, they would only pain you more. You will soon hear enough from another quarter to know where lies the blame; and I hope will acquit your brother of every thing but the folly of too easily thinking his affection returned. Thank God! I am undeceived in time! But it is a heavy blow!—After my father's consent had been so kindly given— but no more of this. She has made me miserable for ever! Let me soon hear from you, dear Catherine; you are my only friend; *your* love I do build upon. I wish your visit at Northanger may be over before Captain Tilney makes his engagement known, or you will be uncomfortably circumstanced.—Poor Thorpe is in town: I dread the sight of him; his honest heart would feel so much. I have written to him and my father. Her duplicity hurts me more than all; till the very last, if I reasoned with her, she declared herself as much attached to me as ever, and laughed at my fears. I am ashamed to think how long I bore with it; but if ever man had reason to believe himself loved, I was that man. I cannot understand even now what she would be at, for there could be no need of my being played off to make her secure of Tilney. We parted at last by mutual consent—happy for

me had we never met! I can never expect to know such another woman! Dearest Catherine, beware how you give your
heart.

"Believe me," &c.

Catherine had not read three lines before her sudden
change of countenance, and short exclamations of sorrowing
wonder, declared her to be receiving unpleasant news; and
Henry, earnestly watching her through the whole letter, saw
plainly that it ended no better than it began. He was prevented, however, from even looking his surprize by his
father's entrance. They went to breakfast directly; but Catherine could hardly eat any thing. Tears filled her eyes, and
even ran down her cheeks as she sat. The letter was one
moment in her hand, then in her lap, and then in her
pocket; and she looked as if she knew not what she did. The
General, between his cocoa and his newspaper, had luckily
no leisure for noticing her; but to the other two her distress
was equally visible. As soon as she dared leave the table she
hurried away to her own room; but the house-maids were
busy in it, and she was obliged to come down again. She
turned into the drawing-room for privacy, but Henry and
Eleanor had likewise retreated thither, and were at that
moment deep in consultation about her. She drew back, trying to beg their pardon, but was, with gentle violence, forced
to return; and the others withdrew, after Eleanor had affectionately expressed a wish of being of use or comfort to
her.

After half an hour's free indulgence of grief and reflection, Catherine felt equal to encountering her friends; but
whether she should make her distress known to them was
another consideration. Perhaps, if particularly questioned,
she might just give an idea—just distantly hint at it—but not
more. To expose a friend, such a friend as Isabella had been
to her—and then their own brother so closely concerned in

it!—She believed she must wave the subject altogether. Henry and Eleanor were by themselves in the breakfast-room; and each, as she entered it, looked at her anxiously. Catherine took her place at the table, and, after a short silence, Eleanor said, "No bad news from Fullerton, I hope? Mr. and Mrs. Morland—your brothers and sisters—I hope they are none of them ill?"

"No, I thank you," (sighing as she spoke,) "they are all very well. My letter was from my brother at Oxford."

Nothing further was said for a few minutes; and then speaking through her tears, she added, "I do not think I shall ever wish for a letter again!"

"I am sorry," said Henry, closing the book he had just opened; "if I had suspected the letter of containing any thing unwelcome, I should have given it with very different feelings."

"It contained something worse than any body could suppose!—Poor James is so unhappy!—You will soon know why."

"To have so kind-hearted, so affectionate a sister," replied Henry, warmly, "must be a comfort to him under any distress."

"I have one favour to beg," said Catherine, shortly afterwards, in an agitated manner, "that, if your brother should be coming here, you will give me notice of it, that I may go away."

"Our brother!—Frederick!"

"Yes; I am sure I should be very sorry to leave you so soon, but something has happened that would make it very dreadful for me to be in the same house with Captain Tilney."

Eleanor's work was suspended while she gazed with increasing astonishment; but Henry began to suspect the truth, and something, in which Miss Thorpe's name was included, passed his lips.

"How quick you are!" cried Catherine: "you have guessed it, I declare!—And yet, when we talked about it in Bath, you little thought of its ending so. Isabella—no wonder *now* I have not heard from her—Isabella has deserted my brother, and is to marry your's! Could you have believed there had been such inconstancy and fickleness, and every thing that is bad in the world?"

"I hope, so far as concerns my brother, you are misinformed. I hope he has not had any material share in bringing on Mr. Morland's disappointment. His marrying Miss Thorpe is not probable. I think you must be deceived so far. I am very sorry for Mr. Morland—sorry that any one you love should be unhappy; but my surprize would be greater at Frederick's marrying her, than at any other part of the story."

"It is very true, however; you shall read James's letter yourself.—Stay——there is one part——" recollecting with a blush the last line.

"Will you take the trouble of reading to us the passages which concern my brother?"

"No, read it yourself," cried Catherine, whose second thoughts were clearer. "I do not know what I was thinking of," (blushing again that she had blushed before,)—"James only means to give me good advice."

He gladly received the letter; and, having read it through, with close attention, returned it saying, "Well, if it is to be so, I can only say that I am sorry for it. Frederick will not be the first man who has chosen a wife with less sense than his family expected. I do not envy his situation, either as a lover or a son."

Miss Tilney, at Catherine's invitation, now read the letter likewise; and, having expressed also her concern and surprize, began to inquire into Miss Thorpe's connexions and fortune.

"Her mother is a very good sort of woman," was Catherine's answer.

"What was her father?"

"A lawyer, I believe.—They live at Putney."

"Are they a wealthy family?"

"No, not very. I do not believe Isabella has any fortune at all: but that will not signify in your family.—Your father is so very liberal! He told me the other day, that he only valued money as it allowed him to promote the happiness of his children." The brother and sister looked at each other. "But," said Eleanor, after a short pause, "would it be to promote his happiness, to enable him to marry such a girl?—She must be an unprincipled one, or she could not have used your brother so.—And how strange an infatuation on Frederick's side! A girl who, before his eyes, is violating an engagement voluntarily entered into with another man! Is not it inconceivable, Henry? Frederick too, who always wore his heart so proudly! who found no woman good enough to be loved!"

"That is the most unpromising circumstance, the strongest presumption against him. When I think of his past declarations, I give him up.—Moreover, I have too good an opinion of Miss Thorpe's prudence, to suppose that she would part with one gentleman before the other was secured. It is all over with Frederick indeed! He is a deceased man—defunct in understanding. Prepare for your sister-in-law, Eleanor, and such a sister-in-law as you must delight in! —Open, candid, artless, guileless, with affections strong but simple, forming no pretensions, and knowing no disguise."

"Such a sister-in-law, Henry, I should delight in," said Eleanor, with a smile.

"But perhaps," observed Catherine, "though she has behaved so ill by our family, she may behave better by your's. Now she has really got the man she likes, she may be constant."

"Indeed I am afraid she will," replied Henry; "I am afraid she will be very constant, unless a baronet should come in her way; that is Frederick's only chance.—I will get the Bath paper, and look over the arrivals."

"You think it is all for ambition then?—And, upon my word, there are some things that seem very like it. I cannot forget, that, when she first knew what my father would do for them, she seemed quite disappointed that it was not more. I never was so deceived in any one's character in my life before."

"Among all the great variety that you have known and studied."

"My own disappointment and loss in her is very great; but, as for poor James, I suppose he will hardly ever recover it."

"Your brother is certainly very much to be pitied at present; but we must not, in our concern for his sufferings, undervalue your's. You feel, I suppose, that, in losing Isabella, you lose half yourself: you feel a void in your heart which nothing else can occupy. Society is becoming irksome; and as for the amusements in which you were wont to share at Bath, the very idea of them without her is abhorrent. You would not, for instance, now go to a ball for the world. You feel that you have no longer any friend to whom you can speak with unreserve; on whose regard you can place dependence; or whose counsel, in any difficulty, you could rely on. You feel all this?"

"No," said Catherine, after a few moments' reflection, "I do not—ought I? To say the truth, though I am hurt and grieved, that I cannot still love her, that I am never to hear from her, perhaps never to see her again, I do not feel so very, very much afflicted as one would have thought."

"You feel, as you always do, what is most to the credit of human nature.—Such feelings ought to be investigated, that they may know themselves."

Catherine, by some chance or other, found her spirits so very much relieved by this conversation, that she could not regret her being led on, though so unaccountably, to mention the circumstance which had produced it.

CHAPTER XI

From this time, the subject was frequently canvassed by the three young people; and Catherine found, with some surprize, that her two young friends were perfectly agreed in considering Isabella's want of consequence and fortune as likely to throw great difficulties in the way of her marrying their brother. Their persuasion that the General would, upon this ground alone, independent of the objection that might be raised against her character, oppose the connexion, turned her feelings moreover with some alarm towards herself. She was as insignificant, and perhaps as portionless as Isabella; and if the heir of the Tilney property had not grandeur and wealth enough in himself, at what point of interest were the demands of his younger brother to rest? The very painful reflections to which this thought led, could only be dispersed by a dependence on the effect of that particular partiality, which, as she was given to understand by his words as well as his actions, she had from the first been so fortunate as to excite in the General; and by a recollection of some most generous and disinterested sentiments on the subject of money, which she had more than once heard him utter, and which tempted her to think his disposition in such matters misunderstood by his children.

They were so fully convinced, however, that their brother would not have the courage to apply in person for his father's consent, and so repeatedly assured her that he had never in his life been less likely to come to Northanger than at the present time, that she suffered her mind to be at ease as to the necessity of any sudden removal of her own. But as it was not to be supposed that Captain Tilney, whenever he made his application, would give his father any just idea of Isabella's conduct, it occurred to her as highly expedient that Henry should lay the whole business before him as it really was, enabling the General by that means to form a cool and impartial opinion, and prepare his objections on a fairer ground than inequality of situations. She proposed it to him accordingly; but he did not catch at the measure so eagerly as she had expected. "No," said he, "my father's hands need not be strengthened, and Frederick's confession of folly need not be forestalled. He must tell his own story."

"But he will tell only half of it."

"A quarter would be enough."

A day or two passed away and brought no tidings of Captain Tilney. His brother and sister knew not what to think. Sometimes it appeared to them as if his silence would be the natural result of the suspected engagement, and at others that it was wholly incompatible with it. The General, meanwhile, though offended every morning by Frederick's remissness in writing, was free from any real anxiety about him; and had no more pressing solicitude than that of making Miss Morland's time at Northanger pass pleasantly. He often expressed his uneasiness on this head, feared the sameness of every day's society and employments would disgust her with the place, wished the Lady Frasers had been in the country, talked every now and then of having a large party to dinner, and once or twice began even to calculate the number of young dancing people in the neighbourhood. But then it was such a dead time of year, no wild-fowl, no game, and the Lady Frasers were not in the country. And it all ended, at last, in his telling Henry one morning, that when he next went to Woodston, they would take him by surprize there some day or other, and eat their mutton with him. Henry was greatly honoured and very happy, and Catherine was quite delighted with the scheme. "And when do you think, sir, I may look forward to this pleasure?—I must be at Woodston on Monday to attend the parish meeting, and shall probably be obliged to stay two or three days."

"Well, well, we will take our chance some one of those days. There is no need to fix. You are not to put yourself at all out of your way. Whatever you may happen to have in the house will be enough. I think I can answer for the young ladies making allowance for a bachelor's table. Let me see; Monday will be a busy day with you, we will not come on Monday; and Tuesday will be a busy one with me. I expect my surveyor from Brockham with his report in the morning; and afterwards I cannot in decency fail attending the club. I really could not face my acquaintance if I staid away now; for, as I am known to be in the country, it would be taken exceedingly amiss; and it is a rule with me, Miss Morland, never to give offence to any of my neighbours, if a small sacrifice of time and attention can prevent it. They are a set of very worthy men. They have half a buck from Northanger twice a year; and I dine with them whenever I can. Tuesday, therefore, we may say is out of the question. But on Wednesday, I think, Henry, you may expect us; and we shall be with you early, that we may have time to look about us. Two hours and three quarters will carry us to Woodston, I suppose; we shall be in the carriage by ten; so, about a quarter before one on Wednesday, you may look for us."

A ball itself could not have been more welcome to Catherine than this little excursion, so strong was her desire to be acquainted with Woodston; and her heart was still bounding with joy, when Henry, about an hour afterwards, came booted and great coated into the room where she and Eleanor were sitting, and said, "I am come, young ladies, in a very moralizing strain, to observe that our pleasures in this world are always to be paid for, and that we often purchase them at a great disadvantage, giving ready-monied actual happiness for a draft on the future, that may not be honoured. Witness myself, at this present hour. Because I am to hope for the satisfaction of seeing you at Woodston on Wednesday, which bad weather, or twenty other causes may prevent, I must go away directly, two days before I intended it."

"Go away!" said Catherine, with a very long face; "and why?"

"Why!—How can you ask the question?—Because no time is to be lost in frightening my old housekeeper out of her wits,—because I must go and prepare a dinner for you to be sure."

"Oh! not seriously!"

"Aye, and sadly too—for I had much rather stay."

"But how can you think of such a thing, after what the General said? when he so particularly desired you not to give yourself any trouble, because *any thing* would do."

Henry only smiled.

"I am sure it is quite unnecessary upon your sister's account and mine. You must know it to be so; and the General made such a point of your providing nothing extraordinary:— besides, if he had not said half so much as he did, he has always such an excellent dinner at home, that sitting down to a middling one for one day could not signify."

"I wish I could reason like you, for his sake and my own. Good bye. As to-morrow is Sunday, Eleanor, I shall not return."

He went; and, it being at any time a much simpler operation to Catherine to doubt her own judgment than Henry's, she was very soon obliged to give him credit for being right, however disagreeable to her his going. But the inexplicability of the General's conduct dwelt much on her thoughts. That he was very particular in his eating, she had, by her own unassisted observation, already discovered; but why he should say one thing so positively, and mean another all the while, was most unaccountable! How were people, at that rate, to be understood? Who but Henry could have been aware of what his father was at?

From Saturday to Wednesday, however, they were now to be without Henry. This was the sad finale of every reflection:—and Captain Tilney's letter would certainly come in his absence; and Wednesday she was very sure would be wet. The past, present, and future, were all equally in gloom. Her brother so unhappy, and her loss in Isabella so great; and Eleanor's spirits always affected by Henry's absence! What was there to interest or amuse her? She was tired of the woods and the shrubberies—always so smooth and so dry; and the Abbey in itself was no more to her now than any other house. The painful remembrance of the folly it had helped to nourish and perfect, was the only emotion which could spring from a consideration of the building. What a revolution in her ideas! she, who had so longed to be in an abbey! Now, there was nothing so charming to her imagination as the unpretending comfort of a well-connected Parsonage, something like Fullerton, but better: Fullerton had its faults, but Woodston probably had none. —If Wednesday should ever come!

It did come, and exactly when it might be reasonably looked for. It came—it was fine—and Catherine trod on air. By ten o'clock, the chaise-and-four conveyed the trio from the Abbey; and, after an agreeable drive of almost twenty miles, they entered Woodston, a large and populous village, in a situation not unpleasant. Catherine was ashamed to say how pretty she thought it, as the General seemed to think an apology necessary for the flatness of the country, and the size of the village; but in her heart she preferred it to any place she had ever been at, and looked with great admiration at every neat house above the rank of a cottage, and at all the little chandler's shops which they passed. At the further end of the village, and tolerably disengaged from

the rest of it, stood the Parsonage, a new-built substantial
stone house, with its semi-circular sweep and green gates;
and, as they drove up to the door, Henry, with the friends of
his solitude, a large Newfoundland puppy and two or three
terriers, was ready to receive and make much of them.

Catherine's mind was too full, as she entered the house,
for her either to observe or to say a great deal; and, till
called on by the General for her opinion of it, she had very
little idea of the room in which she was sitting. Upon looking round it then, she perceived in a moment that it was
the most comfortable room in the world; but she was too
guarded to say so, and the coldness of her praise disappointed him.

"We are not calling it a good house," said he.—"We are
not comparing it with Fullerton and Northanger—We are
considering it as a mere Parsonage, small and confined, we
allow, but decent perhaps, and habitable; and altogether
not inferior to the generality;—or, in other words, I believe
there are few country parsonages in England half so good.
It may admit of improvement, however. Far be it from me
to say otherwise; and any thing in reason—a bow thrown
out, perhaps—though, between ourselves, if there is one
thing more than another my aversion, it is a patched-on
bow."

Catherine did not hear enough of this speech to understand or be pained by it; and other subjects being studiously
brought forward and supported by Henry, at the same time
that a tray full of refreshments was introduced by his servant, the General was shortly restored to his complacency,
and Catherine to all her usual ease of spirits.

The room in question was of a commodious, well-proportioned size, and handsomely fitted up as a dining parlour; and on their quitting it to walk round the grounds,
she was shewn, first into a smaller apartment, belonging
peculiarly to the master of the house, and made unusually

tidy on the occasion; and afterwards into what was to be the drawing-room, with the appearance of which, though unfurnished, Catherine was delighted enough even to satisfy the General. It was a prettily-shaped room, the windows reaching to the ground, and the view from them pleasant, though only over green meadows; and she expressed her admiration at the moment with all the honest simplicity with which she felt it. "Oh! why do not you fit up this room, Mr. Tilney? What a pity not to have it fitted up! It is the prettiest room I ever saw;—it is the prettiest room in the world!"

"I trust," said the General, with a most satisfied smile, "that it will very speedily be furnished: it waits only for a lady's taste!"

"Well, if it was my house, I should never sit any where else. Oh! what a sweet little cottage there is among the trees—apple trees too! It is the prettiest cottage!"—

"You like it—you approve it as an object;—it is enough. Henry, remember that Robinson is spoken to about it. The cottage remains."

Such a compliment recalled all Catherine's consciousness, and silenced her directly; and, though pointedly applied to by the General for her choice of the prevailing colour of the paper and hangings, nothing like an opinion on the subject could be drawn from her. The influence of fresh objects and fresh air, however, was of great use in dissipating these embarrassing associations; and, having reached the ornamental part of the premises, consisting of a walk round two sides of a meadow, on which Henry's genius had begun to act about half a year ago, she was sufficiently recovered to think it prettier than any pleasure-ground she had ever been in before, though there was not a shrub in it higher than the green bench in the corner.

A saunter into other meadows, and through part of the village, with a visit to the stables to examine some improvements, and a charming game of play with a litter of puppies just able to roll about, brought them to four o'clock, when Catherine scarcely thought it could be three. At four they were to dine, and at six to set off on their return. Never had any day passed so quickly!

She could not but observe that the abundance of the dinner did not seem to create the smallest astonishment in the General; nay, that he was even looking at the side-table for cold meat which was not there. His son and daughter's observations were of a different kind. They had seldom seen him eat so heartily at any table but his own; and never before known him so little disconcerted by the melted butter's being oiled.

At six o'clock, the General having taken his coffee, the carriage again received them; and so gratifying had been the tenor of his conduct throughout the whole visit, so well assured was her mind on the subject of his expectations, that, could she have felt equally confident of the wishes of his son, Catherine would have quitted Woodston with little anxiety as to the How or the When she might return to it.

CHAPTER XII

The next morning brought the following very unexpected letter from Isabella:—

Bath, April ——

My dearest Catherine,

I received your two kind letters with the greatest delight, and have a thousand apologies to make for not answering them sooner. I really am quite ashamed of my idleness; but in this horrid place one can find time for nothing. I have had my pen in my hand to begin a letter to you almost every day since you left Bath, but have always been prevented by some silly trifler or other. Pray write to me soon, and direct to my own home. Thank God! we leave this vile place to-morrow. Since you went away, I have had no pleasure in it—the dust is beyond any thing; and every body one cares for is gone. I believe if I could see you I should not mind the rest, for you are dearer to me than any body can conceive. I am quite uneasy about your dear brother, not having heard from him since he went to Oxford; and am fearful of some misunderstanding. Your kind offices will set all right:—he is the only man I ever did or could love, and I trust you will convince him of it. The spring fashions are partly down; and the hats the most frightful you can imagine. I hope you spend your time pleasantly, but am afraid you never think of me. I will not say all that I could of the family you are with, because I would not be ungenerous, or set you against those you esteem; but it is very difficult to know whom to trust, and young men never know their minds two days together. I rejoice to say, that the young man whom, of all others, I particularly abhor, has left Bath. You will know, from this description, I must mean Captain Tilney, who, as you may remember, was amazingly disposed to follow and tease me, before you went away. Afterwards he got worse, and became quite my shadow. Many girls might have been taken in, for never were such attentions; but I knew the fickle sex too well. He went away to his regiment two days ago, and I trust I shall never be plagued with him again. He is the greatest coxcomb I ever saw, and amazingly disagreeable. The last two days he was always by the side of Charlotte Davis: I pitied his taste, but took no notice of him. The last time we met was in Bath-street, and I turned directly into a shop that he might not speak to me;—I would not even look at him. He went into the Pump-room afterwards; but I would not have followed him for all the world. Such a contrast between him and your brother!—pray send me some news of the latter—I am quite unhappy about him, he seemed so uncomfortable when he went away, with a cold, or something that affected his spirits. I would write to him myself, but have mislaid his direction; and, as I hinted above, am afraid he took something in my conduct amiss. Pray explain every thing to his satisfaction; or, if he still harbours any doubt, a line from himself to me, or a call at Putney when next in town, might set all to rights. I have not been to the Rooms this age, nor to the Play, except going in last night with the Hodges's, for a frolic, at half-price: they teased me into it; and I was determined they should not say I shut myself up because Tilney was gone. We happened to sit by the Mitchells, and they pretended to be quite surprized to see me out. I knew their spite:—at one time they could not be civil to me, but now they are all friendship; but I am not such a fool as to be taken in by them. You know I have a pretty good spirit of my own. Anne Mitchell had tried to put on a turban like mine, as I wore it the week before at the Concert, but made wretched work of it—it happened to become my odd face I believe, at least Tilney told me so at the time, and said every eye was upon me; but he is the last man whose word I would take. I wear nothing but purple now: I know I look hideous in it, but no matter—it is your dear brother's favourite colour. Lose no time, my dearest, sweetest Catherine, in writing to him and to me,

Who ever am, &c.

Such a strain of shallow artifice could not impose even upon Catherine. Its inconsistencies, contradictions, and falsehood, struck her from the very first. She was ashamed of Isabella, and ashamed of having ever loved her. Her professions of attachment were now as disgusting as her excuses were empty, and her demands impudent. "Write to James on her behalf!—No, James should never hear Isabella's name mentioned by her again."

On Henry's arrival from Woodston, she made known to him and Eleanor their brother's safety, congratulating them with sincerity on it, and reading aloud the most material passages of her letter with strong indignation. When she had finished it,—"So much for Isabella," she cried, "and for all our intimacy! She must think me an idiot, or she could not have written so; but perhaps this has served to make her character better known to me than mine is to her. I see what she has been about. She is a vain coquette, and her tricks have not answered. I do not believe she had ever any regard either for James or for me, and I wish I had never known her."

"It will soon be as if you never had," said Henry.

"There is but one thing that I cannot understand. I see that she has had designs on Captain Tilney, which have not succeeded; but I do not understand what Captain Tilney has been about all this time. Why should he pay her such attentions as to make her quarrel with my brother, and then fly off himself?"

"I have very little to say for Frederick's motives, such as I believe them to have been. He has his vanities as well as Miss Thorpe, and the chief difference is, that, having a stronger head, they have not yet injured himself. If the *effect* of his behaviour does not justify him with you, we had better not seek after the cause."

"Then you do not suppose he ever really cared about her?"

"I am persuaded that he never did."

"And only made believe to do so for mischief's sake?"

Henry bowed his assent.

"Well, then, I must say that I do not like him at all. Though it has turned out so well for us, I do not like him at all. As it happens, there is no great harm done, because I do not think Isabella has any heart to lose. But, suppose he had made her very much in love with him?"

"But we must first suppose Isabella to have had a heart to lose,—consequently to have been a very different creature; and, in that case, she would have met with very different treatment."

"It is very right that you should stand by your brother."

"And if you would stand by *your's,* you would not be much distressed by the disappointment of Miss Thorpe. But your mind is warped by an innate principle of general integrity, and therefore not accessible to the cool reasonings of family partiality, or a desire of revenge."

Catherine was complimented out of further bitterness. Frederick could not be unpardonably guilty, while Henry made himself so agreeable. She resolved on not answering Isabella's letter; and tried to think no more of it.

CHAPTER XIII

Soon after this, the General found himself obliged to go to London for a week; and he left Northanger earnestly regretting that any necessity should rob him even for an hour of Miss Morland's company, and anxiously recommending the study of her comfort and amusement to his children as their chief object in his absence. His departure gave Catherine the first experimental conviction that a loss may be sometimes a gain. The happiness with which their time now passed, every employment voluntary, every laugh indulged, every meal a scene of ease and good-humour, walking where they liked and when they liked, their hours, pleasures and fatigues at their own command, made her thoroughly sensible of the restraint which the General's presence had imposed, and most thankfully feel their present release from it. Such ease and such delights made her love the place and the people more and more every day; and had it not been for a dread of its soon becoming expedient to leave the one, and an apprehension of not being equally beloved by the other, she would at each moment of each day have been perfectly happy; but she was now in the fourth week of her visit; before the General came home, the fourth week would be turned, and perhaps it might seem an intrusion if she staid much longer. This was a painful consideration whenever it occurred; and eager to get rid of such a weight on her mind, she very soon resolved to speak to Eleanor about it at once, propose going away, and be guided in her conduct by the manner in which her proposal might be taken.

Aware that if she gave her herself much time, she might feel it difficult to bring forward so unpleasant a subject, she took the first opportunity of being suddenly alone with Eleanor, and of Eleanor's being in the middle of a speech about something very different, to start forth her obligation of going away very soon. Eleanor looked and declared herself much concerned. She had "hoped for the pleasure of her company for a much longer time—had been misled (perhaps by her wishes) to suppose that a much longer visit had been promised—and could not but think that if Mr. and Mrs. Morland were aware of the pleasure it was to her to have her there, they would be too generous to hasten her return."—Catherine explained.—"Oh! as to *that,* papa and mamma were in no hurry at all. As long as she was happy, they would always be satisfied."

"Then why, might she ask, in such a hurry herself to leave them?"

"Oh! because she had been there so long."

"Nay, if you can use such a word, I can urge you no farther. If you think it long—"

"Oh! no, I do not indeed. For my own pleasure, I could stay with you as long again."—And it was directly settled that, till she had, her leaving them was not even to be thought of. In having this cause of uneasiness so pleasantly removed, the force of the other was likewise weakened. The kindness, the earnestness of Eleanor's manner in pressing her to stay, and Henry's gratified look on being told that her stay was determined, were such sweet proofs of her importance with them, as left her only just so much solicitude as the human mind can never do comfortably without. She did —almost always—believe that Henry loved her, and quite always that his father and sister loved and even wished her to belong to them; and believing so far, her doubts and anxieties were merely sportive irritations.

Henry was not able to obey his father's injunction of remaining wholly at Northanger in attendance on the ladies, during his absence in London; the engagements of his curate at Woodston obliging him to leave them on Saturday for a couple of nights. His loss was not now what it had been while the General was at home; it lessened their gaiety, but did not ruin their comfort; and the two girls agreeing in occupation, and improving in intimacy, found themselves so well-sufficient for the time to themselves, that it was eleven o'clock, rather a late hour at the Abbey, before they quitted the supper-room on the day of Henry's departure. They had just reached the head of the stairs, when it seemed, as far as the thickness of the walls would allow them to judge, that a carriage was driving up to the door, and the next moment confirmed the idea by the loud noise of the house-bell. After the first perturbation of surprize had passed away, in a "Good Heaven! what can be the matter?" it was quickly decided by Eleanor to be her eldest brother, whose arrival was often as sudden, if not quite so unseasonable, and accordingly she hurried down to welcome him.

Catherine walked on to her chamber, making up her mind as well as she could, to a further acquaintance with Captain Tilney, and comforting herself under the unpleasant impression his conduct had given her, and the persuasion of his being by far too fine a gentleman to approve of her, that at least they should not meet under such circumstances as would make their meeting materially painful. She trusted he would never speak of Miss Thorpe; and indeed, as he must by this time be ashamed of the part he had acted, there could be no danger of it; and as long as all mention of Bath scenes were avoided, she thought she could behave to him very civilly. In such considerations time passed away, and it was certainly in his favour that Eleanor should be so glad see him, and have so much to say, for half an hour was almost gone since his arrival, and Eleanor did not come up.

At that moment Catherine thought she heard her step in the gallery, and listened for its continuance; but all was silent. Scarcely, however, had she convicted her fancy of error, when the noise of something moving close to her door made her start; it seemed as if some one was touching the very doorway—and in another moment a slight motion of the lock proved that some hand must be on it. She trembled a little at the idea of any one's approaching so cautiously; but resolving not to be again overcome by trivial appearances of alarm, or misled by a raised imagination, she stepped quietly forward, and opened the door. Eleanor, and only Eleanor, stood there. Catherine's spirits however were tranquillized but for an instant, for Eleanor's cheeks were pale, and her manner greatly agitated. Though evidently intending to come in, it seemed an effort to enter the room, and a still greater to speak when there. Catherine, supposing some uneasiness on Captain Tilney's account, could only express her concern by silent attention; obliged her to be seated, rubbed her temples with lavender-water, and hung over her with affectionate solicitude. "My dear Catherine, you must not—you must not indeed—" were Eleanor's first connected words. "I am quite well. This kindness distracts me—I cannot bear it—I come to you on such an errand!"

"Errand!—to me!"

"How shall I tell you!—Oh! how shall I tell you!"

A new idea now darted into Catherine's mind, and turning as pale as her friend, she exclaimed, " 'Tis a messenger from Woodston!"

"You are mistaken, indeed," returned Eleanor, looking at her most compassionately—"it is no one from Woodston. It is my father himself." Her voice faltered, and her eyes were turned to the ground as she mentioned his name. His unlooked-for return was enough in itself to make Catherine's heart sink, and for a few moments she hardly supposed there were any thing worse to be told. She said nothing; and Eleanor endeavouring to collect herself and speak with firmness, but with eyes still cast down, soon went on. "You are too good, I am sure, to think the worse of me for the part I am obliged to perform. I am indeed a most unwilling messenger. After what has so lately passed, so lately been settled between us—how joyfully, how thankfully on my side!—as to your continuing here as I hoped for many, many weeks longer, how can I tell you that your kindness is not to be accepted—and that the happiness your company has hitherto given us is to be repaid by——but I must not trust myself with words. My dear Catherine, we are to part. My father has recollected an engagement that takes our whole family away on Monday. We are going to Lord Longtown's, near Hereford, for a fortnight. Explanation and apology are equally impossible. I cannot attempt either."

"My dear Eleanor," cried Catherine, suppressing her feelings as well as she could, "do not be so distressed. A second engagement must give way to a first. I am very, very sorry we are to part—so soon, and so suddenly too; but I am not offended, indeed I am not. I can finish my visit here you know at any time; or I hope you will come to me. Can you, when you return from this lord's, come to Fullerton?"

"It will not be in my power, Catherine."

"Come when you can, then."—

Eleanor made no answer; and Catherine's thoughts recurring to something more directly interesting, she added, thinking aloud, "Monday—so soon as Monday;—and you *all* go. Well, I am certain of——I shall be able to take leave however. I need not go till just before you do, you know. Do not be distressed, Eleanor, I can go on Monday very well. My father and mother's having no notice of it is of very little consequence. The General will send a servant with me, I dare say, half the way—and then I shall soon be at Salisbury, and then I am only nine miles from home."

"Ah, Catherine! were it settled so, it would be somewhat less intolerable, though in such common attentions you would have received but half what you ought. But—how can I tell you?—To-morrow morning is fixed for your leaving us, and not even the hour is left to your choice; the very carriage is ordered, and will be here at seven o'clock, and no servant will be offered you."

Catherine sat down, breathless and speechless. "I could hardly believe my senses, when I heard it;—and no displeasure, no resentment that you can feel at this moment, however justly great, can be more than I myself——but I must not talk of what I felt. Oh! that I could suggest any thing in extenuation! Good God! what will your father and mother say! After courting you from the protection of real friends to this—almost double distance from your home, to have you driven out of the house, without the considerations even of decent civility! Dear, dear Catherine, in being the bearer of such a message, I seem guilty myself of all its insult; yet, I trust you will acquit me, for you must have been long enough in this house to see that I am but a nominal mistress of it, that my real power is nothing."

"Have I offended the General?" said Catherine in a faltering voice.

"Alas! for my feelings as a daughter, all that I know, all that I answer for is, that you can have given him no just cause of offence. He certainly is greatly, very greatly discomposed; I have seldom seen him more so. His temper is not happy, and something has now occurred to ruffle it in an uncommon degree; some disappointment, some vexation, which just at this moment seems important; but which I can hardly suppose you to have any concern in, for how is it possible?"

It was with pain that Catherine could speak at all; and it was only for Eleanor's sake that she attempted it. "I am sure," said she, "I am very sorry if I have offended him. It was the last thing I would willingly have done. But do not be unhappy, Eleanor. An engagement you know must be kept.

I am only sorry it was not recollected sooner, that I might have written home. But it is of very little consequence."

"I hope, I earnestly hope that to your real safety it will be of none; but to every thing else it is of the greatest consequence; to comfort, appearance, propriety, to your family, to the world. Were your friends, the Allens, still in Bath, you might go to them with comparative ease; a few hours would take you there; but a journey of seventy miles, to be taken post by you, at your age, alone, unattended!"

"Oh, the journey is nothing. Do not think about that. And if we are to part, a few hours sooner or later, you know, makes no difference. I can be ready by seven. Let me be called in time." Eleanor saw that she wished to be alone; and believing it better for each that they should avoid any further conversation, now left her with "I shall see you in the morning."

Catherine's swelling heart needed relief. In Eleanor's presence friendship and pride had equally restrained her tears, but no sooner was she gone than they burst forth in torrents. Turned from the house, and in such a way!—Without any reason that could justify, any apology that could atone for the abruptness, the rudeness, nay, the insolence of it. Henry at a distance—not able even to bid him farewell. Every hope, every expectation from him suspended, at least, and who could say how long?—Who could say when they might meet again?—And all this by such a man as General Tilney, so polite, so well-bred, and heretofore so particularly fond of her! It was as incomprehensible as it was mortifying and grievous. From what it could arise, and where it would end, were considerations of equal perplexity and alarm. The manner in which it was done so grossly uncivil; hurrying her away without any reference to her own convenience, or allowing her even the appearance of choice as to the time or mode of her travelling; of two days, the earliest fixed on, and of that almost the earliest hour, as if resolved to have her gone before he was stirring in the morning, that he might not be obliged even to see her. What could all this mean but an intentional affront? By some means or other she must have had the misfortune to offend him. Eleanor had wished to spare her from so painful a notion, but Catherine could not believe it possible that any injury or any misfortune could provoke such ill-will against a person not connected, or, at least, not supposed to be connected with it.

Heavily past the night. Sleep, or repose that deserved the name of sleep, was out of the question. That room, in which her disturbed imagination had tormented her on her first arrival, was again the scene of agitated spirits and unquiet slumbers. Yet how different now the source of her inquietude from what it had been then—how mournfully superior in reality and substance! Her anxiety had foundation in fact, her fears in probability; and with a mind so occupied in the contemplation of actual and natural evil, the solitude of her situation, the darkness of her chamber, the antiquity of the building were felt and considered without the smallest emotion; and though the wind was high, and often produced strange and sudden noises throughout the house, she heard it all as she lay awake, hour after hour, without curiosity or terror.

Soon after six Eleanor entered her room, eager to show attention or give assistance where it was possible; but very little remained to be done. Catherine had not loitered; she was almost dressed, and her packing almost finished. The possibility of some conciliatory message from the General occurred to her as his daughter appeared. What so natural, as that anger should pass away and repentance succeed it? and she only wanted to know how far, after what had passed, an apology might properly be received by her. But the knowledge would have been useless here, it was not called for; neither clemency nor dignity was put to the trial—Eleanor brought no message. Very little passed between them on meeting; each found her greatest safety in silence, and few and trivial were the sentences exchanged while they remained up stairs, Catherine in busy agitation completing her dress, and Eleanor with more good-will than experience intent upon filling the trunk. When every thing was done they left the room, Catherine lingering only half a minute behind her friend to throw a parting glance on every well-known cherished object, and went down to the breakfast-parlour, where breakfast was prepared. She tried to eat, as well to save herself from the pain of being urged, as to make her friend comfortable; but she had no appetite, and could not swallow many mouthfuls. The contrast between this and her last breakfast in that room, gave her fresh misery, and strengthened her distaste for every thing before her. It was not four-and-twenty hours ago since they had met there to the same repast, but in circumstances how different! With what cheerful ease, what happy, though false security, had she then looked around her, enjoying every thing present, and fearing little in future, beyond Henry's going to Woodston for a day! Happy, happy breakfast! for Henry had been there, Henry had sat by her and helped her. These reflections were long indulged undisturbed by any address from her companion, who sat as deep in thought as herself; and the appearance of the carriage was the first thing to startle and recall them to the present moment. Catherine's colour rose at the sight of it; and the indignity with which she was treated striking at that instant on her mind with peculiar force, made her for a short time sensible only of resentment. Eleanor seemed now impelled into resolution and speech.

"You *must* write to me, Catherine," she cried, "you *must* let me hear from you as soon as possible. Till I know you to be safe at home, I shall not have an hour's comfort. For *one* letter, at all risks, all hazards, I must entreat. Let me have the satisfaction of knowing that you are safe at Fullerton, and have found your family well, and then, till I can ask for your correspondence as I ought to do, I will not expect more. Direct to me at Lord Longtown's, and, I must ask it, under cover to Alice."

"No, Eleanor, if you are not allowed to receive a letter from me, I am sure I had better not write. There can be no doubt of my getting home safe."

Eleanor only replied, "I cannot wonder at your feelings. I will not importune you. I will trust to your own kindness of heart when I am at a distance from you." But this, with the look of sorrow accompanying it, was enough to melt Catherine's pride in a moment, and she instantly said, "Oh, Eleanor, I *will* write to you indeed."

There was yet another point which Miss Tilney was anxious to settle, though somewhat embarrassed in speaking of. It had occurred to her, that after so long an absence from home, Catherine might not be provided with money enough for the expenses of her journey, and, upon suggesting it to her with most affectionate offers of accommodation, it proved to be exactly the case. Catherine had never thought on the subject till that moment; but, upon examining her purse, was convinced that but for this kindness of her friend, she might have been turned from the house without even the means of getting home; and the distress in which she must have been thereby involved filling the minds of both, scarcely another word was said by either during the time of their remaining together. Short, however, was that time. The carriage was soon announced to be ready; and Catherine, instantly rising, a long and affectionate embrace supplied the place of language in bidding each other adieu; and, as they entered the hall, unable to leave the house without some mention of one whose name had not yet been spoken by either, she paused a moment, and with quivering lips just made it intelligible that she left "her kind remembrance for her absent friend." But with this approach to his name ended all possibility of restraining her feelings; and, hiding her face as well as she could with her handkerchief, she darted across the hall, jumped into the chaise, and in a moment was driven from the door.

CHAPTER XIV

Catherine was too wretched to be fearful. The journey in itself had no terrors for her; and she began it without either dreading its length, or feeling its solitariness. Leaning back in one corner of the carriage, in a violent burst of tears, she was conveyed some miles beyond the walls of the Abbey before she raised her head; and the highest point of ground within the park was almost closed from her view before she was capable of turning her eyes towards it. Unfortunately, the road she now travelled was the same which only ten days ago she had so happily passed along in going to and from Woodston; and, for fourteen miles, every bitter feeling was rendered more severe by the review of objects on which she had first looked under impressions so different. Every mile, as it brought her nearer Woodston, added to her sufferings, and when within the distance of five, she passed the turning which led to it, and thought of Henry, so near, yet so unconscious, her grief and agitation were excessive.

The day which she had spent at that place had been one of the happiest of her life. It was there, it was on that day that the General had made use of such expressions with regard to Henry and herself, had so spoken and so looked as to give her the most positive conviction of his actually wishing their marriage. Yes, only ten days ago had he elated her by his pointed regard—had he even confused her by his too significant reference! And now—what had she done, or what had she omitted to do, to merit such a change?

The only offence against him of which she could accuse herself, had been such as was scarcely possible to reach his knowledge. Henry and her own heart only were privy to the shocking suspicions which she had so idly entertained; and equally safe did she believe her secret with each. Design-edly, at least, Henry could not have betrayed her. If, indeed, by any strange mischance his father should have gained in-telligence of what she had dared to think and look for, of her causeless fancies and injurious examinations, she could not wonder at any degree of his indignation. If aware of her having viewed him as a murderer, she could not wonder at his even turning her from his house. But a justification so full of torture to herself, she trusted would not be in his power.

Anxious as were all her conjectures on this point, it was not, however, the one on which she dwelt most. There was a thought yet nearer, a more prevailing, more impetuous concern. How Henry would think, and feel, and look, when he returned on the morrow to Northanger and heard of her being gone, was a question of force and interest to rise over every other, to be never ceasing, alternately irritating and soothing; it sometimes suggested the dread of his calm acquiescence, and at others was answered by the sweetest confidence in his regret and resentment. To the General, of course, he would not dare to speak; but to Eleanor—what might he not say to Eleanor about her?

In this unceasing recurrence of doubts and inquiries, on any one article of which her mind was incapable of more than momentary repose, the hours passed away, and her journey advanced much faster than she looked for. The pressing anxieties of thought, which prevented her from noticing any thing before her, when once beyond the neigh-bourhood of Woodston, saved her at the same time from watching her progress; and though no object on the road could engage a moment's attention, she found no stage of it tedious. From this, she was preserved too by another cause, by feeling no eagerness for her journey's conclusion; for to return in such a manner to Fullerton was almost to destroy the pleasure of a meeting with those she loved best, even after an absence such as her's—an eleven weeks absence. What had she to say that would not humble herself and pain her family; that would not increase her own grief by the confession of it, extend an useless resentment, and perhaps involve the innocent with the guilty in undistinguishing ill-will? She could never do justice to Henry and Eleanor's merit; she felt it too strongly for expression; and should a dislike be taken against them, should they be thought of unfavourably, on their father's account, it would cut her to the heart.

With these feelings, she rather dreaded than sought for the first view of that well-known spire which would announce her within twenty miles of home. Salisbury she had known to be her point on leaving Northanger; but after the first stage she had been indebted to the post-masters for the names of the places which were then to conduct her to it; so great had been her ignorance of her route. She met with nothing, however, to distress or frighten her. Her youth, civil manners and liberal pay, procured her all the attention that a traveller like herself could require; and stopping only to change horses, she travelled on for about eleven hours without accident or alarm, and between six and seven o'clock in the evening found herself entering Fullerton.

A heroine returning, at the close of her career, to her native village, in all the triumph of recovered reputation, and all the dignity of a countess, with a long train of noble relations in their several phaetons, and three waiting-maids in a travelling chaise-and-four, behind her, is an event on which the pen of the contriver may well delight to dwell; it gives credit to every conclusion, and the author must share in the glory she so liberally bestows.—But my affair is widely different; I bring back my heroine to her home in solitude and disgrace; and no sweet elation of spirits can lead me into minuteness. A heroine in a hack post-chaise, is such a blow upon sentiment, as no attempt at grandeur or pathos can withstand. Swiftly therefore shall her post-boy drive through the village, amid the gaze of Sunday groups, and speedy shall be her descent from it.

But, whatever might be the distress of Catherine's mind, as she thus advanced towards the Parsonage, and whatever the humiliation of her biographer in relating it, she was preparing enjoyment of no every-day nature for those to whom she went; first, in the appearance of her carriage—and secondly, in herself. The chaise of a traveller being a rare sight in Fullerton, the whole family were immediately at the window; and to have it stop at the sweep-gate was a pleasure to brighten every eye and occupy every fancy—a pleasure quite unlooked for by all but the two youngest children, a boy and girl of six and four years old, who expected a brother or sister in every carriage. Happy the glance that first distinguished Catherine!—Happy the voice that proclaimed the discovery!—But whether such happiness were the lawful property of George or Harriet could never be exactly understood.

Her father, mother, Sarah, George, and Harriet, all assembled at the door, to welcome her with affectionate eagerness, was a sight to awaken the best feelings of Catherine's heart; and in the embrace of each, as she stepped from the carriage, she found herself soothed beyond any thing that she had believed possible. So surrounded, so caressed, she was even happy! In the joyfulness of family love every thing for a short time was subdued, and the pleasure of seeing her, leaving them at first little leisure for calm curiosity, they were all seated round the tea-table, which Mrs. Morland had hurried for the comfort of the poor traveller, whose pale and jaded looks soon caught her notice, before any inquiry so direct as to demand a positive answer was addressed to her.

Reluctantly, and with much hesitation, did she then begin what might perhaps, at the end of half an hour, be termed by the courtesy of her hearers, an explanation; but scarcely, within that time, could they at all discover the cause, or collect the particulars of her sudden return. They were far from being an irritable race; far from any quickness in catching, or bitterness in resenting affronts:—but here, when the whole was unfolded, was an insult not to be overlooked, nor, for the first half hour, to be easily pardoned. Without suffering any romantic alarm, in the consideration of their daughter's long and lonely journey, Mr. and Mrs. Morland could not but feel that it might have been productive of much unpleasantness to her; that it was what they could never have voluntarily suffered; and that, in forcing her on such a measure, General Tilney had acted neither honourably nor feelingly—neither as a gentleman nor as a parent. Why he had done it, what could have provoked him to such a breach of hospitality, and so suddenly turned all his partial regard for their daughter into actual ill-will, was a matter which they were at least as far from divining as Catherine herself; but it did not oppress them by any means so long; and, after a due course of useless conjecture, that, "it was a strange business, and that he must be a very strange man," grew enough for all their indignation and wonder; though Sarah indeed still indulged in the sweets of incomprehensibility, exclaiming and conjecturing with youthful ardour.—"My dear, you give yourself a great deal of needless trouble," said her mother at last; "depend upon it, it is something not at all worth understanding."

"I can allow for his wishing Catherine away, when he recollected this engagement," said Sarah, "but why not do it civilly?"

"I am sorry for the young people," returned Mrs. Morland; "they must have a sad time of it; but as for any thing else, it is no matter now; Catherine is safe at home, and our comfort does not depend upon General Tilney." Catherine sighed. "Well," continued her philosophic mother, "I am glad I did not know of your journey at the time; but now it is all over perhaps there is no great harm done. It is always good for young people to be put upon exerting themselves; and you know, my dear Catherine, you always were a sad little shatter-brained creature; but now you must have been forced to have your wits about you, with so much changing of chaises and so forth; and I hope it will appear that you have not left any thing behind you in any of the pockets."

Catherine hoped so too, and tried to feel an interest in her own amendment, but her spirits were quite worn down; and, to be silent and alone becoming soon her only wish, she readily agreed to her mother's next counsel of going early to bed. Her parents seeing nothing in her ill-looks and agitation but the natural consequence of mortified feelings, and of the unusual exertion and fatigue of such a journey, parted from her without any doubt of their being soon slept away; and though, when they all met the next morning, her recovery was not equal to their hopes, they were still perfectly unsuspicious of there being any deeper evil. They never once thought of her heart, which, for the parents of a young lady of seventeen, just returned from her first excursion from home, was odd enough!

As soon as breakfast was over, she sat down to fulfil her promise to Miss Tilney, whose trust in the effect of time and distance on her friend's disposition was already justified, for already did Catherine reproach herself with having parted from Eleanor coldly; with having never enough valued her merits or kindness; and never enough commiserated her for what she had been yesterday left to endure. The strength of these feelings, however, was far from assisting her pen; and never had it been harder for her to write than in addressing Eleanor Tilney. To compose a letter which might at once do justice to her sentiments and her situation, convey gratitude without servile regret, be guarded without coldness, and honest without resentment— a letter which Eleanor might not be pained by the perusal of—and, above all, which she might not blush herself, if Henry should chance to see, was an undertaking to frighten away all her powers of performance; and, after long thought and much perplexity, to be very brief was all that she could determine on with any confidence of safety. The money therefore which Eleanor had advanced was inclosed with little more than grateful thanks, and the thousand good wishes of a most affectionate heart.

"This has been a strange acquaintance," observed Mrs. Morland, as the letter was finished; "soon made and soon ended.—I am sorry it happens so, for Mrs. Allen thought them very pretty kind of young people; and you were sadly out of luck too in your Isabella. Ah! poor James! Well, we must live and learn; and the next new friends you make I hope will be better worth keeping."

Catherine coloured as she warmly answered, "No friend can be better worth keeping than Eleanor."

"If so, my dear, I dare say you will meet again some time or other; do not be uneasy. It is ten to one but you are thrown together again in the course of a few years; and then what a pleasure it will be!"

Mrs. Morland was not happy in her attempt at consolation. The hope of meeting again in the course of a few years could only put into Catherine's head what might happen within that time to make a meeting dreadful to her. She could never forget Henry Tilney, or think of him with less tenderness than she did at that moment; but he might forget her; and in that case to meet!—Her eyes filled with tears as she pictured her acquaintance so renewed; and her mother, perceiving her comfortable suggestions to have had no good effect, proposed, as another expedient for restoring her spirits, that they should call on Mrs. Allen.

The two houses were only a quarter of a mile apart; and, as they walked, Mrs. Morland quickly dispatched all that she felt on the score of James's disappointment. "We are sorry for him," said she; "but otherwise there is no harm done in the match going off; for it could not be a desirable thing to have him engaged to a girl whom we had not the smallest acquaintance with, and who was so entirely without fortune; and now, after such behaviour, we cannot think at all well of her. Just at present it comes hard to poor James; but that will not last for ever; and I dare say he will be a discreeter man all his life, for the foolishness of his first choice."

This was just such a summary view of the affair as Catherine could listen to; another sentence might have endangered her complaisance, and made her reply less rational; for soon were all her thinking powers swallowed up in the reflection of her own change of feelings and spirits since last she had trodden that well-known road. It was not three months ago since, wild with joyful expectation, she had there run backwards and forwards some ten times a-day, with an heart light, gay, and independent; looking forward to pleasures untasted and unalloyed, and free from the apprehension of evil as from the knowledge of it. Three months ago had seen her all this; and now, how altered a being did she return!

She was received by the Allens with all the kindness which her unlooked-for appearance, acting on a steady affection, would naturally call forth; and great was their surprize, and warm their displeasure, on hearing how she had been treated,—though Mrs. Morland's account of it was no inflated representation, no studied appeal to their passions. "Catherine took us quite by surprize yesterday evening," said she. "She travelled all the way post by herself, and knew nothing of coming till Saturday night; for General Tilney, from some odd fancy or other, all of a sudden grew tired of having her there, and almost turned her out of the house. Very unfriendly, certainly; and he must be a very odd man; —but we are so glad to have her amongst us again! And it is a great comfort to find that she is not a poor helpless creature, but can shift very well for herself."

Mr. Allen expressed himself on the occasion with the reasonable resentment of a sensible friend; and Mrs. Allen thought his expressions quite good enough to be immediately made use of again by herself. His wonder, his conjectures, and his explanations, became in succession her's, with the addition of this single remark—"I really have not patience with the General"—to fill up every accidental pause. And, "I really have not patience with the General," was uttered twice after Mr. Allen left the room, without any relaxation of anger, or any material digression of thought. A more considerable degree of wandering attended the third repetition; and, after completing the fourth, she immediately added, "Only think, my dear, of my having got that frightful great rent in my best Mechlin so charmingly mended, before I left Bath, that one can hardly see where it was. I must shew it you some day or other. Bath is a nice place, Catherine, after all. I assure you I did not above half like coming away. Mrs. Thorpe's being there was such a comfort to us, was not it? You know you and I were quite forlorn at first."

"Yes, but *that* did not last long," said Catherine, her eyes brightening at the recollection of what had first given spirit to her existence there.

"Very true: we soon met with Mrs. Thorpe, and then we wanted for nothing. My dear, do not you think these silk gloves wear very well? I put them on new the first time of our going to the Lower Rooms, you know, and I have worn them a great deal since. Do you remember that evening?"

"Do I! Oh! perfectly."

"It was very agreeable, was not it? Mr. Tilney drank tea with us, and I always thought him a great addition, he is so very agreeable. I have a notion you danced with him, but am not quite sure. I remember I had my favourite gown on."

Catherine could not answer; and, after a short trial of other subjects, Mrs. Allen again returned to—"I really have not patience with the General! Such an agreeable, worthy man as he seemed to be! I do not suppose, Mrs. Morland, you ever saw a better-bred man in your life. His lodgings were taken the very day after he left them, Catherine. But no wonder; Milsom-street you know."—

As they walked home again, Mrs. Morland endeavoured to impress on her daughter's mind the happiness of having such steady well-wishers as Mr. and Mrs. Allen, and the very little consideration which the neglect or unkindness of slight acquaintance like the Tilneys ought to have with her, while she could preserve the good opinion and affection of her earliest friends. There was a great deal of good sense in all this; but there are some situations of the human mind in which good sense has very little power; and Catherine's feelings contradicted almost every position her mother advanced. It was upon the behaviour of these very slight acquaintance that all her present happiness depended; and while Mrs. Morland was successfully confirming her own opinions by the justness of her own representations, Catherine was silently reflecting that *now* Henry must have arrived at Northanger; *now* he must have heard of her departure; and *now,* perhaps, they were all setting off for Hereford.

CHAPTER XV

Catherine's disposition was not naturaly sedentary, nor had her habits been ever very industrious; but whatever might hitherto have been her defects of that sort, her mother could not but perceive them now to be greatly increased. She could neither sit still, nor employ herself for ten minutes together, walking round the garden and orchard again and again, as if nothing but motion was voluntary; and it seemed as if she could even walk about the house rather than remain fixed for any time in the parlour. Her loss of spirits was a yet greater alteration. In her rambling and her idleness she might only be a caricature of herself; but in her silence and sadness she was the very reverse of all that she had been before.

For two days Mrs. Morland allowed it to pass even without a hint; but when a third night's rest had neither restored her cheerfulness, improved her in useful activity, nor given her a greater inclination for needle-work, she could no longer refrain from the gentle reproof of, "My dear Catherine, I am afraid you are growing quite a fine lady. I do not know when poor Richard's cravats would be done, if he had no friend but you. Your head runs too much upon Bath; but there is a time for every thing—a time for balls and plays, and a time for work. You have had a long run of amusement, and now you must try to be useful."

Catherine took up her work directly, saying, in a dejected voice, that "her head did not run upon Bath——much."

"Then you are fretting about General Tilney, and that is very simple of you; for ten to one whether you ever see him again. You should never fret about trifles." After a short silence—"I hope, my Catherine, you are not getting out of humour with home because it is not so grand as Northanger. That would be turning your visit into an evil indeed. Wherever you are you should always be contented, but especially at home, because there you must spend the most of your time. I did not quite like, at breakfast, to hear you talk so much about the French-bread at Northanger."

"I am sure I do not care about the bread. It is all the same to me what I eat."

"There is a very clever Essay in one of the books up stairs upon much such a subject, about young girls that have been spoilt for home by great acquaintance—'The Mirror,' I think. I will look it out for you some day or other, because I am sure it will do you good."

Catherine said no more, and, with an endeavour to do right, applied to her work; but, after a few minutes, sunk again, without knowing it herself, into languor and listlessness, moving herself in her chair, from the irritation of weariness, much oftener than she moved her needle.—Mrs. Morland watched the progress of this relapse; and seeing, in her daughter's absent and dissatisfied look, the full proof of that repining spirit to which she had now begun to attribute her want of cheerfulness, hastily left the room to fetch the book in question, anxious to lose no time in attacking so dreadful a malady. It was some time before she could find what she looked for; and other family matters occurring to detain her, a quarter of an hour had elapsed ere she returned down stairs with the volume from which so much was hoped. Her avocations above having shut out all noise but what she created herself, she knew not that a visitor had arrived within the last few minutes, till, on entering the room, the first object she beheld was a young man whom she had never seen before. With a look of much respect, he immediately rose, and being introduced to her by her conscious daughter as "Mr. Henry Tilney," with the embarrassment of real sensibility began to apologise for his appearance there, acknowledging that after what had passed he had little right to expect a welcome at Fullerton, and stating his impatience to be assured of Miss Morland's having reached her home in safety, as the cause of his intrusion. He did not address himself to an uncandid judge or a resentful heart. Far from comprehending him or his sister in their father's misconduct, Mrs. Morland had been always kindly disposed towards each, and instantly, pleased by his appearance, received him with the simple professions of unaffected benevolence; thanking him for such an attention to her daughter, assuring him that the friends of her children were always welcome there, and intreating him to say not another word of the past.

He was not ill inclined to obey this request, for, though his heart was greatly relieved by such unlooked-for mildness, it was not just at that moment in his power to say any thing to the purpose. Returning in silence to his seat, therefore, he remained for some minutes most civilly answering all Mrs. Morland's common remarks about the weather and roads. Catherine meanwhile,—the anxious, agitated, happy, feverish Catherine,—said not a word; but her glowing cheek and brightened eye made her mother trust that this good-natured visit would at least set her heart at ease for a time, and gladly therefore did she lay aside the first volume of the Mirror for a future hour.

Desirous of Mr. Morland's assistance, as well in giving encouragement, as in finding conversation for her guest, whose embarrassment on his father's account she earnestly pitied, Mrs. Morland had very early dispatched one of the children to summon him; but Mr. Morland was from home —and being thus without any support, at the end of a quarter of an hour she had nothing to say. After a couple of minutes unbroken silence, Henry, turning to Catherine for the first time since her mother's entrance, asked her, with sudden alacrity, if Mr. and Mrs. Allen were now at Fullerton? and on developing, from amidst all her perplexity of words in reply, the meaning, which one short syllable would have given, immediately expressed his intention of paying his respects to them, and, with a rising colour, asked her if she would have the goodness to shew him the way. "You may see the house from this window, sir," was information on Sarah's side, which produced only a bow of acknowledgment from the gentleman, and a silencing nod from her mother; for Mrs. Morland, thinking it probable, as a secondary consideration in his wish of waiting on their worthy neighbours, that he might have some explanation to give of his father's behaviour, which it must be more pleasant for him to communicate only to Catherine, would not on any account prevent her accompanying him. They began their walk, and Mrs. Morland was not entirely mistaken in his object in wishing it. Some explanation on his father's account he had to give; but his first purpose was to explain himself, and before they reached Mr. Allen's grounds he had done it so well, that Catherine did not think it could ever be repeated too often. She was assured of his affection; and that heart in return was solicited, which, perhaps, they pretty equally knew was already entirely his own; for, though Henry was now sincerely attached to her, though he felt and delighted in all the excellencies of her character and truly loved her society, I must confess that his affection originated in nothing better than gratitude, or, in other words, that a persuasion of her partiality for him had been the only cause of giving her a serious thought. It is a new circumstance in romance, I acknowledge, and dreadfully derogatory of an heroine's dignity; but if it be as new in common life, the credit of a wild imagination will at least be all my own.

A very short visit to Mrs. Allen, in which Henry talked at random, without sense or connection, and Catherine, wrapt in the contemplation of her own unutterable happiness, scarcely opened her lips, dismissed them to the extasies of another tête-à-tête; and before it was suffered to close, she was enabled to judge how far he was sanctioned by parental authority in his present application. On his return from Woodston, two days before, he had been met near the Abbey by his impatient father, hastily informed in angry terms of Miss Morland's departure, and ordered to think of her no more.

Such was the permission upon which he had now offered her his hand. The affrighted Catherine, amidst all the terrors of expectation, as she listened to this account, could not but rejoice in the kind caution with which Henry had saved her from the necessity of a conscientious rejection, by engaging her faith before he mentioned the subject; and as he proceeded to give the particulars, and explain the motives of his father's conduct, her feelings soon hardened into even a triumphant delight. The General had had nothing to accuse her of, nothing to lay to her charge, but her being the involuntary, unconscious object of a deception which his pride could not pardon, and which a better pride would have been ashamed to own. She was guilty only of being less rich than he had supposed her to be. Under a mistaken persuasion of her possessions and claims, he had courted her acquaintance in Bath, solicited her company at Northanger, and designed her for his daughter in law. On discovering his error, to turn her from the house seemed the best, though to his feelings an inadequate proof of his resentment towards herself, and his contempt for her family.

John Thorpe had first misled him. The General, perceiving his son one night at the theatre to be paying considerable attention to Miss Morland, had accidentally inquired of Thorpe, if he knew more of her than her name. Thorpe, most happy to be on speaking terms with a man of General Tilney's importance, had been joyfully and proudly communicative;—and being at that time not only in daily expectation of Morland's engaging Isabella, but likewise pretty well resolved upon marrying Catherine himself, his vanity induced him to represent the family as yet more wealthy than his vanity and avarice had made him believe them. With whomsoever he was, or was likely to be connected, his own consequence always required that theirs should be great, and as his intimacy with any acquaintance grew, so regularly grew their fortune. The expectations of his friend Morland, therefore, from the first over-rated, had ever since his introduction to Isabella, been gradually increasing; and by merely adding twice as much for the grandeur of the moment, by doubling what he chose to think the amount of Mr. Morland's preferment, trebling his private fortune, bestowing a rich aunt, and sinking half the children, he was able to represent the whole family to the General in a most respectable light. For Catherine, however, the peculiar object of the General's curiosity, and his own speculations, he had yet something more in reserve, and the ten or fifteen thousand pounds which her father could give her, would be a pretty addition to Mr. Allen's estate. Her intimacy there had made him seriously determine on her being handsomely legacied hereafter; and to speak of her therefore as the almost acknowledged future heiress of Fullerton naturally followed. Upon such intelligence the General had proceeded; for never had it occurred to him to doubt its authority. Thorpe's interest in the family, by his sister's approaching connection with one of its members, and his own views on another, (circumstances of which he boasted with almost equal openness,) seemed sufficient vouchers for his truth; and to these were added the absolute facts of the Allens being wealthy and childless, of Miss Morland's being under their care, and—as soon as his acquaintance allowed him to judge—of their treating her with parental kindness. His resolution was soon formed.

Already had he discerned a liking towards Miss Morland in the countenance of his son; and thankful for Mr. Thorpe's communication, he almost instantly determined to spare no pains in weakening his boasted interest and ruining his dearest hopes. Catherine herself could not be more ignorant at the time of all this, than his own children. Henry and Eleanor, perceiving nothing in her situation likely to engage their father's particular respect, had seen with astonishment the suddenness, continuance and extent of his attention; and though latterly, from some hints which had accompanied an almost positive command to his son of doing every thing in his power to attach her, Henry was convinced of his father's believing it to be an advantageous connection, it was not till the late explanation at Northanger that they had the smallest idea of the false calculations which had hurried him on. That they were false, the General had learnt from the very person who had suggested them, from Thorpe himself, whom he had chanced to meet again in town, and who, under the influence of exactly opposite feelings, irritated by Catherine's refusal, and yet more by the failure of a very recent endeavour to accomplish a reconciliation between Morland and Isabella, convinced that they were separated for ever, and spurning a friendship which could be no longer serviceable, hastened to contradict all that he had said before to the advantage of the Morlands;—confessed himself to have been totally mistaken in his opinion of their circumstances and character, misled by the rhodomontade of his friend to believe his father a man of substance and credit, whereas the transactions of the two or three last weeks proved him to be neither; for after coming eagerly forward on the first overture of a marriage between the families, with the most liberal proposals, he had, on being brought to the point by the shrewdness of the relator, been constrained to acknowldege himself incapable of giving the young people even a decent support. They were, in fact, a necessitous family; numerous too almost beyond example; by no means respected in their own neighbourhood, as he had lately had particular opportunities of discovering; aiming at a style of life which their fortune could not warrant; seeking to better themselves by wealthy connexions; a forward, bragging, scheming race.

The terrified General pronounced the name of Allen with an inquiring look; and here too Thorpe had learnt his error. The Allens, he believed, had lived near them too long, and he knew the young man on whom the Fullerton estate must devolve. The General needed no more. Enraged with almost every body in the world but himself, he set out the next day for the Abbey, where his performances have been seen.

I leave it to my reader's sagacity to determine how much of all this it was possible for Henry to communicate at this time to Catherine, how much of it he could have learnt from his father, in what points his own conjectures might assist him, and what portion must yet remain to be told in a letter from James. I have united for their ease what they must divide for mine. Catherine, at any rate, heard enough to feel, that in suspecting General Tilney of either murdering or shutting up his wife, she had scarcely sinned against his character, or magnified his cruelty.

Henry, in having such things to relate of his father, was almost as pitiable as in their first avowal to himself. He blushed for the narrow-minded counsel which he was obliged to expose. The conversation between them at Northanger had been of the most unfriendly kind. Henry's indignation on hearing how Catherine had been treated, on comprehending his father's views, and being ordered to acquiesce in them, had been open and bold. The General, accustomed on every ordinary occasion to give the law in his family, prepared for no reluctance but of feeling, no opposing desire that should dare to clothe itself in words, could ill brook the opposition of his son, steady as the sanction of reason and the dictate of conscience could make it. But, in such a cause, his anger, though it must shock, could not intimidate Henry, who was sustained in his purpose by a conviction of its justice. He felt himself bound as much in honour as in affection to Miss Morland, and believing that heart to be his own which he had been directed to gain, no unworthy retraction of a tacit consent, no reversing decree of unjustifiable anger, could shake his fidelity, or influence the resolutions it prompted.

He steadily refused to accompany his father into Herefordshire, an engagement formed almost at the moment, to promote the dismissal of Catherine, and as steadily declared his intention of offering her his hand. The General was furious in his anger, and they parted in dreadful disagreement. Henry, in an agitation of mind which many solitary hours were required to compose, had returned almost instantly to Woodston; and, on the afternoon of the following day, had begun his journey to Fullerton.

CHAPTER XVI

Mr. and Mrs. Morland's surprize on being applied to by Mr. Tilney, for their consent to his marrying their daughter, was, for a few minutes, considerable; it having never entered their heads to suspect an attachment on either side; but as nothing, after all, could be more natural than Catherine's being beloved, they soon learnt to consider it with only the happy agitation of gratified pride, and, as far as they alone were concerned, had not a single objection to start. His pleasing manners and good sense were self-evident recommendations; and having never heard evil of him, it was not their way to suppose any evil could be told. Good-will supplying the place of experience, his character needed no attestation. "Catherine would make a sad heedless young house-keeper to be sure," was her mother's foreboding remark; but quick was the consolation of there being nothing like practice.

There was but one obstacle, in short, to be mentioned; but till that one was removed, it must be impossible for them to sanction the engagement. Their tempers were mild, but their principles were steady, and while his parent so expressly forbad the connexion, they could not allow themselves to encourage it. That the General should come forward to solicit the alliance, or that he should even very heartily approve it, they were not refined enough to make any parading stipulation; but the decent appearance of consent must be yielded, and that once obtained—and their own hearts made them trust that it could not be very long denied—their willing approbation was instantly to follow. His *consent* was all that they wished for. They were no more inclined than entitled to demand his *money*. Of a very considerable fortune, his son was, by marriage settlements, eventually secure; his present income was an income of independence and comfort, and under every pecuniary view, it was a match beyond the claims of their daughter.

The young people could not be surprized at a decision like this. They felt and they deplored—but they could not resent it; and they parted, endeavouring to hope that such a change in the General, as each believed almost impossible, might speedily take place, to unite them again in the full-ness of privileged affection. Henry returned to what was now his only home, to watch over his young plantations, and extend his improvements for her sake, to whose share in them he looked anxiously forward; and Catherine re-mained at Fullerton to cry. Whether the torments of absence were softened by a clandestine correspondence, let us not inquire. Mr. and Mrs. Morland never did—they had been too kind to exact any promise; and whenever Catherine received a letter, as, at that time, happened pretty often, they always looked another way.

The anxiety, which in this state of their attachment must be the portion of Henry and Catherine, and of all who loved either, as to its final event, can hardly extend, I fear, to the bosom of my readers, who will see in the tell-tale compres-sion of the pages before them, that we are all hastening together to perfect felicity. The means by which their early marriage was effected can be the only doubt; what probable circumstance could work upon a temper like the General's? The circumstance which chiefly availed, was the marriage of his daughter with a man of fortune and consequence, which took place in the course of the summer—an accession of dignity that threw him into a fit of good-humour, from which he did not recover till after Eleanor had obtained his forgiveness of Henry, and his permission for him "to be a fool if he liked it!"

The marriage of Eleanor Tilney, her removal from all the evils of such a home as Northanger had been made by Henry's banishment, to the home of her choice and the man of her choice, is an event which I expect to give general satisfaction among all her acquaintance. My own joy on the occasion is very sincere. I know no one more entitled, by unpretending merit, or better prepared by habitual suffering, to receive and enjoy felicity. Her partiality for this gentleman was not of recent origin; and he had been long withheld only by inferiority of situation from addressing her. His unexpected accession to title and fortune had removed all his difficulties; and never had the General loved his daughter so well in all her hours of companionship, utility, and patient endurance, as when he first hailed her, "Your Ladyship!" Her husband was really deserving of her; independent of his peerage, his wealth, and his attachment, being to a precision the most charming young man in the world. Any further definition of his merits must be unnecessary; the most charming young man in the world is instantly before the imagination of us all. Concerning the one in question therefore I have only to add—(aware that the rules of composition forbid the introduction of a character not connected with my fable)—that this was the very gentleman whose negligent servant left behind him that collection of washing-bills, resulting from a long visit at Northanger, by which my heroine was involved in one of her most alarming adventures.

The influence of the Viscount and Viscountess in their brother's behalf was assisted by that right understanding of Mr. Morland's circumstances which, as soon as the General would allow himself to be informed, they were qualified to give. It taught him that he had been scarcely more misled by Thorpe's first boast of the family wealth, than by his subsequent malicious overthrow of it; that in no sense of the word were they necessitous or poor, and that Catherine would have three thousand pounds. This was so material an amendment of his late expectations, that it greatly contributed to smooth the descent of his pride; and by no means without its effect was the private intelligence, which he was at some pains to procure, that the Fullerton estate, being entirely at the disposal of its present proprietor, was consequently open to every greedy speculation.

On the strength of this, the General, soon after Eleanor's marriage, permitted his son to return to Northanger, and thence made him the bearer of his consent, very courteously worded in a page full of empty professions to Mr. Morland. The event which it authorized soon followed: Henry and Catherine were married, the bells rang and every body smiled; and, as this took place within a twelve-month from the first day of their meeting, it will not appear, after all the dreadful delays occasioned by the General's cruelty, that they were essentially hurt by it. To begin perfect happiness at the respective ages of twenty-six and eighteen, is to do pretty well; and professing myself moreover convinced, that the General's unjust interference, so far from being really injurious to their felicity, was perhaps rather conducive to it, by improving their knowledge of each other, and adding strength to their attachment, I leave it to be settled by whomsoever it may concern, whether the tendency of this work be altogether to recommend parental tyranny, or reward filial disobedience.

Rinehart Editions